"Hilarious. . . . If you can imagine a chocolate truffle with a cayenne center, you can get the flavor of *Love, Stars, and All That*. . . . A charming book about looking for love. . . . Narayan's ear for dialogue is exceptional, as is her ability to select small details that evoke whole cultural patterns."

—Roz Spafford, *San Jose Mercury News*

"Astute, funny, and gracefully composed, Kirin Narayan's wonderful novel penetrates to the heart that unites cultures in a single, ever perplexing, always fascinating humanity."

—Michael Dorris, author of *Working Men* and *The Broken Cord*

"A delightfully funny cross-cultural romp and . . . a most satisfying love story."

—Lynette Lamb, *Utne Reader*

"The characters in this delightful look at modern India and Indians in the United States are deliciously and bitingly drawn—both those in India and those in academe, especially Berkeley. A good read for all."

—Barbara Maslekoff, *Library Journal*

"Witty . . . intelligent . . . and revelatory of what it is like to be an American born in India. . . . *LOVE, STARS, AND ALL THAT* is full of promise. It makes one feel that Narayan is that very rare bird, a born writer, and that she may fly far."

—Dom Moraes, *India Today*

"A beguiling blend of romance, humor, and perceptive social observation. . . . Witty, enjoyable, and even a bit educational, *Love, Stars, and All That* is a delightful read."

—Nadine Goff, *Wisconsin State Journal*

Also by Kirin Narayan

*Storytellers, Saints, and Scoundrels: Folk Narrative
in Hindu Religious Teaching*

Love, Stars, and All That

Kirin Narayan

WASHINGTON SQUARE PRESS
PUBLISHED BY POCKET BOOKS

New York   London   Toronto   Sydney   Tokyo   Singapore

This book is a work of fiction. Names, characters, places and incidents are products of the author's imagination or are used fictitiously. Any resemblance to actual events or locales or persons, living or dead, is entirely coincidental.

WSP

A Washington Square Press Publication of
POCKET BOOKS, a division of Simon & Schuster Inc.
1230 Avenue of the Americas, New York, NY 10020

Copyright © 1994 by Kirin Narayan
Cover design by John Gall
Front cover photograph by Brent Nicastro

Library of Congress Cataloging-in-Publication Data

Narayan, Kirin.
    Love, stars, and all that / by Kirin Narayan
        p.   cm.
    ISBN: 0-671-79396-9
        1. Women graduate students—California—Berkeley—Fiction.
    2. Man–woman relationships—California—Berkeley—Fiction.
    3. East Indians—California—Berkeley—Fiction.   4. Berkeley
    (Calif.)—Fiction.   I. Title.
    PS3564.A68L68   1994
    813'.54—dc20   93-26084
                                                                CIP

First Washington Square Press trade paperback printing
January 1995

10 9 8 7 6 5 4 3 2 1

WASHINGTON SQUARE PRESS and colophon are
registered trademarks of Simon & Schuster Inc.

Printed in the U.S.A.

To Ma

for the hot cups of tea and shoulder rubs

Contents

Contents

PART 2: Quests

PART 1

❀

Arrivals

1
Love, Stars, and All That

On Saturday nights, Gita washed her hair. She squeezed out water from dripping black strands and twisted these into a turban towel. Later, at her desk, she loosened the towel, shaking her head as her hair uncoiled. Damp, fragrant, it fell like a cloak around her. As she read, she worked at snarls with a coconut-shell comb. She started at the ends. When the comb slid smooth, she progressed higher. Past her waist, past her breasts, high up to touch her scalp. It was satisfying when the comb finally glided free, her arm straightening to her hair's full length. Books might be tumbled about her desk, assignments a muddle of index cards and incomplete outlines; but when the comb met no obstacles in that soft, scented mass, Gita felt there was a flow and order to her life. This is how, in Berkeley, Gita spent her Saturday nights.

*   *   *

Bet, her housemate, thought it was abnormal.

"What's normal?" asked Gita, immediately embarrassed that she might have been rude. Bet was standing in a dressing gown at the open door of Gita's room. Gita was cross-legged on the floor, books open before her on her board-and-bricks desk.

"Normal is hot-blooded," said Bet. "Normal is interest in things like men and sex. Hey, I'm celibate by default. It's not as though I ever take a vacation from finding a guy. I'm only in bed watching *Singing in the Rain* for the hundred millionth time because I couldn't scare up a damn thing else to do tonight. But you—you don't even *try*."

"Graduate school is so much work," said Gita. She looked back at her books in their cozy halo of lamplight. She was reading an interesting article about how the past is known only through the narrative forms that shape it. She wished she could shake Bet off and get back to her own handwriting moving across the page, appropriating the article in tidy notes. Remembering that the paper using this article was due on Monday squeezed tension into her breath: how could she yet again perform the sleight of hand that transformed blank pages into coherently argued, typewritten ideas? Twiddling a damp strand of hair, Gita said, "With all this work, there's just no time to think of anything else."

"Bullshit!" Bet's blue eyes narrowed. "Given a chance, don't tell me you'd put schoolwork before a date!"

Date. The word rustled with the turning pages of Archie comics or Mills and Boons romances that girls at her convent school used to read under their desks. She had been out to lunch and dinner, yes, but never on a *date*. Dinaz Ganjifrock-wala's cousin-brother, Firoze, who was also a graduate student at Berkeley, had gone out with her to eat *idli-dosa*s at a local South Indian restaurant a couple of times. But he was such a boy, with his crumpled *kurta* and irritating habit of referring to the Third World as though he'd forgotten the name for India, he didn't count. A Date carried the image of a car door being held open by a sardonic, experienced, older man—

4

possibly a widower. As usual when Bet brought up this subject, Gita didn't know what to say. At college in Delhi other girls had gone out on dates; according to rumors some had even Done It. But what with being a day scholar and out of the right social circles, none of this had ever slid into Gita's horizon of the possible. She groped for ammunition to protect herself.

"Look, I don't need to waste my time dating because I know when things will change," Gita said, sitting straighter. "My Saroj Aunty's astrologer has already told me: in Chaitra twenty-forty I'll meet the right man."

"Get out of here! Twenty forty? Is this some sort of pension plan or one of those *next* lives you people believe in?"

Gita didn't know the Hindu calendar beyond the date that Ganeshan Kaka, the astrologer, had authoritatively declared. To say Chaitra 2040 instead of the March 1984 that came far more readily to her lips was to claim a cultural authenticity that she knew was fake. But in America, it seemed the only thing that would shield her difference, protect her boundaries, so she could do the work she had taken on in coming here: to be alone and to study.

"God-is-good-and-luck-is-with-us," Ayah used to pronounce, rolling out this stream of English whenever a princess and prince had been finally united in one of her stories. Slicing at a betel nut with a clipper, she would smile with the stubble of betel-worn teeth, adding, "Heavenly Father Bhagavan made the *jori*. May God bless you too, Baby."

A *jori*, a pair. To Gita, the word always conjured up the image of rubber "Hawaii" slippers, leather Kolhapuri *chappal*s with bright red tassels and gold thread, shiny black Bata shoes, daubed white tennis Keds. All these forms of footwear were lined up in her room: two by two, a matched precision. When Gita sat listening to Ayah as a sole little girl, she sensed that somewhere out in the world was the young prince who should be beside her, taking in the same story. If she thought of Him too hard she had such a strong sense of one shoed foot awaiting its mate that when she stood up she had to suppress a limp.

Ayah, Gita's nursemaid, only sounded like a Christian when she spoke English. She actually worshiped at a suitcase full of assorted framed Hindu deities, which she hauled out from under Gita's bed and opened up each morning. With the end of her white sari pulled up over her gray hair, lips moving in a mutter over ground-down, yellowed teeth, Ayah would wave a stick of incense before the gods. When the stick burned down to a sprinkle of scented ash, the gods went back into the suitcase.

As Ayah told stories about these brightly colored gods or conjured up princesses suffering from separation, she was most comfortable speaking colloquial South-Indian—accented Hindi. Yet decades of attending to the children of missionaries or Western diplomats had left her with a fragmentary and pious English. It was with English that she marked moments of closure or formality.

"Foreign exposure," Kookoo Das, Gita's mother, would tell visitors, her painted eyes flashing emphasis. "So many of these local girls just pinch one's makeup and drug the children with opium! But this woman, she came with *references*. It's absolutely the best for little Gita." If little Gita happened to be listening, she was told to "Shoo, dear, go to Nanny." It was a profound and ongoing source of irritation to Kookoo that the transformation of Ayah into Nanny was never complete. Ayah just could not be persuaded to swap cotton saris for a nice white frock. Further, it seemed to Kookoo that Ayah indulged Gita too much—always talking to her, always telling her stories.

Gita had thought of Ayah on the gusting monsoon day in Bombay when Saroj Aunty had arranged for the astrology session. In Ayah's stories, astrologers often appeared to foretell catastrophes or issue advice on how fate could be overcome. Now Saroj Aunty had summoned Ganeshan Kaka, the astrologer, because Gita was about to leave for graduate school in America.

Saroj Aunty and Harish Uncle Shah weren't really Gita's relatives by blood. Childless themselves, they had adopted all their friends' children as adored nephews and nieces. While most of these children showed up every few years to be plied with homemade *kulfi* ice cream and taken for an evening walk on the beach, Gita was one of the more needy of their circle of fictive kin. Ever since she entered boarding school at the age of six, she had spent most of her vacations with the Shahs.

Ganeshan Kaka was a regular visitor at the Shahs' home. Gita had known him for many years as another *kaka*—uncle. He was a small man, so thin that he was almost two-dimensional, and with a voice that could rise into an emphatic squeak. When people asked him questions about their lives, he would whip a pen out of his shirt pocket and work furiously on calculations. Somehow, as a child, Gita had never seriously viewed what he was doing as a consultation with destiny; it really had seemed more like an amusing party trick. Yet Saroj Aunty's summoning Ganeshan Kaka to dispense predictions for Gita's trip abroad gave him the aura of a magical tale. Horoscope predictions made at a child's birth invariably threw a kingdom into disarray. Knowing the stars brought hardship, conniving, sudden flukes of altered fate, and yet always, it seemed, a final harmony.

"I never even knew I had a horoscope, Aunty."

"But of course, darling." Saroj Aunty had the face of a friendly owl, with wisps of gray hair curling around her head and glasses magnifying her slightly crossed eyes. "I had it made up for you *years* ago. Don't think I don't know how Kookoo carries on about it all being native superstition. But the way people draw these lines! That stepfather of yours is pukka-positively convinced that astrology is hocus-pocus. Just talk to him some more and you find that he is one hundred and *one* percent sure that wearing gems produces scientifically proven effects. You've seen how he's always off to the jewelers ordering up another coral, topaz, or God only knows what kind of ring to help him out, whether it's blood pressure, constipation, or problems with his diplomatic posting abroad! So if Kookoo and Dilip want to pooh-pooh astrology, I just sit quiet. It's not as though I didn't already have your birth date, time, and place from Vinay."

Gita looked down when her real father, Vinay, was mentioned. He had been a famous man involved in the Independence movement. But he had died before she could remember, and so she was never quite sure how to claim him. She did know that the Shahs had really been *his* friends, though how and why were never discussed. Along with Kookoo, Dilip—the bejeweled stepfather whom Gita was unable to think of as "Daddy"—sometimes visited the Shahs. It was clear, though, that they did this out of duty more than enjoyment. Gita thought about her mother's imported nylon saris and Saroj Aunty's starched, hand-printed handlooms. Kookoo arranged gladioli and tuberoses in tall vases; Saroj Aunty ordered the servants to float fleshy *champa* blossoms in bowls of water or to string jasmine into fragrant garlands for the hair. Dilip insisted on Western toilets with imported seats that sank with a sigh under your thighs. But at the Shahs' house there was a sunken ceramic latrine with two white footrests for squatting. Kookoo's "staff" all spoke some English and wore monogrammed white uniforms; even though Dilip had by now retired from his diplomatic missions, for special dinners the servants still dressed in black Nehru jackets with buttons of bright brass. The Shahs' servants, on the other hand, shouted in Marathi and chewed tobacco. At all meals, the Maharaj appeared from the kitchen, in a sleeveless muslin undershirt and a crumpled cotton *dhoti* pulled between his ample legs, to berate and cajole guests who didn't eat well. Gita was unable to name the exact underlying difference between these two households, but she knew for sure it wasn't a simple matter of "Westernization."

"So, Aunty, how does this astrology and all work?" Gita asked.

"Simple," said Saroj Aunty. "The stars are in a certain pattern at your birth. Then they keep moving on to highlight different parts of the pattern. All this endless uncertainty, darling, it's really a bother. Happiness, heartbreak, happiness again—what on earth are we to make of this muddle? When you think of those planets moving, it really helps. Not that everything has to be *exactly* as the stars predict. Planets simply outline a story that you can fill in in so many different ways. Anyway, darling, what our Kaka does is astrology all right, but he mixes it up with some sort of German numerology."

"I see," said Gita, though she didn't quite understand. At this time, she was still waiting for the day when everything made sense; a magical moment when she would finally arrive at the horizon of being grown up. She was sure that a destined He was somewhere out there, but it was too difficult to see anything beyond the sheer precipice of her departure for America.

Saroj Aunty and Gita were sitting indoors with the lights on. Around them windows rattled, coconut trees whirled, waves flung themselves high against the garden wall. Because Bombay roads easily became rivers when it rained, Harish Uncle had decided not to go into town to his office today. Instead he was lying on the big bed in the next room, reading Agatha Christie and listening to a tape of *sarodh* music. Faint twangs mixed in with the din of the storm.

"Kaka should be here any minute," said Saroj Aunty. "Time for tea. Tukaram! Muktabai!"

As Saroj Aunty instructed the servants about what kind of spices to pound for tea, Gita slipped into the next room. She had dressed up in a sari in honor of looking more grown up, but being unused to saris she periodically felt the urge to straighten her pleats. Standing before the mottled almirah mirror, she pulled the front part of her sari out from its anchor in the petticoat. With the index and middle fingers of her right hand anchoring one side of the pleats, and her thumb the other side, with her left hand she guided the sari material into a neat fan. Then she straightened the border that rose toward her left shoulder to fall from the back. After brushing the material down, she stopped and examined her reflection. As always, whenever she stared at her own face, she could hear her mother clucking that she was *sooo* dark, poor little thing, why didn't she remember to keep out of the sun and apply Pond's cold cream nightly? She could also hear the girls at the convent school groaning about what *lovely* long lashes she had, so lucky, *yaar*. The face looking back through the cloudy glass had hair pulled tightly from a high forehead, serious black eyes with circles beneath them. It looked earnest, worried. Gita turned her face sideways so that the roundness of her young cheeks gave way to a line that might, with luck, someday transmute into well-defined cheekbones. She straightened her back, wondering if she would ever grow beyond her frail-shouldered, bony-wristed five foot three.

"Lovely, darling." Saroj Aunty looked up in her cross-eyed way to smile as Gita returned. "And we're all so proud of that scholarship you've won! But I'm sick with worry about whether that stipend will be enough. Who's going to look after you? You know how the government is about rupees leaving the country, and what with your brother's health problems it's not as though Dilip and Kookoo can offer much help. There *are* people out there, but God only knows where all, it's not just that California-Shalifornia of yours. I believe that Kalpana's brother-in-law is in New Jersey, quite a nice fellow with specs, someday we'll have to *definitely* get you together. And Neeru, darling, she's in Mad something—Madison, I tell you, just like her to go to a place like that. Harish's cousin Maheshbhai is in a place called Queens. Don't tell me you haven't heard about him, it's one of Harish's absolutely favorite stories! Years ago, Maheshbhai's plane abroad was eight hours late because of one of these monsoon storms. I swear it, when he came back from the airport to rest, we could distinctly hear that he'd already gone and developed an American accent!" Saroj Aunty let out a high-pitched titter. For a woman of her broad bulk, her laugh was unexpectedly small. "Such a huge-huge country, darling," Saroj Aunty continued, her voice softening as she stared at the windowpanes swirling with gray water. "A country as big as our Arabian Sea. Or bigger. Who'll look after you out there?"

"I can look after myself," Gita said. After all, that's what she'd been doing ever since she'd been sent off to boarding school.

"We'll have to find you a nice boyfriend," said Saroj Aunty. She raised a shoulder and smiled coyly over it, fingers reaching out to touch Gita's cheek. "Ganeshan Kaka will tell us *all* about him."

Gita looked down, unable to admit the interest she felt. She wished she could say something smart and nonchalant. It was terrible how words got stuck in her throat, sounding stupid before they were said, and if she did speak them how they came out whirling, nosediving into flat air.

Ganeshan Kaka arrived late because of the flooded roads. "*Sala,* this rain is like the end of one bloody *yuga!*" Kaka cackled as he slipped out of his sopping sandals and folded his black umbrella by the wall. He emerged from the bathroom a few moments later, his freshly washed feet leaving imprints on the marble floor. After warming up with spiced tea, he examined the notebook in which Gita's horoscope had been drawn. His mouth worked furiously around his false teeth as he muttered calculations, counting on the joints and tips of his fingers. He wrote out Gita's full name and added up each letter. Then he drew a five-pointed star around which he arranged an explosion of numbers.

"Tell us about love, Kaka," prompted Saroj Aunty.

Ganeshan Kaka snorted a laugh. "Baba, everyone is so interested in this love, stars, and all! Hold on, girls, hold on. I will be telling you everything." He brought out a Hindu almanac and continued with his calculations as Saroj Aunty shot Gita a conspiratorial smile. To Ganeshan Kaka, everyone younger than himself, even bald Harish Uncle in the next room, even his tiny wife who always stayed at home, was a boy or girl.

"*Ahma Saraswati no ashirvaad bau saras che,*" he finally informed Saroj Aunty. Kaka was originally from Madras, but he had held a job as a bank clerk in Bombay's Fort District for so many decades that he often spoke rapid-fire Gujarati with the Shahs. Among the servants, both he and the Shahs switched to Marathi. Ungrammatical Bombay Hindi was used for random interactions—for example, bargaining with the fruit-*walas* over the price of the mangoes in the baskets on their heads or giving directions on the street. English was also used much of the time with visitors, especially if, like Gita, they weren't familiar with Marathi or Gujarati. Ganeshan Kaka repeated in English for her, "Look here, girl, you've got very fine blessings from Saraswati."

"The Goddess of Learning, darling," put in Saroj Aunty.

"Come on, Aunty, I know *that*," Gita said, ducking her head at the end of the sentence. She didn't mean to sound disrespectful. Kookoo would have berated her manners, but Saroj Aunty continued to beam. Gita allowed herself to smile too. She thought of Saraswati seated in a fragrant white lotus, garlanded with white flowers, holding a musical instrument against the folds of her white silk sari.

Ganeshan Kaka continued, "With Saraswati's blessings, what is the problem then for studying? Baba, this girl will just take away all the gold medals and all. Going abroad, job, everything will come from her mind." Actually, he inserted a *y* before all vowels, so these words sounded like "yall," "yabroad," and "yeverything."

"We already know *that*, Kaka," said Saroj Aunty. "We don't need astrology to know how brainy our Gita is. But what about *matrimony?*"

Ganeshan Kaka lifted a scrawny wrist, studying his watch as Saroj Aunty's voice rose to form a question. "Eleven fifty-three!" he shot out the moment her question was complete. Then he hunched over to proceed with further calculations. Gita stared at her feet, reflecting that her sandals had been abandoned at the front door. "Shani Maharaj . . ." Kaka finally said in a low voice. "This Saturn is one troublesome bugger. Not that he doesn't teach and all, but so much problems he gives! Difficulties, disappointments, all his doing. Later on you might thank him . . . Humph!" Kaka briskly jotted down a stream of numbers as he paged further through the almanac beside him. "Before Chaitra twenty forty there's no chance for this marriage business. March nineteen eighty-four Anyway, Gita girl, you listen to your Kaka. I am simply telling you that by twenty-three years, seven months, and five days you will surely be getting a boy."

Saroj Aunty clapped her plump hands. Glass and gold bracelets tinkled on her wrists. "Wonderful, darling! We'll all look forward to Him."

Gita twisted the end of her braid, feeling a blush rise from her ears.

"But this Shani . . ." Kaka's false teeth rattled fiercely. He narrowed one eye and raised the sheet of paper parallel to his face. "Listen, girl, when you see those pots of oil that Shani's devotees who wear black and yall bring out on Saturday, you just throw some coins in the oil, yokay?"

There were people in black on Telegraph Avenue, which jutted out from the main gate of the campus. These people wore outfits of black leather with metal spikes. Their faces were frighteningly white, with hair blacker than black, or partially shaved, or dyed bright colors and combed into absurd creations. They loitered amid the dense smell of grease outside pizza parlors. Other people, dressed less formidably, hiked by with backpacks full of books or careened along the sidewalks on skateboards. Men with matted hair sat by the walls of the decrepit hotels, their palms outstretched. Vendors chatted with each other beside stalls filled with unaffordable things. Gita walked briskly, anxious about wasting time or money. On this street, there were absolutely no caldrons of sesame oil to toss a glistening American president into.

Saturn, then, had remained unpropitiated when eighteen months rolled along, presenting Gita to March 1984. Gita had thought a lot about this month: on days when she was lonely but felt she must not break her routines, on days when she gave in and dawdled, drinking tea and talking to her housemate, Bet. March had come to represent the moment when everything would change and Heavenly Father Bhagavan would bless her with a mate. It was odd, Gita thought, heart unfolding in a smile of anticipation, that despite almost two years of classes she still hadn't met any nice boys. Sorry, men. Gita had to keep reminding herself that here even people younger than she were women and men, the Ganeshan Kaka principle in reverse. At twenty-three, Gita had to admit that she still saw herself as a girl. "Woman" hung awkwardly, with too much space and unapologetic certainty in its outlines.

On the first day of March, Gita woke up to find a card by the phone. It was from Bet, who stayed up late and always slept until after Gita left for the library. The card had foxes on it. Their tongues spilled out obscenely over their jaws, and their ears were flattened as they chased ahead. "Happy Hunting," Bet had written inside. *Hunting?* That was wrong, thought Gita, as she put the kettle on. Whoever He was, He would come to find her once she had shown herself. Like a princess holding a heavy garland of jasmine and roses, she had only to recognize Him. She would stretch her arms, He would bow His dark head, she would slip the intoxicatingly fragrant wreath around His neck, over His broad chest. Lush red silk, a shimmer of gold brocade, a *kurta* of startling white. The red and white together made her breath tighten.

During her midmorning break from the library that day, Gita went to drink tea at a café. Ordinarily she never went to cafés. Fifty cents a cup per day meant fifteen dollars a month. Fifteen dollars from her scholarship stipend might buy a book instead. It was better to walk back to the apartment and brew up a pot. To the apartment was a good eighteen-minute walk, but the bus was another fifty cents, and anyway this counted as exercise for which there was no other time. Luckily it was a pretty walk, past houses in old neighborhoods, past gardens that bloomed all year long and sometimes displayed makeshift crosses for people killed in Central America, past dogs and cats that were stretched out in wait of passing, petting hands. This month, though, Gita was determined not to always rush back to her room during empty patches of time. It was too important to be alert and attuned to the principles of romance for the moment when He arrived.

Two convoluted articles were assigned for class. Gita took out her ruler and pencil for underlining key passages, and began writing comments on an index card. (She clutched this card, glancing down to be refreshed, when during a seminar the inquiring faces and sudden silence set her ideas faltering, her words dissolving in the constriction of a thumping heart and reddened face.) But her eyes wandered from the text. She soon noticed that there was a handsome man at a table nearby, a most positively handsome Indian man. He looked like Shashi Kapoor once had: with delicate nostrils and hair very black against the nape of his fair neck. He was sitting alone, intent on the paper. Gita drank her tea slowly, conscious of His presence as she tried to anchor the words she was reading onto the page. Could it really be He? Had He seen her? As far as she could tell, the man never looked up, not even once. He kept reading and sipping his cappuccino. She set to jingling her glass bangles, pretending to look for something in her bag: surely the trembling clank was a sound He should recognize. No response, and she didn't have even a single point outlined on her card. Oh well, this man was probably an Arab or Latin American or Italian or something. It was not always easy to tell with people of that complexion. After a while she collected her books and took refuge in a library carrel.

On March 2, a man with a dimpled, expectant smile rang the doorbell. Unfortunately, all he wanted was a donation for disarmament. Gita took out a precious dollar, hoping he might ask her name. But he only asked for her signature, one among many pages on a petition. He didn't even look up to smile good-bye.

By March 5, she wondered whether tall, American-born Rakesh in her French class might be a possibility—it made conjugating verbs that morning a thrill—but then she saw him under the campanile sharing a sandwich with a girl. They were sitting very close. With true love there could never be a question of competition, and that was the end of Rakesh. Anyway, she could never have respected a man whose American accent seemed to stand between him and the correct pronunciation of his own name.

The same evening Bet brought home a man who asked Gita a lot of questions about India while she warmed up her dinner in the kitchen. He looked her deep in the eyes when he talked about how he had a guru and was learning to fly, so far just flopping, in a cross-legged position, but soon he hoped to lift off the ground. Gita felt guilty for wondering if this could be He when perhaps he was Bet's. But after he left, Bet said he was gay. "Like, what do you expect? These are hard times, kid. All the guys are married or gay."

March 9: a party organized by a classmate. Instead of pleading too much work, Gita went. There was a man there with glasses whose brown hair was so dark it could almost have been black. He was a veterinarian. Gita thought of *Reader's Digest* articles about kindly vets and grateful animals that the sisters at her convent school had loved to read. He started telling a story about the time he had volunteered to canvas for the homeless. In the San Francisco Marina neighborhood, a plump woman came to the door in her nightgown. "The deities sent you!" she had exclaimed. "Come on upstairs and I'll write you a check." Gita slid away in mortification as everyone laughed. She filled her glass with more orange juice. But when she came back it turned out that the woman had been performing a Tibetan Buddhist ritual and needed a witness for the last lamp lit. Even with this explanation, Gita couldn't bring herself to talk more to him.

Another man at the same party worked for the Democratic campaign, and said Gandhi was his hero—he had seen the film five times. Gita mentioned that her father had been portrayed in the film, even though it was a marginal role. The man lit up and gave her his card, saying he would like to "talk more about your country." He was too blond and too chatty. She didn't know what he would expect if they went out alone, just the two of them. She took the card and then, almost as if it were dirty, she tossed it in a garbage bin outside. (Bet, waiting at home to hear what happened, extravagantly shook her head. "No, no, no!" she said. "Cut out this first-sight crap. Next time you *save* the card of a man who's available!")

Each day in March was harder to live through than the last. Every morning began with hope, with increasing care for the face in the mirror that He might also see. She began underlining her eyes with a little finger rubbed with *kajal*. She brought out different earrings. Absolutely nothing happened. The thought that most girls her age had at least been kissed began to creep up on her, to ambush her no matter what she was trying to do. Furthermore, there had been no blue aerograms from India for a while. It seemed clear that she was on the margins of absolutely everyone's life, had always been, and would always be. When Gita was a small child, Kookoo was always sending her off to Ayah; when Dilip appeared, the "run along, dear"s increased, seconded by a gruff "jolly good," as she disappeared out of sight. Then Kookoo was recurrently ill and Gita was sent off to boarding school, and Ayah was retired. Gita had received one—or was there a second?—letter from Ayah, written by a village scribe and addressed to "Baby." But then somehow the letters had stopped. Ayah had never been heard of again. Who had she been? Gita now wondered about this woman whom she had once unquestioningly accepted as part of her life and whose comforting body she could still feel. Why had she worked for a living? What had her real name been? Did she still chew betel nut because servants ate so late, and she was hungry? Had she worn white because she was a widow or because Kookoo thought it hygienic? Who had there been for Ayah to return to in the village? The pathos of being a woman unprotected and alone had never before struck Gita so forcefully.

Certainly the Shahs had always seemed happy to see Gita when they took her in during vacations through the years that Dilip was posted abroad, but why did they do this? Was it charity? A promise made to her father? She wasn't their daughter or even really their niece. Why, after all, would they care?

Around this issue of the missing mate, Gita felt every form of affection she had ever known blacken and shrink like leather mildewed in the monsoon air. By the third weekend in March Gita was so low that she decided to spend the time and money to see a movie. But standing in line in the bright sunshine for a matinee, she noticed that everyone around her had someone with them. They licked at each others' ice cream cones, held hands, talked animatedly, tied shoelaces for children. Tears scratched in her chest and she abruptly left for the library.

Sunday morning, March 18, Firoze Ganjifrockwala rang up to ask if she'd heard the news that Dinaz would be the Lyril soap girl, whirling under waterfalls on Indian prime-time television in every city and all the villages connected by satellite: vivacious, buxom Dinaz. Firoze was happy that his cousin would earn a real packet of cash, and Gita listened attentively through the receiver as he voiced his worries about the commoditization of the peasant imagination and the creation of artificial market-mediated needs. He then asked if Gita would like to meet midweek for lunch at the Indian food and pizza place near campus. Gita felt a stir of possibility: here, after all, was a male seeking her out.

Though Firoze wasn't exactly a strapping hero, he wasn't bad-looking either, with his fair Parsi complexion, pronounced nose, thick straight brows, hazel eyes. But his habit of lecturing, hardly bearable on the phone, was unendurable in person. He seemed to be the very incarnation of earnestness as he carried on about the colonized Indian mind. There was an inkspot spreading out from the pocket on his chest. He was apparently growing a beard. He had shifted from computer science to political science, he said, and had begun to study Spanish on the side. He was also taking a course in women's studies for reasons that Gita couldn't decode. The lunch was partially unfrozen vegetables doused in *garam masala*. It was all depressing: no sardonic widowers or red roses, just this confused boy holding forth in a place that had someone else's mathematical calculations scratched in ballpoint pen on the plastic tablecloth. Gita worried that the waiters might think she was involved with him. She worried that he might get the wrong idea about her if they kept lunching out like this. She made a point of telling him how hard she had to study to renew her scholarship next year, and that there was no question of ever going to films or any other sort of social life. As they left, a thin boy standing by the door with a stack of red leaflets handed one to each of them.

"Must be about the march on Saturday," said Firoze, sticking the paper in his shoulder bag. He continued with his analysis of how kicking out Coca-Cola from India had at least been an important symbolic statement, even though Campa Cola, Thums Up, Rim Zim, and other home-grown imitations had taken over the market. Gita glanced down at the leaflet. "Has that wonderful person with the extra something yet crossed your path?" the sheet of paper inquired. She whipped the paper into her own bag. Later, in her library carrel, she unfolded it.

> *Has that wonderful person with the extra something yet crossed your path? Why be alone in the land of sweet dates? Let Krishna "Chris" Patel be your Kama of Karma.*
>
> *CHRIS CROSS: Dedicated to the hearts and lives of Bay Area South Asians and those Americans with love for our ancient spiritual traditions.*
>
> *CHRIS CROSS: Your multilaned highway to happiness.*
>
> *Call CHRIS CROSS today for free information. Astrological counseling included in package deal.*

Gita held the paper, thinking that no one in India ever called it "South Asia" and how even a phone call involved her own effort. Truly, the unseen He should have known where she was and come galloping in. Tears began to close in around the corners of her vision, and it was with a valiant effort that she returned to taking notes for the next day's class. She felt enormously grateful for the excuse to fill out index cards with smooth, neat writing.

The Thursday afternoon seminar had gone well. At a moment when two adamant young men had been deadlocked in an argument, with even the shaggy professor looking dismayed, Gita had lifted her index card and spoken out in quiet tones that caused the entire class to lean forward, transfixed. Through the rest of the seminar several people had referred back to her point. The professor had praised her for articulating the "Eastern perspective, from which we can all learn." One of the young men had come up to her afterward with congratulations for "shutting up that asshole, I grooved on what you had to say." (For a flickering moment Gita had regarded this loud giant with hope, but she saw almost immediately that he was just too grotesquely huge, and furthermore so vain that he hadn't even registered his own silencing.)

Gita was reflecting on her success, sipping tea, and leafing absently through Bet's newspaper when the telephone rang. It was for her, Gita. It was an unknown man.

"You don't, umm, know who I am," he said. "My name is Timothy Stilling. But I have this gift for you from the Shahs." He had met them, he said, at Heathrow airport, where all the flights had been delayed due to a bomb scare. She could picture Saroj Aunty, wearing her printed silk traveling sari, spotting the San Francisco tag on this man's luggage and nudging Harish Uncle out of the P. G. Wodehouse he always read on trips. They had started a conversation, charmed this Mr. Stilling, persuaded him to carry something for Gita. Probably Saroj Aunty slipped off to buy it at the duty-free shop as Harish Uncle held him captive with charming stories.

"I, well, live in San Francisco," Timothy Stilling said. He had a deep, honest voice. "I'll be up in Berkeley for a reading at, uh, Cody's Books next week. If you could manage to make it over there, I could hand deliver your package."

"A reading?" Gita asked. She hated that her voice thinned like the finest silver filigree whenever she spoke to unknown people on the phone.

"Oh yes, I'm . . . a poet."

A poet! This was the kind of coincidence about which minstrels sang. Poetry: the very word was filled with miraculous shades of emotion. Gita occasionally wrote poetry herself. When she was at boarding school in Ooty she would disappear to the old British cemetery or onto the terrace of the dormitory to write when feelings were glowing with their own unearthly light. At Our Lady of Perpetual Succour Convent they read Wordsworth, of course. And some Shelley and Shakespeare sonnets, and Ravindranath Tagore on the mind without fear. Yet it had been Saroj Aunty who introduced her to modern poetry. Saroj Aunty in her big bungalow with all her servants and art gallery openings and silk saris, each lying named in its own box, had read poetry almost all her life. She kept Eliot, Lorca, Faiz, Yeats, Mahadevi Varma, Neruda, and others on her bedside table along with Sanskrit and English versions of the Upanishads. Some of her saris had names of poems she liked. Meghaduta was a smoky blue silk, Waste Land was printed lilac, gray, and blood red.

According to Saroj Aunty, Gita's real father had written poetry too. He used to recite inspirational pieces about freedom for Mother India after he'd had a few drinks with his Communist comrades. Saroj Aunty had once taken out a book of Rilke's poems to show Gita the inscription on the flyleaf in Gita's father's brisk, thick-nibbed hand: "For Saru, a blossom with stillness, Vinay." Gita was dimly aware that once Saroj Aunty had been a Communist too. But there were other connections between the families. Gita's father's father had been a barrister who advised the people from the minor princely state that owned the haunted villa near Harish Uncle's Juhu place. Her father and Harish Uncle's mother's brother had once played on the rocks at low tide as boys, pretending to spot smugglers. Then, if you started excavating, there were still more overlaps. Gita's mother's great-uncle had settled in Tanzania for business at the same time as Saroj Aunty's second cousin. And so on. Sometimes it seemed as if all the people of that class and those generations were interconnected across India. Now these ties were spreading across the globe, encircling others as they went.

✳

"Holy cow! Not Timothy Stilling." Bet squinted one eye open. She was soaking in the afternoon sun on the deck in case she was called back for an audition.

"Who is he?" Gita asked, so excited that the name was recognized that she forgot to wonder if Bet was making fun of her. She was never sure whether people in California only said "Holy cow" to Indians. She was also trying to ignore the expanse of nude flesh before her. Thank goodness Bet was lying on her stomach; it would have been quite difficult the other way.

"Well, he's sure a Bay Area celebrity. I don't know how well he's known elsewhere. One of those postmodern Susan Sontag kind of men. He's in the *Chronicle* sometimes. I read an interview about him once; I think he writes essays and poetry. You'd better get your little ass right over to the Telegraph Avenue bookstores to check out his writing. Well! It looks like that astrologer of yours has something going for him."

"Nothing," said Gita, smiling broadly. She stopped, listening to her voice. She hadn't used the word that way in months, maybe years. It was the way girls at the covent had said "Shut up" or "Nonsense." Na-*thing*—it seemed to fling away the other person's position even if you suspected it was right.

"Before you go, remember to pick up, will you? I already told you I might have some folks stopping by."

"Sure," said Gita. That was the arrangement: if either of them had a visitor they had to issue advance warning. She put her books in her room, closed the door, and sped off through streets festive with pink blossoms.

There were two slim volumes of poetry by Timothy Stilling in stock. The back covers were filled with praise but no picture, alas. Gita turned a few pages and soon she felt that she was visiting an old, dear friend. The bookstore bustle disappeared. He was holding up a mirror for her to see herself. He understood the nuances of what she had never been able to express. He spoke about places inside her she would like to discover. She felt herself hugging, hugged by his words, felt herself expanding to incorporate his mind.

If the books hadn't been hardbacks she would have bought them both even though they weren't assigned for a class. Instead she checked them out of the library, reading and rereading them with someone else's marginal notes (yes, he was worthy of a paper, maybe even a dissertation!). She calculated that there was a fourteen-year age difference between them, the right amount of time for someone to grow wise. She stopped dressing up and forcing herself into cafés. It was clear now, she was to be devoted to this man. But being shy, she did not let on to anyone, though it was all she thought about most of the time. Shani Maharaj, with all his weight and presence, and seven gyrating moons, was slowly lumbering ahead.

He was not handsome. Hardly the dark-haired, broad-shouldered prince Gita had always expected. Timothy Stilling was very skinny and quite bald, and the hair hanging low around his scalp was a nondescript brown. His eyes were small under the jutting forehead. His shoulders sloped. If she took him home to Delhi surely everyone would laugh. "Couldn't you have done better, dear?" Kookoo would say in an undertone, leaning forward as she handed back the salad spoons to the uniformed servant standing behind her chair. Dilip would bring out imported whisky and invite Timothy to have a few pegs, then remark later that it was a pity the old chap wasn't much of a drinker, and a terrible shame about cricket and those Yanks. Riding with Timothy on the train to Bombay would be a disaster too; she could already feel the heat of the stares from other passengers. How he would be received by the Shahs wasn't clear yet: after all, they must have liked him if they had forwarded him onward.

As soon as he started introducing his poems, her opinions began to shift. His voice was filled with golden light. His eyes shimmered, blue, wise. His hands were long-fingered and eloquent when he spread them out to make a point. Even the teeth, set so tight and crooked in his mouth, were charming. Yes, Saroj Aunty had picked the right kind of man. Sitting in the back row, Gita became conscious of her breath pumping into her stomach, playing intoxicatingly out over her upper lip. She had felt this way only a few fleeting times before in her life. She remembered the thrill of algorithms taught by the sole male teacher who was not in robes, a nervous young man whom every girl in the convent school longed for but who disappointed them all by getting married over an Easter vacation. She thought of the neighbor's son in Delhi with his short shorts and hairy legs, off with a tennis racket in the early mornings, and how when the parents got together for dinner she had once spent an entire evening in his room wondering what to say as he sucked, scowling, on a cigarette. Before she had pricked up her ears at college for the kinds of things one might talk about with a boy, he had gone off to England on a Rhodes scholarship. It was sad but true that though Gita was so accomplished in other spheres of life, when it came to romance she felt like an ignoramus. Even if Bet was sometimes so awfully condescending, it might not be a bad idea to open up to her in search of advice.

Gita had dressed in Indian clothes for the poetry reading. Before March she had mostly tried to disappear into crowds by wearing jeans and running shoes, hair severely braided down her back. But this day she had loosely anchored her hair in a bamboo hair clip and spent the time before the reading ironing a red-and-black tie-dyed *kurta* to wear over tight-fitting black *churidar*s. Saroj Aunty had chosen this outfit from a boutique in Bombay run by two elderly sisters pledged to natural fabrics and vegetable dyes. It bore luck. As Gita waited for the crowds to clear away from Timothy Stilling when he finished his reading, she felt pretty and unique.

Women were fluttering around him, men were shaking his hand, books were thrust before him for a signature. A short Indian (Pakistani? Bangladeshi? Sri Lankan?) girl with a halo of hair around a self-possessed, smiling face went up and extended a hand, accentuating Gita's awkwardness to herself. He was taller than most people, Gita observed. That bald head would be like a white beacon in any crowd, in any situation of the shared story that was rising up with such certainty before them. Finally he was left with just one man.

"I am Gita," she presented herself, conscious of her voice being different, a "charming lilt."

"Gita? Oh yes—" He was puzzled but smiling down at her with all those wonderful crooked teeth.

"Gita!" the other man said. He was short, tanned, with wiry black hair and glasses. "I've seen you around Feeler Hall, haven't I? Aren't you a new graduate student?"

"Yes." It seemed to Gita that she could do nothing but smile as though her cheeks would split.

"Oh no. The present," Timothy Stilling said. "I knew I forgot something. I'm so sorry you had to come all this way. This is terrible. I've been doing this kind of thing lately— there's just too much going on with, you know, the British editions coming out and proofreading for the new book and all the traveling."

"At least you made it here on the right day, Tim," the other man said. "Right month, right time. That's something."

"Oh, cut it out, Norvin," said Timothy. "This is Norvin Weinstein, Gita. He's kidding around because I, umm, wrote down a reading in Cambridge wrong in my calendar. I got there a month early."

Gita was wishing she could disappear. She recognized the name Norvin Weinstein. He was a famous professor, someone her adviser had suggested she take a course with sometime.

There was no reason to feel publicly shamed at what wasn't even an obvious assignation, but she did. The professor would surely know that she could have been decoding Foucault's *The History of Sexuality* this evening instead of looking for her March Man. "And then?" she asked, her smile suddenly awkward in its fit.

"Well, nothing. The bookstore folks were stunned. I stayed on to hear the other reading. Then I had to fly back and go out again. The whole experience was like walking into someone else's nightmare. I really am sorry about your package. I even put it near my car keys, but at the last minute the phone rang."

"Look here," said Professor Weinstein, "why don't we all go out for a drink? You can always give her the package later. Gita, I've been wanting to get together with you. I was in India in the Peace Corps. Nasik, Maharashtra. Sixty-six to sixty-eight. I'm sure you know the place. Where did you go to school?"

"Our Lady of Perpetual Succour Convent, Ootacamund," said Gita, wondering why Timothy pressed his lips hard so he wouldn't smile, and the professor let out a whoop.

"Fabulous," said the professor, grinning with what seemed like all thirty-two teeth. "Just fabulous. We've got to talk. And what are you working on?"

What a question! To say she didn't know yet would show her up as a graduate student so young she was still floundering for a Topic. Gita thought rapidly on her feet, bringing an inspirational folklore course she'd been sitting in on into the same frame as Ayah. "The intellectual paradigms underlying colonial folk-narrative collections on the Indian subcontinent," she said.

"Hot stuff!" said the professor. "You can work in intertextuality, imperialism, invented traditions, all the rest of it. Terrific. Well, let's go for a drink. My car's down the street."

By now it was time for Gita to have been studying her daily chapter in the French for Reading Knowledge book. But it was the professor who was insisting. That eased the responsibility.

*   *   *

By the time they had all sat down, she was using their first names. Norvin explained that he and Timothy had been undergraduates together at Harvard. (Harvard! Gita thought—even the convent sisters wouldn't just dismiss this as a nest of long-haired protestors but would associate it with respectable citizens.) They had met the first day, when Timothy was singing a Bob Dylan song with his guitar and Norvin came by from the next dorm room to say the E major chord should really be minor. Norvin, it turned out, was right. It appeared that he went through life being short, dark, handsome, and right. They became friends. When Norvin was in India, Timothy was in Paris. Later they were both in graduate school at Yale. Now they were both stars in their own right. Norvin was known for his contributions to poststructuralist, neo-Marxist literary criticism and Timothy for his postbeat poetry. Gita had heard at some graduate student party that Berkeley had had to create a special endowed Doolittle Chair in order to keep Norvin, he was wanted by so many other universities. And neither of them was yet forty!

Norvin was trying to speak to Gita in Marathi. *"Mazha nav* Norvin *ahe,"* he said. *"Me* America *la rahatath, Mazha vadhil* lawyer *ahe. Tumcha nav kai?"*

Gita nodded, too awestruck to tell him that she didn't speak Marathi, she wasn't from that part of the country. *"Ho, Ho,"* she assented, remembering that this was how Saroj Aunty's servants said yes. She wished he would stop so Timothy could say something wise. "Walking into someone else's nightmare" had been so poetic. She had no idea what Norvin was talking about except when English words made their way through his Brooklyn accent. She looked nervously around through the clatter and cigarette smoke in the café. There was a clutch of Iranian students at the next table, unrolling posters of tortured people. There was a group of girls—probably undergraduates—sharing a jug of beer and laughing loudly at each other's stories. "Give us Bruce Springsteen!" someone shouted at a friend poised by the jukebox. In the midst of this there were people with books open before them, some studying hard and some looking around wistfully. Luckily nobody she could recognize from her classes.

Timothy was drinking herbal tea, which gave her the excuse to order some tea too without looking unsophisticated. As Norvin carried on, Timothy twirled the cup around and around on the table. He began to shred the paper napkins and rearrange the white pieces into different patterns. Then he took a small book out of his breast pocket and wrote something down.

"A poem?" Gita asked hopefully, even though Norvin was midway through some unintelligible narrative. When Timothy took out the pen she felt as if she were stepping into a temple, lamps flickering in the innermost sanctum. She could smell incense and burning *ghee* and feel the presence of freshly bathed Ayah.

"No, not exactly," said Timothy, fidgeting with the book as he slid it back into his pocket. "Just, umm, a reminder for me to make an international call. I keep forgetting to do these things. Everyone ends up mad at me."

"Well, to cut a long story short," Norvin said, "I managed to convince them that I didn't have to be followed around with a chair, I was quite capable of sitting cross-legged. It took all that! Sorry, Timothy, I really wanted to practice my Marathi. I hardly meet anyone I can talk to anymore. It's important to keep up on all one's languages."

"Very important," Gita ventured.

"I speak six," said Norvin, "twelve if you bring in the reading knowledge. You guys want anything? Sure? I'm going for another beer." As Norvin stood up, Gita noticed that his shirt was textured purple handloom, probably made in India, and just the fashionable amount too big. Timothy's shirt was actually too tight, blue checks that might have been better on a kitchen table, its cut accentuating his bones and angles. And it didn't even have buttons, it had snaps! Thinking that Timothy didn't know current men's fashions made her feel protective.

"People should understand that you're busy," Gita said,

leaning forward and looking into Timothy's long harlequin face. "I mean, being creative and all is hard work."

"It's not the creativity," Timothy said, "it's the being on display. All the expectations and demands. You know how that is?"

"Oh, *yes,*" said Gita, flattered that he thought she might. She had to force herself not to flinch as his eyes connected with hers.

"At this point in my life I just want to have enough time alone to keep writing, but that's not what anyone else seems to understand. I mean, fulfill expectations and time becomes this leaky faucet, drip, drip, unrelenting drip."

"Oh, I know *exactly* how it is," Gita said. "Here in America it's something that you have to always be rationing."

"Ration," said Timothy. "Great word." He took out his notebook again and wrote it down. Wrote her word down! What else could she say?

"There's a famine on time here," Gita said carefully. "Everyone works but is hungry inside." She waited for him to write this down too. He didn't, and the pole of attention went back from her point of view to his. "You must look after yourself," she said. "Can't you get a secretary to make those calls and all so you can write?" She paused, then said in a rush, "Your poetry is lovely. You must give yourself maximum time."

Her ears began to burn as soon as she said this. She looked into the dregs of her rosehip tea. Lovely was such a tame word, and really what she meant was: you need a wife.

"Thank you," said Timothy. "I'm glad you like my work." He had the kindest smile that pierced blue-eyed through her heart right to the other side.

Gita began to see bald men everywhere. They sat in front of her at talks, they disappeared around street corners, they wandered through stacks and lifted their heads from carrels in the library. It always gave her an electric shudder. She discovered entire typologies of baldness. There were men whose hair was thinning around a whorl at the top of their heads, men whose hair crept backward from the front. There were erudite elongated foreheads, and entire expanses of skull-stretched skin. She thought of how Timothy's skull had glistened under the lights that night, how smooth it would be to run fingers over, very, very, gently.

But none of these bald men was ever Timothy. March was running out, and he still hadn't delivered the present. What would happen if Shani Maharaj was blocked from doing whatever he was supposed to do in the set framework of time? Could planets be wrong, like Dilip had always said? She worried about Ganeshan Kaka's powers of prediction. Yet Saroj Aunty had trusted him, hadn't she? Gita started studying in her room in case Timothy called and was too tongue-tied to leave a message on Bet's machine. But attended telephones, like watched water, stay maddeningly still.

Whenever Gita saw Norvin on campus, she went in the other direction. Once she even hopped into a bathroom so she wouldn't have to talk to him. It was mortifying: suppose he had seen how she felt about Timothy? Suppose he had changed his mind over whether someone with a scholarship could spend an evening in a café with two men? She imagined him talking about it at a faculty meeting. "Gita Das passing her exams? But that girl is obviously smitten with Timothy Stilling. Are you sure she has the concentration to do the Ph.D.?"

Timothy had said he read the *New York Times,* everything but the business section, like an addiction each day. Gita had thought of herself as too busy to read anything more than the headlines of Bet's local paper, but she now made a point of looking up the *Times* in the library when she arrived each morning. It gave her comfort to know that he was reading the same pages, maybe even at the same time, and she wondered what kind of fantastic thoughts were sprouting in his mind as he too located himself in this enormously complicated world. She learned more about the empty words of jolly-faced Reagan, about stones being thrown on the West Bank, about the first reports on the mysterious disease called AIDS. She learned about discotheques in Abu Dhabi, religious fundamentalists in India, punks in Australia, and the flow of alpha waves in meditation. She found herself composing notes in her head about passages he might like.

Gita was not used to having girlfriends to confide in, but when the loneliness of waiting was unbearable, she let out her feelings in hesitant spurts to Bet.

"How d'you know he's not attached?" Bet asked over the hot hiss of an iron. She was doing the neighbor's clothes. Along with walking the neighbor's dogs and baby-sitting their children, this was her main form of income in the long waits between plays in which she was paid.

"He's not," said Gita. "It doesn't say anything about any special women in his dedications or acknowledgments. Except his mother, that is."

"Yeah, but those books are old, and you can't tell everything about a person's life from their *books,* anyway. I wouldn't be surprised if he's one of those goddamn passive men who just lie there waiting to be *seduced* and lap up all the attention."

"Oh no, Timothy's not like *that,*" Gita said hastily. The word *seduction* wasn't part of her repertoire. Or his. He lived inside her now, she knew him like her oldest friend.

"Or he might be the driven sort," Bet continued, holding up the dress on which she had just worked through the gathers of puffed sleeves. With its cinched waist, it was too small for her. "You know, no time for romance, that kind of crap. Always *producing.* I dated a playwright for a while. Bill Jones. You'd have heard of him if you'd grown up here. It was awful with Bill, creativity came first. He'd even get out of *bed* if he had an idea. You have to watch out for famous men."

"Timothy is very busy," Gita said. "He forgets to ring up people." She thought of the little notebook. Maybe this very minute, wherever he was, he would whip the book out of his pocket and write: "Call Gita." Call Gita. Please, she's waiting. You looked into her eyes when you smiled. You know how this feels: "like an impaled cork," your poem on page 65 of the first book says.

"Anyway, it's just a week or so. People don't get back to each other that soon," Bet said. "You might as well lay easy and trust your astrologer."

In the end it was Norvin who called. ("What kind of nerdy name is that?" asked Bet, summoning Gita with a hand over the receiver.) Gita struggled against calling him "sir" on the phone. Timothy would be coming over the bridge on Saturday night, he said. Would Gita like to go out to dinner and dancing with them? Of course she didn't have the time (when would the university ever allow her time?) but she had to go. Timothy must have asked Norvin to call, being so busy himself. Anyway, in America it was freer for professors and students to mix. Better Timothy with Professor Weinstein than no Timothy at all.

"First you must get rhythm," Gita said in her thickest Indian accent. She clicked her tongue against the roof of her mouth. TSK tsk tsk tsk, TSK tsk tsk tsk. With every fourth beat, she clicked her fingers too. She had been too proud to tell them she didn't drink and was now suffering the consequences. She began reciting so the clicks exploded on the second syllable.

> Oh COME to me my love, oh COME,
> I've LOVED you from the last au-TUMN
> I've LOVED you from my heart's bot-TOM
> Oh COME to me my love, oh COME.

She paused. "And then he raised one significant eyebrow and said to the girl, 'NAAA-ice, no?' "

They were all laughing. It was really a very silly story but worth telling to unveil Timothy's crooked teeth. It all began with the man on the train asking the foreign girl if she liked "potry" and then standing up to orate before a crowded and spellbound compartment.

"Fabulous," said Norvin. "I had these kinds of encounters on trains and buses in India all the time. People always trying out English on me. 'What is your good name? Hearty condolences for your President Kennedy, very, very fine man. Like avatar of Vishnu, so very fine.' 'Oh come to me, my love.' Fabulous little jingle. Maybe we could do a Lacanian analysis of it in my graduate seminar. I wonder if it could be worked into an article. Hmm. Very interesting. So did it work?"

"What?" asked Gita.

"Did he pick her up?"

"Pardon?"

"Pick her up. You know," Norvin pressed. "Was the pass successful?"

"Was it—umm, a pass?" asked Timothy.

"I don't know," said Gita, beginning to twist at her napkin under the table. "It's just a story. It's supposed to have happened to this girl from Aspen School, which is American and up in the north. We told it in my school just like that." This happened to her in conversations where she was trying to be sophisticated; suddenly she was floundering right out of her depth.

"And 'come' is in the same code there as here?" asked Susan, the editor from New York who had sleepy red eyes, short black hair, and was dressed entirely in black, with boots though it was spring. Gita had the impression that she was someone's old girlfriend but couldn't quite figure it out. All evening Susan had seemed mildly impatient, as though she understood that Gita didn't belong with this crowd.

"Pardon?" asked Gita again.

"Good question," said Norvin. "Bravo, Susan. Here we enter the unexplored dimensions of sexual slang in Indian English. Or shall we say Indish? 'Come' is a great place to start. 'Oh come to me, my love.' Clickety-click. So, Gita, does it mean the same thing?"

Gita figured that it was better to act authoritative on this matter than admit that she hadn't the faintest idea what they were talking about. "Of course," she said.

"There's something so primal about rhyme," said Timothy, "I, umm, have to write more that rhymes. Autumn, bottom. Caught in, stopping."

"Oh come on, Timmy," said Susan, "you went through that ridiculous phase of limericks on postcards to everyone. I don't think rhyme is your style."

"That was years ago," said Timothy. "I was revving up for my prime. In rhyme." Under that high forehead, it seemed as if his blue eyes just fizzed with wit. His eyes caught and held Gita's across the table.

"All sublimation," said Susan. "Can't fool me." She blew smoke and patted Timothy on the shoulder. Timothy smiled—indulgently, Gita thought. How could any woman talk so disrespectfully to him?

"And what about sex education at Our Lady of Perpetual Succour?" asked Norvin, leaning toward Gita. He had thick chest hair showing where the shirt was unbuttoned. A few hairs were white. He looked as if he should be wearing a gold chain, but he wasn't.

"We had biology," said Gita. Feeling this was too dull for present company, she fumbled for something entertaining and quickly discarded the Malayali biology teacher's celebrated dictum that "menstrruation is the bloody teearrs of the frrustrrated Yoo-terrus." "The nuns told us we'd get pregnant if we wore sleeveless clothes. Someone brought a Beatles record to play on our house phonograph at school, but the Sisters didn't like them. 'Dirty, sexy!' Sister Bernadette said."

"Wait, wait!" said Norvin, taking off his glasses and pinching the bridge of his nose. "Dirty, sexy, yes, what a wonderful juxtaposition, power, eroticism, and the colonial experience all right there. But that poem of yours is triggering my memory. All the Marathi poems: *Ye re, ye re pausa, tula deto paisa.* You must know that one. No? You don't? 'Come come, rain, I'll give you cash.' Oh, I've got to dig out those old textbooks so we can look them over together. *Ye re,* that means 'come' too, I'm quite sure that's right. Oh my! That offers us a different angle on the jingle!"

"So what's new with Rachel?" Susan asked Norvin, though it was Timothy who seemed to jump. He took out his appointment book with the little gold pen and wrote something in it. Maybe it was her birthday, Gita thought. She had learned this evening that Norvin was married, but it was a long-distance relationship as Rachel, being brilliant, followed her own career at a faraway university.

"Well, she's fine, I guess," said Norvin.

"How's the commuting working out?" Susan blew more smoke, and Gita had to repress the impulse to wave it away.

"The pits. She wouldn't do the Valentine's Day trip though it was her turn. She said she had to submit a journal article. What did a week's difference matter? It's not like we're still scrambling for tenure and need to add up points with publications. I mean, I've put off deadlines a couple of times to go see her."

Gita reflected that couples should stay together; it seemed so odd for the wife to go off and work in another city. Norvin wasn't a bad fellow, actually—it was sad that his wife left him by himself. Gita had been very touched that he had insisted on paying for her tonight. "I know what it's like to be a graduate student," he said. "Everyone forgets later, how you finger books you can't afford to buy and weigh all the pros and cons before shelling out even a few coins. You bring sandwiches to libraries with you, and they're soggy by lunchtime. I know it all. It's such an amazing relief when you don't have to think about money anymore. I mean, at least not all the time. I've arrived. When you get there you can take some student out too, to pass this on. Good karma, what do you say?"

"Oh, umm, let me," Timothy had said, alerted to gallantry. Gita had melted when he said that. But Norvin stood firm. Nobody spoke about treating Susan. Gita felt that this was one more reason for Susan, so sophisticated in her black, to send black thoughts in her direction. Bet had things to say about the psychic effects of wearing black.

"Let's dance," Susan now said. "We're at this club to dance and we're just sitting around bullshitting and getting buzzed."

"You guys go out there and dance," said Timothy. "I want to go watch the disc jockey first. I love the moment when a new record drops. For years I've been wanting to write about it."

"Can I see the disc jockey too?" Gita asked. He had been looking at her as he said that. She didn't want to be left without him.

"Sure," said Timothy, giving her one of his crooked-teeth smiles. Following Timothy through the crowd it seemed perfectly natural that they should hold hands. Like children on a school outing, so they didn't get separated, Gita thought. His fingers, she noticed, were cold; they badly needed warming.

They were standing together on a balcony above the disc jockey in his booth when she leaned against Timothy. She couldn't help it. It was way past her normal bedtime, she'd had at least one entire glass of wine. All her heaviness slumped against him. Her hair was hanging loose and tousled (Bet's fashion advice). He adjusted his arm so it was around her.

"Are you OK?" he asked.

"Yes," said Gita. She loved the smell of his leather jacket. She wanted to close her eyes.

"Look," said Timothy. "There's this moment when one song finishes and he drops another record down so there's no break. Do you see? It's like seamless time. Transitions just happening."

"Yes," said Gita. The bass beat was scattering her thoughts from any clear direction. It seemed as though he was saying that suddenly you realized you were in love with someone, that there was a new song playing in your life. "Do you know that my name means song?" she asked, looking up with her cheek pressed against his chest.

"Your Aunty told me," Timothy said. He said "ahnty" like an Indian. "But I think I knew it from the, umm, *Bhagavad Gita* too. By the way, don't forget you have that—umm, was it perfume?—they sent in Norvin's car."

Gita didn't budge. The music was throbbing around and through them. She wondered if she could have heard his heart beat without the music. She wondered what poems were fermenting in there, what they revealed about the world that she couldn't see yet.

"Boy, it's getting late, we should be going out there soon to join them. I have to fly to Chicago at some god-awful hour tomorrow morning. I guess by this point it's later today. The Chicago Art Institute has this exhibition I wanted to see before my reading."

Gita still didn't move. She could feel Timothy tensing around her, his arm shaking at her shoulder. She didn't care. She closed her eyes, drawing inward to the comfort of her body against his at last. He had to kiss her before this evening was out: a token they would not be separated ever again. He could go lecture anywhere but still be with her, hers as she was his. "Hey there," said Timothy. "We've got to get going." Then it happened. There was a pause, his fingers crept into the hair against her scalp, his lips puckered dryly against hers. "Let's go," he said, moving away. Losing his support, she almost fell. Swift, swirling thoughts: I have been kissed—it's happened to me—the licorice, the hair. If Bet's up I will tell her. When he comes home I'll run out to meet him in our driveway. We'll be grandparents, old side by side.

Gita reached for Timothy's hand again as they pushed through the crowds to join the others. She pressed it without even thinking this was bold. She brought her other hand forward to caress the long fingers she had stared at all evening. Timothy didn't twitch, and he turned to give her a look she couldn't understand. Gita pictured Shani Maharaj, rolling along in the vast darkness of outer space.

The dance floor was built over what had once been a swimming pool. They danced in the moonlight and the neon glare of a tall Marlboro sign. The music was so loud it pulsed through them all like shared blood. It connected them, like the words in the *New York Times* each morning, like the slow movements of the planets. Timothy's scalp glinted white. He was a loose-limbed dancer, a marionette being shaken on all its strings. Susan's bloodshot eyes were closed; she seemed to be moving through water in her sleep. Norvin, though, was spry on his feet: all compact movement. He came over and gave Gita a whirl. "You should leave your hair loose more often," he shouted above the music. "It's fabulous. Let's plan on getting together soon to work on my Marathi." Gita couldn't quite catch everything he said, but she liked the friendly drift, the steadiness of his arm around her waist, his breath entangled by her ear. Timothy's friends were her friends, leveling the divide between professors and students. She could just picture Saroj Aunty's cross-eyed smile behind her heavy glasses when they exchanged garlands at the wedding, she and Timothy. I and he: we, encircled in fragrance. Would a white silk *kurta* hang too awkwardly on him, his legs like sticks in *churidar*s? How could he be anything but a prince? Catching his eye at last, Gita smiled up at Timothy. He looked above her head and over her shoulder before he smiled back. She twisted her hands like a Kathak dancer: for him, she tossed her cloak of hair. In this story, she was sure, radiantly sure, that she had secret and certain access to the end.

Kookoo Das

Sometimes in the afternoon I lie awake, thinking. Dilip, well, how can I put it, he breathes through his mouth. He can sleep even through power cuts. I lie awake in pools of frightful perspiration, listening to the crows, the servants banging dishes about, and those dreadful little scooties putt-putting past. Silly mind, it just won't turn off in the heat. At night it's not hard since we usually have our social schedule keeping us up quite late. Then too, I always have my few little pegs in the evening that make it easier to sleep.

I was selecting new cloth napkins at Cottage Industries earlier in the morning when I ran into Ratna. She was looking at the mirror-work cushions and bedspreads, which are practically in the same section. She's gone so gray lately that it's hard to recognize her. Really, I don't know why women do this to themselves when there are so many good things on the market. Even Indian-made dyes aren't as bad as they used to be. All kinds of Chinese girls in town with beauty parlors where they'll do the job, and thread your eyebrows as you wait. At first I was going to stand behind a pillar and ignore Ratna. But then the overhead air conditioner must have given out because the ceiling began to drip. When I moved out of the shower she called out in that brisk voice of hers.

"Hullo, hullo, do I see Kookoo?"

"My dear Ratna!" I responded. "What a lovely surprise to find you here."

"Wedding," she said. She gestured at a block-printed green-and-red double bedspread, the sort that would surely run colors and could never be put into a machine. "My girl's gone

39

and done it, found a young man. Bengali fellow from the air force. These days it seems like all we do is shop, shop, shop."

"You mean your dear little Natasha? Don't tell me! Last thing I remember she was just so big. She's always been the sweetest little thing."

"Sweetest my foot," said Ratna. "Nutty's as headstrong as they get. There hasn't been a day without a major fight about this, that, and the other related to the wedding. And how is your Gita?"

"Fine, thank you," I said. "Studying away out there. She's always been such a studious little thing."

"I saw Saroj in Bombay," said Ratna. "She showed me several of those small square pictures that students out there are always sending home. Gita looked well. Saroj didn't mention anything about a boyfriend, so I won't ask. Of course, some of our smartest boys go out there; it probably is the very best place for her to meet a good catch. Nice that her circle is growing, isn't it—that dinner in San Francisco and all? It can't be easy going alone to a place like that, but at least our girls are doing what we couldn't." Ratna ran her hands through that hair of hers that's absolutely shrieking out for some color. "The way the children are growing up! We're all becoming old fogies before our time. Anyway, so tell me more about Vicky. And how is his health?"

What am I to say after a meeting like that? Insults through and through. First of all she boasts about Nutty, then she rattles on about Saroj knowing more about Gita than I do, she rubs my nose in never taking up that Radcliffe scholarship, she accuses me of looking old, and she brings up the problems with Vicky. All she held back on was Dilip. I'm surprised she didn't put in a jab about his drinking. How dare she say that Gita sends Saroj photos but doesn't send any to me?

Of course, there are all sorts of rumors about why Saroj can't have children. I'd be the last one to bring up her involvement with the Communist party and their believing in free love or whatever it is that those people wanted. People would say anything about spirited young women in those days. I suppose they still do, and for good reason. Saroj never mentioned anything about coat hangers to me, of course, but one picks up these things. It could always be something wrong with Harish. I'm not the sort who spreads rumors, but I can't help remarking sometimes that Harish doesn't have quite enough facial hair to really grow a beard. When you look at him, he seems, well, too soft and—how should I put it?—smooth.

I've heard that even in college Saroj was quite independent-minded; she helped set up a printing press and was always traveling around by third-class train with political pamphlets. Good thing she was able to nab Harish with all his money and his big house. It was all passed off as arranged, of course, and so convenient that he was of the right caste. I don't believe that he had those same ideas about the lumpen elements, wanting to make them equals or whatever. It's all very well if you have stocks and bonds to carry on like that. They seem to get on well together, I suppose, but I can't help wondering about all that interest he takes in choosing her saris. I mean really! Of course, I wouldn't know anything, and I'm hardly in the habit of passing on aimless gossip. All the same, why haven't they had children of their own? Why does Saroj always have to be claiming Gita?

There's no doubt that little Gita would never have received the right kind of education if she had been with us abroad. One wouldn't want a girl to go to school if one was, say, posted in New York. What kind of continuity would she have? And the moral standards! After all the heart operations for Vicky we've had to do quite a lot of work at home and couldn't always be monitoring a young girl. When it comes to convent schools I still think that our Indian ones are among the best. It was a good thing for Gita that those Sisters knew how to discipline. She had been quite spoiled by that Ayah of hers, silly woman that she was with those rambling stories. The nuns were so very good with the girls' nail inspection. I was glad to hear that they even inspected underwear, getting the girls early on feminine hygiene. They know very well how

*to raise little ladies at the convent. It's a good thing we sent
Gita there, a very, very good thing that Dilip insisted. Just
look how obedient she is and how well she's done with her
studies.*

*"Mrs. Das, your daughter is a tribute to our convent,"
Mother Superior herself said to me when we visited Ooty on
our home leave. Of course, those nuns were always so thrilled
when some important parents came to visit, they had the love-
liest flower arrangements in our honor. Huge colored mums
and all, hill stations make me long for clippings, but then
bring the plants to Delhi and the air just stunts them. These
days pollution is absolutely out of hand, all those dirty little
scooties puttering about, and the buses starting up in those
great clouds of smoke. "Why, thank you," I said to that dear
Irish Mother Superior about Gita, "I wonder who she gets it
from!"*

*It's not that I haven't had my chances for higher education
with that scholarship to Radcliffe. If my aunt the doctor had
been married too I suppose I would have gone. One of India's
first lady surgeons, poor thing, and because of all that education no offers ever came in for her. When I won the scholarship, everyone was sure that I'd lose all my chances too. Even
Leela Aunty, dried-up thing that she was, came personally to
stop me with all this "don't ruin your life" business. Everyone
became frantic about marrying me off at once.*

*Of course, Vinayji was well known in those days. Even now
everyone is aware of his role in Indian independence, though
I must say that the actor who played him in the film Gandhi
simply didn't get the right accent. Vinayji had a proper British
education, none of this garbled Indian singsong that the actor
was using. There's no denying that Vinayji was quite the catch.
Not that he was terrifically wealthy or handsome, but he was
well regarded and my father admired him no end. No one had
ever thought he'd marry. But then he saw me that time at
Bubbly's wedding and just stood there, staring. I was so embarrassed I had to look down, even though I knew very well
I was gorgeous with my fair skin in that pink-and-silver bro-*

cade sari and with lipstick borrowed from Mummy. I remember that he was wearing a white achkan, with a collar tight and high. He was already quite bald, but he had those eyes, black-black eyes, those eyes that Gita has got, eyes that fix on you and bore right in. "Good morning, Uncle," I finally said.

"Are we related?" he asked.

"No, Uncle," I said. I found myself smiling, which I tried not to do. I looked down again, and when I looked up, he was still watching.

"If we're not related then I'm not your uncle," he said. When he smiled his eyes creased, and his hair seemed to slip farther down on his head.

"Even then, Uncle," I began. I didn't exactly mind having this one-pointed attention from someone whose pictures I'd seen in Papa's newspapers. Just then Papa came bustling up to say Mummy was looking for me.

"So she's yours, Pankaj," Vinayji said. They spoke for a few minutes and as we turned away, he called out after me, "Remember, I am not your uncle."

How could anyone guess that he'd go have that wretched heart attack so soon after we were married? It all happened that year: first my father, and then Vinayji going like that, so suddenly. Gita was less than a year old, and I wasn't even twenty. I actually met Saroj the first time when she came by for condolences. It was a week or two later, I think. She and Harish had come up from Bombay. She wore white, like everyone else who was mourning. I was so sick and tired of white. I was sick and tired of the wailing too, everyone telling me I was so young and it was such a shame, everyone expecting me to be a widow for the rest of my life. And this little dark baby who wouldn't stop wetting her nappies, and wouldn't stop crying, no matter how much she was held by Ayah. Saroj had on these dark glasses, I remember, and not seeing her eyes made me nervous. Harish had had to leave for some appointment. We talked a little—what can you say at a time like that? Then, all of a sudden, Saroj picked up Gita, who'd been brought in to be shown. "I'll take her around the garden for a walk," she announced, tucking the baby over one hip. *How do you like that? Without so much of an if-you-please or by-your-leave?* I should have seen into her plots for Gita right then and there.

My marriage to Dilip wasn't much publicized, what with it being a second marriage for me, and the wrong caste, and the way people are in this backward Indian society. Saroj somehow heard about it, though; maybe it was even that wretched busybody Ratna who told her. Saroj sent a gift through some relative traveling to Delhi. I can't remember anymore what the gift was—a sari, I suppose—but I clearly remember that line in her card: "If you ever want Gita off your hands, remember we'll be happy to take her, for however long it is." We didn't need to take up the offer until Dilip got his diplomatic postings abroad. Maybe we should have sent for Gita more during vacations, but what with her traveling alone and Vicky's health problems, it was never possible. Not that Dilip isn't fond of her. And of course *we* were being generous to a childless couple. But just look at where this generosity has got us—impertinence from people like Ratna. Oh well, no point in thinking too hard, it just tires the brain. Gita's always been a strange little thing anyway. I can barely wait for the day that she gets married too. We'll put on a wedding that will shut up that gloating Ratna and the others once and for all.

2
The Eiffel Tower Does Not Meet the Grand Canyon

Gita sat in the uppermost floor of the U.C.-Berkeley library, books open before her and her mind in Bombay. She was trying to take notes for the afternoon seminar. But for the last few weeks, her concentration had been flickering: winds of memory and desire blowing, until in the present there was only a blackness focusing and dissolving diverse shapes.

Saroj Aunty came down the front steps of the bungalow. She moved slowly, one hand poised lest she should fall. She had had a cataract operation recently. The new spectacles she wore magnified her eyes as she peered out at the arrangement of cane chairs in the garden bordering the beach. She was wearing a fresh sari after her nap: "It's that *feeling*, you know, of smooth, crisp cloth," she said. "Such a sensualist!" Harish

Uncle grinned. "Oh, shoo," said Saroj Aunty, smiling back. "Who insists?" Most days her saris were starched cottons: handlooms or block prints. But on Sundays, out came the silks from boxes in which they lay named.

Timothy would like that, naming saris. Gita couldn't have exactly defined postmodern, but she was certain that this practice of Saroj Aunty's must be as postmodern as the critics described Timothy's poems to be. Cultures and histories were all mixed up in Saroj Aunty's cupboard. "Darling," she would say, "do you think that today is a Nefertiti day?" (Nefertiti: austere ivory and turquoise, with black outlines like kohl around lovely eyes.) "For that dinner party with H.H., wouldn't you say that Moonlight on the Ganges would be just right? Maybe it's a cool silver occasion. Or Kadambari—it could always be one of those royal *magenta* nights." This sort of consultation took place beside the open cupboard lined with cardboard boxes bearing names. It was mostly addressed to Harish Uncle, who had always taken a great interest in his wife's clothing, even buying jewelry to match the *bhavana*, the mood of a particular sari. "No Saru," he might say. "It's going to be a Bombay high-society catty event. How about something truly evil, like Idi Amin?" Or else it could be Gita sitting on the bed, watching and agreeing, a little too shy to have an opinion. Now, from Berkeley, she imagined Saroj Aunty addressing Timothy: gangly, smile askew, his blue eyes would be very amused as he read the lines of names penned in with black marker in Saroj Aunty's splashy handwriting.

It was Saroj Aunty, after all, who had chosen him at Heathrow airport and sent him into Gita's life. Gita thought of the wise old holy man in the stories who gave a prince a golden mango that would speed him on his path toward the princess; or was it an old woman with an apple? Sometimes those tales of Ayah's got mixed up with others that she'd read. Even if Timothy wasn't quite as black haired or regular featured as she had expected, he did fit into the contours of such stories. Yet three Sundays had now passed since, in the quiet hours of the morning, Gita had stood on her porch, waving good-bye to Timothy and his friends as she prepared to step indoors. Twenty-three days, and Gita had not heard from him. He was with her every moment, tugging every thought toward himself, but that was the Inner Timothy. The outer one had revealed his identity and vanished. Every weekend when the rates were low, Gita stayed home by the phone, thinking that maybe he was traveling again and just might ring up long distance.

On weekends, reflected Gita, all kinds of people visited the Shahs. Visitors arrayed themselves in low cane chairs around the swing, facing each other or looking out to the sea. Servants poured out of the house with sequences of spiced tea, freshly squeezed and slightly salted lemonade, plates of hot fried snacks. Timothy would enjoy the assortment of people; maybe he would be inspired to write a prose poem with them all in it. (She could see it already: the reviews remarking on the expansion of his creativity since he married that multicultural young woman.) There was His Highness of Pindapur, also known as H.H., who played cricket and arrived each time with a different dimpled young woman. "Little lady" was what he had always called Gita as she sat on the margins, observing, unless she was absolutely forced to speak. His wife, the Maharani, came too, but on weekends when he wasn't around. Puffy faced and with smeared lipstick, she warned Gita about getting too much education: "You know, these men like women a little backward." Then there was Ganeshan Kaka with his jutting nose and jutting chin, bony wrist bearing a watch lifted for close scrutiny as he made predictions: "Ask me a question, ask, ask, ask . . ." There was Manjuben from Surat, the cousin who arrived laden down with boxes of crumbly *nankhatai* biscuits and proceeded to direct the servants in simmering fragrant hair oil, sewing quilts from old silk saris, or sunning pickles on the roof. She only spoke Gujarati, but she and Gita managed to smile a good deal at each other. And then there were the Parsis.

Gita had not put the Parsis in a clump before. But Timothy had said over that magical dinner, "I'm rereading all of

Nietzsche. *Thus Spake Zarathustra* is next on the list, maybe for the plane to Chicago. What do you know about actual Zoroastrians?" Shining with the authority of someone who could be consulted, Gita had put down her fork and begun, "You mean Parsis." But then Norvin had turned from the conversation with Susan that he had mercifully left them for to jump right back in. "Parsis!" he exclaimed. "Did I hear you say Parsis? I tell you, in India, everyone thought I was a Parsi. Russian Jewish stock, you know—fair, black hair, striking features. Very Parsi. They emigrated from Iran, sort of like Jews with all that wandering, talent, eccentricity. Parsis are great. Terrific Anglophiles, 'Our Queen Victoria' and all that. Fabulous names: Screwwala was my favorite. Maybe I should write my next article under a pseudonym, something like Dr. Cowassjee Screwwala. Or else I could be Norshirvan Daruwala. *Daru,* you see, means liquor—it's not unlike *wine.* Oh, by the way, Timothy, what happened to those New York poems you used the pen name for? Did you decide to include them in the new collection?" Gita sat with stories churning inside her as the conversation swerved off in an entirely different direction. Through the last three weeks as she waited for Timothy, these memories had been refined. She wished Timothy would reappear so that she could tell them to him.

Harish Uncle had a soft spot for Parsis. "For every Gujarati in Bombay, they're a sort of alter ego," he used to say. "You know, the way the Parsis speak Gujarati with all those ups and downs, and the hard *d*s, it just makes it into a musical performance."

"Stravinsky!" said Jimmy Seervai, a regular Sunday visitor with a jerking neck. "Béla BARTÓK. Admit it, Harish, you say music but you're secretly thinking CACOPHONY. You know, that Ram's American wife still doesn't speak Gujarati because every time she tried to learn it, his family would gather around, laughter, ABSOLUTE hysteria, because they thought she spoke like a Parsi."

"That's Ram's family," said Harish Uncle. "I tell you, I appreciate Parsis. Bombay would be lost without them. Even India would. After all, why do you think I founded the—"

"P.W.S.B.," said Jimmy. "The Parsi-Watching Society of Bombay."

"Like bird-watching," said Jeroo, Jimmy's pretty daughter. A few years older than Gita, she was already wearing lipstick and seemed very sophisticated. She was lying flat on the swing that was as large as a bed, letting her hands trail over the edge as she addressed the sky. "Parsis are worth watching. All inbred, genes doing mad-mad things all over the place. Geniuses, idiots, everything we've got. Great tics. Observe Daddy's neck. Uncle, have you arranged for your club to document this?"

"Don't be IMPERTINENT," said Jimmy, readjusting his neck in a motion like a Bharat Natyam dancer. "Or Harish will start telling us about other tics he's seen. You were raised on those stories, child. He's the one and only member of this blessed Parsi-Watching Society, he's the chairman, the librarian, the CURATOR. You've undoubtedly heard ALL about his Parsi assistant who repeated the last two words of any sentence you said like a stuck record. 'How are you?—Are-you, are-you, are-you, are-you.' Or that government official who poked a cheek filled with air and made the rudest noises."

"Just don't demonstrate, Daddy," said Jeroo. Gita marveled: she would never have spoken like this to Dilip. In fact, she barely spoke to him at all. Since his first appearance when she was five, his arms full of sickly sweet tuberoses, Gita had been trained to stand up straight, be polite, and swiftly disappear.

"Impertinence!" said Jimmy. "Proachie, why don't you teach your *dikri* some manners?"

"Trying, dear," said Proachie, his wife, turning from a conversation with Saroj Aunty.

"Anyway, there are plenty of normal Parsis too," Jeroo stated, slipping one smooth leg off the swing to set herself in motion. "Upstanding moral citizens. But you and your society, you're just looking for another Gemini circus. Daddy can be the chief clown. If you HAVE to perform and all"—she turned her head—"why not do the train to Ooty?"

"The train to Ooty!" Gita repeated. She was at a boarding school in Ooty at the time and dearly loved the small train with its steam engine that climbed up from the plains into the blue-green hills. She had also heard Jimmy impersonate the train many times through the years in which she had spent her vacations with the Shahs. "Oh yes, Uncle, please do the train."

"Have I had enough pegs?" asked Jimmy.

"More whiskey inside," said Harish Uncle, a grin already spilling across his face. "Come on, Jimmy, be a good sport."

Jamshed Seervai sat up straight in his cane chair. He adjusted his collar, neck moving in a countermotion of its own. "Che. Che. Paise. Che. Che. Paise," he began, shoulders pumping back and forth. This was the train taking off, its wheels circling at a leisurely pace. One hand gestured, right angles from a sharp elbow as the train snaked uphill. It sped up, "Che-che paise, che-che paise, che-che paise!" The whistle blew, Jimmy's hand held upright beside his nose. "TOO-TOO! TOO-TOO!"

Out over the sea, the sun was disappearing, elongated orange, then shrinking to a crimson sliver followed by a split-second flash of blue. The group was bent over with laughter, chairs creaking beneath them. Gita worried that she might pee, her stomach hurt so much. The train got faster yet, a tongue-twisting, waving-hand dynamo. It creaked, "Kheeey, kheeey." A climax of staccato whistles. "TOO-TOO-TOO-TOO-TOOOOOO!" Then the train began to slow down: "Che. Che. Paise. Che . . . che . . . paise." It sighed out the last of the steam. "Pooo-ooo-ooh." Jimmy slumped into his chair, limbs at all angles, quite spent.

"Bravo, Bravo!" cried Saroj Aunty amid the claps. "A safe arrival!"

*   *   *

All this was going on inside Gita's head, when she should have been reading about poststructuralism. She found herself back in Berkeley, looking out through the library window. The panes were grimy, graying the April brilliance outside. The book for the day's seminar still lay open with a pencil aligned along its crease. After a while she lifted the pencil, but instead of making ticks in the margins she drew a block capital T. With slow deliberation she thickened it and then outlined its shadow: upward, to the right. In her head, she turned over an Indian folktale she had recently read in an old British journal she was researching for a term paper. She idly wondered if Ayah had known this story.

Once upon a time there was a holy man of the sort that Hindoos call a sadhu. *Being a man who renounced the world, he had withdrawn to the jungle, maintaining only his loincloth. Each day he was offered food and drink by pious villagers who felt honored to have this great soul performing such heroic austerities in the adjoining jungle.*

Now, day and night, the holy man meditated, toiling extensively for the achievement of enlightenment. But there was a rat who gnawed on his loincloth. Angered by the animal's impertinence, the holy man requested that the villagers bring him a cat to ward off the rat. Yet to feed the cat, fresh milk was required. Few days had passed before the holy man requested a cow. However, the cow required tending and this distracted the holy man from his profound meditations. He requested a servant. A servant was brought, and then the servant was lonely and fetched his wife. The wife desired companions in this lonely jungle place, and she persuaded her married brothers to move there along with their wives. Soon enough, a small township had sprung up around the cave. Unable to meditate any longer, the holy man resigned himself to the worldly life and so he himself took a wife. For this reason, the Hindoos say, "Attachment leads to further attachment. Even a loincloth can make an entire worldly life."

"Here's the Song of Songs!" Gita's reverie was broken as a hand clamped her shoulder. She jumped. Professor Norvin Weinstein in a turquoise polo shirt was smiling down at her with a glint of gold-rimmed glasses.

Gita threw shut her book. "Good morning, sir," she stammered. She felt that she had been caught red-handed. Had he seen the *T*? How did he know what her name meant? Could Timothy have told him what she had said and then what had happened? "I mean, hello, how are you?"

"Great to see you up here with the *B*s," said Norvin. "I'm very attuned to the intellectual topology of call numbers. *BL*s, I see. Researching religion or something?"

"Studying," said Gita. "Just reading for class."

"Oh. If you're not bound to this place, I'd recommend the *G*s. *GN*, *GR*. Anthropology, you know: wild stuff. You see some real characters down there, clanking camel jewelry, batik shirts, that sort of thing. The *D*s aren't bad either if you're interested in India, great old compendiums of customs by British officials. Sati, thugs, beds of nails—it's just fantastic. I'm thinking of looking into all this for an article sometime. Or who knows, maybe another book. The place I always steer clear of is the *P*s—there's always the danger you could be waylaid by a novel. So how're you doing?"

"Fine, thanks," said Gita. This was untrue but automatic. "Actually, there are windows on this floor—it's nicer to read by real light."

"Fabulous, fabulous. Pragmatism wins again."

Norvin was speaking as though he were addressing a lecture class without a microphone, and as if to balance his volume Gita had been muttering and swallowing her words. *"Shhhh"*: the hiss she had been anticipating slithered from a nearby cubicle.

"Oops!" Norvin's voice dropped, and he knelt beside her. He smelled of aftershave like Harish Uncle's; also faintly of browned cumin. Gita thought with a lurch of the raw scent of a leather jacket. "I told you," he whispered, leaning into her ear, "seminarians come up here. They sit here meditating on the glory of God and don't like to be reminded of mundane things. Want to talk outside? Can I take you out for a cup of *chai? Kai, tula chai paijai? Bara bara, ye ye. Amhi chalte.*"

Even the threat that he would carry on in what Gita assumed was pidgin Marathi could not counterbalance the lure of information about Timothy. And it wasn't as though she were getting much work done these days, what with her mind roaming out the window to San Francisco, Boston, Chicago, wherever that man with the long fingers, high forehead, eloquent Adam's apple might be. "Thank you," she said. Norvin had already picked up her book for her, and she followed him out of the library, anxious that he not open to the page betrayed by the edge of protruding pink rubber to see her doodle.

"Café Depresso," said Norvin, as they walked into the dark interior rife with the aroma of roasted coffee beans. Gita scanned the crowd inside and was relieved that no one she knew was present. It made her stiffen and cringe to be seen publicly with a professor. She didn't want people to get the wrong idea. How would they know he was Timothy's friend and that this was a respectable link? She studied the board trying to decide what kind of tea to order. But Norvin had already ordered and paid for two large glasses of steamed milk with amaretto. "I said *chai* but all you'll get here are those insipid, unboiled bags. Milk is good for the nerves. You know, this academic environment!"

"Yes," said Gita. She really would have preferred caffeine.

"And so what are you working on these days?" asked Norvin, clearing aside a crumpled *Daily Cal* from a table.

Gita felt the blood rush to her ears. "Nothing much," she said, drawing her finger around a wet ring left by the last person's glass. "There are always books to read and papers to write."

"That's graduate school for you. When you're in it, it seems like prison and drudgery, but you'll look back to think these were the best years of your life. It seems to me that you're working too hard. Have you been out dancing lately?"

"No time," said Gita. She cleared her throat in an attempt to sound nonchalant. "By the way, have you—have you heard from Timothy?"

"Timothy disappears," said Norvin. "I don't hear from him for weeks at a time, and then, hey, presto, he's there. That was a great outing we had. You were enchanting with your hair down. I never did understand why Indian women with that fabulous thick hair always went in for braids. Two braids hooped up with ribbons for little girls. Two braids hanging down for those a little older. One braid through adolescence. A braid or a twisted bun for married women. When I was in the Peace Corps in Nasik I sometimes just wanted to go up to women and loosen their hair."

Gita drew her braid closer to herself. "It's more convenient," she said. Trying to keep a note of irritation from her voice, she added, "Also, Nasik is not all of India. So many other communities, like Christians or Parsis, wear their hair short. And even among Hindus and all, since that film actress Sadhana bobbed her hair, short hair became known as a Sadhana cut. Since you were there, things have been changing in India all the time. If you go now, you'll see a lot of women with short hair."

"Parsis," said Norvin, as though he hadn't heard anything else she'd said. "I love Parsis. Everyone in India—"

"—thought you were a Parsi," Gita said.

"How did you guess?" asked Norvin. "That's exactly what happened. Well, Russian Jewish stock, you know, we are absolutely indistinguishable . . ."

Gita dipped her finger in the ring of water, smoothing it out into an asymmetrical blob. How could she possibly steer the conversation back to Timothy? He was as close to her as her own breath, his absence hurting with each intake of air. Yet she had no phone number for him, not even an address. She stared at the couple at the table beyond them, both engrossed in their books yet holding hands on the marble top. "There were lots of Parsis at my convent school," she said, plotting conversation.

"Oh yes, Our Lady of Perpetual Succour," said Norvin. "Outstanding name for a convent school. Pray tell me more about it."

He laughed, a sort of neigh, and Gita examined him coldly. "The nuns were concerned about our manners," she said.

"Manners," repeated Norvin. She could see that he found something quite amusing about that, but she didn't care if he did. "What kind of manners?"

"You know, courtesy. Please and thank you. Table manners—we even used knives and forks for *chappatis*. Letters. We always wrote thank-you letters. Oh, by the way, I need to write a thank-you letter to Timothy—it was so kind of him to carry that perfume from my friends."

"Delightful," said Norvin. "Emily Post, Dear Abby, and all that. I'm always telling my wife, Rachel, that she's a lousy letter writer. She's become a terrible communicator, actually, doesn't even talk much on the phone since the move to North Carolina. Letter writing is probably the only thing that keeps long-distance relationships alive. Unlike phone calls, you can reread and hold on to letters."

"I need his address," Gita said.

Norvin had begun to fiddle absentmindedly with the buttons on his polo shirt. Gita looked away from the luxurious black chest hair tinted with gray. "Sometimes I wonder if Rachel took the job because she wanted to opt out of the marriage," he said. "I mean, why didn't she tell me if that was on her mind? It's a drag for two academics to be in the same field and she was right about this being a chance for her to be the star for a change. She used to moonlight around here, you know, picking up a course here and there. She went with tenure. I don't see why she's so hung up on finishing this book that she won't let me visit and won't come here herself. We haven't even been able to coordinate conferences recently."

"Timothy's address," repeated Gita. She had been so

smooth, so sly, and now she was having to underline how badly she wanted to be back in touch with Timothy.

"Timothy's address," repeated Norvin. He had taken off his glasses, and his mouth had turned down, his eyes faraway. He focused back at her, a searching direct look that made Gita drop her eyes. "Sure, Gita, I'll give you Timothy's address. A thank-you note! You know, you are just a breath of fresh air."

When she came home that night they went out dancing, the event seemed like a prism scattering shoals of rainbows through her mind. Her body gulped to incorporate the pleasures and promises the stars had brought her way. She couldn't sleep till dawn, as she replayed the moment Timothy's mouth had brushed against hers, fast-forwarded to the kinds of names their children might have, names that wouldn't sound awkward in India or America: Nicholas-Nikhil, Anita, Deven-David, Sheela. She tried to recall what song the disc jockey had been playing when she and Timothy went off alone to watch him change records. If not for the switching of songs, they might have spent the whole evening chaperoned by Norvin and that weird woman from New York. If she could remember the song it could be like the anthem of their life, something to play at the wedding and anniversaries, standing hand in hand and looking into each other's eyes. She imagined Timothy picking over the keys of a poetically battered typewriter, and herself stepping in to set a cup of hot tea at his side. The great works that would flow from him as she guarded his time, answered his phones, prepared meals! She would learn how to cook, tracking down recipe books and apprenticing with Saroj Aunty's Maharaj. The fragrance of bay leaves and cloves in the *pullao*s she would feed him rose in her nostrils, the rich, round scent of onions reddening in *ghee*. With her, he would no longer be so scarecrow thin. He would fill out with the substance of a Husband.

He had said that he would be in Chicago for a few days, and she wished she knew exactly how long. Part of her had hoped he would make some wildly romantic gesture from Chicago—a long-distance call, the delivery of one red rose, perhaps even a small gem of poetry—but another part of her protected him, saying he was too busy. After all, she gathered from his poems that it was for his creativity ("Mistress Muse, leather caprice") that he had remained single so long, almost into his forties.

"Don't make excuses for him," said Bet, trying out a bright comb in her hair as she stood before the bathroom mirror. She was preparing to go off to a rehearsal. Recently, cheered on by Gita's astrological successes, Bet had consulted a psychic who held consultations at a card table unfolded on Telegraph Avenue. For five dollars, he had informed her that her name, Elizabeth Johanssen, carried bad professional vibes and a better substitute would be a plain and simple Krista. He also told her that patchouli oil would extend the power in her aura and that eating licorice would improve her pheromones. Whatever it was, following his advice seemed to have changed Bet's fate. After a long spell of doing odd jobs, she had at last landed a part in a play. Unfortunately, this meant that she was at home a lot less, leaving Gita's heart to short-circuit whenever the phone rang. Gita craved company as she faced the desolate expanse of Timothy's silence. When Bet was back in the apartment, there was nothing else Gita would rather talk about than Timothy, sifting through all the reasons why he possibly could have vanished.

"Excuses," Gita agreed, hanging back from the sink and feeling a rush of gratitude that Bet would discuss this at all. She wasn't quite sure what Bet meant. Early in life she had found that repeating people's words made them feel they were engaged in a meaningful conversation.

"Exactly," said Bet. She turned her head, then removed the comb and set to brushing her golden hair again. "He's being chicken. Scared-male behavior. He's running away."

"Oh no," Gita said, "he believes in love."

"Love! You just met this man. You've spent something like a total of six or eight hours with him, and you think you know him from the two books of his poems I see you poring over night and day. Look, Gita, everyone can be obsessive and think that a nice time means a happily-ever-after. I've done it myself when I was much younger. But you just have to understand it's more complicated. If he ever reappears, you have to begin with just getting to *know* him, and I don't just mean in the Biblical sense. Why not look up the psychic dude on Telegraph? I hear he's good with the Tarot too."

"But I already know from Saroj Aunty's astrologer," said Gita. "He said March 1984, and he was right."

"I know," said Bet, blowing some mousse into the front of her hair. "But does Timothy know about this astrologer guy? Is he willing to go along with the prediction? So do you think I should go for the comb in my hair or not?"

"Let's see." Gita inspected as Bet turned her head from side to side, neck raised as though before a vigorously clapping audience. "I don't know, really—it seems nice both ways."

"Come on," Bet sighed. "How are you going to be ready for this man if you don't ever allow yourself to have a strong opinion?"

After Norvin wrote out Timothy's address Gita held on to it for several days. Finally, when there was still no sign of him, she brought herself to write. It was an awkward business: how was she to address him, so close to her that she knew him from within, yet so far away outside? Finally, after several drafts, she wrote out a note in her best pearly handwriting. She used special stationery that Saroj Aunty had given her, outlined in orange and presided over by a small, rotund, orange Ganapati. Timothy wouldn't know that one invoked this elephant-headed god at the beginning of any venture. But Gita hoped, fervently hoped, that Ganapati-Bappa would do what he was supposed to do: remove obstacles.

Dear Timothy,
Thank you again for a lovely evening, and also for bringing the perfume. I hope that your Chicago trip went off very well, and that you were able to visit the museum

as planned. Please do let me know when you will be in Berkeley again. I can also take the BART to San Francisco if you are giving a reading. You asked me about Zoroastrians (Parsis). I have a few stories that you will enjoy. I look forward to sharing them with you sometime.

With all my best wishes,
Gita

P.S. In case you have lost my number, here it is again.

Gita went in person to the post office to mail the letter, but once the blue lid had swung closed, she was full of remorse. Had she been too formal? Should she have mentioned the kiss? Did including her number again seem plaintive? Would he judge the word "share" as too Californian? How should she really have signed off? Adding "with all my" to "best wishes" had made it less of a cold formula, but maybe she should have opted for something more casual. But what? "Sincerely" certainly wouldn't do. But if she had inserted the word "your" before "Gita," this would have shown him that she was truly his. Being a poet, he would be so sensitive to all the possible meanings of words. Why oh why had she posted that letter?

A week went by, a week of increasing voltage when the telephone rang. Lifting the receiver, she would be out of breath, heart bouncing out of her chest. She waited restlessly for each day's visit from the postman (sorry, postperson—it was a shapely Chicana), and felt close to tears when the box was banged shut, leaving nothing of substance inside. Letters from India came, but somehow these didn't matter as much anymore. She found herself skimming a letter in Saroj Aunty's splashy looped writing for some mention of Timothy, disappointed by the mere allusion: "Darling, it's simply wonderful that my *plot* to get a gift to you worked out. I will always be on the lookout in airport lounges. Who knows what other couriers I'll find?" Why didn't Saroj Aunty acknowledge that she had sent Gita this wonderful man? Why did she reduce him to one among many possible couriers? It seemed, these days, that everything in Gita's life was being stripped of value unless it could somehow be related to him. She found herself writing feverish poems. "This is someone else's nightmare," the first of the series began.

Two more weeks of waiting, and barely keeping up with work. Then she tried to telephone. But there was only an answering machine so full of static one couldn't even savor his voice. When it seemed as though even getting up in the morning had lost all meaning, there was a lone postcard in the mailbox. It was of the Eiffel Tower and bore French stamps. Timothy had tiny writing slanted slightly to the left.

> Gita: The age of mechanical reproduction is upon us. To walk the Louvre is to scatter simulations through the world. Degas in San Francisco bathrooms. Van Gogh shrunk to a postcard. Zubin Mehta is a Parsi, but rumored to be an Israeli citizen. What must it be like to be a Parsi in Paris? À bientôt, Timothy.

What did it mean? What was he trying to say about their future together? Did he mean something about children (why should it be mechanical?). How long had he been in Paris? When was he coming back? Did he love her? She clung to the word *Parsi*. At least that had interested him. It suggested intimacy, private communications, more puckered kisses. She would have to telephone the one Parsi she knew in Berkeley so she'd have more data by the time he returned.

"So why don't you go out and get him a postcard of the Grand Canyon?" asked Bet after she'd examined the postcard, turning it over several times. "Sending the goddamn Eiffel Tower, he's just asking for it."

"I can't write back," Gita said, wanting to cry as her world slid off at the edges into a blankness as mysterious as the margins of a medieval map. Parsi: it was the only thing that would keep him from slipping out of reach. "I don't even have a Paris address."

* * *

As usual, Firoze Ganjifrockwala was late. They had arranged to meet at the fountain on Trowel Plaza at noon, but the campanile chimes had long since lapsed into silence. Gita sat at the edge of the fountain, watching the crowd. The stocky woman in her long black robe who limped about blowing profusions of iridescent bubbles into the faces of scurrying students. The thin, bearded man in a miniskirt who aimlessly wheeled a pram, appearing and disappearing through the crowd. The tables manned by earnest talkers ready to transact a certain brand of ideology right next to an opposing faction. The procession of Hare Krishna in saffron Indian clothes that just didn't look right with thick wool socks and Birkenstocks. Gita watched glumly, her eye tuned on bald men. Who knew?—there was always a chance that Timothy would return and make a surprise visit to Berkeley. One of the poems in his first book had been about Harvard Square at high noon; maybe he could come here for comparative purposes sometime. When she saw Norvin emerging from the crowd, she felt a mixed impulse to studiously examine a copy of the *Daily Cal* and to wave at him. She had no choice: he had seen her.

"*Namaskar,*" he said, ceremoniously folding his hands by his chest. "*Kasa kai? Bara ahe ka?* Hi there, Gita, we never did do anything about the Marathi conversation lessons. *Me marathi boltat.*"

When was Gita going to break the news that she didn't speak Marathi and never had? She shouldn't have let him carry on that first night she had met Timothy. Now she was afraid that she would lose the one golden thread that linked her to Timothy if she confessed. "*Ho, ho,*" Gita agreed, again mimicking Saroj Aunty's servants as they were given instructions on what kind of drink to bring out for a guest. "*Bara.*"

"Like to go get a sandwich?" asked Norvin.

"Well, actually . . ." Gita began.

"Or a burrito. Great burritos you can design yourself. I recommend avocado and sour cream together, calories be damned."

Gita was embarrassed to tell Norvin that she was meeting

a boy for lunch. Norvin might think she was hitched up with Firoze or something, and he might tell Timothy. Then Timothy would write sad poems about her (a critic had noted that he was good on abandoned love) and she would never hear from him again. "I'm, umm, meeting a Parsi," she said.

"A Parsi!" said Norvin. "How outstanding! Where did you find a Parsi in this place? I hope it's a little old lady who wears her sari pinned up with a brooch and talks about how 'sweet Queen Elizabeth was as a gull.' Oh, this must be your Parsi."

It was indeed Firoze. He had appeared beside Gita, unkempt as usual, a *jhola* filled with books hanging off one shoulder. "Hello," he said, giving Gita an inquiring hazel look under his straight line of brow.

Gita wished she could just merge into the fountain like a water nymph. As she introduced the two men she felt compromised on both sides. Firoze would wonder what she was doing with a professor, and Norvin would see that the few contacts she had in Berkeley weren't as sophisticated as the circle that he moved in with Timothy. She also worried about Firoze overhearing himself labeled as "her Parsi."

"*Namaskar,*" said Norvin. "*Majha nav* Norvin *ahe. Me* America *la rahathat . . .*"

"Howdy," said Firoze. "Are you speaking an Indian language or something?"

"Marathi," said Gita quickly. "He knows me because of this gift that my Saroj Aunty had sent, with, er, his friend. I know Firoze because his cousin Dinaz was my classmate. He's studying computer, no, sorry, political science." Oh good, she thought, now I've explained that I don't belong to either of them.

"You mean you don't speak Marathi?" asked Norvin, looking up at Firoze and, Gita feared, taking in the uncombed hair, the half-grown beard, the *kurta* that could have used ironing.

"Oh no," said Firoze. "My parents live in Bombay, but I was mostly in boarding school up north and I never picked it

up. Actually, I'm ashamed. I took French as my language op-
tion. I speak very bad Bombay Hindi. I follow Gujarati but
can't really speak it. I wanted to be properly literate in at least
one Indian language, so I'm taking a course here in Hindi."

Just like Firoze, Gita thought with irritation. He had to
come all the way to America to study Hindi! How would he
ever get a Ph.D in any one thing if he ambled through departments in this irresponsible way?

"Gita is going to help me brush up my Marathi," said Norvin. *"Meethu meethu popat,* that sort of conversational thing.
Not that I have a research project in mind just yet. It's just
always advisable to keep up on all one's languages."

"You speak Marathi?" Firoze asked Gita. "If you were a
kid in Delhi and all, how did you pick up Marathi?"

"Well, actually I . . ." Gita faltered.

"All I need help on is the basics," Norvin said. He grinned,
teeth bared all the way back to his molars and several fillings
flashing. "It's also a chance to get to know Gita. Marvelous
girl."

Firoze looked at Gita. She had always struck him as so
serious, so restrained. Not that she wasn't quite attractive
those rare times she laughed. She had the most enviably dark
complexion, a true shade of Indianness, and lovely black eyes.
And she was clearly smart. But she made him nervous by the
way she stared straight through him with all the censure of a
maiden aunt. That she had become chummy with this professor fellow, that he seemed to have quite a crush on her, that
she knew Marathi: all this was quite perplexing. Firoze tried
to catch Gita's eye to see whether she would want to have
Norvin join them for lunch. She appeared to be examining the
end of her braid with enormous concentration.

"So! I hear you're a Parsi," Norvin said. "I can't tell you
how it improves my life in Berkeley to know there's a Parsi
community around."

"Are you Parsi or something?" Firoze asked.

Gita came to life with a broad grin. "Would you like to
have lunch with us?" she asked Norvin. "You don't mind, do

you, Firoze? I mean, we can all talk about India, and Parsis, and all."

"Of course, please join us," said Firoze. "So *are* you Parsi?"

"Not at all," said Norvin. "See what I mean, Gita? Just anyone from India who meets me thinks I'm Parsi."

"I wouldn't have actually thought unless you said . . ." Firoze began. What was all this about Parsis anyway? But Norvin was off on his own track, addressing Gita with an occasional beaming glance through his gold spectacles in Firoze's direction.

"Fabulous!" he said. "Just fabulous. I can't tell you what it does for me to be mistaken for an Indian again. When I think of India I'm back in a time in my life when, well, things seemed so *fresh*. Everything was possible then. The academic community hadn't even heard from me. I'd already met Rachel, but we were still so young, writing each other long, idealistic letters in many shades of ink. All that rich *puran-poli*, all those fried *bhajiya*s, no thoughts about a diet . . . So, where shall we eat?"

They settled for an assortment of food from the carts on the sidewalk. Then, armed with swatches of napkins, they arranged themselves on the lawn by Trowel Hall. It was a glorious day, the sky benevolent, a glitter on trees and a sheen to faces. Cars drove by on the street adjoining campus: a procession of colors, reflections, glossy surfaces. After many weeks of wishing she were in another time or place, Gita unexpectedly felt glad to be right here, in the present, with sour cream on Norvin's chin and Firoze giving her a bewildered look from under that perfectly horizontal line of brow. Two people from her French for Reading Knowledge class walked by. She waved, pride surging up over the embarrassment of being seen with not just one but two men.

"Tell us all about your background," said Norvin to Firoze. Gita smiled at him. Here they were, she and Norvin bonded in research for Timothy.

"Well, what is there to say? I guess I have the regular background of any elite city person in a previously colonized society. I'm more Western than Indian. I think in English. I'm estranged from traditions that should be mine."

"Marvelous, marvelous," said Norvin. "The postcolonial intellectual. I understand your identity dilemma perfectly. Fanon, Cabral . . . have you read any Edward Said?"

"Actually, yes," said Firoze. "I'm reading quite a bit these days. Of course, there is the complicating factor of being an immigrant minority, even if the immigration was many centuries ago, and having some Western blood too. But all the reading actually helps me see that what I thought was a personal problem is actually historical and cultural, shared all over the Third World."

"The Turd World," said Norvin. "I've always thought it should be renamed. All that shit on the sidewalks."

"Well, that's part of the problem of inequality. Bathrooms with Italian marble in my grandfather's old house on Malabar Hill exist side by side with slums where people have to choose between railway tracks or the sidewalk."

Gita's sense of the moment's perfection was eroding fast. This was going in the wrong direction—no mention made of Parsis yet. Why did Firoze always have to talk in this serious way?

"Tell about your grandfather," she said.

"Ah, your grandfather!" Norvin seconded.

"My grandfather?" Firoze asked. These two were quite a duo, but he might as well humor them. "Well, what do you want to know about him? He's an old chap now, goes to the Willingdon Club or fire temple, or sits at home in his chair with carved tiger paws, reading Dickens and writing 'How true' in the margins. He built up the ready-made clothing business that his father had started, and that gave us our name. He went to Britain to study management in the twenties, and then spent some time in Paris. He met my grandmother taking ballroom dancing lessons. She was French, you know. But she died before I was born. So, what else can I tell you?"

A Parsi in Paris! The rest of the story shrank beside this

fact. "Did you know that Timothy is in Paris?" Gita blurted out to Norvin.

"Is he?" asked Norvin. "I wondered where he was off to this time."

"He sent me a postcard," Gita said.

Norvin crumpled up his napkin and tried to aim it at a nearby bin. It bounced off the edge and fell outside. "Damn," Norvin said, getting up to retrieve it. "So I guess Marie-Claire is on again. Other people seem to manage keeping up these things long-distance, I don't see what Rachel's problem is. I mean, not that I would set Timothy and Marie-Claire up as ideal—he gets all his creative jolts from ambiguity. But all the same, San Francisco to Paris makes Berkeley to Chapel Hill look like kid's play."

Marie-Claire? Who was Marie-Claire? It was one of those moments when the light seemed to grow yellow, to snap and flicker and remind one of the darkness that was always an engulfing presence beyond the patches of warmth that people made. Gita didn't say anything. She tried to swallow the last of her falafel down a throat that felt very tight.

Firoze looked on, embarrassed. The professor chap had taken off his glasses. His lips curled downward and he tweaked the bridge of his nose. Gita was looking past Firoze with such intensity it made him want to turn his head. Without knowing what the problem was, he could see that they badly needed distraction. Whatever this fascination was with Parsis, it would keep them entertained.

"Do you know about the Tower of Silence?" he asked.

"That's how I feel," said Norvin. "I just keep getting her answering machine and she won't even call back."

"So it's true that Parsis put out corpses in the tower for vultures to eat?" Gita asked, her convent manners triumphing over tears.

"That's it," said Firoze. "The idea is to feed another creature. We call it the *dungarwadi*. Anyway, in Bombay, with all those new skyscrapers, there are all sorts of rumors circulating about how the vultures visit the tower and then stop off on balconies for a munch. The stories tell of hands being dropped off, or pieces of thigh. Not that it's happened to anyone I know, but everyone claims that *they* know a friend who has a friend who lives on a twenty-first floor somewhere. Imagine a fat Bombay hostess taking her guests out for a cocktail and finding a fragment of the latest deceased Parsi in the potted plants!"

"Really?" said Gita. She had a vision of her mother trying to deal with such a situation and granted Firoze a bright grin before she remembered that she didn't want to give him the Wrong Idea. She swiftly summoned up her scholarly self. "You know that business about hearing it from friends and its being in multiple versions makes the story qualify as urban folklore. You should definitely go contribute it to the folklore archives on campus."

"Oh, right," said Firoze. He was glad to see Gita smile, so he didn't ask why on earth she thought such silliness should be stowed in an archive.

"Dismembered," reflected Norvin, sadly. "It can also happen while you're still alive."

Gita was timid; she believed in love of which minstrels sang. But Gita could also have great courage when she understood that she was not being treated right. She had no class that afternoon, and so, after Firoze set off and she had listened some more to Norvin's troubles, she came right home and dialed Timothy. She had rehearsed the message she would leave on the answering machine during her walk back from campus, an icy message the gist of which was that she would appreciate it if he would care to call her back. Bet was not at home, and the apartment, cool after the sunshine outside, seemed to be thumping and trembling in its own stillness.

"The absent presence signifies desire," his answering machine began. "At two five eight, one seven one two, your message—" At this point, Timothy's voice broke through the static. "Hello? Hello, wait a minute, I'm turning this thing off."

"Hello," Gita affirmed. The way he spoke so matter-of-factly, with that amber-honest voice: she had missed that edge of his uniqueness. "Timothy, this is Gita."

"Gita, how are you?"

"Fine, thanks. I wanted to thank you for your postcard from Paris."

"Oh, umm, yes. Your letter too, thanks. Very Dada with the elephant's head."

"How long have you been back?" She was dead set on confronting him, but she had to warm up first.

"About ten days or so. I'm going back tomorrow for the summer. Some thoughts of moving there. There's nothing like a café to catch poems in—it's as though they dive like flies into the saucers of coffee."

"Diving like flies"—she felt a simultaneous thrill for his use of language and a distance flavored with hurt pride. Why did everything he said always have to be so *poetic?* She would not bring up Marie-Claire, that was stooping too low. "Why did you . . ." Gita began to lose her nerve. She rearrranged the collection of pens beside the phone book, though everything was already immaculate, thanks to Bet. She dared herself to speak that word, compromising herself as if she'd been besmirched. "Why did you kiss me?" she asked.

"What?" asked Timothy.

"Kiss me, why did you kiss me that night? I mean, not that it matters or anything. I just would like to know why."

"Kiss you? Gita, I didn't kiss you."

"We were watching the disc jockey," Gita said.

"The DJ? Oh, that. I, well, gave you a peck if I can remember, but I wouldn't really call it *kissing*. You know."

"Oh," said Gita, furiously humiliated.

"Maybe in India . . ." Timothy said. "Look, I'm sorry. This must have meant something to you if months later it's still on your mind. I mean, I wouldn't want to imply that you're not, umm, kissable or anything. You are, you know . . . attractive. But you are, well, very young."

Young! This was piling insult on injury. "I'm twenty-three years old," Gita said, "even if I don't drink."

"It's a matter of experience," Timothy said. "Gita, look, we don't know each other at all. I have to apologize if I did something that didn't seem right. You admire me. I appreciate that. But do you know what it's like to be put up on a pedestal? You can only slip. I didn't ask to be on your pedestal."

"I see," Gita said. She had no idea what else to say. All her pride had been pulled out from under her.

"Look, my experience with attraction like yours is that it's often trained on something you haven't developed in yourself. In real life there's usually tarnished ambivalence," said Timothy. "It's only crushes that shine."

He was saying that she was young, that she had worshiped him, that she had had a crush. All this was true, but it was worse than horrible to hear him point it all out. He, who was once her dearest Protector, cherished by every atom of her being. She kept silent.

"Look, I want to assure you that this is between the two of us; I won't ever mention anything to, umm, anyone we both know. I'm sorry that you've felt this way. I don't know what else to say. When I get back, let's get together for an espresso."

"I don't drink coffee, I drink tea," Gita said. "But yes, thank you very much, that would be nice. It was so nice talking to you. Hope you have a wonderful trip. Do look after yourself. Bye-bye." Thank goodness for the nuns.

She was imagining a cup of tea. A cup of tea filled almost to overflowing, a muddy brown against swirling yellow stoneware. The tang of lemongrass, of ginger, of cardamom and cloves. If you had a cough, turmeric staining the mixture. Bubbles of buffalo milkfat gleaming on the surface. The sweetness of granular sugar, bought on a ration card from a *banya* shop facing the road. Shouted for and shouted at, Tukaram would have served this on an oval silver tray. A breeze whipped up from the sea as she sipped.

"Darling, have another," Saroj Aunty said. "What is this, aren't you eating anything? Come o-o-on, at *least* have a biscuit."

Norvin was unshaven. He had bags under his eyes and seemed to be putting on weight around the jowls. "Why does she have to write to me at the department? It's not as though she doesn't know our home address or phone number. I go into this faculty meeting with a pile of mail and, wham, I feel like a bomb is let off into my entire intellectual system. I couldn't even argue my case for the distinguished lecturer we need to bring in. The rest of the faculty voted for this arrogant tycoon whose face I hate to see on this campus. You should have seen the review he did of my last book. Writing to the department, just one more innocent-looking envelope with a typed address! It's hitting below the belt."

"It's unfair," agreed Gita.

"My therapist says that she's always resented my work. Sees herself in competition. It's all to make up for the fact that she didn't want a child. Next thing I know there'll be sideswipes in journals. Here, be careful, you'll trip over these fishing rods."

They were out for a walk at the Berkeley marina. They paced along the wooden pier that jutted into the bay. San Francisco shimmered across the waves, its spires and towers like a science fiction city removed in time. To their left, cranes like enormous horses of Troy loomed against the horizon. They could hear the distant clink of sails from the boats lodged at the other end of the marina, the call of sea gulls, lapping water, and an intermittent honk that Gita thought was perhaps to warn boats. The air smelled different out here. A few men fished along the sides of the boardwalk. A couple with a dog was walking toward them.

"I can't tell you how much I appreciate your listening to all this. It's difficult with my colleagues, you know—everyone is a friend of hers and is professionally connected to her as well."

"It's no problem," said Gita. It was lulling to hear Norvin's troubles. These days, every minute that she didn't think of Timothy she felt she had accomplished something. It was as though he'd packed all her worth and taken it off with him to Paris. Even when she got A's on papers or people in class listened attentively to what she said, it didn't seem to matter. It felt good to be with a man exactly Timothy's age who didn't seem to think that twenty-three was too young to understand life and its complications.

"This is all so petty. It's like goddamn sibling rivalry. Because I was given the chair she feels she has to go get herself a lover. And a woman lover! I mean, I *know* Rachel's heterosexual, I know it for a fact. This has to be one of her flirtations with radical feminism or something. Too much theory goes to the head, or should I say to the . . . Oh, well."

"Oh no!" said Gita. She examined the shifting peaks of the waves and looked back over her shoulder at the reassuring line of the Berkeley hills. How was she to change the subject? "Is, uh, Marie-Claire a feminist?"

"Who? Oh, you mean Timothy's friend. I suppose you could say so. She's his mother's age, sort of a nineteen eighties Colette. Frizzed gray hair and leather bracelets with studs. You know the sort. I believe she might ride a motorcycle, or maybe that was just for a piece of performance art. I never thought about it; I guess she's feminist. These days most women are, you know—the question is what brand."

So he had wanted a crazy old woman instead of her. Something dropped inside Gita, echoing downward as it clanked. "I'm sorry about Rachel," Gita said. "It might help if you see all this as her problem, not yours."

"Wise," said Norvin. "Oh, that's wise. Yes, there's a lot of taking that perspective. I just feel so—how can I say it . . . This is a woman I had sex with for fourteen years. And it was good sex, too, I'm sure of it. She can't have been putting me

71

on all that time. What would she want with a woman? I mean, all those sound effects if—"

Gita was desperate to change the topic, and she lit upon the first thing that came to mind. If she had to respond to what Norvin was saying it would soon be apparent that she had never even been properly kissed. "Remember you said you were interested in Parsis? Would you like to hear about a Parsi who was possessed by a train?" As though stopping up her ears, she talked, all the stories she had prepared for Timothy spilling out helter-skelter. For once, she did not even allow Norvin to break in.

"Fabulous, fabulous." Norvin was smiling by the time she paused for breath. "What a simulation! You mean, your uncle actually founded this Society? How about a Berkeley chapter with you and me in it?"

"We can only watch Firoze," Gita said, "and he's too serious. He's not even very Parsi."

"Ah," said Norvin, "Parsi is a floating signifier. Parsi is a state of mind. You don't have to be born a Parsi to be a Parsi. Everyone who's innovative, a wonderful character is a Parsi. There are Parsis everywhere in the world! Academe is strewn with them."

On behalf of Jimmy Uncle, Gita felt affronted. "They're Zoroastrians," she said. "They have a history. They might be a small minority in India, but with so many talents they're famous all over the country. There are people with names you can immediately recognize as Parsi in science, industry, law, music. This isn't just an abstract category you can switch around because you feel like it." She felt proud to be arguing with an older man who only a few weeks ago she would have automatically deferred to.

"In language, anything is possible." All Norvin's teeth were showing again. "Anything, but anything, can happen when you start narrativizing events. So tell me more about this Jimmy's performance pieces."

Gita couldn't help it, she had to smile. "Well, sometimes he would also pretend to be his great-aunt's car, an ancient

Dodge, revving up. Saroj Aunty accused him of sounding constipated when he did the car show, so it wasn't quite as popular as the train."

"The train! Let me perfect this train. It could be a great non sequitur for my next distinguished lecture. Especially when you think of all the trains we have known in literature. Paul Theroux, move aside. Let's go. Cha. Cha. Cha. Bombay Central, Victoria Terminus, here we come."

Gita had begun to laugh, her head thrown back, stomach pumping, mouth wide. It made her so happy to be connecting Bombay to Berkeley. "Che. Che. Paise," she enunciated for Norvin with a rush of warmth. She reached out both hands to press his palm backward toward his wrist. There was hair at the back of his hands, she noticed, and that faint, not unpleasant smell like roasted cumin coming from him. "Right angles, as though you're snaking up a mountainside. Now roll your shoulders around and around. By the way, do you know, I actually don't speak Marathi?"

"POO-POO!" Norvin cried. "POO-POO, POO-POO. Oh dear, here are some kids coming who I think I recognize from my big lecture class. Well, let them see that professors have lives. Hey, Gita, am I doing it right?"

Firoze Ganjifrockwala

Here we sit in the latest Indian food disaster on Telegraph Avenue. *Bapuji no Bistro* is the name of this one. I don't give it more than a few months. The food is hopeless, just some generic spices thrown around in oil. There are misshapen batik apsaras on the wall, empty Kingfisher and Taj Lager beer bottles lined up along the windows, and plastic roses in plastic vases on the tables. Gita is on one edge of her chair as though she's expecting a cockroach to creep up from the side. And of course coming to this place was my idea.

I'm trying to get Gita into a conversation about Simone de Beauvoir. I think that de Beauvoir is fantastic, even if everything she says doesn't hold up cross-culturally. She really gets to the heart of the phoniness involved in this whole virginity business and inequality between the sexes. I mean, *genders.* OK, gender, whatever. Not that I would use words like virginity or sex *with* Gita. It would only make her stiffen her back: the sacred is tabooed with interdictions, just like Durkheim said. I have just been outlining the general principle of Woman as Other for her.

She sits there fidgeting with the pita bread that is supposed to be a chappati, soaking it up in that awful lentil soup they've sprinkled with curry powder and passed off as dal. Those big, haunted eyes, those delicate veined hands, that hair hanging over one shoulder, and her mind definitely somewhere else. It makes me feel like a bastard to be talking *at* her. I think that at this point neither of us is paying much attention to what I have to say, but I can't seem to stop the lecture.

She's weird. The way she keeps a distance—in the clipped

conversation, in the averted eyes, the body held taut across the table—I tell you, man, it makes me feel bad. It makes me feel as though I've got some sort of hidden criminal tendencies and if she doesn't watch out I'll be pouncing in a flash. This kind of attitude is really a problem with Indian women. OK, I don't mean to essentialize, let's say some Indian women. It's the whole cult of virginity. The quest for the perfect hero, to whom they will finally surrender themselves. Women end up being too bloody paranoid. They're afraid that if they loosen up a little it means they'll completely let go. When they get to America, there's so much damn sex in the air that if they're the uptight sort they go into deep freeze.

OK, so I know that men back in India can be awful when a woman gets into a crowded train compartment or a bus. Delhi buses are apparently the worst—if you're a woman you get completely fingered. In the crush, men take the opportunity to grab at buttocks and squish breasts. She went to college in Delhi—no wonder she's so anxious about this sort of thing. But it's not just her, though, it's just about every second deshi woman you meet out here, whether she's from Bombay or Calcutta or Madras. And the ones who aren't uptight end up getting involved with foreign guys. I swear it: foreign. It's the difference that adds mystery and erases any residue of fear or guilt. For example, Najma. We're in the same feminist theory class. She's the sort who will smile right at you and laugh at double meanings in words. The kind of girl—well, woman— who can really be your friend. And who's she involved with? Guess. Some American scientist type. When I was an undergrad out at Boston it was the same thing. Either they're nervous and dart off or they're already taken by some foreign bugger.

Dinaz said, "Look after Gita. She's damn brainy but she's a mouse who keeps to herself." So I call up Gita at least once a month and we go out to eat together. What I don't understand is, if she's so brainy, why the hell is she so insecure about what she thinks? You try to start an intellectual conversation, and she mostly agrees, looking at a spot just beside *your left ear. If she says anything, it comes out apologetic. I mean, what's wrong with the Indian educational system if intelligent women can feel inadequate just because they're intelligent? Because it disqualifies them to be wives who listen sweetly at their husbands pontificate? What does it do to you if nothing you ever say is challenged? We talk about the oppression of women, but we need to also think about the psychological effects on men.*

A month or two ago I was trying to explain to her about us all being products of colonialism. She was more with me that day, a mind like a whip, cracking out dates. What year the East India Company got to India, what year the Battle of Plassey made British power dominant over the French, what year the first War of Indian Independence was, when Gandhi started his agitations. I can't remember all the dates now, even if I tried. But the thing is, she doesn't see that this all relates to her, that all the impact of all those dates is inscribed in every elite Indian's mentality. I don't know what sort of Indian she is—Das is probably something from the north. But look at the weirdness of it all: me originally from Iran but settled in Gujarat, then Bombay, for God knows how many generations. That's at least on my Indian side. Her from somewhere in north India. Both of us eating fake Indian food in Berkeley, California, and we're not speaking Farsi or Gujarati or Bengali or Punjabi or Hindi but English *to each other. I mean, just think about it for a minute.*

If she's so smart, why is she just applying her mind to those books and not out to actual life? Insecurity? Could be. As though she has to have some corner of the world in which she's stable before she starts questioning anything else. It's probably those goddamn nuns. You should hear Dinaz on the subject of that convent they all went to. I know it was the nuns who drove Dinaz to her big revolt of taking up modeling. What's so depressing about it all is that Dinaz thinks that showing up in a bikini is revolt. How can the inequalities in Indian society ever be overturned if women are wasting their energies on these petty revolts? I bet that Gita thinks that going out for a walk alone with that professor fellow is something so scandalous it's titillating. I saw how flustered she was when I met them getting into his car near the marina. And all it is is a walk. Big bloody deal. All I can say is that I wish the professor good luck. Even if he has some strange ideas about being reincarnated as a Parsi. There's something about her that . . . oh hell, to melt her primness even a big important man like him is not only going to need luck but supernatural intervention.

So my thoughts are running one way and my speech is still carrying on. Gita is still watching me with this distracted, weary look.

"So that's de Beauvoir," I say. "You might not agree that it's all universal—in fact, anthropologists are looking into whether there are any societies where the genders are equal. But you have to acknowledge that for our backgrounds, at least, it sort of fits."

You know what Gita says to me after this whole long monologue? She focuses right on my face and she asks, "Firoze, do you think there's a postal strike on in Bombay?"

Now what the hell sort of response is that?

3

A Nipple
in the Air

"It's that dude Norvin again," said Bet, stark naked and trailing the long telephone cord into Gita's room. She put one hand over the receiver. "*Norvin*, Jesus! It makes you think of someone with dandruff on his blazer."

Gita turned down the classical music playing from the little tape recorder by her desk. She avoided looking at the expanse of skin before her, the pink-tipped breasts that dangled as the phone was handed over, the patches of blond hair. Through their months sharing the same apartment, Gita had never once allowed Bet to see beyond her shoulders or above the knee. This was old habit from boarding school. In all Gita's ten years of living in a dormitory under the watchful eyes of the Sisters, no girl had ever appeared nude. The damp bathrooms had been for bucket baths, not for the privacy of changing clothes. Every Our Lady of Perpetual Succour graduate was a verified expert in the art of decent changing in public: wrestling with one thing over your head as another slides down underneath, pulling bras off through one sleeve, stepping out of panties with a skirt still on, and, in a pinch, groping about in the sieved light under a bedspread.

"Thanks," said Gita, withdrawing toward the receiver. She spoke to Norvin briefly. When she finished, Bet was still standing behind her, spreading lotion over her stomach.

"So what did he want *this* time?" Bet asked.

"Well, it's about Friday."

"Friday. You mean you have a date with him on Friday? Didn't you just go for a *walk* last Sunday? And the weekend before that? And meet him for coffee during the week? Come on, Gita, something has to be going on."

"He's a professor," said Gita. She kept her eyes on the bare floorboards directly in front of the scented flurry of motion. She really had to buy a cheap dhurrie or something for this floor when she could save a little from her stipend. "He's married. These days he's, I suppose, sort of depressed and so he—"

"About to *divorce* from the sound of it," said Bet. "And anyhow, being married never stopped anyone. Especially professors. I've already told you what happened to me when I was an undergrad. Sure, it was one of those teaching assistants who grabbed me, but a professor is just one step removed."

"The party is at Firoze's house." Gita now trained her attention to the wall over Bet's head, onto the miniature reproduction she had bought in Delhi before she left. An expectant young woman stood at a doorway, gauzy orange scarf outlined with gold, as three white cranes swooped into the swollen monsoon sky. "Firoze invited us both. Norvin was just checking up on whether I wanted to be picked up."

"Picked up!" Bet snorted. She went into her room and returned with a sheet of newspaper and a nail clipper. "Quite a choice of words," she said, spreading out the paper. "And I suppose he'll *take you home* too? Watch out, Gita. Beware. I bet he's the generation that just *assumes* every woman—"

"Norvin is not—"

"And you're not exactly the world's *expert* on these things, Gita." Bet's words were punctuated by methodical clicks as bits of toenail tumbled across the newspaper. "I'm telling you this for your own good. I don't think you should go out with this Norvin. A Norman would be bad enough, but a name like Norvin, Jesus Christ!"

"You haven't met him," Gita said, trying to swim through the black tides of mortification unleashed with Bet's suggestions. How could Bet insinuate such things? Bet had had lovers, of course, and lately, with fair advance warning, she'd occasionally been bringing home the man who worked the lights in the play she was in (Gita hurrying to get out the door in the morning so she didn't have to mutter polite nothings to an unshaven stranger). Bet believed that this acting role and the man too were entirely thanks to the advice of the psychic on Telegraph Avenue, and she had been pushing Gita to go for a consultation. Gita worried that this psychic might want her to change her name to something like Phyllis or Elaine, so she kept repeating that she already had an astrologer, thanks.

Bet said that she wasn't in love, the guy was too young, but heck, he was available, the sex was nice, and he thought her newfound stage name, Krista, was cool. No obsession, just a mutual understanding: a diversion once in a while. Gita had no objections to Bet discussing her own love life: it was most interesting and educational, if scandalous. But her discussing Gita's projected sexual career made Gita want to lather up with Mysore sandalwood soap under a hot, cleansing shower. Despite Gita's most puritanical objections, she somehow just couldn't resist such conversations. "Poor fellow, Norvin can't help his name. He's really not a bad chap. He's lived in India."

"So?"

"I, well, I trust him."

"I don't," said Bet, scraping at the inner rims of her nails. "Since no one *else* around here is looking out for you, it's my job to see that nothing terrible happens."

Gita didn't know what to say to this. She examined her fingernails, trying to judge whether they had extended beyond the length of brisk typing and no unsightly grime. At Our Lady of Perpetual Succour there used to be nail inspection each Monday morning, the girls all lined up with outspread hands. Sometimes the Sisters brought along rulers and did hemline inspection at the same time. "Bet, when you're finished, will you please pass your clipper?"

"Homely and beautiful girl seeks match," said Firoze, entering the crowded room to hand around some *papad* he had just roasted over the stove. There were black streaks and yellow turmeric stains on the rough texture of his *khadi kurta*. A smell of roasted onions mixed with *masala*s hung in the air.

"Come on, *yaar*," said his housemate, Ravindran, immaculate as ever with a line of talcum powder at the back of his dark neck. *"Parents* seek match for fair, homely, and beautiful girl. Domesticated, maybe even housebroken."

"Oh, shut up you," said a short woman with spiked hair whose name Gita hadn't caught. She had been introduced as an Indian from Singapore, and now she sat next to Ravindran on the sofa. The hand-printed bedspread covering the sofa was puckered around their bodies, the material drawn inward to expose springs and splotches. "And I mean *shut up you,* like a film actress would say, one flapping wrist and all. *Homely* is standard, same as *domestic.* But I never read anything about domesticated, house-trained, and the rest of this rubbish. You make it sound like getting a pet."

"A pet wife," said Firoze. "Well, wouldn't you say that most arranged marriages assume the hegemony of patriarchy? Husband as God to be served eternally, husband as sole altar of sexuality. I tell you, India is just not going to go anywhere as long as women aren't allowed their full potential. Actually, you could say that this isn't specific to India. *Pativrata* happens to be a Sanskrit term, but it could be applied to women's ideological subordination elsewhere."

"Don't be so heavy, *yaar*," said Ravindran. "This isn't your feminist theory seminar. Back to the *funda*. Did you hear about the fair groom, one hundred sixty-five centimeters, age twenty-six, four-figure salary, good family, limps only while walking?"

"He married the girl who stutters only while talking," said Gita. They all laughed, turning to her. She adjusted the woven sari border high over her breasts, unable to confess that this was actually Harish Uncle's joke. One of her ears was trained toward the kitchen, where Norvin had last been seen discoursing on the merits of the 1979 Sonoma zinfandel he had brought three bottles of. There were no wineglasses in this household, and the wine had been poured into small glasses that looked as if they had been filched from a cafeteria. When these ran out, the wine was painstakingly poured into empty jars that Gita suspected had once held mango pickles. "Charming, charming," was Norvin's comment. He looked around the walls filled with Spanish woodcut posters displaying guerrillas or women with headscarves, adding, "All this just takes me back to the sixties."

"Firoze told me you're a friend of his cousin Dinaz," said Najma. She was a small woman with a cloud of black hair parted in the middle and a perpetually amused expression on her round face. She wasn't plump, but everything about her was rounded, as though you'd get precise circles if you were to slice from any angle. Gita vaguely remembered seeing her at Timothy's reading and around campus. There was a warmth she carried, like sun slanting on crimson bougainvillea. "Lovely perfume!" she said, lowering herself onto the floor beside Gita.

With most other people Gita would have been embarrassed that perhaps she had doused herself in too much of the Saroj Aunty perfume if it was commented on. But with Najma, she found herself smiling. "Thanks," she said.

"So you're one of those Our Lady of Perpetual Succour convent school girls!" Najma grinned. "Did you know Annunciation Madeira by any chance? She must have been a few classes ahead of you. I came to Bombay once about ten or fifteen years ago—my father had some work—and we stayed with her family in Bandra."

Gita did indeed remember Annie Madeira, who had been her senior. They agreed that Annie had been quite a firebrand, and wasn't it too much that she had become so famous for agitating for higher wages to be paid to the women who carried endless loads of sand and bricks in Bombay construction work? In the meantime, this making of mutual connections had spread through the room.

"What year were you at Pillani? Did you know Groovy Singh?"

"Oh God, don't tell me you know *Groovy!*"

"That word *funda, yaar,* and I can sniff an I.I.T. wallah a mile away. Which one was it, Delhi? One of my classfellows . . ."

"Did I hear I.I.T. Delhi? My sister's brother-in-law's cousin taught physics out there. Really? You know her, damn brainy dame?"

"Remember that guy Lund who was Groovy's best friend? I just met him in Washington, he works in the World Bank. You should have seen him turn maroon in his three-piece suit when I brought up that school name!"

"St. Stephens, oh hell, *Doon School* and St. Stephens: with this kind of *maha*-elite combo I think I'll just have to leave the room, *sarr!*"

"Really, I can swear I saw you at the jazz *yatra* many years back."

"But tell me, why was he called Lund anyway?"

Norvin returned in the midst of this. He smiled broadly at everyone in the room and settled himself cross-legged on the carpet even though there was a chair available. Gita sensed that since he had a few gray hairs and was the only professor present, he was trying to make a point of being one of the crowd. He was wearing a raw silk *kurta* that seemed a little tight around the shoulders. "I was in Nasik in the Peace Corps," he announced to an ash blonde with a blunt pageboy cut, one of the other visibly non-Indians present.

"Agnostic?" she reported politely.

"No, no. *Nasik*. It's near Bombay. In India."

"Yah, yah," she said. "Me, I have never been there." She was staring across the room at Firoze. Gita studied Firoze's face. Catching her eye, he smiled. He looked exceptionally fair amid the other Indians, but then nothing as fair as this blond woman. Gita couldn't make out if this woman was just a classmate from the feminism class or if something more was going on. What was it with these Indian men in America that they always seemed to go for pale girls with light hair (and, Gita secretly suspected, eyes more brightly devoted, opinions more bleached than those of the most dutiful of Indian wives)?

"Once I was waiting to use a phone booth in Delhi," Ravindran said. "There was this huge Punjabi woman using the phone. She'd just been to inspect a boy. You know what she said? *B.A. Fail, par passa-nalitee bari changi hai!*'"

"Oh wow," howled the woman whom Gita had decided to label Spike-Hair. They had not had a chance to be introduced so far, and as the woman seemed focused entirely on the men it was unlikely that there would be a chance to properly meet. "Passa-nalitee. Ravindran, you're too much, the way you've got down that accent."

"What did she say?" Norvin asked. "When I went to India I was told to expect B.A. Fail on calling cards, but I never actually saw one. Maybe calling cards went out with independence. If you speak Marathi I'll understand. *Kai, koni Marathi boltat?*"

"He's failed his B.A., but his personality is very good," explained Firoze, hazel eyes earnestly fixed on Norvin. "That's what the woman said."

"Oh," said Norvin, laughing without enthusiasm, though the blond woman seemed to find this very funny.

"The humor is because she's using that English word *personality* and was saying it in a very slurred Punjabi sort of way," Firoze continued.

"C'mon, *yaar*, don't be so heavy," said Ravindran. "You can't *explain* a joke and still expect people to laugh."

"Murder to dissect," muttered Gita, who had been reading

Wordsworth those few minutes she counted as her own before she switched off the light for sleep. These days she felt that by always analyzing everything in terms of hidden structures, themes, intentions, she was losing the pleasure of a good read. Whatever she turned to brought ideas now, not feelings. Of course, she had written those poems about Timothy and submitted them in a bundle to the campus poetry competition. Yet in the aftermath of Timothy's departure, she wasn't even sure she believed in either poetry or love. She was to be Norvin's research assistant this summer so she could earn some money. Though survival continued to be a problem, there was little in the big flat desert of an unmated future she could see as worth looking forward to.

"Oh, Indian English! I love Indian English," Norvin said. "It has to be the most creative dialect going. I tell you, sometimes I wonder if going to graduate school in English wasn't brought on by the years I spent in the Peace Corps in India. Joyce would have had a heyday. The prime minister and president had a telephonic exchange. Antisocial elements are undermining communal harmony. On the buses there is increased Eve teasing."

"Especially in Delhi," said a thin mustached man with glasses. "In Madras there are special seats for women."

"Hey, *yaar*, Firoze," said Ravindran. "Tell that story about your dad in Madras."

"You mean the nipple one?" Firoze asked.

"The *what?*" asked Najma, giggling. Gita shrank. He would repeat it, that word.

"The nipple. The story goes that my father was visiting Madras on business. The temperature dropped to a mere ninety-five degrees. Everyone brought out their woolens. My father passed this old chap out for his morning constitutional. He waved a stick, adjusted the muffler around his head, and when my father said, 'Good morning,' he replied, 'There's quite a *nipple* in the air.'"

"A muffler on his head?" asked Norvin. "Was he having car trouble or something?"

This suggestion brought the house down. Gita worried that someone would tip over a glass or jar. "A muffler is a scarf," she said to Norvin, half of her finding him hilarious, the other half empathizing. Poor fellow, how could he know?

"I see, muffles the cold," said Norvin with goodwill.

"Oh no, a car muffler around the head, imagine it," laughed Spike-Hair, still in stitches and falling over toward the man from Madras.

"How many of you have a rubber story?" asked Ravindran. "Put your hands up!"

"Boy," said Norvin, "did my imagination boggle when I saw that kids were requested to bring a pencil and *rubber* with them to school. I thought that this was catching them early for family planning campaigns."

"Erasers," said Najma, grinning away. "E-ra-ser. We have to all practice the word. Eraser, eraser, eraser. We should all recite it fifty-one times each day."

Gita actually had a rubber story, but there was no way she would tell it. A few months after she'd first arrived, she'd been in the International House study hall late at night writing the first draft of a paper in pencil. At one point, she had gotten up to tiptoe barefoot across the room and ask the sole other occupant, a studious-looking man, if he had a rubber with him. He had blanched. "No, I'm sorry, I can't help you," he said with a nervous smile, immediately turning back to his books. Much later Gita had chanced with horror upon the American meaning of this innocuous word, and when she looked back, it seemed that the studious man had been avoiding her, even shrinking into a corner of the elevator whenever she got on.

"We forgot one great matrimonial ad," said Firoze, stroking at the scruffy growth on his chin. "The *bar-bar* one."

"Oh *no!*" objected Spike-Hair, going into further paroxysms on Ravindran's right shoulder. The *papad* in her hand was crumbling in yellow bits onto the Bukhara carpet (sent by Firoze's mother) so out of place in the mismatch of yard sale and Salvation Army furniture.

"Singles bars, yah?" enquired the ash blonde.

"*Bar-bar*," repeated Firoze. "It means 'again and again.' You tell it, Ravindran, you've got the style."

"No, *yaar*, there are ladies present."

"All emancipated," put in someone from the kitchen doorway. "Anyway, this joke is hardly nonveg."

"And of course all the ladies are supposed to be pure vegetarians!" said Najma. "Let me tell you that I've heard that joke at least five thousand times. I even tell it myself. What's all this sweet little innocent Indian woman *nakra?* Don't you ever pick up those books that Firoze brings home? I mean, let's have some consciousness-raising around here!"

"OK, OK." Ravindran crossed his arms. "There was this Indian guy in America who wanted to put in a matrimonial advertisement."

"Was he in America?" put in the slim man from Madras. "I heard this was in the *Times of India.*"

"Literalist!" shrieked Spike-Hair.

"Just listen. He put in a matrimonial ad, OK? Let's just shelve the fine points of where he was at the time. The poor guy was lonely, he wanted a wife. So his ad said: Wanted, fair-complexioned, educated, homely, and beautiful girl. Caste no bar. Age no bar. Sex *bar-bar.*"

"Fabulous!" cried Norvin. "I knew that the spirit of the *Kamasutra* was still alive." Everyone was laughing and Gita was forced to join in.

"Do you know about the Sardarji who ordered a hot dog in Manhattan?" Najma asked, eyes shooting mischief and tiny, pearly teeth exposed in a big smile.

Gita felt an embarrassing spurt. Before the evening was out, she would definitely have to change. But if she went to the bathroom with her bag, wouldn't everyone guess? As Norvin began to discourse on how he'd once been interested in Hindu spirituality but that the *Bhagavad Gita* didn't really hold up on an Indian train, Gita began to think through what she

should do next. If she'd worn *salvar-khameez* she could have
at least moved to a wooden chair and smoothed the *khameez*
out so it was draped behind her rather than sat upon. That
would have set her mind at rest.

"Got my chum," the girls at school used to acknowledge
occasionally if they were sitting out from sports. On the
whole, it wasn't exactly a publicized thing. "Uncle's visiting,"
others said. Once in a while someone—generally a girl who
had joined from another school—would talk about an "M.C."
and she didn't mean a tuxedoed master of ceremonies with
Brylcreem in his hair. It was only the Sisters who referred,
lowering their voices and hastily swallowing the words, to
"the curse." Being a day scholar at college in Delhi had made
for a lot of loneliness, and Gita had not been on such confiding
terms with any other girls. Rukmani Aunty, the family friend
with whom Gita mostly stayed, expected her to be back by
5:30 each day but pretty much left her to herself, which included emptying her own dustbins.

During the vacations, when Gita's mother and stepfather
were at home, there was no problem either. There was a basket in the bathroom of the room that Gita used but never felt
was her own because of the long stretches that she was away
from it. A female sweeper came each morning, faded sari hiked
up around her knees, and dealt directly with that betraying
container. The only terrible moment had been the first time
Gita came back from school with the need to buy sanitary
napkins, and so, to confess to her mother. She found she had
no presentable words for this request. Instead of saying anything she had spirited away dozens of cotton handkerchiefs to
her room. It was the time that Vicky had chicken pox. Because
of his bad heart, there was special worry. Then too, worrying
about Vicky was one of Kookoo's most pressing preoccupa-
tions, tied into her daily routine as closely as the anxiety over
menus for the next diplomatic event. So she was in a terrible
flutter over the chicken pox. Searching Gita's bathroom for
some Aspro, she came upon a phalanx of freshly washed white
cotton squares. And then it all had to be explained, and it was

miserably embarrassing, with her mother smuggling emergency supplies from their hiding place among the saris in her own cupboard, and saying "oh, nothing" in a too loudly uninterested voice when Dilip asked what was going on.

The real nightmare, though, was visiting the Shahs during the vacations when her parents weren't home. In the Shahs' big bungalow, Gita occupied the room that had once been Harish Uncle's mother's. (Gita could vaguely remember her, an old woman wearing white and spinning cotton for hours at a stretch, a habit she had never given up after Independence.) It was a spacious room. A fan hung down from the high ceilings, and gusts of coolness blew in off the sea. A portrait of Harish Uncle's father wearing a long black coat with a high collar, a red turban, and pince-nez presided over the room. Also, there were framed posters of plump, multiarmed, pinkish goddesses or blue gods. Since the old woman had died, the Gujarati volumes had been supplemented with the spillover of books from other parts of the house. *I'm OK, You're OK* and an Erle Stanley Gardner mystery flanked a collection of hymns from Gandhi's ashram. A two-volume Russian edition of *The Brothers Karamazov* bought by Saroj Aunty at a book fair was separated by the hefty *Tulsi Ramayana*. A book picked up by the Surati cousins at a railway station and titled *How to Choose a Wife: Bold, Frank, Easy Approach, a Psychopragmatic Analysis of Interpersonal Relations Based on the Calculation of the Analytic Rate of Personality Between the Bride and Groom (To Be)*, written by one Dr. S. K. Vinayaka, was shelved beside Sartre's *Nausea*. Gita had spent hours looking for things to read in this room, and whenever she returned, she could immediately spot any rearrangements.

But the problem with this room was that the attached bathroom had no basket in it—nothing. If you wanted to throw something away you had to bring it back to the open waste basket so prominent beside the door. Gita smuggled sheets of newspaper into the bedroom and slit them four ways. With her capable fingers and the years of needlework at school, she folded everything—even packages to be thrown away—with precision. Tukaram, who swept the floors each morning, must have at first thought anything so carefully wrapped must contain something valuable. Tobacco bulging in one cheek, he had set down the flicking tongue of broom. Without rising from his squatting position he dipped a hand in the basket and began to unwrap a sample package. Gita was not sure she would ever get over the mortification of that moment. Ears burning, she had tried to continue sorting clothes that had arrived freshly ironed from the *dhobi*'s. Tukaram got up and splashed under a tap. Since then, he never unwrapped but gave Gita what she took to be knowing and disgusted looks when such packages were found in the wastebasket.

One Christmas vacation the humiliation of her body's rhythms being broadcast had been too much to take. She hid four days' worth of packages in a corner of her cupboard with the intention of walking them to the nearest dump. But of course, people were watching there too. At least they were strangers and she hoped she would never see them again. As the emaciated dogs with tails tucked between their legs gorged themselves on the mess of stinking garbage, Gita abruptly tossed out the bulging bag she had saved. She swiftly walked away, not daring to turn for fear of seeing swollen-bellied children leap in through the rotting vegetable peels and fermenting rice to examine what she might have left behind.

How was she to make an exit here, either to the bathroom or to the relatively unscrutinized safety of her own apartment? After the potluck meal—each dish from a different region and prepared with varying amounts of skill—Gita went in search of Norvin. She found him talking to Firoze by the kitchen sink. "For me, those were truly happy years. It was a time of idealism in my life, before I realized that everything has a dark edge and that no cause provides the only answer. I felt I was helping people through the Peace Corps."

Firoze was pouring water into a pressure cooker. He had

prepared excellent vegetarian *dhansak* so that everybody present, regardless of community and level of orthodoxy, could eat it. Gita noticed that there was black mold where the tap emerged from the wall—the sort of thing that Bet would pounce upon with cleaning powder and exclamations of disgust. "Even if all the causes are imperfect one has got to keep trying for change," Firoze said. "It can only come about step by step." He saw Gita and smiled at her over Norvin's shoulder. She stood there patiently, not quite having the courage to poke Norvin from behind so as to catch his attention.

"Idealistic youth," said Norvin. "It's the trope of the vanishing pastoral. Shows up in constructions of the past and, of course, in autobiography. There's always this moment after which you realize that you just can't change the world and make it into a beautiful place. All you can do is try to carve out a good life for yourself."

"Excuse me, but I don't agree. What you're saying is cynical. Hi, Gita, do you need something?" Firoze turned off the splashing water.

Norvin turned with an enormous grin. "Gita! The Song of Songs! Well, hello there. I'm having the most fabulous time here with your friends. Just sniffing the curries in this kitchen I'm transported back almost twenty years."

"Would you, umm, mind going home soon?" Gita asked. Seeing Firoze throw her a startled look, she clarified. "I mean, taking me home. Sorry, I mean, you know: would you mind dropping me off where I live?"

"C'mon, Gita," said Firoze, "Girish has even brought his *sarodh*. We were just revving up for a performance after *chai*. The semester's over; what could you possibly have to do?"

That was a bind. Usually she had work to duck behind, great walls of work that shielded her when she didn't want to interact. "Some very pressing things," she said vaguely. "Also, my housemate likes me to . . ."

"Certainly, if you want to go I'll take you," said Norvin. Gita was relieved that he immediately got the point. "Whatever you'd like. How often is one requested to do anything by someone in so regal a costume as a sari?"

It seemed that Firoze was trying to smother a grin. He turned his face away slightly, but she could catch that lifting of cheeks under the scraggly growth of hair that couldn't yet be termed a beard. She suspected that it was the word *costume* that he found hilarious, as though everyone in India attended an extended Halloween party. Or could it be that he found Norvin's solicitude amusing? Lifting more dishes into the sink, Firoze swept a look over her. "By the way, you look damn good in a sari, Gita," he said.

"I just love the way that area around the waist is revealed by saris." Norvin inspected Gita too. "Boy, that's a beautiful one."

"My Saroj Aunty names her saris," said Gita, brusque and uncomfortable with compliments. She had always admired people who could smile, throwing a light thank you and moving right on. She couldn't quite meet the eyes of either of the men. "I used to go stay with her and Harish Uncle on school vacations. Saroj Aunty gave me this one too. She knows these two sisters who have taken a vow to only wear handloom materials with vegetable dyes. They have a boutique with really exquisite traditional saris and things. Synthetics are apparently bad for the ozone layer or something. Also they put all these weavers out of work."

"In other words, fashion can be socially conscious and ecological," said Firoze. He was thinking that maybe there was some hope for Gita after all. And she really did look quite striking this evening.

"Naming saris! I love it!" said Najma, who had come bustling in behind them to check whether the water for tea was boiling. "Hey, Firoze, do you guys have any ginger or anything around here? *Elaichi?* Tell, Gita, does this sari have a name?"

"No name," Gita said. "That was only for Aunty's silk collection."

"We must definitely name it," said Firoze. "Just look in that cupboard, Najma, one of the old mustard bottles. Ginger's probably in the door of the fridge. See it?" Gita averted her eyes as the fridge door opened, revealing shelves that were piled high and spilling over. She felt sure that the many yogurt containers were filled with decaying leftovers and that in the drawer vegetables lay in pools of slime.

"A name," repeated Norvin, quite mesmerized as he stared at the folds of the sari. This meant that his vision was trained somewhere near Gita's crotch. "Ineffable, deep, and inscrutable, singular name."

Gita squirmed. She just wanted to get home quickly, away from the dirtiness she felt in her body and the rot in this kitchen. Now all three were examining her from every angle. She felt like a mannequin in a showroom. She would have liked the earth to open up and protect her, as it had once done for Sita. The sari was Orissan: black and white and deep, round red. There were checked patterns and trails of tiny woven flowers and fish.

"Flamenco," said Firoze. "All that drama. Or how about Sandanista?"

"Come on," Najma laughed, "those sound like seedy bars in five-star Bombay hotels. Alhambra cocktail lounge. I can just see it."

"Mandela," Firoze began, but Norvin had leapt into action.

"Why go cross-cultural?" Norvin asked. "Why not be consummately Orientalist and Indian? How about Shakuntala? Think of the effect of those early translations on the German romantic imagination! Or Kalidasa; can't you just see the poetry, the swimming sensuosity in that sari?"

"Can we go now?" Gita asked.

"Hold on," said Najma. She had not stopped grinning since she entered the kitchen. Gita knew that she was not grinning *about* her, but she wished she herself found all this amusing enough to join in. "My vote is for Joan Armatrading."

"Joan who?" Firoze asked.

"A singer," said Norvin, suddenly dropping his voice. He didn't look anyone in the eye as he said, "British. Originally from Trinidad or Jamaica or someplace like that."

"The thing is her voice." Najma stopped pounding carda-mom, and she spoke with luminous eyes. "It's *so* rich and beautiful, with little rivulets of texture. She has, you know, a red, black, and white voice. Especially red, blood red, wine red, forehead's spot of *kumkum* red. For your information, Firoze, if you're into feminism you should really start listening to the right music! Great stuff on being vulnerable and want-ing love but wanting independence too. Do you know her stuff, Gita?"

"No," Gita said. "I'm not exactly up-to-date . . ."

"Oh you must! She's just wonderful, *maha*-wonderful. Let's meet for lunch sometime and I'll bring along a tape. By the way, where do you live? Benvenue? My goodness, this is too much. I live *so* close by."

"Let's go, Gita," said Norvin.

Norvin's car was parked out front. Gita could read its glow-in-the-dark bumper sticker, HONK IF YOU ARE JESUS. When they had settled in, Norvin sat still in the driver's seat. He neither started the engine nor flicked on the lights. Crickets were humming and creaking around them. A car went past with a swerved arc of illumination. There was a faint scent of mock orange in the air. Gita sensed that he wanted to be quiet, and so she didn't say anything either. She sat very straight, knees together, hands in her lap.

"That hurt," Norvin finally said. "I was having such a good time, and then, bam, Rachel was brought in."

"I didn't hear anyone say anything about Rachel," said Gita. Though she felt mature and important when Norvin con-fided in her, it also sometimes seemed that he suspected razor blades and wedges of glass associated with his wife to be hid-den in all interactions. "Honestly, I don't know what you heard. Was it feminism? I'm sure . . . I'm just sure it wasn't meant."

"Feminism," said Norvin. "*That* I can handle. To survive in the university I'll have to. It was the mention of music that she likes. I've got to admit, Joan Armatrading is very good. Extremely dynamic. Imaginative. But I think back to her song about a woman who has two lovers she's double-crossing. It's called something about 'the weakness in me.' Rachel loved that song. I wonder how long she's been involved with this woman. How long was it going on before I was told? When we went to bed at Thanksgiving, was the awkwardness because she'd just been with a woman and found a man with his *appendages* weird, or was it really only that she couldn't remember if she'd salted the turkey stuffing? She *says* this is her first relationship with a woman. I don't know, maybe she was with others as flings, not relationships. I just can't get these questions out of my mind."

"I'm sure she wouldn't lie," said Gita, wishing Norvin would keep such revelations to himself.

"I mean, we had sort of agreed at the start that we didn't own each other and that we could both explore other people if the chance came up. Conferences, research trips abroad, overnight stays with old friends, those sorts of things. Not that it happened much, but, heck, life's short, isn't it? The idea was that we never told each other unless it was important. Maybe she was screwing her so-called *woman* friends in hotel rooms between the portions of the conference that she'd circled on the program as important."

"Maybe we should go?" Gita asked, quite horrified. What was she doing talking to a man who moved in such a disorienting and distasteful world? She was also thinking of how the people inside might wonder why the car hadn't taken off yet. She squeezed herself closer to the door.

Norvin revved up the engine. The gold rims of his glasses gleamed with the occasional streetlight. "I'm hurt," he said. "I'm really hurt. So here goes this marriage the way of fifty percent of all American marriages. I mean, off goes a relationship hijacking all your trust and hope. Sorry, I'm rambling. Gita, I know you're busy, but would you mind just stopping in at a café or something and talking some more? Please?"

If there was one thing that Gita had no defense against, it

was a request that made her feel needed. How could she desert Norvin when he seemed close to tears? How could she, as a decent person, lead him to believe that the world presented unscalable walls of turned backs and pressing routines? Poor Norvin, she understood exactly what he felt. Well, a café would at least have a bathroom. It would be nothing unusual to take a purse along, and no one would ever identify anything dropped off in the bins. "All right," Gita said. "But please, not too late."

They parked near Telegraph Avenue. The bookstores were open late, and the streets were wheeling with people. Kids on skateboards hurtled past. A bedraggled woman with five shopping carts roped together and two cats on leashes pushed her way toward People's Park. At one corner a man was playing the saxophone, sad sounds floating up through the upper stories of the buildings. Through the glass panes of cafés, people were leaning forward in earnest conversation. Gita walked with her head bent low. With one hand she hoisted the rim of her sari up out of the dirt. She was hoping that no one who knew her would see her out alone, at night, with a professor. Not that she was in his class or anything, but still, who knew what they might think?

After a stretch that was relatively quiet, Norvin turned in at a place that seemed to be a small house. There were candles flickering inside. They were ushered through the underwater ripples of shadows in different rooms to a table with a starched white cloth, a single red rose, and a candle. There was no one else present. Gita disappeared immediately into the bathroom. She returned to find Norvin studying the menu.

"What'll you have, Gita, steamed milk? Liqueur? Dessert?"

"Milk, thank you," Gita said.

"With amaretto? Good, I'm glad to see you've taken up my tastes. I'll have the same." He waved for the waitress, who slid over, a curly-headed blonde who was all smiles and bright agreement. Gita watched the woman leaning toward Norvin and wondered if she saw him as an attractive man. He was on the short side by American standards, but this made him compact, light as an acrobat on his feet. His head seemed a little large in proportion to the rest of his body. His features were even, though the nose pressed down a little as a camel's might. His skin seemed perpetually tanned. The gray in his black hair gave it a nice, springy texture; it almost seemed to invite patting hands. Not that he was dazzlingly gorgeous, but he wasn't bad-looking, he really wasn't. You could even say he was handsome.

After ordering, Norvin leaned across the table, *kurta* parting to reveal grizzled chest hair. "Gita, I'm sorry to have been carrying on about myself. We could talk about what I'd like you to find in the library for me. But we can do that during hours you're paid for next week. Tell me, now, what do *you* think about marriage?"

"Well." Gita squared her shoulders. "First of all, I think it should be for life."

"Marvelous, marvelous," said Norvin. He was smiling again, his big toothy smile. He seemed to be revived, possessed of himself, a man with a last word for everything rather than a man thinking aloud as though no one else were present. Gita wasn't sure which Norvin she liked better. The confident one seemed to supply endless full stops and exclamation marks; the confiding one was all ellipses, parentheses, commas. Both were embarrassing, both in their own ways quite likable. "And what else?" asked Norvin.

"People should love each other. They should adjust." Gita took a deep breath. She hauled her thick rope of braid over one shoulder and began to fidget with the tapering end. "They should not, I mean, sleep with other people."

"Fabulous," said Norvin. He crossed his arms, beaming all the while. "Tradition rides again. I can't tell you what good it does the heart to see that someone around here still believes all this. Rocks of the ages. I take it your parents are still married?"

"My parents . . ." Gita was reluctant to talk about them. She took refuge in sipping the froth of fragrant milk before her. "Actually, one of the best marriages I know is between Saroj Aunty and Harish Uncle."

"Ah, the Parsi Watchers," Norvin said. "You've mentioned them before. The woman with Idi Amin snuggling up to Cleopatra in her cupboard. So what makes their marriage so good?"

"They read together in the afternoons," Gita said.

"They *read* together?"

"Yes, after lunch, and after the long ritual in which she makes *paan*—you know, stuffed betel leaves—from her assortment of brass boxes, they lie on the big double bed and they read. Two different books, but it's just so—so *companionable*. I mean, they're not talking to each other or anything, they're just there together. And then Harish Uncle is so interested in Aunty's poetry, sometimes she reads that aloud to him. He is always choosing saris and jewels and all for her."

"Any children?" Norvin asked.

"No," Gita said.

"Too much reading," Norvin surmised.

Gita decided to ignore this comment, which she found to be in extremely poor taste. "They just never had children, that's all. They've adopted all the children of their friends as nieces and nephews. In India, for people like us, everyone older becomes an Aunty or Uncle, or in special cases Masi or Chacha or Kaka. But Harish Uncle and Saroj Aunty are different. It's not just a title. If you've been adopted, they're, well, they're *always* there for you."

"Sending perfume." Norvin nodded his head.

Gita never blushed. It was her ears that burned, blood rushing in from the neck and throbbing along the upper rims. The allusion to perfume brought in Timothy, like an uninvited guest drawing up another chair at this table. These days she did not want to think about Timothy. It held up a mirror in which she was too young, inexperienced, a girl with a crush staring mutely up at a man. Well, Timothy should see her now, in a fancy restaurant on a Friday night, making conversation that might almost be rated sophisticated, fragrant with the perfume he had carried. He should see her speaking by *candlelight.*

"Sending all kinds of presents," said Gita. She reflected that that had been her mistake: thinking that Timothy himself, meant as courier, was a peculiarly wrapped gift for her to keep forever.

"And what do you think about sex?" continued Norvin.

"Pardon?"

"Sex. What are your views on it? For example, if you believe in monogamy in marriage, would you extend that to celibacy before marriage? Would you advocate marrying someone without a trial, like taking home a pair of shoes with the hope that they'll just fit?"

Here Gita was in a bind. How was she to reply? If she said what she frankly thought, Norvin might write her off as Timothy did, someone so swathed in white veils of naïveté that she couldn't even distinguish a friendly pucker from a passionate kiss. On the other hand, if she said something too filled with bravado, Norvin might take her seriously. "That's highly context-specific," she said, reaching for the sort of terminology that she was rapidly becoming proficient at around seminar tables, but whose level of vagueness actually seemed a way for people to hide. "It's all a question of the hegemony of a particular discourse."

Norvin seemed to know what she was talking about, even if she wasn't sure herself. "That's right," he agreed, "it's vital to incorporate a paradigm of multiple and disparate subjectivities, else there's that old problem of how to explain radical changes in ideology."

"Quite so," Gita said in the wisest tone she could muster. Not that she didn't understand this language: she was just unused to taking it away from classrooms and into everyday life.

The doorway to Bet's room was open when Gita crept up the stairs.

"Is that you, Gita? Jesus, it's past midnight—what were you doing out so late? Come on in and tell me all about it."

This was way past Gita's usual bedtime, and she would really have preferred to sink into the oblivion of a hot shower and bed. "I thought you had a rehearsal tonight," she said, setting her purse down by the telephone table and stepping into the doorway of Bet's room.

Bet was lying on her water bed with a paperback open and a box of half-eaten truffles beside her. "That goddamn director decided to quit; he wants to move to New *York* or something. It just makes me puke the way these artists in the Bay Area always think the big life is somewhere else. It's like the weather here is too good for creativity or something. Not that I was being paid much, but at least I was acting. This means that Tom moves back up to Mendocino too, so that's the end of my little affair, if you could even call it that. I never saw a worse bunch of *morons* than directors. By the way, while I remember, would you make a point of remembering to open the bathroom window enough for the moisture to get out? There's mold growing on the ceiling."

"Sorry," said Gita. Try as she might, there were always little things that she did wrong. Bet had lived here for years and years and had her own way of managing the apartment. "I'm sorry about the thing with Tom not working out."

"He wasn't anything great. It's just that with the pickings around here in terms of men . . . Oh well, so did Norvin the Nerd try to paw you?"

"He did not," said Gita, deciding to omit Norvin's taking her left hand in both of his as her right hand balanced on the handle of the car door. He had leaned toward her, perhaps to offer her a kiss on the cheek, but she had leaned away. His palms, she remembered, were as warm as the hothouses in the botanical gardens, hot as Bombay in October. She rubbed her own hands against each other to see what they might have felt like to him; probably just icy. The thought struck her that perhaps on some future occasion it was in her power to tilt her face toward him. She suppressed a smile. "Honestly, Bet, he's quite a nice fellow."

"Well, I'm glad to see he could keep his creepy-crawly professor tentacles off you for at least *one* evening. So, tell me more about this party. Any interesting single men?"

"Not really," said Gita.

"What about this Firoze?"

"He's nothing."

"He seems to call you often enough. I've taken at least *four* messages from him in the last few weeks. Oh, by the way, speaking of messages, you have one from that Korean girl. Korean, Taiwanese, whatever she is. I guess she's interested in borrowing your lecture notes again. Someone new too, called Marshall. I never heard about *him*."

"He's in my French for Reading Knowledge class, probably wants to know about the homework assignment. Bet, really, don't raise your eyebrows that way, he's married and all."

"So?"

"No, I mean really, he just had a birthing party when his wife delivered."

"OK, so this guy Marshall is crossed out for you. Well, *your* social life is sure picking up; I guess students are more friendly than theater folks. Tell me more about that cute Firoze."

"First of all, he's not really my friend," said Gita. Ever since Firoze had once walked her home after a lunch, Bet watching through the upstairs window, he had become a part of these dissections. "I told you, he's my classmate Dinaz's cousin. He was telephoning to make arrangements for the dinner, so each person brought one dish and we had a full Indian meal. I swear, he's not my type. The latest thing is that he's planning to go to law school and to change the world."

"Sounds interesting to me." Bet rearranged herself. The bed began to lap around her. Gita ignored the thigh that was now exposed.

"He's too serious," Gita said. "Bet, I swear that every man I talk to is not some great prospect. Anyway, I think that

Firoze is getting hooked up with some Swede or something. When he went to show her the bathroom light I thought he came back with some lipstick. On his mouth."

"Oh well, so he'll be out of circulation for a while. You can have a deferred plan."

"Bet, I swear—"

"And what did Norvin have to say about his *wife* today?"

"He didn't mention her at all," said Gita. When had this begun, her confiding everything in Bet as though she were some sort of Mother Superior? It seemed boorish to feel resentful when Bet was taking such a concerned interest. "Bet, I'm really sleepy, I'm going to go to bed."

"But you didn't tell me what you talked about when you drove back and forth. The way you don't see anything that's going on, you need someone more experienced to interpret the signs. If he's moving on from his wife, what's next in the agenda for conversation?"

"Nothing much." By saying that Rachel had never been mentioned, Gita found herself unmoored from truthfulness. It felt great. "He told me about the technological shortcomings of the village where he worked in the Peace Corps."

"That's got to be one of the weirdest come-on routines that *I* know. The Peace Corps? What's he trying to say, that he'll bring progress and expansion to the most backward areas of your being?"

"Bet, really. I don't think he's trying to say anything." Gita hesitated, almost relenting. "He's just lonely and I suppose depressed."

"Watch out for depressed men," Bet ominously stated. "They always grab you as a solution. I've already told you that you don't have enough experience to decode any of this."

"Good night," said Gita. She turned into her own room, closed the door, and flicked on a lamp. She stopped and surveyed herself for a moment in the mirror. In America, her dark complexion had taken on a touch of mystery, even for herself. When she wore *kajal* in the lower rim of her eyelids, her eyes really did look larger; she should wear it all the time.

Maybe she should pluck her eyebrows too. She folded Joan Armatrading with care, smoothing her hand over the sari as though they shared a pact.

Saroj Aunty had made the *kajal* at home, burning almonds and collecting the soot on the edge of a silver spoon. A little camphor was mixed in too. She had pressed it all into a tiny round silver container inscribed with two parrots facing each other, and mangoes around the borders. "Here, darling," she had said, holding it out in one broad palm. "For you to take over there to that America. It's women's power, you know, in these little things."

"Power, Aunty?" Gita said. To her, power meant Indira Gandhi inspecting troops that stood at attention in blazing sun, chests puffed under insignia. Or Mother Superior hauling someone into her office to demand an explanation for why they were getting letters every other day from the same return address, and to repeat that girls from Our Lady of Perpetual Succour were from Good Families, they set Examples, they were always above Scandal.

"Certainly. Power is when you have ways of controlling your own life. You know, so other people can't push you around. Brains are power, charm is power, beauty too is power, and I don't just mean the looks you're born with but all the aesthetic *fit* of everything you do."

It had struck Gita at the time, even before the meager stipend of graduate school, that Saroj Aunty hadn't mentioned money as power, it was just taken for granted. She knew that Saroj Aunty had once been in the Communist party and had owned only two homespun saris. But all that had changed when she married Harish Uncle. They now swam in comfortable wealth. It brought a shine to the floors, lifted sea breezes through spacious rooms, put them in the backseat of their white Ambassador.

"I'm not one who ever says that social change should root out beauty, darling. Of course, we all hope that socialism will bring equality for everyone, even between men and women. But that shouldn't mean the end of lovely saris and cut-glass bangles and gardenias floating by the bedside table. Of course, there are ways and ways of being a gracious woman." Saroj Aunty smiled, looking like a happy cat as wisps of gray hair blew around her face. "Not like Jimmy's girl Jeroo, with that nail polish and those—what do you call them?—*hot* pants? She is really becoming quite a little vamp!"

"Quite a little vamp"—the phrase had stuck with Gita whenever a piece of clothing bore the threat of breaking away from her subdued, covered, style. At college, girls who had one long plait and wore saris were called Bahenjis; those who went in for bell-bottoms and short hair were Mods. Gita had been able to escape both titles by keeping her own style, monitored by Saroj Aunty during vacations and sponsored by discreet envelopes of money bestowed by her mother. Exquisite rare handlooms, however, "traditional and all," had also to be acknowledged as "hip, *yaar,* quite fab." If there was one thing that Gita couldn't bear from all her years of boarding school onward, it was trend-monitoring cliques. She always stayed a little aloof, reading, even if it meant she was eternally labeled "brainy."

Sometimes Saroj Aunty talked about how things had been for girls in her own youth. Parents were fighting for Independence. Fathers had often been educated abroad, but mothers tended to remain at home. Saroj Aunty's mother had strict ideas about menstrual taboos. Saroj Aunty's father said that this was all "primitive superstition," but her mother had prevailed: through perseverance, without argument, house keys jingling at her waist. You couldn't touch anyone for three days. You had to sit on a low, rectangular wooden stool out on the balcony. Your meals were brought to you, and you washed your own dishes, not to mention your collection of rags. On the fourth day, you bathed and washed your hair. "Three full days to read!" Saroj Aunty said. "I tell you, I went through a novel a day. I read most of Dickens, the Brontës, Hardy, lovely Jane Austen this way." Gita, muttering and

mumbling (ashamed, even then, to confess to Saroj Aunty anything about herself in this regard), had asked whether it wasn't
awful to have everyone in the house know what was going
on. "But why, darling? It was expected. It's *natural*, isn't it?"
Yet even Saroj Aunty saying this wasn't convincing.

Once Uncle Jimmy Seervai had entertained a Sunday gathering with the tale of going through customs at Goa (then still
a Portuguese preserve). There were tampons in Aunty Proachie's bag, and the officials suspected them of being cigars. The
story was told with full dramatization, Uncle Jimmy striding
around the room and changing his voice. He even brought out
a collection of pens from his upper pocket to examine, sniff,
stick experimentally between his lips. "What is this fuse doing
here?" one of the customs officials supposedly asked. Now in
Berkeley Gita thought about how everyone had laughed, and
how though she had never seen a tampon herself, it had
seemed that the joke exposed her in some sinister, underhand
sense.

Gita just hated Sunday mornings; the libraries on campus
didn't open until one, and if you went wandering anywhere
else there were always too many entwined couples and happy
families sunning themselves on benches outside bakeries or
groups of friends walking to brunch. She had even taken to
doing her laundry during the work week so that she wouldn't
have to go out on Sundays.

Bet had been for a run and brought in a copy of the *Chronicle*. She had read aloud Gita's horoscope for the week to her
from page 16 of the pink section. She had made a few calls,
the phone drawn inside her room and the door closed (leading
Gita to suspect that at least one call was for the lights man,
Tom; perhaps breaking up was not as easy as Bet had made
it sound). Then Bet had taken off to walk Max Weber, the
neighbor's dog, who was her charge when they went out of
town. Gita sat cross-legged at her desk, staring at books she
needed to read this summer. It was sunny outside but at her

desk she needed a lamp. She could have read the newspaper, but that had lost its glamour since Timothy went out of her life. How did world events really affect her survival on this scholarship with orals just a few months away, how did any of it fit with the books she had to know about?

When the doorbell rang, Gita trudged downstairs. It was sure to be one of those endless Berkeley causes requiring donations. But it was Najma.

"Hi!" Najma beamed. "I brought you a tape and some banana bread. We've been baking this morning."

"Come in for some tea," said Gita, quite delighted. She had never had anyone drop in for a visit since she moved from her room in International House to this apartment. It was one of Bet's rules that visitors should be prefaced by fair advance warning, and anyway, Gita had been too busy to invite people over. "I thought that maybe you were the Jehovah's Witnesses. They come almost every Sunday, you know."

"Oh yeah, I just spoke to them." Najma followed her upstairs. "I had a heyday telling them what they'd probably say to a Muslim. Or a Hindu for that matter. Not that I was brought up very religious. Anyway, I told them that no one around here wanted to hear about a heathen religion, that we would stop up our ears from blasphemy, and that their magazine was destined for the burning fires of hell. That sort of thing."

"You didn't!" Gita began to laugh.

"Of course I did. I carried it off with a straight face, too. I mean, what else can we do but give people back their own stereotypes? I mean, let's talk about finishing food on a plate for the starving children in the Bronx! Let's mention the urban squatters in People's Park, or ritual and superstition on Telegraph Avenue. Oh, what lovely things in this room. You know, I have the exact same miniature—the set from the Delhi Museum, right?"

"Right," Gita agreed. She looked around her room, realizing that there was really no place for a visitor to sit. It was either the bed, the floorboards, or the mirror-work cushion beside the desk. "Shall we go into the living room?"

"Sure, whatever. I'll take your tape recorder along with us. I think you'll just love Joan Armatrading. Hey, I see you have some Amjad Ali Khan. He's good, isn't he? And Prabha Atre: fantastic! Can I borrow this sometime and make a copy?"

Najma looked around the kitchen as Gita put water on for tea. Joan Armatrading was already blasting away in the next room. "My God, this place is just too spotless. Speckless. I mean, everything *shines*."

"My housemate is quite particular," Gita said. "It was in the ad posted at the housing office that she wanted someone neat and quiet."

"My God, I'm such a slob, I'd steer away from an ad like that. My boyfriend and I do really slob plus things like just dropping our clothes in a pile. When the pile is too high to get between the bed and the closet, or when it all gets this really moldy smell, we push it all into his station wagon and take it to the Laundromat. Oh good, here's a cutting board. Where's a knife?"

"You have a boyfriend?" Gita asked, flattered by the way that Najma was bustling around the kitchen. She must like me, Gita thought. She herself already liked Najma too much to pass Our Lady of Perpetual Succour judgment on her living with a man. So, Najma was one of those girls who had crossed the big divide. "Was your boyfriend at the party?"

"No, he had some experiment he was watching in his lab. He's in chemistry."

"Is he . . . Indian?" This was a delicate question. Until Timothy came along, Gita had never questioned that she'd marry an Indian. Certainly one with thick black hair, and possibly one with Shashi Kapoor lashes. Yet Ganeshan Kaka's prediction about when she'd meet the man she'd marry coinciding with gawky, bald Timothy had loosened that certainty.

"Oh no, hardly!" Najma's laugh swirled out. "When you meet him you'll understand why I think that's funny. Noah is black. If my grandmother ever saw him she'd probably scream."

"Oh," said Gita, bringing the tea to a second boil along with the milk. It seemed hair-raisingly sacrilegious to talk about one's own man this way. Thinking about how color conscious people could be in India made her wonder if Najma would really have the courage to allow her grandmother to meet Noah.

"He's a good chap," said Najma. "It's quite fab, isn't it, the alliteration and the rhyme? Najma and Noah. N and N. Sometimes I tease him about that being why I picked him out. Actually he's three years younger than me—you know how these scientist types are so precocious. So, is there anybody in your life just now? I couldn't be sure if there was anything going on with that funny fellow who came with you to Firoze's party."

"No, nothing," said Gita, pouring out the tea into two of Bet's mugs. She realized as she slid into that old habit of denial that she might be losing her chance to claim a sympathetic and most likable listener. "Well, actually, I don't know. He's this big shot on campus, with a chair and all. But he keeps wanting to confide in me. We go for walks and things. He's getting a divorce, and because his wife knows all his professor friends he feels he can't talk about it with them. He's desperate for sympathy, I suppose."

"Succor," said Najma, following Gita into the other room. They both sat down at the table. "Poor chap, he was actually quite sweet, the way he carried on about India to all of us. It was as though he really wanted to belong." She chewed her banana bread and added, "He's *quite* sexy too."

"He *is?*" Gita asked, a guilty grin creeping over her face. "I mean, how?"

"Oh, c'mon, Gita, you know what I mean. You don't want me to go into what they call locker room talk!" Najma giggled. "He's that age you begin to call distinguished. I bet he's a great lover with all that experience behind him. The one thing I'd worry about is his being newly divorced. Oh look, where did this dog come from?"

There was Max Weber, the neighbor's shaggy poodle. A minute after the amiable, tail-wagging entrance, Bet herself appeared in a faded blue jogging suit. She stood in the doorway and stared at Najma. She definitely did not look welcoming.

Gita mumbled hasty introductions, turning down the music and adjusting the plates so they were neat and symmetrical on the tablecloth. She realized with panic that she had left the loaf of banana bread out on the kitchen counter, and that the pot with tea leaves still stood in the sink. It was too late: Bet was already in there, opening the refrigerator and banging around. Gita excused herself to Najma for a minute and followed her in.

"Sorry, Bet," she said in an undertone. "I mean, I'm sorry. I really didn't expect you back."

"The arrangement is that we're supposed to *inform* each other if we're bringing someone home," Bet hissed. "You can't just have strangers all over the living room and not be *prepared* for it. I had this horrible conversation with that stupid idiot Tom this morning, and the last thing I need is having to deal with people I don't know."

"She just dropped in," pleaded Gita. "Really, I'm sorry."

"Can I help wash up?" asked Najma from the doorway. She was carrying the plates and mugs. "Did you try my banana bread, Bet? Oh, you *must*—this is a special recipe from my boyfriend's mother. She's very worried that he'll destroy his stomach enzymes if he lives with me and my so-called 'curries.' The joke is that he does most of the cooking—it's hardly that I'm pumping him up with spices."

"Thank you," said Bet, refusing to look directly at Najma. She helped herself to a piece on a plate, elaborately clearing crumbs off the sideboard and depositing them in the trash. Then she withdrew to her room, calling Max Weber after her, and slamming the door.

"So, what should we do now?" Najma seemed undaunted,

oblivious. She brimmed over with as much jaunty energy as before. "Do you want to go to the bookstores on Telegraph Avenue, or should we go up the fire trail back near the old Deaf School? Let's call up this Norvin of yours for a fuller inspection. Or we can go visit Noah in his lab. Or check the temperature of this thing Firoze seems to be getting into. My God, the way that woman was gawking at him—did you see it too? Were you wondering too about that whole *nakra* about wanting to use the bathroom—'Firoze, Firoze, please show me the light?' The poor guy. Anyway, I wish him all happiness. Oh, c'mon, Gita. This is the first weekend of summer vacation—let's do something really *fun*."

Instead of books or walking or dropping in on unsuspecting men, Najma and Gita meandered through clothes stores on Telegraph Avenue. Najma tried on hats, some with speckled veils. Gita inspected sales racks of shoes. Najma modeled in running shorts, Gita looked into a mirror with a dress held up against her on a hanger.

"You have to buy that!" Najma ordered.

"I don't wear dresses," said Gita, who still had the residual sense that there was something risqué about showing her legs.

"Oh, c'mon, *yaar,* this is *too good* on you—it's a perfect summer dress."

"Too much money," said Gita. "It's made in India anyway, and when you convert to rupees . . ."

"But at least try it on properly," Najma said.

When Gita was twisting and twirling in front of the mirror, Najma applauded. "This is yours, Gita, it's meant for you, I swear. I'll lend you the money if you need it. Forget this rupee business, you'd never find it there. Just go for it, *yaar.*"

And so it came to pass that Gita was sitting on Norvin's patio in the Berkeley Hills, wearing this very dress as she balanced a glass of champagne. The dress was off-white, with woven clumps of color shot through with turquoise, purple, magenta, gold. It had a boat neck, short sleeves hanging off the shoulder, and a swish of folds down below the knee. Its overall looseness was gathered in by a sash with the same brilliant colors but in a different weave. And everything was soft cotton; Saroj Aunty's handloom sisters would have been proud. Although the dress showed some leg, even Saroj Aunty would agree that it was lovely; there would be no question of being labeled a vamp.

Gita felt sophisticated and slim-waisted in this dress. There was something about wearing saris to every major occasion that had been making her feel old-fashioned, as though she were holding on to every vestige of fixed difference from this rapidly moving American world. Now she felt she blended perfectly with Norvin's other guests: she could finger the stem of her glass and appropriately incline her head when he put on some jazz. She could lean forward from the black leather sofa to the transparent coffee table and delicately dip a blue corn chip in guacamole. She could mutter appreciatively with the rest of the group when Norvin led them to the collage of bottle caps he had recently acquired in his collection of works by local artists. She could look out at the patterns of lights scattered ecstatically in the city below them and half turn with the verdict, "Lovely setting."

They had just finished dinner, interwoven with discussions of each ingredient, every preparation process, and exclamations of appreciation directed toward the cook. Gita felt as though the others were speaking a strange dialect that only she and the Spanish novelist didn't seem to understand. Warmed loaves of *Semifreddi baguettes; mesquite*-grilled salmon; pasta with *sun-dried* tomato sauce; a salad with *arugula*, goat (not sheep!) feta, *balsamic* vinegar, and *extra-virgin* olive oil (virgin, the others agreed, just wasn't good enough, and Gita tried not to squirm). Now a lime sorbet made by Norvin in his own ice cream machine was on the way.

"Oh, Norvin," sighed Miranda, who had close-set eyes and a soulful expression. Earlier in the evening she had informed

Gita that she Did Art. "You're just a ge-ni-us, this is such a symphony on the palate."

"This is as good as Chez Panisse," said John, her husband, who was apparently a physicist. "Don't you think, honey, the last time we went there—"

"Cheese Penis," said Alejandro, the Spanish novelist.

"Fabulous, fabulous," said Norvin, putting out crystal bowls.

"Can I help?" asked Gita for the umpteenth time.

"No thanks, I'm all set. By the way, one of my ex-graduate students was in town last week. He's been exiled to some terrible place in Nevada, you know—one of those first job deals. He took ten pounds of dark, unsweetened chocolate back with him. Also one pound of fresh mozzarella and five loaves from the Bread Board that he said he would freeze."

"Oh, I think it's absolutely *terrible* what deprivations people who leave the Bay Area have to go through," said Miranda. She reached into her little snakeskin purse as though looking for a tissue. "It's tragic what graduating can do to you."

"Calm down, honey," said John. "Did you really say *ten* pounds? Incredible. This might be worth an entry in *Choco-holic News*. One of my old graduate students started a Laun-dromat, he couldn't bear to leave Berkeley. Not that he didn't have offers from good places, like all the others working in our group. Norvin, this sorbet is just so, so . . . piquant. Did you say you used a dash of raspberry liqueur? Marvelous. So, Alejandro, will you be with us long?"

"My visiting appointment has yet to be renewed," said the novelist. "The deans—"

"Oh, don't even mention deans," Miranda cried. "John will have a fit. You won't believe what the deans did with the tenure case in his department! And then these negotiations with the TAs!"

"Take it easy, take it easy," said John.

Gita listened, entranced. She didn't understand everything that was being said, but it seemed that at last she was in the midst of the real, grown-up world. This was how life should be lived: among intelligent, accomplished people with many experiences behind them. She was quite happy to sit here feeling decorative. After finding out that she was a graduate student, both Miranda and John had stopped directing questions to her. But she was Norvin's confidante, after all, and this made her feel central to the group. Every now and then she caught Norvin's eyes and he smiled so warmly she just had to smile back. Once or twice, the Spaniard had challenged her to stare at him, but at those moments she had simply looked down.

"Oh, what a *perfect* night," Miranda said as the crickets started up and a full moon appeared through the eucalyptus trees. "So, are we all going to squeeze into the hot tub?"

"Sure, if you want," said Norvin. "I can go get it ready."

"Oh, a hot tub is essential," said John. "It would just cap off the perfection of this meal. Why can't all of life be like this? The espresso just right and no classes tomorrow."

"A California custom," said Alejandro. "My next novel may be entirely set in a hot tub."

Gita froze. Hot tub? Nobody had warned her that Norvin had a hot tub. She thought of the light bulb joke someone had repeated over a meal at I-House. "How many Berkeley Hills residents does it take to screw in a light bulb?" "In the Berkeley Hills, people don't screw in light bulbs, they screw in hot tubs." Gita knew that it was something like a little swimming pool or a large bathtub that people got into together. Naked, probably. She imagined Norvin's wet hip slithering against her, the novelist's toes touching her ankles like nibbling fish. Of course, they were surely too gentlemanly to presume anything more. But what a nightmare! How was she to climb out of this jam of limbs and save face as a sophisticate at the same time?

As the others began to discuss the best kind of wood to construct a hot tub with, Gita's mind raced with all the ways she could get out of this. Could she suddenly develop a cold, sore throat, headache, or infectious skin disease? But how— wouldn't it be transparent if she'd shown no symptoms before? Could she have to make an urgent telephone call and talk to the humming line about how, yes, of course she would come immediately? But she didn't have the acting skill to pull this off. Could she say that Hindus only bathed communally in Ganges water and temple tanks? But then Norvin would have some argument, some story from his days in the Peace Corps, that would show her up as a fraud. Should she simply say, "Sorry, I don't appear naked in public. I don't even appear naked at home. I even sleep in a long nightgown with my underpants on." But that would be paying obeisance to the Young and Inexperienced girl already rejected by Timothy. If she admitted what she really felt, Norvin might never invite her to a party again; he might withdraw into the upper echelons of his life as professor.

Gita's consternation began to thump in her ears. She reached for her hair to twist the end of it. But her plait was pinned up high in what she had decided was a salon hairdo, twisted and decorated with barrettes borrowed from Bet. In raising her hand to the back of her head, a possible solution sprang out. She could let down her hair. It was long hair even by Indian standards, falling almost to her knees. Mostly it was a burden, taking ages to comb and wash, and, Gita felt, looking distinctly unfashionable with its severe middle parting and practical long braid. But today her hair's grand moment had arrived. She would hide behind her hair and would keep her eyes focused on the foreheads of the other people. It would be a huge, daring thing to do. Mother Superior would not approve, and certainly Bet wouldn't either.

"Does anybody want a swimming suit or anything?" Norvin asked when he returned from the garden.

"How quaint," said Miranda. "Swimming suits?"

"I mean, Rachel wasn't exactly thin, but there could be something of hers lying around."

So he had sensed her hesitation! Gita could have wrenched Norvin's hand with gratitude. "Oh no," Gita replied, "I don't require a bathing costume, thank you very much."

Luckily there was no bright light out in the corner of the

garden where the hot tub was placed. There was an arbor of honeysuckle and night-blooming jasmine planted around it. Moonlight drifted through to make dim and swirling patterns on the water. Occasionally fireflies darted above the hedge. People had undressed indoors—and came out with towels. Gita kept her eyes to the garden path as she followed the others out. The terrible moment was letting go of her towel; she never thought she could feel so bonded with a towel. But then it was off, and she stepped into the tub with her hair swinging loosely around her. She balanced on the seat—thank goodness there was a lot of room—and pulled her hair forward so two thick clumps covered each breast, already mercifully submerged in water. The Jacuzzi whirled, caressing, licking, whispering excitement and depravity. She prayed that the long hair wouldn't get stringy, parting and opening around her body when it was wet. As the others discussed whether the Monterey Market or Berkeley Bowl was better for fresh strawberries, she found her body growing golden heavy and her mind swimming like quicksilver moonlight off to Saroj Aunty's.

It had been a Sunday gathering, somewhere around the time that Gita was waiting to hear about admissions and scholarships from the handful of American universities she had applied to. Pandit Prem Kumar, a well-known *sarodh* player and an old friend of the Shahs', had just returned from a concert tour of Europe and America. He arrived in a muslin *kurta* with gold studs, *paan* reddening the corners of his mouth as usual.

"Oh, what a *tapasya* it is to go to these places where people just sit through concerts without a sound, and then at twelve o'clock you must stop playing," he sighed, shaking his head. "*Arre*, what's even worse is those Americans who have studied our music and just keep rolling from the neck and putting in *wah-wah*s at odd times. Of course, some are very accomplished, they are playing very well. But *bhabhi?*"—he had leaned across his belly to address Saroj Aunty—"I have got the story of the season for you." Laughter was already gurgling in his throat, and as he told the story in Hindi, he had to stop from time to time to wipe his bald spot and tears from his eyes. Saroj Aunty tittered helplessly beside him, Ganeshan Kaka cracked his skinny fingers, and Harish Uncle slapped Panditji's proffered hand each time there was a particularly hilarious point. His Highness of Pindapur was in stitches, while his latest dimpled woman sat with her hands folded in her sari, bright lips twisted in a Mona Lisa smile. Gita listened, quite embarrassed but enormously intrigued, glad that no one had thought up an errand for her to run inside.

According to the story, Panditji had been invited to give a private concert somewhere in California. It was to be at the home of a millionaire renowned for his support of Indian artists, and so Panditji was especially anxious that everything should proceed just right. He emerged from the limousine he and the tabla accompanist had been picked up in, and they both set down their instruments for a moment as they rang the bell and smoothed their hair. A maid in a uniform answered the door. but beyond her—could they possibly be seeing things?—everyone, absolutely everyone in the big room with French windows, was naked. The women had makeup on, some even had elaborate hairdos. There was a scent of ganja in the air. The host came hurrying out, wearing only a huge gold medallion around his neck. He extended a hand as he neared Panditji. Panditji didn't want to look down. He didn't want to stare over his host's shoulder at all that revealed flesh. He was worried that he and his accompanist would be obliged to strip for the performance. He smiled broadly, looked resolutely into his patron's eyes, and put out his own hand in greeting. He found his hand curling, though, not around another hand but something else. Shock registered on his host's face, and in his confusion, Panditji found himself tugging as he might a cow's udder in the village of his childhood. "This," said Panditji, laughing into his drenched handkerchief, "this is the kind of thing that happens to Indian music in America."

"What happened to him?" asked Harish Uncle. "Your host?"

"What do you expect with such a grip?" said Panditji, laughing harder.

"And did you have to disrobe?" Saroj Aunty asked through her small, high-pitched giggles.

"Oh no, we could do what we liked. After we had some ganja and some drinks we were also quite happy, quite *mast*. We were set up by the pool and everyone listened from the water. Who knows how we played, but then I don't think anyone cared."

"Foreign buggers," wheezed Ganeshan Kaka.

"Jolly good, old chap," said His Highness of Pindapur, throwing a look at his Mona Lisa friend. "Oh, what a jolly, jolly time."

❁

"And how was it?" asked Bet the next morning. "I fell asleep waiting. Well, did that Norvin try any tricks?"

"No," said Gita, combing out her freshly washed and conditioner-fragrant hair. They were standing on the deck, which was still in shadow though the day was resplendent with sunshine. "There were lots of people there."

"Lots? How many?"

"Oh, about a hundred or so. It was a catered event."

"Don't tell me. One of those stupid necktie things that professors have?"

Gita's ears began to burn as Bet said the word *neck*. Thank goodness her hair was all around her, falling over her cheeks and, if she bent just a little, hiding most of her face. After the hot tub, everyone had gotten dressed. Miranda and John began to mutter about their baby-sitter. Norvin invited Alejandro and Gita to stay late, but the novelist was expecting a call from his agent in Spain. Gita said that she'd like to go home. Norvin drove them down the snaking roads and breathless inclines of the hills, the city shimmering at their feet, the bridges winking and tumbling like amusement park rides.

He dropped off Alejandro first. Outside Gita's house, they sat for a moment with moonlight drifting in through the windshield. Gita offered Norvin a hand in thanks for the lovely evening, thanks so very much, a really fine dinner, such a lovely time. He walked her to her door, seeming preoccupied. Just as she was turning to go in, he had reached for her upper arms. Gita went soft and pliant. Experience! Here it arrived! With precise care, Norvin parted the hair hanging damp around her. Gita leaned back, like Scarlett O'Hara, but unlike Scarlett she kept her eyes wide open to see what would come next. Her mouth remained set; it was her neck he was bending toward. He pressed slippery, kneading lips to the side of her neck. His breath was hot, with little catches. Gita shivered as she thought back. The experience had been most surprisingly delicious, sweetening strange places. She adjusted her hair again so her nipples would not poke through the dressing gown and into sight.

"All the men were wearing formal jackets," she reported. "There were hired musicians who played waltzes. Some people took off their shoes and danced in the garden. With the fireflies."

"Holy cow, it sounds like quite a bash! Why waltzes?—that's bizarre. Maybe it's some sort of trend with those academics—they're always a little out of sync with the wider world, it seems. And so *Norvin* brought you home?"

"Oh no, it was the department secretary, this nice woman who was once a nun."

Gita watched butterflies fluttering yellow across the lawn below. Her comb was now sliding clear from the scalp down. Her hair fell straight around her, heavy black satin with tints of blue. At the earliest possibility, she would telephone Najma.

"So I guess the party didn't break up until really late," Bet reflected.

"People were still out dancing when we left," Gita said. "You know, the moon—it was very, very bright."

Y. M. Ganeshan

Whatever language I am speaking, that language only I think in at that time. Just now this Sarojben has come with one foreigner girl wanting predictions and everything is English, English, English. Even if we use a single other word this girl is wanting an explanation. On the table she has kept one tape machine.

"What did he say?" she asks Sarojben. "Could you repeat that, please?"

"Just listen to your Kaka," I tell them as I assemble pen, paper, and all.

Girl looks upset. "What does he mean?" she asks. "He wants us to listen to . . . ? I know some doctors tell you to look, but I didn't know this was another Indian oracular form . . ."

"Kaka means uncle," says Sarojben, giggling in that way of hers. "Like ben means sister. There's a silly joke that Harish loves to tell about the Gujarati man who went to London to see Big Ben. He's been trying to get me to name a sari after that clock tower ever since."

Sarojben is wearing blue sari with black borders. The foreigner is dressed in something with shoulders, arms, neck, back, legs, sala everything showing. So thin she is, like a pole of bamboo. Even then, people from the next building are all lining in their windows for the free show. Woman from opposite balcony has stopped her cooking to watch the fun of Kaka being visited by a people who came in one Ambassador gari. Downstairs—I can see it—so many people have gathered around the car and driver. The cows and pigs from the rubbish *heap at crossroads have also come to see if the car has got anything good to eat.*

"Anyway, Kaka," Saroj says, "as we were saying, Fiona here thinks she might include you in the piece she's doing on Indian prediction traditions for a British fashion magazine. Proachie's friend Mrs. Rastoji of the Time and Talents Club had heard about those astrological predictions you did for Jimmy last year, and so they packed Fiona in a taxi and sent her off to Juhu."

"So how much you know about our India and predictions?" I ask this Fiona-Biona. She is wearing some scent that fills up the room.

"I've done an awful lot of traveling, actually," she tells me. "I've already covered the usual street prediction traditions: all kinds of palmists, parrots that choose cards, pulse-diviners. I've visited famous astrologers and the shadow-measuring men. I even consulted with the Bhrigu up north."

"Did he have your leaf?" asks Saroj.

"Yes! As a matter of fact I was one of the names called out that day! I was over the moon at finding that some sage, centuries ago, had foreseen my visit. The old palm leaves actually had my ancestors' names written down in Sanskirt. It was splendid! Even described these stomach problems I've been having and what to do about them."

Baba! What I am to tell a dame like this whose every future movement has been mapped out by so many people up and down the whole country? Whatever I say now can only come as anticlimax. But she has a sweet smile and I must not disappoint. Also I am wondering how to drop a hint to Sarojben. "Since you are having so many personal predictions," I say, "today you can study astronumerology with your Saroj Aunty asking the question."

"Aunty?" Those big blue eyes get even bigger. "Oh, all right."

"I'm everyone's aunty when I'm not being a sister," says Sarojben.

"Ask me a question," I instruct Sarojben, lifting my hand for a good look at the watch. "Ask, ask, ask."

Sarojben closes her eyes and breathes in, filling her lungs with that European perfume. "OK, so tell me about our Gita."

"Twelve twenty-two!"

"The Bhagavad Gita?" Fiona asks. Poor girl, she is trying.

"Gita Das, my niece," says Saroj.

So she didn't ask me about her situation, but Gita's. Of course, I already know Gita's full name, date of birth, lunar ascendant, and other biodata. As I begin to do the calculations and draw the star, the British dame starts snapping photos. So many she takes! Wife comes in with coffee and tells me in Tamil that I should change into proper clothes. After all, I was sitting here in checked lungi and vest when they came. I respond in English. "This is all natural," I tell her. "No posing." The Fiona takes one shot of me and my Mrs. together, which makes the Mrs. happy. Mrs. returns to kitchen.

"Main thing for Gita," I tell Sarojben, "is that someone out there is J."

"J?" my foreign correspondent looks up. "For Jesus?"

"J for jealous," I tell her. "Jealous, understand? Look here, people get used to another person being a particular way. If possible, they like to feel sorry for a person because it makes them look big. Then if that person improves somehow, something good happens to her, it is very tough for others to understand. They will find some reason to have a fight, some reason to put on some blame. Always, they would prefer to control. That's what I mean by J. Get it?"

"Ah," says Fiona, leaning so close I simply have to turn my head away from that loose blouse—Baba, I am too old for all these things. "Would you mind telling me a bit about how you calculated this?" she asks.

I explain Kaka's ABCs of astronumerology. I also tell her that since my nephew moved to the U.S.A. I have been getting inquiries from there also. I calculate according to the moment of the postman's arrival. Fiona says that if I moved to America

I could make a lot of money, especially if I went to California. I tell her that sala *money is not everything. I have lived my entire life without being a rich man, so now in old age why to worry? Sarojben is not listening to what we say, she sits with one worried look on her face, looking out the window but not seeing the people on the opposite buildings. Actually, adults have gotten bored, and only children are now watching. When I finish up the interview, Sarojben asks, "You don't mean her mother, do you?"*

"How should I know who and all, girl?"

"Man or woman?" asks Sarojben. "She wrote me something about a professor she'll be working for for a summer job. I could see that if she started to show that she was more brilliant than he there might be some trouble."

"That and all how I am to say? You think the stars, numbers, and all are so specific as to tell about sex of the influence?"

"But what should Gita do?" Sarojben asks. "Come on, Kaka, you can't just issue predictions without giving some clues about how to handle them."

"Baba, what she is to do except try not to advertise anything good that is happening to her and not another person? Look here, girl, you can't always control the timing of actions or reactions. Life is whole the time giving us lessons. I told you, that Saturn, bloody bugger, started a new influence in her life this year. But what the exact moment of influence becoming action is, how I am to know? You think your Kaka is one gentleman clairvoyant?"

"I just don't want to see her hurt."

"Hurt and all, that's life. How you can go through life without some hurt? At least you learn something. Some things that are bad in the beginning, you never know—they can turn into some type of knowledge that will help you later on. Just you don't worry."

What I can't openly tell Sarojben is that I have been following her chart, and it is she who I am more worried about than Gita. Gita will pick up. She has got so much ahead of her.

But something big is going to change with Sarojben. In her life she has had one big sadness already, around age twenty-eight. That same cycle with a tough conjunction is returning. Then too, numerologically speaking, with the last name Shah there is some problem. What and all I can't say.

"Look here." I aim my remarks at the Fiona. "I don't know if you are interested in your own life predictions or the predictions of fashion for your magazine. But you just take down what I tell you. Take it down. You see how Sarojben asked about Gita before she asked about herself? This is love. Love, get it? In life there are so many kinds of love. There is love that parents have for children, there is love between friends, or the love between partners, man and wife. All these kinds of love. But out there in your West, everyone is whole the time looking for the love found in a couple. Love, romance, ooh and aah and stars and all the rest of these things. Thinking too much about that love, you can sala forget all about the other kinds. But then too, what is life without loss and change? Now if one sort of love is lost, do you think that the others go away? No, my dear girl. It is precisely by keeping alive many kinds of love that a person will always stay sane. Now repeat it back to me: what did I say?"

4
Dashing
Means Danger

As Gita walked home from the library she reflected
that the stop signs in Berkeley had all been co-opted. At every
corner, the octagonal red boards were embellished with white
spray paint. STOP Reagan. STOP AIDS. STOP War. STOP
Rape. STOP Nukes. STOP El Salvador. Through the chain of
associations that continually lured her back to Norvin's futon
bed, she thought about the two sets of signs at the crossroads
in her head. STOP circling hands, sliding tongues, rising heat.
STOP Sister Bernadette's moral science classes, chaste heroines
of Hindu mythology, judgments that would make Najma a
fallen woman and leave Gita herself more sullied by the week.
STOP. And STOP! Brakes squeaking, she somehow had to
avert a head-on collision.

"But tell me, how did it all start?" Najma, freshly back
from Yosemite, was full of exuberant congratulations. "It's

obvious he's been lusting after you for ages, but how did you get into this routine?"

"I don't know," Gita said, craning her neck so she could see down the stairs as she held the phone. Bet had gone out some time ago, but it was now ingrained in Gita to be furtive as she spoke. "It just, like, you know. After that night on the porch things sort of, you know, well . . ."

"What? Speak up, Gita."

"Things sort of just happened."

"Tell, *yaar*. What happened? Step by step. I mean, of course, you don't have to if you don't want to, but I'll admit I'm dying to hear about it all. So he dropped you home. And then?"

"Well, actually, I had a nine o'clock appointment in his office the next morning. I was supposed to hand him some notes on what I found for his research in the library."

"Thank God you're not his student. He'd have all sorts of scruples then. But a research assistant is a different matter! It's probably been a cover for professors to get close to pretty students for quite some time. Meet me in my office! Meet me in the library stacks! Meet me for a cappuccino as we discuss your findings! And no problems about the ethics of grading. All at the university's expense too."

"Come on," said Gita, "this is serious research I'm doing. It's even helping me with my dissertation proposal. It's not just a front or anything."

"Not just a *front,*" Najma repeated with mischief. "Hmm, sounds *very* promising. OK, so you went to his office in the morning, all dressed in some discreetly fabulous outfit, and then? Let's hear it with full jing-jang *masala*. But hurry, because Noah's setting up an experiment and then he'll be coming by and honking for me. It's one of our Laundromat dates. Start the story at least, but also plan to come over tomorrow. Noah's off to some conference and we can keep talking. Lunch?"

*   *   *

When Gita had tentatively knocked that morning, Norvin extended an arm as he opened the door. He led her inside and shut the door. His face was serious; it was Gita who found herself grinning. She wanted to giggle at that intense look on his face, accentuating the way his head seemed a little too big for his body and his nose pressed down at the end. She quickly reprimanded herself not to act like a schoolgirl but a Woman involved in serious romance. Neither of them said a word as he pressed his mouth against hers. This time Gita remembered that she wasn't raising her lips to a tall hero. She stood straight, trying to reorient her image of what a kiss should be. Why didn't anyone ever mention the problem of spittle, surely *jhuta* of the worst sort and tasting faintly of mint toothpaste, almond essence, and stale milk. She had to admit that this was quite wonderful, especially when one got the knack of letting lips grow pliable, then knead and explore with a will of their own. Yes, Timothy was right: that really hadn't been a *kiss* kiss before.

Past Norvin's ear on one side she could see the windows of Trowel Hall. Could anyone possibly be armed with binoculars in there, all the secretaries in the registrar's office, for instance, getting up on a chair and taking turns to look? She thought of the Lovers—men and women nestled together against the high walls that sloped down from bungalows on Juhu beach. The presence of a walking companion, whether Harish Uncle, Jeroo, or H. H. Pindapur's latest acquisition, had always restrained Gita from taking a good look at whatever those Lovers were up to. But groups of young men out for a beach adventure were less inhibited. With tight pants, the haircuts of film heros, and arms wrapped over one another's shoulders, these young men would stand transfixed before the Lovers, sallying a loud commentary between themselves. After a while, the Lovers usually broke away from each other, the woman ducking as she rearranged her sari, the man's profile turned in a distant, furious silence. Gita also remembered Dinaz's description of kissing a cricket star turned bush-shirt model in the back of a Bombay taxi. The Sikh driver had watched them through his rearview mirror, then pulled over to one side of the road and informed them if they didn't stop right now there would be an accident. *"Accident ho jayega!"* Dinaz had laughed her hoarse, braying laugh. "As though kissing is all it takes for an *accident!"*

Kissing perpendicularly with half one's mind roaming out the sunny window or toward passing footsteps in the corridor was altogether different from kissing prone in an empty house on a balmy summer night. That had been the next step, when he invited her over to dinner. He had told stories about Nasik like a nervous tic, and she had picked at her plate, wondering when they could resume that luxury of bodies pressed close. He had finished the bottle of wine single-handedly before he sat down beside her and took her hand—finally! It was now an unspoken understanding that arranging to meet for an evening walk to the Marina, the Rose Garden, or up to Tilden Park meant that they would end up entangled somewhere in his house.

Kookoo Das believed that holding children in your lap messed up your sari, and even Vicky had to sit beside her. "Good boy, now sit up straight." It was Ayah who had comforted Gita, hugging her close if she scraped her knees or was left behind when Kookoo and Dilip went out: "No, baby, no crying," she would say before starting into a story. During the Delhi winters, Gita had sometimes left her bed for Ayah, who lay curled on the floor beside her, a bastion of safety and warmth. She had missed being able to creep to someone when the wind rattled the shutters at boarding school. How many years had it been since she lay close to someone in a bed, close enough to feel breath filling a chest, and the rhythm of a different heart? Of course, everyone lounged in the afternoon on Saroj Aunty and Harish Uncle's expansive double bed, under the fan amid trays of iced fruit or burnished brass boxes for *paan*. But lying around, separated bodies, in the same shared space was not the same as snuggling. After such prolonged starvation, Gita found she could not imagine surviving without those rich slabs of nourishment that Norvin's body brought her way. She hardly heard or even judged what he was saying anymore; it was like a movie with the sound cut off. He had moved into soft focus, each shot a close-up so near that he was blurred. These days, every moment that Gita was doing something else, she wondered when she would be alone with him again in a soft, darkened interior.

Firoze was already ringing the bell for Najma's apartment when Gita arrived at the stoop of the house.

"Oh, hi, Gita," he said. "How are you? Haven't seen you for a while."

Gita tried not to suppress her irritation as she said, "I'm invited to lunch. What are *you* doing here? I mean, in this part of town?"

"Well . . ." Firoze cleared his throat. His voice still seemed a little clotted with sleep. He looked down, adjusted the strap of his shoulder bag, and then, with his head still lowered, looked up at her sideways. A huge and unmistakably guilty grin was spreading across his face. He had probably been over at that Swede's place. Gita stood her ground, refusing to smile back. She noticed with distaste that he hadn't shaved that morning; if he had decided to do away with that awful beard, why didn't he stick with the decision? With this thought, Norvin's evening cheeks rose up, rough under her fingers. Now it was her turn to dart a glance at the bits of lint and shriveled leaves on the communal porch. "I have this friend who, well, lives quite nearby," Firoze was saying. "I was dropping in to ask Najma about some posters. Ah, Najma, here you are!"

"Hi, hi! Come on in! So you decided to bring Firoze along?"

"Well, actually," Gita and Firoze began at the same time. As though their voices had collided, they both drew back into silence and followed Najma inside. Najma's hair was a wet circlet of snakes around her shoulders, and she was wearing a cotton Bengali sari. ("I like to at home, you know. It's a different sort of feeling about being myself," she had once told Gita.) In the apartment everything was low: embroidered cushions, mattresses with bright printed spreads, woven cotton dhurries to sit on, a door balanced on a few bricks serving as a table. There were angular white Warli stick figures on sacking material, Van Gogh's self-portrait, Kangra miniatures from the Delhi Museum, a red, yellow, and black Madhubani painting of a huge-eyed and multiarmed goddess, and a misty Monet landscape.

"Whenever I come over I have this strange sense that I could be somewhere in India." Firoze said what Gita was thinking.

"Intellectuals' India," said Najma. "Artsy-craftsy cottage industries, government emporiums, handloom-house India. I mean, come on, Firoze, you'd be the first to say that it's socially irresponsible to think that the ingrown stratum we move in is all of India." She went back to kneading dough with her knuckles, periodically flicking in water from the bowl beside her.

"OK, OK," said Firoze. "I agree, let's say that it's the home of a postcolonial intellectual with roots in India, who is now settled just about anywhere in the world. This could be Nairobi or Toronto or Southall. Traveling culture. Is that better?" He dawdled by the door of the kitchen. "Actually, Najma, I don't mean to stay. I just heard that you were back in town and wanted to ask about the posters."

"Oh, come on," said Najma. "Just look at these *aloo paronthas* I'm assembling. How can you resist? Here, Gita, can you mash the potatoes?"

"*Aloo paronthas*! I can't resist. At least not *this* sort of resistance." He rubbed thoughtfully at his chin, as though missing the beard.

"Glad to hear it," said Najma. "Here's the mint. Clean it, then chop it fine."

He could at least have hesitated for courtesy's sake, thought Gita, mashing aggressively at the potatoes as Firoze started picking through sprigs of mint. All that talk of feminism, and he couldn't even see that everything was different with a man around! What kind of sensitivity did he have if he just butted in, sending unsaid confidences flapping off in different directions? For Najma, though, she shouldn't sulk or be too openly belligerent. "Isn't it funny," Gita said, "that here we all cook together and become such experts while at home it would just be servants producing things behind the scenes in the kitchen?"

"Or adoring mothers," said Najma. "The whole South Asian food-is-love equation."

"Not mine," said Firoze. "We have all these servants from Surat. Though occasionally she likes to get into the kitchen to make cakes and pastries."

"I don't think my mother even knows where the light in the kitchen is," Gita said. "Not that she's not an expert at planning menus and clipping out recipes. But even when they lived abroad they had a cook with them. She reads aloud recipes in the drawing room. If there's a boy, he goes back and forth with the instructions, otherwise it's the cook who has to keep coming out after every step. She sends thank-you notes and New Year's cards on mornings when she's cooking like this."

Firoze eyed Gita. He had never heard her speak of her family before. He wondered how to keep her talking. "So they live in Delhi now?" he asked.

"Just now, yes," said Gita.

Firoze waited. She didn't say any more. Instead she asked Najma, "What are the posters for?"

"Shakti," said Najma, kneading the dough with her knuckles and sprinkling more water from the mug beside her. "You know, our South Asian feminist organization that I've been trying to get you to come to. We have this fantastic speaker coming in next week. It's our one and only summer event, and we're hoping we can get enough people together. We had this huge success in boycotting that Manorama's Panorama place with all the bullshit about *Kamasutra* Love Secrets. It turned out all the women they employed had brown makeup base smeared all over, not an Indian tit in sight. Anyway, what was the title of that lecture again, Firoze?"

"Difference, Alterity, and the Return of the Jaina Repressed: A Transnational Decentering of Phallogocentric Hegemony."

"Wow!" Gita looked up from the potatoes. "What's the lecture about?"

"Actually, I don't know," said Firoze. "But it's sure to be brilliant."

"Oh," said Gita.

Firoze looked extremely earnest. "Kamashree has done important work on deconstructing *pativrata* ideology in all its cross-cultural variants."

"Actually, even when you hear her speaking it's often hard to tell what she's talking about," said Najma. "Jaina repressed! That should really have professors here scratching their heads. How would they know about the pure life-style of the Jaina community? No eggs, no meat, and for the really orthodox, no garlic, onions, or even tomatoes. Don't they carry nonviolence to such an extreme that some nuns and monks even wear face masks so that they don't breathe in any insects by mistake?"

"I think so," said Gita. "Isn't it part of *ahimsa*?"

"Look," said Firoze, "if you can sprinkle texts with fancy French terms, what's wrong with a little Sanskrit? Can't you see that it's a product of colonialism that prestige value is attached to one language rather than the other? Why should the West continue to set the terms for our discourse? I think it's a terrific political tactic for Kamashree to use South Asian terms when she speaks."

"So who exactly is this person?" asked Gita.

"Kamashree Ratnabhushitalingam-Hernandez," said Najma. "One of those hyphenations that makes travel agents groan. Think of all the suffering that goes into bibliographies." Najma smirked. "God! These *lingam-lingam* Southie names are really too much. Anyway, Firoze, if you're done with the mint, will you chop these onions?"

"Professor Goddess-of-Desire Jewel-Studded Phallus," said Firoze, absentmindedly handling the knife that Najma had given him. "After my Hindi course I keep seeing meanings in all these names. There's this guy on campus who is Professor Padmanabhan, Lotus-Navel. What would you be, Gita? Miss

Song?" He was smiling down a her, under those thick brows. "And then doesn't *Das* mean 'servant' or something? No wonder you're such a total slave, so devoted and all to your work. My God, what a burden to carry!"

"Shut up, Ganjifrockwala!" Gita made an attempt to glare, but her lips pressed into a grin. He could almost be nice sometimes. "Ganji-frock-wala, you have no right to say anything with that collection of male underwear and female garments floating around in your surname."

"Sort of like drag," giggled Najma. "Really, Firoze, it's now up to you to combine the best of male and female qualities in yourself."

"I'm aiming to be postgender." Firoze's eyes sparkled under that black line of brow as he looked at the two women. "Though I couldn't, well, exactly claim to be postsexuality."

"Bravo!" Najma clapped. "What a two-in-one combo!"

"Give me those onions." Gita grabbed the chopping board from Firoze. He was doing a coarse, inept job. "How did Hernandez come into it?" Gita asked.

"Hernandez was this Salvadoran guerrilla," said Firoze. Gita was getting gumption too, he observed. That bossy way she took charge of the onions—it was so unlike her.

"What rubbish." Najma turned from the stove where she was greasing a flat pan. "Hernandez was from Goa. That's a Portuguese name, and he was as Indian as any of us. He was supposed to be a Naxalite, into helping out the tribal groups who're being screwed by caste Hindus everywhere, and she married him so that he could get asylum during the Emergency."

"Bull*shit,*" said Firoze. "I definitely heard he was from El Salvador. For your information, she had the name even in her earliest publications, and those date back to a time before she had a green card in America. By her second book she didn't even bother to thank him."

"Maybe he was a Salvadoran who came to India and was trying to pass as a Goan," said Gita, smiling to herself as she recognized the tack of trying to learn about someone by reading the acknowledgments in their works. "And then what happened in her second book?"

"New men," said Najma, putting dabs of the potato, mint, and onion mixture into the dough and rolling it out with brisk, sure strokes. The first *parontha* hit the pan with a sizzle. "New acknowledgments. Firoze, would you mind getting out the plates?"

"Norvin knows her too," said Firoze, reaching into the cupboard. "Quite well, I believe. He helped raise some money from his department for her talk. Her fee was of course much more than Shakti could afford, we're talking about a *major* academic star here. Has he said anything about having a reception for her at his house, Gita?"

"No, he hasn't," said Gita shortly. Was her seeing Norvin already such an established social fact? "Give me the plates and I'll set the table." She didn't look up as she took the plates from Firoze. None of them matched. Nor did the cutlery. It was all unmistakably part of a graduate student hoard gleaned from thrift stores, church sales, yard sales, the hand-me-downs of friends moving away to first jobs. All the same, the collage of different patterns had its own charm on the low, rectangular table surrounded by square cushions on which *ikat* fish met *ikat* flowers.

Though Saroj Aunty meticulously matched sari ensembles, when it came to food she felt that the items used for serving should not be related to each other but to the food at hand. Main meals were always on burnished brass *thali*s with delicately tilting rims. But beyond that there was variety renewed every few years when a white-bearded Sikh potter trained long ago in Japan came to Bombay for exhibitions. In the summer, concentrically cut white onions were laid out with pale jade cucumbers on a cerulean blue platter, a blue bluer than the brightest midnight sky. Iced pomegranate seeds arrived at the big bed in cool, individual bowls the color of foam on the waves. Fresh mangoes of assorted varieties were sliced in different hues of saffron on a speckled plate the colors of dry and wet sand on Juhu beach. The accompanying bowl for peels—mottled green on one side, stringy orange on the other—was as black as the rocks revealed at low tide, with a metallic sheen.

"All this about sets and pairs is nonsense," Saroj Aunty had once said. "It *absolutely* undermines individuality."

"What about *jori*s?" Harish Uncle teased. "Aren't you and I a *jori*, a real matching pair?" He and Saroj Aunty eyed each other, little smiles twisting at the corners of their mouths. Gita again could not help thinking of shoes, and how though the two didn't really *look* alike, they really did match well.

"Two *pukka* crazies," Jimmy Seervai put in with a twist of the neck. "Utter and complete, I tell you; only mad-mad people like you could tolerate each other. I tell you, how many couples would sit around naming a collection of saris?"

H. H. Pindapur had cleared his throat, uneasy beside the latest young lady he had brought to visit.

"Whole the bloody thing is destiny," Ganeshan Kaka stated. "*Sala,* those planets and numbers at birth."

Well, Norvin had showed up in March, that was true. Yet she had been so sure that Timothy was The One and that Norvin was just a pseudo-Parsi that it was hard to recast him with all the transcendent shine of Fate. Yet if she was carrying on with Norvin in this shameless way he had to be The One, her *jori*. It wasn't as though anyone else had been pushed into form by the ponderous rotations of Shani. It wasn't as though anyone else had ever stroked her long hair and declared it to be the finest satin.

Norvin was waiting for her under the tall gray campanile. He sat on the long bench facing the bay. He had dark glasses on and appeared to be catching up with the book reviews in one of the endless journals he subscribed to, which lay in helter-skelter piles on top of his desk. Gita knew she wasn't being paid to pick up his office, but whenever she was there she couldn't help readjusting some of the piles so that at least they were straight.

"My Song of Songs!" Norvin reached out a hand. Gita looked around before extending her own. Luckily very few people came to the library on a Sunday afternoon in the summer. Not that she had ever taken a class with him, or that they were even in the same department. She allowed their fingers to interlace for just the briefest of moments.

"Sorry I'm late," she said. "I was having lunch with Najma." It was so nice to have someone waiting for her, a hub of her own in the huge emptiness of a Sunday afternoon; so nice to have someone she checked in with regularly enough to make even the smallest events into news. She sat down beside him. "So how's it going?"

"Terrific," said Norvin. "The usual bagels with the *Times* this morning. Then I had a couple of phone calls. My mother is playing her part, worried about whether I'm getting enough to eat. Actually I'm putting on weight. It's not as though I didn't manage alone when we were married. Rachel wasn't exactly around, as you know."

"Yes," said Gita. She had heard a good deal about Rachel these last few weeks. She had heard how they met at Peace Corps training, though Rachel went to Africa. She had seen the picture of Norvin's polished black shoe poised over a wineglass at their wedding, and the picture of them both in tie-dyed shirts on their honeymoon. She had discerned that Rachel was given to dieting and was responsible for the many tins of weight-loss programs still occupying the kitchen cupboards. She knew that Rachel did not approve of Norvin's catching up with popular culture and had the annoying habit of switching off the television when she wanted to talk to him. Also that Rachel had smoked, while Norvin believed in a smoke-free environment. Rachel's new lover apparently managed a construction business, which Norvin interpreted as a case of Going for the Proletariat.

"It's no good having two academics racing along the fast lane in the same household," Norvin was saying. "You're just always signaling that you want to pass, it's your turn to get ahead. Always speeding. Never in the same car at the same time."

"Ah," said Gita. She looked away from Norvin's mouth to the tree-lined avenue before them. Far away, the Golden Gate Bridge quivered in a haze of heat and sea.

"Being an only son has its burdens," Norvin continued. "My mother's been worried for years about my continuing the family line, all those rabbinically refined intellectual genes. I actually had some sperm frozen a couple of years ago, you know. It was around the time that Rachel told me that her career had to come first. Interesting how in India this sort of thing isn't an issue at all. People just assume that marriage will come with children. Of course, I know that those Parsi Watchers of yours, that Aunty and Uncle—"

"What?" Gita snapped back to attention. "What about the Shahs?"

"I was just saying that they probably didn't plan not to have children. I bet it was a disappointment that it never happened. Was she infertile for some reason? In India, with that tropical climate, it just seems so natural to luxuriantly reproduce."

"Saroj Aunty never said why," said Gita. "I mean, she has nieces and nephews, like me."

"All the same, I bet it was a disappointment," continued Norvin. "When I was in Maharashtra, the headman in the village actually married three wives . . ."

Gita was off, luxuriating in Norvin's soft bed. When Norvin's fingers crept toward her breasts Gita always pulled away; also when they edged up her skirt or against the inner seam of her jeans. Stop signs loomed precipitously above these areas. It was like the *National Geographic* magazines with articles on "primitive" tribes that arrived in India with rectangular black patches stamped across all areas demanding modesty. The comfort of arms around her, body relaxed, eyes turned inward, mouth straining for more: this was enough. Gita thought of the signs lettered in white against the parapets of steep curves on the roads up to hill stations, whether Ootacamund, Lonaula, or Simla: DASHING MEANS DANGER. But immediately she thought of the other set of signs that instructed BETTER LATE THAN NEVER.

How late was late? "Late is all relative," Saroj Aunty had said. In the American terms surrounding her she was already hopelessly, spinsterishly late. She knew she was being boring: if she were a character in a book, for example, wouldn't this foot-dragging, this lack of exciting action get on a reader's nerves? Yet on the score of sex, she seemed unable to be a page turner. On the other hand, if he was really Her Man— he *had* to be, if she was carrying on with him this shameless way—what was wrong in cutting short the progression of "late" toward "never"? Why not, her body demanded, even now as he carried on about Maharashtra and she observed the way hair curled black at the back of his fingers. Why not grab at "never" so it metamorphosed in her hands to a "now" filled with throbbing potential? Why not suggest they leave for his house right this moment, and then unsnap her bra, airing the constriction beneath? PLEASURE YOUR CURVES. Why not allow those fingers so expert in stroking her stomach descend into the damp areas in her panties? Why not let the panties be slipped down, hair springing up in release, thighs parting to the great unknown? Gita! A CHANCE TAKER IS AN ACCIDENT MAKER. How could she even think these things?!

But he really is brilliant, Gita, she told herself. Just look at the way his mouth moves—such conviction!—as he's lecturing just now. You have only to step inside the library and slide a microfiche into the machine to see all the books written and edited by him. This is a man that even Yale and Harvard have bid for, a man whose name is surely in the bibliography of practically every article in the journal he has lying on his thigh. (Firm, warm thigh, so close to That place. Quick, back away from that thought, THE LIFE YOU SAVE MAY BE YOUR OWN.) It would be wonderful to send his curriculum vitae to Mummy to flutter over. "This distinguished professor is actually a friend of our little Gita's. He gave her a copy of his biodata himself. She's keeping such fine company out there at her university. Who would have ever expected it of her, poor little thing—she was always so shy." There was really no need to make any decision about anything right now. NO HURRY NO WORRY. If she continued to help him, maybe there would be books to send home too, the acknowledgments ending *Special thanks to Gita Das, whose meticulous research made this work possible.* Why not even a dedication? *For my Song of Songs, with enduring thanks.*

"Don't you want to hear about what I've dug up in the library?" Gita burst out.

"Oh yes, of course," said Norvin, who had apparently been quite carried away by what he was saying, for his spectacles were off and he was tweaking the bridge of his nose. "Quite right. It's terrific that you remain right on course. So, let's hear what you've found on the beds of nails."

Gita straightened her back, glad to have returned to solid land, where references could be cross-checked and she knew her own mind. "Well, it's all over the place, as you say, quite a dominant trope in the American construction of India. The missionaries were quite taken with it. There's a woodblock in the *Missionary Herald* put out from Massachusetts in 1824, accompanying an article on how immoral and filthy the Hindu ascetics are, spending all their time lounging around on nails and doing other impractical practices instead of contributing to society. It's the same woodblock, though, that Reverend Ward, the British missionary, had in his book. So it seems that American images are actually building on ones deriving from a colonial interaction in which descriptions of lazy natives and misguided practices served to justify domination and conversion efforts."

"Fabulous, fabulous," said Norvin. "And so they become caricatures by the time they reach here. What about the other figures I suggested we look into? How about Sati? The luscious wife with streaming hair and rolling eyes, arms raised as she prepares to jump onto her husband's funeral pyre? I've got to say I've always admired Indian women for courage like that."

"I think they were mostly pushed," said Gita. "From what I gather they were drugged too; it was the in-laws insisting. Or society at large. Nobody really tried to interview the women, so it's hard to say."

"Yes, of course," said Norvin. "The old problem of documenting the subaltern mentality. Fabulous, fabulous, a great angle on iconicity. You're a treasure, Gita. Could you start typing out the notes on index cards?"

"Certainly," said Gita. She straightened her back, enjoying the sense of feeling reliable, needed.

"By the way, before I forget, do you think you could help me arrange a party at my place? This Indian woman, a real dynamo, will be in town to give a lecture next week. I thought of having a sort of dinner reception afterwards, you know, with Indian cuisine. It would be a way to have your friends over too. That Parsi boy and all the others."

"Of course," said Gita. *Dear Mummy, Professor Weinstein, who occupies the Doolittle Chair on campus, asked me to be the hostess at his party for a most distinguished guest lecturer . . .*

"So that's settled," said Norvin. "Now, tell me, have you found anything on the snake charmer who entrances his own phallus? And what about the fabulously wealthy maharajas?"

H. H. Pindapur had been educated at Eton and Cambridge. He spoke with an impeccable British accent and played a fine game of cricket. Apparently he had been in the Debating Society with Gita's father at Cambridge. This was why he was a visitor in the households of both Saroj Aunty and Kookoo Das. For some reason he never brought his changing assortment of girls to her mother's house. Not that Kookoo didn't know about them, for Gita had often heard her sniff, "It would be fine if he just stuck with the *foreigners,* but the way he goes in for these Anglo-Indians, actresses, dancing girls . . . Of course, I can't deny they're *pretty* little things, but their breeding . . . !"

After the privy purses had been abolished, H.H. had had some financial worries. He had turned his summer palace into a museum and charged a high admission. Other maharajas had made their palaces into hotels, but H. H. Pindapur said he couldn't abide the thought of anyone else living in the same spaces as the copulating ghosts of his ancestors. "At least in a museum they will have their own peace and quiet at night."

H. H. Pindapur only drank Patiala pegs of scotch. A Patiala peg is as high as the distance between pinky and index finger. It was named after the infamous Maharaja of Patiala, whose very name conjured up rivers of liquor and a sweaty reek of debauchery.

After a few Patiala pegs, H.H. liked to tell jokes, which he then explained. The more the pegs, the dirtier the jokes, while Saroj Aunty snickered in Bombay, and in Delhi Kookoo twittered like a bird at sunset.

"I say, old boy, how do you make a hormone?" H.H. asked Jimmy Seervai as they sat indoors one summer afternoon with *khas* wet and fragrant, fans blowing, and frosted glasses full of assorted drinks in their hands. Harish was rubbing the women's feet. Currently it was Proachie, but Jeroo was sitting close beside her, barely able to keep still until it was her turn.

"A hormone?" Jimmy Seervai asked. "Interesting question. Are you getting into SCIENCE or what, and how do you expect PRESENT COMPANY to give you an answer?"

"How do you make a hormone?" repeated H. H. Pindapur.

"Is this a joke?" Harish Uncle inquired. He lay down Proachie's arched foot, while Jeroo swiftly presented him with hers.

"Don't interrupt, old boy. I say, anyone around here know how to make a hormone?"

"Not knowing," said Ganeshan Kaka. "This modern science and all."

"Tell, tell, Uncle, hurry up then," Jeroo urged on H.H.

"Proachie, IMPERTINENCE!" cried Jimmy.

"Yes, darling," Proachie said serenely. "So, how *do* you make a hormone?"

"You make a whore moan if you don't pay her."

The line was met by laughter, applause, groans, silence. "You see, whores have got to make their livings, the blessed girls . . ." The compulsory explanation was already under way.

"You old bore!" said Saroj Aunty with affection. "So, shall we have dinner put on?"

At Gita's parents' house they would all be in the sitting room surrounded by knickknacks collected from diplomatic stays in different parts of the world. A Swiss cuckoo clock, china shepherdesses from England, Dresden plates, Thai dolls, and a three-foot-long replica of a German mechanical pencil. Ramchand would have put on his white livery with shining brass buttons to become bearer for the night and would be serving fresh hot kabobs wrapped in *rotis* as the hors d'oeuvre.

"This chappie was found wandering on the Simla Mall late at night," H.H. would conversationally begin after a few pegs.

"Oh dear," Kookoo fluttered, "I do hope it's not that old father of Brigadier Trivedi's—he's rather given to wandering about alone. I told Tutu to keep a better eye on him. I do hope that he wasn't attacked or anything. Crime has gotten terrible at Simla—it's not like the good old days. I suppose it would be in the papers if he was stabbed."

"Didn't see anything about it in the papers," said Dilip. "The riffraff, lumpen elements, are taking over the nation. Violence everywhere."

"Listen, please. This chappie was walking around on the Simla Mall on a frightfully cold night. He was absolutely nude below the waist."

"It doesn't sound like Tutu's Uncle at all, not at all. Perhaps it was that dear old Mr. Lall. I heard he was losing his marbles after retirement from the ICS. Gita, darling, would you run and see what Vicky is doing in his room?"

"The police stopped him. He explained, 'My wife sent me out like this. You see, the other day I didn't have on a scarf and I got a stiff neck, so tonight she said I should go out without—"

"Gita, be obedient, dear, haven't you learned any manners

at your school? To think of all the expense we went to, and you don't even get up at once. There's a good girl—"

"—without trousers. You see, she hoped that he'd, well, be *stiff* enough to . . ." The explanation came trailing after her, then was displaced by the arguing of servants as Gita went down the hall toward her younger brother.

Norvin had to go to dinner at the house of one of his colleagues. Though he had invited Gita to come along she simply did not want to. How could she face these professors as she balanced a glass of wine she didn't dare drink, when someday she might yet be answerable to the opinions they held forth in classrooms? Studying with Norvin, she'd already decided, was altogether out of the question at this point. Too bad— just recently her adviser had mentioned that his course on the imperial imagination would be helpful for her dissertation.

Gita walked home feeling a fondness for her life. She was grateful to have a friend like Najma who allowed her space to be herself, who listened but did not pry. Even Firoze had turned out to be quite sweet today; maybe he was actually developing a sense of humor. Norvin was a good man, though he did talk an awful lot. She felt a special gratitude to him for opening such luxurious spaces out around her, even as he respected her boundaries. She was enjoying this summer job much more than last year's at the Middle Eastern restaurant. Her dissertation topic was genuinely interesting, and she'd recently found rich folk-narrative materials in the *North Indian Notes and Queries* set up by colonial officers in the last century. Now it was a benevolently golden summer evening, with cats musing outdoors, the scent of barbecues in the air, barefoot children playing on the sidewalk. She walked to the accompaniment of water sprinklers. Upright sprinklers, like showering trees of the sort always featured in Divali fireworks. Low, arched sprinklers that revolved like radars. Sprinklers that hissed all in one direction. At one spot, with sprinklers making a sheet of water, she glimpsed two translucent bands of rainbow. Yes, when one did not have a paper due tomorrow morning, life really could be enjoyable.

As she unlocked the door, she sniffed baking chocolate. Oh no. Bet was home. Well-being, so jaunty a moment ago, dropped limp. She held her breath in the effort to be absolutely silent as she tiptoed upstairs. When Bet baked brownies it meant she was depressed and had eaten large amounts of chocolate in hopes of consolation. By now she was probably undressed in her water bed, watching television.

But Bet was sitting at the telephone table at the top of the stairs. "Hi," Gita said.

"Your *boy*friend just called," said Bet. "Aren't *you* sorry you missed him!"

"Who?" asked Gita.

"Look, don't do that innocent little girl full of succor number on me," said Bet. "You might have stopped informing me of your comings and goings, but it may not have occurred to you that I have *eyes*. Especially with no plays on at the moment I have plenty of time in this apartment to notice what's going on."

"Ah," said Gita, craning her neck to see the message. She really didn't want to bridge the gap her silence had created, for she had the feeling that given the chance, Bet would rush over, colonizing every square millimeter of her interaction with Norvin.

"I don't know what's happened to you," continued Bet, "and I'm not sure I even care. But you might have the decency to respect my life in this apartment."

"May I see the message, please?" Gita asked, straining against every nerve that demanded she apologize. It was an unusual feeling to be cast as a bad girl, an awful, disobedient person who gave others grief. Looking at the slip of paper she had to suppress a chortle.

> *Firoze called. He says that* cum kaam, *the goddess of desire, has changed the date to Thursday, but same time and place.*

"It's not my idea of a joke to ask someone else to transmit

obscene messages in a language they're not supposed to understand." Bet had stood up and was standing at her door. "I don't give a damn if you're screwing around, but you can leave me out of it. If I hadn't asked him a couple of times for the spelling that I couldn't get with that accent of his, he would never have switched to the English translation, 'Oh, she'll understand!' he kept saying. He must have been snickering up his sleeve. Your *boy*friend, that Firoze."

Even though it was giving Bet data, Gita opened her mouth to say, "He's *hardly* my boyfriend." But Bet's bedroom door was already closed.

There was a large colored poster on the door of the Indian Foods and Goods Boutique. It showed a young woman wrapped in a scanty sari, her arms, legs, and hair bedecked with the gold jewelry of a bride if not an actual celestial damsel. She knelt, head demurely inclined, eyes lowered, palms joined in a *namaste* below her lovely profile. HAVE A NICE DAY instructed the English logo she faced. All around her there were smaller announcements taped up: for Indian classical concerts, for forthcoming festivals to be celebrated at the Hindu temple, for musical extravaganzas featuring Indian film stars and play-back singers on triumphant world tours.

"Do you keep pretty active in the community?" Norvin asked as he held open the door.

"Not really," said Gita, "I've been so busy studying."

Norvin seemed to have divined the other reason, which she did not mention. "I guess these events are steep on a student budget. Well, let me know if you'd like to go to anything. I could always take you as a research expense."

The store smelled of roughly ground spices, sawdust, and incense. There were shelves spilling with products whose colored packaging from recycled paper had a faded look compared to the sleekness of what was available in American supermarkets. A long line of bins filled with whole grains, flours, and spices dominated the center of the store. Steel and aluminum utensils were stacked together in a corner: pressure cookers, vessels with large rings on both sides, flat griddles, coconut scrapers, tongs to lift pots, multitiered tiffin containers. There were guides to Indian cooking beside mythological comics and paperbacks with titles like *How to Bring Up Your Child as a Hindu, What's That Dot on Your Forehead? 22 Favorite Questions about Indian Culture, A Beginner's Guide to Palmistry,* and *An Investment Handbook for Non-Resident Indians.* A card rack held endless shots of the Taj Mahal and the Livermore temple, along with an assortment of enormous-eyed and multiarmed deities. The shop was fairly empty because it was a weekday, and the wizened old woman in the Gujarati sari and windbreaker who presided over the checkout counter eyed Gita and Norvin curiously. Gita looked away, determined not to be embarrassed.

"You know what this reminds me of?" Norvin asked. He was clutching a canvas basket as he followed Gita down the aisle of bins.

"Maharashtra?" asked Gita, shoveling garbanzos into a paper bag. She was contemplating the sign that advertised Texmati rice, *basmati* grown in Texas rather than imported from monsoon-flooded fields. "The Peace Corps?"

"Oh yes, that too," said Norvin. "No, I was thinking of shopping expeditions with Rachel when she got into women's lib and insisted we go together to the supermarket. I thought it was really sweet that you didn't make a big deal about my coming along."

"But I don't have a car to get here," said Gita. "I don't drive either." She wanted to add, And it's your party anyway.

"Oh, it's no problem to drive you around," said Norvin. "It's refreshing. So, was it fifteen people or twenty at the last count? By the way, Timothy will be here too."

"Timothy?" Gita stopped short. "I thought he was in France."

"Oh, he's here just briefly to meet with people at the Press; he has some ideas for the layout of his new book. Of course, there was no way he would miss a talk by Kamashree. She's legendary. So that's one more. I thought you'd enjoy seeing him again. Not that you and I wouldn't have met anyway in the course of time, but that perfume certainly helped speed things along."

Oh no, thought Gita, why did he have to reappear now? But she swiftly edited the lines rolling through her head. Good! Let Timothy see how nicely Norvin's parties can be catered while he sits letting flies dive into his saucers at cafés. Let him see how wonderful I can look in a brocade sari while his Oedipal displacement goes around in her leather. Let him see how productive Norvin is going to be when I type his index cards. Let him see how Norvin and I . . . Here she paused, unsure about what she wanted him to see. "Let's also stop at a supermarket to get some ricotta and half and half," she said.

"Whatever you say," said Norvin.

It was the American recasting of a *rasmalai* recipe that made the last-minute complications. Other dishes had been prepared over the course of several evenings with Gita in charge and Norvin alternating between Wimbledon, "Star Trek" reruns, breaks for kissing, and active helping. Now there was no space in Norvin's fridge, and this had to be chilled. Gita asked Norvin to drive her home on their way to the talk. He waited in the car, fiddling with radio knobs while she went upstairs.

Bet was sitting at the table with a newspaper spread out before her. It was either the personals or employment, for she had a red pen out and was circling something as Gita looked in.

"Hi, Bet," said Gita, rearranging plastic containers in the fridge so it would accommodate the bowl of soft, cardamom-flavored *rasmalai* floating in saffron-tinged half-and-half. At the last minute, she planned to scatter red rose petals on top from plants on Norvin's patio guaranteed by the Korean gardener to be without pesticides.

Bet snorted. Gita went into her room and swiftly wrapped her best brocade sari around her. She also picked up an aerogram with her mother's handwriting that Bet had set on the telephone table: she could take this with her and scan it later.

But just as she was setting off down the stairs, she remembered that the dessert should also have some freshly ground cardamom sprinkled on it, and returned to the kitchen.

"So where are *we* off to?" asked Bet, eyeing the glittering green sari.

"To a lecture," said Gita.

"Sure," said Bet, "dressed like a Christmas tree. Don't give me that crap."

"Well, there's a reception later," said Gita, furiously pounding cardamom as she looked at her watch.

"Oh, I forgot, the *goddess* of desire has her hanky-panky to attend to. Sorry I asked."

"Look, Bet, I have to run. I'm leaving this bowl of dessert in the fridge and I hope it's not in your way."

"Don't mind me," said Bet. "I don't exist in this apartment." Gita tried to swallow away the bitterness of this interaction as she ran down the stairs. They drove toward campus. As Norvin listened to an interview with practicing witches of the Bay Area, Gita reflected that sometime soon she would have to sit down and spend enough time with Bet to wash away this mud and slime that seemed to darken every conversation.

The room in Feeler Hall was already full, abuzz with conversation, when they arrived. From the door, Gita could see Timothy's bald head, ivory white, partly obscuring a small woman who she presumed must be the speaker. Other professors hovered about, probably awaiting a moment's audience. An invisible hierarchical barrier separated the graduate students, who either stood at a distance or looked on from their seats.

"Come on, Gita," said Norvin, taking an elbow to steer her toward the cluster of faculty, "I'll introduce you."

"No thanks," said Gita hastily, drawing away. How many eyes had swerved to Professor Weinstein's entrance with That Indian Girl? How many eyes were taking in her sari and—horrors—perhaps pronouncing her overdressed. After all, this *was* a talk, and in this heat none of the men even had jackets on; quite a few people were in shorts. She desperately wanted to join her own tribe and searched the crowd for any familiar graduate student face. From a seat against the wall near the front, Firoze caught her eye and waved. The chair beside him seemed to be vacant.

"Smashing sari," said Firoze as Gita sat down. "You really look great."

"You don't think it's too much, do you?" asked Gita, rearranging the folds at her shoulder. Needless to say, Firoze's double woven blue-and-purple handloom shirt hadn't been ironed.

"Just take a look at Kamashree!" said Firoze.

The crowd had cleared as Norvin made his way to the podium to stand beside Kamashree. She was a short woman, perhaps even shorter than Gita, but she had a presence that filled the room. She had pronounced jaws and hair cut with fashionable asymmetry so that on one side it was practically shaved around the ear, but on the other it dipped toward her chin. Her eyes were black and intense behind fifties-style narrow, curved spectacle frames sporting a diamond at each end. She was dressed in a batik sari featuring emerald and purple peacocks against a turquoise blue background. Above this, she had on a Nehru jacket with epaulets and a variety of buttons that were hard to read from afar. Beneath the sari, she seemed to be wearing high-heeled leather boots. She unsmilingly scanned the faces around the room, as though taking command.

"Isn't she splendid?!" Firoze inquired.

Readjusting his raw silk Indian tie, Norvin had begun his introduction: Kamashree's postcolonial educational background, her sequence of postmodern publications, her unchallenged supremacy in the posthumanist era of postfeminism as deconstructed by diasporic women of color. Kamashree stepped forward and unfolded a small plastic stepladder. She now towered in the room, a veritable warrior queen. Adjusting the mike to her new height, she thanked Norvin and promptly proceeded to correct his pronunciation of her name, his pronunciation of the school she had gone to in Madras, and the wording in the title of her fourth book. She congratulated the organization Shakti for honoring women's power and moved into an analysis of power juxtaposing Foucault, the Dharma-shastras, and pronouncements by Angela Davis.

"Right on!" muttered Firoze.

Stepping momentarily from her elevation, Kamashree briskly chalked "Ramrajya Fascism" on the blackboard. Gita could see professors in the front row twitch forward, faces creased with worry, write this out on their yellow pads. Timo-thy's Adam's apple bulged and he looked pitifully skinny as he gazed at the board with a beatific expression that led Gita to suspect that he was composing poems around this assem-blage of letters: "Ration . . . I must write that down. Ram-rajya rations, I woke as if from someone else's nightmare . . ." Maybe someday Gita would write a poem about him compos-ing poetry. Kamashree talked briskly, with a ringing and roll-ing Tamilian-British accent. Very soon Gita had altogether lost the drift of what she was saying. It seemed like a lot of words rarely used in everyday conversation slapped together in a suc-cession so rapid-fire there was no time to remember what these terms were supposed to mean. After a few moments Gita slit open the aerogram lying in her lap. Firoze squirmed beside her; he surely thought this was sacrilege.

Gita lowered her eyes to read as unobtrusively as she could. Since Kookoo had the habit of planting emotional bombs in her letters, Gita liked to skim them first, steeling herself for whatever insinuations or allegations were being leveled across the seas. But what she saw now went beyond the dynamic they had become locked into as mother and daughter. She wished she could return to the moment before she had opened the aerogram, and so erase the truth of what it contained. With unsteady breath and grief rising into her cheekbones, she began at the beginning and read each word.

Dear Gita,
How is our little scholar? I haven't heard from you

recently, you must be ever so busy. I'm disappointed that your letters have been irregular. I do hope that you haven't been falling behind on your discipline about writing home weekly that the Sisters instilled so beautifully.

Your daddy and I read in the papers this morning that Harishbhai Shah has passed away. Of course, I tried to ring poor Saroj at once, but the line seems to be out of order—you know how it swings that wretched way between palm trees in Juhu, and now in the monsoon it's more usual for a line to be out than to be working. I've told Saroj for years that they should think of moving to a part of the city where phone lines are more reliable. Someplace more central, like a nice apartment building near Warden Road or Breachcandy. That wall directly beside the beach has always worried me—you never know when some hooligan might just climb over. They should at least put glass slivers on top of the wall, the way we've done here in Delhi. No doubt Saroj will move now. Imagine being all alone in that enormous house. I had the driver take a telegram down to the post office. It didn't look good for us not to send anything, especially since the Shahs have been so especially kind to you.

Ratna's dear little girl Nutty has just gotten married. When I thought of how the two of you used to go to Lodi gardens with your nannies I had to take out my hanky at the ceremony. Nutty was a beautiful bride. I suppose I should call her Natasha now. Thinking of the Russian connection, I wonder if Ratna was also part of that Communist crew that Saroj and people used to sympathize with. The young man she married is ever so promising. He's in the air force and of the very best Bengali Brahman family, a nice tall boy. Tea gardens, I believe. I wasn't told where they met but I'd certainly be very curious. Ratna is triumphant. I don't suppose you come across young men like that out where you are. I know you have to study, but don't forget, you're not getting any younger.

This morning I am instructing cook on how to make a trifle. That wretched *mali* wants to know what to do with the roses I set him to repotting, so I will sign off. Vicky's health remains delicate, though he is much better. We hope you won't be too emotional about Harish. Such a shame they went to the trouble of a bypass, and that too *abroad* in England, and then to have this happen! You must have learned the format for a letter of condolence at the convent. Be sure to write dear Saroj—that's a good girl.

Your loving,
Mummy

Gita's heart pitched forward, tumbling and bruising again and again. Harish Uncle dead. What did it mean? Beyond the form that was already wavering in her mind—gray hair, large nostrils, smooth, smiling face—there was the sense of him positioned near the center of a secure world. No Harish Uncle meant Saroj Aunty unpaired, eating in silence until bossy Maharaj emerged from the kitchen to dole out another helping. It meant saris lying unnamed. A blank spot on the big bed. Not that she'd ever been as close to Harish Uncle as to Saroj Aunty, but he had always been around, a kind and amused presence. It was as if a portion of the sky had crashed down: instead of predictable blue, there were black spaces where unknowable firmaments whirled, Shani Maharaj among them. How would Saroj Aunty stand up straight and keep going without her *jori?* With such terrifying fissures around routines, professions, plans, how could anyone ever bear to be alone?

Gita thought of Norvin's hairy shoulders. She wished she could rest her cheek against him and be held safely. He was laughing now at something Kamashree had said, her head held high and face unmoving as the audience roared. Norvin caught Gita's eyes and raised his palm, smiling in a greeting just for her. Gita smiled back and it seemed that there was a compel-

ling beauty in the still moment before her heart rose again to
lurch.

There was a rush for the podium after the talk. When Norvin introduced Gita, Kamashree swept an unsmiling look over
her and immediately turned back to Firoze. Gita wanted to
tell Norvin about Harish Uncle, but not in this crush. She
stood behind him, reading the buttons pinned onto Kamashree's jacket as he debated some point about the intertextuality of colonialities with one of his colleagues. WAR IS
MENSTRUATION ENVY, proclaimed a red button. TO XEROX IS
TO KNOW, said another. There was one in Hindi that read,
PREM SE KAHO HAM SAB INSAAN HAI—"Say with love that
we're all human"—that Gita recognized as an inversion of the
slogan touted by political parties who wanted a religious
rather than secular Indian state: "Say with pride that we're all
Hindu." Another button warned, WEARING BUTTONS IS NOT
ENOUGH.

Looking around the room, she also caught sight of Timothy.
His head was inclined as an animated young woman looked
up into his blue eyes. Gita watched, observing that no electric
field seemed to shimmer from his bald spot anymore. Come
to think of it, he was really sort of scrawny and couldn't be
much fun to hold.

Kamashree came with them in the car. She sat regally in the
front beside Norvin and they gossiped about someone or the
other being lured someplace or the other by the promise of
one course a year and a private secretary, and a salary even
more than so-and-so's! In the backseat, Gita looked out the
window and thought of Saroj Aunty in widow's white. Would
she really sell the house with its high ceilings, splotched walls,
bowls of jeweled pomegranate seeds? It would be an unthink-
able expense to telephone India, but then between Norvin's
bed and Harish Uncle's death, what was thinkable these days?
Maybe she would call tomorrow morning.

Only the hall light was on when Gita retrieved the *rasmalai* from the fridge. There was a sealed envelope marked "Gita" propped up by the telephone. Gita scooped this up on her way back to the car. If it was trouble like further complaints about Firoze, she just couldn't cope right now. It was more important to reach Norvin's house before the other guests did and to start pulling out, warming, serving the evening's array of food. She took up her post in the kitchen, and rapidly all the graduate students present who had looked at Norvin's bay view, Norvin's contemporary art, Norvin's three televisions, and Norvin's distinguished gathering made their way to offer unsolicited help.

"What happens when you cross a Mafia boss with a post-structuralist?" asked Ravindran, pulling the plastic wrap off deviled eggs.

"You get an offer you can't understand," said Firoze, looking up from the coriander he was washing at the sink.

"No fair," said Ravindran, "you already heard it. Anyway, this is really the empress's new sari syndrome. Why can't this Kamashree dame speak regular English?"

"She wouldn't have a fancy chair worth a hundred thousand a year if she did," said Najma, drawing *papad* over the gas flame.

"So do you all consider yourselves women of color or what?" Ravindran appeared to find this very funny.

"Sure," said Najma. "In this setting, at least."

"What about you, Gita?"

"I actually hadn't ever thought about it that way," said Gita, rummaging in Norvin's drawers for serving spoons. "I mean, I *am* darker than the average American, but in terms of grouping myself with all women who are not white, well . . ."

"Lookit, Ravindran," Firoze said. "You've got to understand that identity is fluid, it's tied up with where we are. In India, who would think to call ourselves South Asians, but here with the Bangladeshis, Pakistanis, Sri Lankans, Nepalis, and all there's a different context for identity. Or take England: there, Indians are blacks."

"I still think it's a phony act," said Ravindran. "How can

some Brahman woman with thousands of years of privilege behind her, sitting in some Ivy League castle, put herself in the same category as Hispanic farmworkers and inner-city blacks? I mean, how can anyone from the elite, the bloody six percent of English speakers in India, seriously pass themselves off this way?"

"If the terms for discourse are set by white males in both places, then why not?" asked Najma. "Anyhow, even within Brahman communities, women weren't exactly given status beyond that of Shudras: laborers!"

"You've got to accept the assumption that women are an oppressed group," said Firoze. "Identity politics is essential for solidarity and resistance."

"Bloody hell," said Ravindran. "Solidarity with whom? Those hotshot profs out there? I bet she hires graduate students to be her slaves. If there's all this female solidarity, then why isn't she throwing her arms around Najma and Gita here instead of hobnobbing with that poet guy and the rest of them out there?"

"Like I said, we all probably belong to many groups simultaneously, and it's a matter of multiple positions that we shift between," said Firoze. "Different events or circumstances bring out different sides of ourselves."

"OK, Philosopher, you're talking as though everyone's got this grand mobility and choice. Some villager employed to do backbreaking work on my father's fields, who has TB but smokes anyway because he's hungry, and who's worried about when the moneylender's going to get him—a man like that is not exactly going to have the mental space for all these multiple identity crises."

"No, you don't get the point at all. He's a laborer in some circumstances, the master of a household in others . . ."

Gita hated it when men began to argue, and she saw an argument coming. This was what Saroj Aunty called "gorilla warfare," tittering this information into a handkerchief as some duo at a gathering wrestled and grunted over their own vehement opinions, and everyone else was reduced to onlooker. Even Harish Uncle could get into this mode sometimes: Gita could remember an occasion when he and Jimmy Uncle had a furious wrangle over some fine point of the Parsi-Watching Society's bylaws, even though, as their wives tried to interject, they were actually agreeing. Gita wanted to get away from this group, but she didn't want to join the distinguished visitors in the other room either. She wanted to be alone for just a few minutes, cry a little to relieve the acrid incrustations of unhappiness in her joints, deal with Bet's note, which was nagging at the back of her mind. Dinner could be a few minutes late, another round of drinks wouldn't hurt anyone. She crept out onto the redwood balcony beside Norvin's office. Sitting with her chin on her knees, she breathed in the scent of eucalyptus from the hills behind. She stared at the sun hovering over the bay and the distant city washed with gold.

The setting sun reminded her of Saroj Aunty. It also made her wonder where it was that Harish Uncle had gone. In Juhu, the sun always sank into the gray-blue expanse of the Arabian Sea. To the left, apartment buildings of downtown Bombay caught fragments of light in their windows, burning a red as brilliant as the setting sun. Some days, the sun seemed to lose its spherical shape as it dropped lower. It elongated at the top and bottom, grew thick between. As it was swallowed up into the water there was always a silence among the group gathered on wicker chairs in Saroj Aunty's gardens, as though speaking might hold up the descent. Sometimes, as the last sliver of red vanished, there was a violet-blue flash on the line of horizon.

Someone was coming into Norvin's office, and Gita edged further over to the side, where she was hidden by the curtain.

"We can look through the reprints I keep in here." It was Norvin's voice. "Or I have a complete set at the department—making things easier for biographers, you know. I could have the secretary send out a Xerox."

"For the review essay I will be needing it just now only." That was Kamashree's rolling Tamil-British accent. There was a sound of files being taken off the shelf and thumping on the desk. "So how is your love life doing these days?" she asked. Gita imagined her nailing Norvin with a stare from behind those curving spectacles.

"Well, uh. You know that Rachel and I are now formally divorced. Did I ever send you this kamikaze raid I made when she gave my last book a bad review? Which idiot editor sends things to an *ex*-wife, damn it? We never used the same last name, but you'd think he would be more tuned to the sociology of the profession."

"Don't switch the subject, Weinstein—are you sleeping with that sweet morsel who's managing your kitchen or what?"

"She's a terrific cook, actually," said Norvin. "Gets all these recipes written out by this woman in Bombay who names saris. This woman even sent us a recipe from one of her relatives in Queens that substituted ricotta cheese for boiling down milk. I see you've given up leather and are back into saris after all these years. Have you thought of naming them? You know, you could name your saris after theoretical concepts: Hegemony could be one of those two-toned silks, dark with a shimmer in the light. Binary Oppositions could be little checks, and as for these peacocks you're wearing now, hmm . . ."

"Holy Jesus!" When Kamashree said this it sounded like Wholly Cheese-us. "Let's talk evasion! I am simply not interested in naming my saris. I have lectures, books, and articles to name, thank you. The lacunae in your language suggests you are still turned on to Indian women. Haven't as yet got rid of that Orientalist idea of us all as custodians of *Kamasutra* secrets, is it?"

"Actually," said Norvin, "you're wrong, it's not like that at all with Gita."

"Balls, Weinstein—don't tell me she's your cook and research assistant and you haven't arranged to screw her too. Don't you want full service?"

"Kamashree, listen," Norvin said. "These things are serious to her; it's not like the rest of us. This is someone who went to a *convent* school."

"I did too, and look where it got me! They say that when the ex-convent girls go wild, they are wilder than anyone else."

"She's untouched by the postpill, pre-AIDS ideological complex. I have to respect her even if I'm, well, sometimes, you know . . . This is mind over matter. Gives me a new angle on medieval poetry. Elevated ideals, honor . . ."

"Oh, I see," said Kamashree. "Male wimp. Fear and awe at virginity. But what a discovery, no wonder you're looking so pleased with yourself these days! A young thing all to yourself who'll never compare you, who can be trained into sex just as you like it. What a treat! It's been a while since I had a virgin to myself—it's a vanishing species in America."

Norvin glared, but then he laughed, a sort of braying neigh. "You always did have a good head, Dr. Ratnabhushitalingam," he said. "I mean—brains."

"Thank you," said Kamashree. "Call me Professor. I'm glad that you remember these things. So you want some help with, as you say, getting your rocks off as you wait it out with this virgin? This door has got a lock or what?"

"Thanks, actually, I appreciate it, but no thanks, really. I think we should rejoin everyone, I hope you don't mind . . ."

"No problem," said Kamashree, "I'm into younger men these days myself. I was only suggesting it as a favor."

They left the room. Gita crept out. She went into the bathroom, looked into the mirror, and burst into tears. A few minutes later she opened up Bet's note and started to cry all over again. She must not have locked the door, for all of a sudden it opened and Norvin was there.

"Oh, excuse me, I didn't realize . . . Gita, what on earth is wrong?"

"Harish Uncle died," said Gita, not caring if tears were dripping onto and possibly staining her silk sari, not caring that her *kajal* was probably running all over her face. "Bet's asked me to move out of the apartment and I'll never find a place at this time of year. And that woman . . ."

Norvin was holding her tightly. "What woman?"

"She called me a virgin!" bawled Gita. "I was sitting on your balcony and I heard."

"Do you mean . . . ?" Norvin stopped short as he thumped her back. "Did I misunderstand something?"

"It was so . . . patronizing."

"Are you? Did you? I'm sort of confused here, honey."

"It's the label." Gita snuffled into his shoulder. "She made it seem so backward and crude and public."

"Don't mind Kamashree, she's like that with everyone." Norvin pressed his ear tighter against hers, rocking slightly from side to side. "You saw how she publicly corrected me for mispronouncing all these things."

"Yes." His arms were already helping, relaxing her limbs, easing and loosening the knot in her heart.

"Good, you've stopped," said Norvin, standing back. "Here's a tissue. We've got to serve up dinner before everyone drinks themselves into the floor. So, why don't we get married?"

"What?"

"I'm asking you to marry me. I know the bathroom's not the best setting for these things. Sorry about the timing. Come live with me. Sleep with me. Study in the spare room. Cook all the time."

Gita had begun to cry again. "I don't know if I love you," she said, wiping her lip so snot would not trickle into her mouth.

"Don't worry about *that*, honey—love is just a bourgeois invention. In Berkeley at this time of year it's easier to get married than look for an apartment. Of course, if you prefer, you can just live here and we wouldn't need to get married, but I have the feeling that you and all those nuns in your superego would be happier if we got into the wedlock stuff."

"Everyone is waiting outside for dinner," Gita said.

"I know, I know, but let's get this settled. I miss you when you're not around." Norvin held her very tightly. "Really I do. You're the song playing the strains of my midlife crisis. Isn't that what professors who turn forty are supposed to do?

Divorce their first wives and marry graduate students? We might as well submit to the scenario. So what do you say, should we take out the champagne and make an announcement?"

Gita had been raised to see marriage as a pinnacle to be scaled, a place of safe arrival. She thought of her mother at Nutty's wedding, and of Saroj Aunty stripped of jewelry. She thought of Ayah who had expected her to someday find a *jori*, of Ganeshan Kaka stating that *sala*, everything was destiny, of Norvin showing up in March. She thought of Firoze spending the night out in strange places, of Najma so cheerfully independent in her relationship, and of Ravindran, who would surely joke that some North Indians pronounced *wedding* as *bedding*. She thought of how everyone else knew about sex and she stood outside, an object of fun. She thought about the dissertation she had yet to write, the problems in applying for a fellowship yet another year, and the hassles of moving into a new apartment. All these thoughts and Gita felt out of control, floundering in a plot that was not of her making. A huge exhaustion came upon her.

Norvin felt her relaxing in his arms. "That's great," he said, giving her a kiss. "I tell you, you're going to love being married, it can really be cozy. Let's hope that your friends took the hors d'oeuvres around. Now, shall we start serving dinner?"

PART 11

❊

Quests

5
The
Ethnic Shelf

On Saturday nights, Gita hoped to attend the foreign film series at Whitney College. In the town of Whitney, Vermont, the local movie theater catered to the lowest common denominator in adolescent fantasy: action with extraterrestrials, romance with vampires, and comedy with oversized amphibians. To find more movies required an hour's drive to the nearest "city," though there was not a skyscraper in sight. Gita had no car. Each week she checked the calendar of campus film events posted on the refrigerator and tried to guess which one of the strangers she was surrounded by might possibly be coaxed into an early dinner before the film. Sometimes the film did not beckon. Often there was no company to be found. Instead, Gita roamed through the record collection that the people she was subletting from had left behind. As music filled the empty chairs, drifted over the kitchen counter, wafted upstairs over the neatly made bed, Gita underlined key passages in books she would teach the following week. When sense could no longer be squeezed from sentences even after several rereadings, she took refuge in the phone. On the West Coast it was still afternoon: someone was bound to be home, willing to extend company across the darkening continent. There were evenings when she met only rings or recorded voices. Then Gita would scour the bookshelves in search of some other reality to escape into. Though there was a television set around, it would need cable services for the flickering hiss to sharpen into recognizable shapes or voices. Cable TV reminded her of Norvin. So, the set became just another surface for piling library books she should go through: if not this weekend, the next.

Gita now washed her hair on Sunday mornings.

Saroj had woken from her nap, changed into a freshly starched cotton sari, and sat down at the polished dining table. She was equipped with her telephone book and a sandalwood letter opener with elephants lined up along one side. She started by dialing other women who might attend the next Save the Bombay Trees Association meeting. As expected, Tukaram soon brought in the afternoon mail. One hand cradling the phone, Saroj lifted her glasses and leaned down to ferret through the stack of letters. There were notices for exhibition openings on stiff handmade paper, wedding invitations with gilt edges and rotund gold Ganapatis, a messily written postcard from a servant's village (she hadn't looked carefully yet, but she could tell), and a glossy American aerogram.

"It must be Gita," Saroj said to Kalpana Vats, who happened to be at the other end of the line. "So, as I was saying, darling, if we don't all gang up now, this ridiculous municipality will just keep on widening the roads. Of course, we have these traffic jams, but the solution can't be cutting down all the trees. We Bombayites are positively *living* on the oxygen from these trees. We'd never survive the summer without their shade. And all that those trees have witnessed: they're living history from the days of the British, some even from the time there were just fishing villages. Yet all over the city, cement grows higher and the trees come down!"

"For those of us at home and all its's OK," said Kalpana, "but for children going daily on the school bus it's so bad for the health. That's why we put Varun-Tarun in boarding school. Did you read that article on pollution and children's asthma in the *Sunday Express?* Baba, even taking the dogs for their walk morning and evening—"

"The darling," Saroj muttered as she slit open the aerogram with her sandalwood opener. She was pouring good energy into the letter, hoping that it would unfold in good news. Lately each letter from Gita had brought a constriction of anxiety.

"Pardon?" asked Kalpana. "Which one do you mean? Pinky or Tommy?" These were Kalpana's Pomeranians, who lay at her feet, panting against the cool marble floor.

"I was talking about Gita, I'm opening the letter."

"Ah, U.S.A.," said Kalpana, stroking the dogs' curved foreheads. "We received photos some time back from our Ajay in New Jersey. Simply hopeless he is. Still a bachelor. For so long we have tried to arrange something. Even before he went to the U.S., when his mummy was still alive, she wanted to find a nice girl. But he said no. He said he was a student. Then he received his Ph.D. and all, and still he said no chance. Now he has got a very fine job, earning so many dollars monthly. He even has some gray hairs. But he keeps on saying nothing doing. So we are doing nothing."

"Did you ever try?" asked Saroj.

"Try? Of course, elder brother is head of family, and so Varun's daddy always is feeling the responsibility. So much worry this Ajay has caused us. The last time Ajay came down, two years back, Varun's daddy had put an ad in the *Times of India*'s matrimonial column."

"My, you must have been flooded!" Saroj said. "*Green card* holder and all that. Then too, Ajay has always been a good-looking boy. I can just imagine how *all* the girls and their parents just wanted to fall at his feet."

"Baba, let me tell you, we received over five hundred letters with photos of girls! Some were very pretty. Fair and all; beautiful really. Good families. My mother-in-law and all, if she was alive, she would have insisted on a Brahman girl. But we know Ajay has always made it a point to be a little forward-minded. We put 'caste no bar' in the paper. Even then, let me tell you, even then, the responses were from the very best families. This stupid fellow Ajay—Can you imagine?—he wouldn't even look at a *single* letter? The way he can sulk. 'I'll find my own girl,' he said. 'Baba, how old are you getting?' I asked him. 'Thirty-six? You want to grow old all by yourself? You think that's fun?' Hello, can you still hear me?"

"Hello?" Saroj said, "It must be the line." Her face had sagged, mouth drooping downward and eyes slackening from their focus. She smoothed her gray hair with the hand that was free, and stared out across the table, through the open door and toward the sea. Tukaram was sweeping in one corner of the room. Without ever rising from his squatting position, he stalked bits of dirt with his broom. He looked up warily, Adam's apple gulping above the collar of his white *kurta,* as Saroj's gaze drew in from the sea and pinned him down.

"Hello." Kalpana confirmed she was still on the other end.

"Just wait." Saroj cupped the receiver in her palm and loudly accused Tukaram for forgetting the corners. She yelled at Muktabai for putting yellow roses together with pink at the center of the table: didn't she understand anything about color? She bellowed toward the kitchen to ask what exactly Maharaj was up to if tea hadn't appeared yet. When she returned to the phone, there was a renewed vigor to her voice. "Hello? Are you still there? These servants!"

Kalpana was used to these interruptions whenever she spoke to Saroj. She didn't actually speak Marathi herself, but having married into a family that had lived in Bombay for a few decades, she could more or less follow the drift. As she waited, she had skimmed the recipe page in the latest issue of *Eve's Weekly*, "So, how is your Gita?" she now asked.

The fan whirled humid October heat away from Saroj. The blue aerogram fluttered in her hands. She took off her glasses and brought the paper up very close to her eyes. "She's quite well," said Saroj after a moment. "Overworked, of course. The way those people work out there, all this emphasis on *careers*. Not that we don't have careers over here too, but it seems to be more in perspective. And my! A press wants to publish her dissertation. Our Gita a professor *and* an author too! I tell you, the best compensation for growing old is to see babies grow up and blossom this way."

"But she is so thin," said Kalpana. "Even in that photo you have kept in the sitting room she is looking too weak. Has she put on since then? This dieting and all, absolutely cracked."

Saroj giggled. "Oh, shoo! Gita is naturally thin. It's that *mother* of hers who's preoccupied with dieting. No doubt that I, and, well, you too, darling, should think of cutting down once in a while, but life is so *short*. Whenever I went in for the hot lemon and boiled veggies, Harish said I was doing all this *tapasya* and penance for the diet deity he called the Diety. But then too, Harish . . ."

"Hello?" said Kalpana. "Hello?"

"Nothing," said Saroj. "What were you saying?"

"That Gita is too thin. With marriage at least she should have improved."

"But dar-ling, could you *blame* anyone who works so hard for being thin? Just look at all she's done these past few years. Imagine what it takes to do a dissertation. And then, going out to face whole mobs of those gigantic American students. And moving! That is the most *peripatetic* continent on the face of the earth, people just swarming all over the place. Harish used to call it peri-pathetic! Well, I suppose there's Australia, of course, the way those aborigines move around, but at least the wandering out there in Australia has some sort of *pattern*. From what I understand, it happens in groups, too, so people aren't always so lonely."

"Ajay also," said Kalpana. "We have scratched out two, three pages in the address book for him only. Anyway, *ji*, we were talking about Gita. What is the news of that professor? Norman? He has moved also?"

"His name is Norvin," Saroj said.

Kalpana waited. Saroj didn't say more. Lately she had been acting like this when Gita was mentioned. This was intriguing, for Saroj was usually willing to pour forth all the news one could want. Kalpana pondered the rushing traffic and horizon of sea stretching out beneath the flat. A group of Arab women with what looked like beaks on their faces were out on a joyride in a horse carriage, but otherwise it was the same old whizz of black-and-yellow taxis, small Maruti cars, red double-decker BEST buses. After a moment Kalpana tried again. "That Mrs. Das was so proud when she came for tea to your house that time. My son-in-law this and my son-in-law that. Oh, Baba!"

"Just *like* Kookoo," tittered Saroj. "Take any subject under the sun, and it's always her who has the indisputable best. Have you heard her on the subject of her hemorrhoids?"

"No. But that Do-Nothing Chair she was so proud about the professor occupying! Oh, Baba! And the way he was making Gita do all his research."

"Ah," said Sarojben. She rubbed her index finger along the ridged backs of the sandalwood elephants.

"So, that professor, he has moved with her?"

"For your information, he has not," said Saroj.

"Ah!" said Kalpana, unable to suppress a note of glee. "So then . . ."

Saroj sensed the jangle of phones connecting a gossip network through Bombay. She gripped the receiver tighter. "But of course you *must* know that they've been divorced for quite a while."

"Quite a while!" Kalpana repeated. "Nobody told me."

"Darr-ling!" said Saroj, lying through her dentures. "We've all been talking about it. You mean you *just* realized?"

Kalpana was silent, so silent that Saroj could hear the whizz of tires and toots of horns along Marine Drive. "Foreign marriages," Kalpana finally said. "Out there it always happens, this divorce."

"Out there? My dear, just look into our own Bombay backyard. There's our Jeroo showing some common sense at last by walking out on that chinless wonder of a Jhunjhunwala husband, no matter how rich he is. And my goodness, why go as far as Peddar Road apartments, didn't your Gangabai just run off with the company driver? Oh God, TUKARAM. You won't believe that he's emptying the dustpan through the window!"

"But *Hindu* marriages, they are sacred," said Kalpana, when the volley of Marathi abuses had ended. "Not like for these minority types, small castes, foreigners, and all. Hindus recognize the meaning of dharma. Wife must stay with husband, whether he is rich or poor, good or bad."

"Oh, don't be so *boring,* darling. Of course that's the standard line, but we don't have to swallow it. Personally, I'm all for divorce. It's wonderful when people are so *brave* as to see they have emotions, and then do something about it. I mean where would all the poets and storytellers and film directors be if everyone was caught up with being good and dutiful all the time?"

"Ummm," said Kalpana. Really, this Sarojben! Getting on in age and all, but frivolous as ever. Even as a widow, the way she continued to deck up in all sorts of named saris and jewels. If Varun's grandfather hadn't been Harish Shah's financial adviser in the old days, it was possible that Varun's daddy might not approve of Kalpana talking to a woman of these views. But Varun's daddy was off in his executive suite, and there was no way that he could know what was being said. Kalpana smiled. "So, you were saying earlier, there is this Save the Trees meeting. But I also heard that there is a

good exhibition on of Pochampalli saris. Would you like to
drop in over there afterward?"

Gita had sublet from the Davidsons, a couple on sabbatical.
It was a small white house, with delicately carved posts on
the porch by the front door, paned windows, high, creaking
stairs, and upstairs rooms in which the ceilings were all angled.
From the back windows, there was a view of fields, forests,
and rising moons. The front windows faced the road. Traffic
moved past in the mornings and evenings, as the community
drew in to its focal point, the college. Otherwise, people called
out to each other as they walked their dogs. Young children
bicycled without fear. Toward dusk, the ski team whizzed by
on roller skates with a metallic rush of wheels and a thump
of poles.

Subletting had saved Gita from having to stock up on household things: electric blenders, comforters, or bookshelves. She
loved tending the plants, though she had to be sure to clean
her fingernails when she was required to look respectable
(which, as visiting assistant professor, was most of the time).
She liked the use of the answering machine and stereo system.
The record collection, spanning baroque and the blues, was
intriguing. The Davidsons had a set of very sharp knives, and
fortunately she had brought her own pressure cooker. Gita
removed the frilly duvet from their queen-size bed and spread
out the handloom, hand-blocked, red-and-orange bedspread
Saroj Aunty had sent as a wedding present through Harish's
cousin Max. Gita took down calligraphed Christian religious
poems and stored them in the attic, putting up the Kangra
miniatures she had had framed while married to Norvin. She
spread her books on the Davidsons' shelves.

When the phone cut through silence hanging so dense in the
house, Gita's spirits would straighten, grow bright. Yet lifting
the receiver, she often found that the call was not for her at
all. Gita fielded calls for the Davidsons from students with
incompletes from last semester, from the town librarian, from

old friends who suddenly had the impulse to say hello, from colleagues in desperate quest for certain references while writing papers over the weekend. It was a pleasure to inform salespeople that the lady of the house was not at home and would not be for twelve months—sorry, good-bye—but apart from that, she often felt reduced to a shadowy presence siphoning the Davidsons' absent lives.

Not knowing anyone well had made a large windswept space around her. In conversations, she found her words gliding off: she could control what she said but not what her words said about herself. It was as though she had been stripped of all her stories. It was eerie to have no inner dimensions in other people's minds: to start afresh, with every conversation, in building up a past. She had never felt so dark in Berkeley. Colleages from other departments addressed her in emphatically enunciated sentences at faculty barbecues. With them and during office hours for her classes, she fielded questions about *The Jewel in the Crown* reruns, and the exact relationship between the Mahatma and Rajiv Gandhi. There were skiing stores and bookstores in this small town, but the closest that Gita could get to Bedekar's mixed pickles or Lijjat *papad* was beside oyster sauce, taco shells, and canned litchis on a single ethnic shelf at the health food store. Without Berkeley's World Music program, there was absolutely no hope of tuning in to a raga on the radio.

As an old and respected small liberal arts college, Whitney catered mostly to Caucasian students from wealthy families on the East Coast. Gita's first few classes left her with a blurred sense of blond hair, designer clothes, and ruddy health. Certainly, the college was trying hard to bring in financial aid students from a diversity of backgrounds, but there was a certain truth to defacement of the *n* in the Whitney sign by the main gate. No matter how often campus authorities repainted that sign, or how often the small white campus security car patrolled past, that *n* continued to be missing.

Most people who taught at Whitney College appeared to be married. There were few employment opportunities beyond the campus, and spouses who did not teach were often employed by the college too. College couples seemed to live safe and bounded lives with station wagons containing baby car seats, bags laden with groceries, and large dogs. On weekends they gardened. They got together for potlucks to discuss the shortcomings of the local school system, the (college) president's policies, drinking in the fraternities, and who, among the new faculty, might be showing signs of pairing up with whom. Everybody could recognize everyone else's car, and a favorite sport was to drive through town—with or without babies and dogs—guessing who was possibly out to dinner with whom.

Gita's teaching schedule blocked out Mondays, Wednesdays, and Fridays. This left Tuesdays, Thursdays, and weekends open for office hours, grading, preparing classes, and revising her dissertation. When she wanted to write, she hid herself in a cubicle on the top floor of the college library. Amid the musty scent, there were no phones, no knocks on the door, no reminders of a life beyond the manuscript. With her favorite ink pen, she marked in sections that needed to be changed. She filled out index cards with the latest references on the subject and wrote longhand insertions on yellow sheets that she would then go home and type into the computer. As she wrote, she found herself haunted by a certain story she had found in a collection from the Punjab in the 1880s that struck echoes in a tale Ayah had told her many years ago. Thinking of the story, she could hear the rustle of the mat that Ayah unrolled to rest on in the hot afternoons, and smell faint and musty DDT from the closet where the mat was stored.

> *A girl and her mother lived together, so poor that each day the mother had to go begging for them to eat. The mother ate a large wheat cake. She gave the daughter a small one. But as the girl grew up she was hungrier. One day, she ate her mother's larger portion. The mother was crazed: "Give me my wheat cake, give me my wheat*

cake!" she demanded, chasing her daughter. The girl fled into the forest. She took refuge in a tree above a stream. A king hunting in the forest stopped to drink water. Leaning down to fill his water pot, he saw a beautiful reflection in the water's surface for the single moment before his pot dipped in and the image rippled away. He looked up and spied the girl. He bore her off to his palace, where she became one of his queens.

After some years, the mother made her way to the palace. She was still in her crazed state, her hair matted, her body covered in dust. "Give me my wheat cake, give me my wheat cake!" she cried. The queen was now cloistered far within the palace, but her serving maid told her of this strange apparition that had arrived. All in a panic that she would be discovered and would lose the king, the palace, her position, she paid off a palace servant to kill the old woman and bring the body to her. She hid the body in a trunk in the beams of her room.

It so happened that the king's eyes rested on the trunk when he entered her apartments that evening. He demanded to see what was inside. He would not take no as an answer. All in a panic, the queen prayed to her oil lamps that she be saved. She took a deep breath, and opened the trunk. There was a priceless necklace inside. "Who gave this to you?" the king stormed. "My mother," said the queen. "Such a mother!" the king said. "And you have been hiding this from me. Let us all go, the entire court, on a visit to her palace."

The queen prayed to the oil lamps again. The court set off in the direction where the broken-down hut had once been. There was a fabulous castle in its place, with walls inlaid with jewels, rustling fountains, and satin bolsters on its beds. There were sumptuous meals and servants who served them. There was even a dignified couple who appeared to be her parents. The queen held her breath. The king was deeply impressed.

After a day or two the court set off again. The king's

barber suddenly remembered that he had left his shaving things behind. He turned around. But when he reached the place where the castle should have been there was a desolate clearing with just one withered tree. No leaves, no flowers, not even a bird. On the tree, swinging slightly in a chill breeze, was his bag. When the barber caught up with the court again, he mentioned this to the king. The queen pulled the veil further down over her face.

"How was this done?" the king demanded.

"Don't ask me or I'll die," murmured the queen.

"I must know at once," the king insisted. It was a king's prerogative, after all, to issue orders. Furthermore, he had other wives.

As the queen related the truth about herself, she grew fainter. "We lived together," she began, "and we were very poor." When she reached the end of the story, that was the end of her too.

Whenever Gita thought about love, that castle in the forest came to mind.

"Look, you were there when it was all beginning." Gita lay in bed, receiver pressed against one ear, with the lights off. The first chill of fall evenings crept in through the open window, bringing a coziness to her flannel sheets. Beside her, the glowing hands on the alarm clock indicated that it was getting on toward one o'clock. She would need many cups of coffee the next day. But it was a rare treat to have Najma linked back into the U.S. telephone system. "Why didn't you just stop me?"

Najma laughed, a long, gurgling laugh. Gita grinned into the darkness, though she wasn't quite sure yet what the joke could be. "Stop you! My God, who could have? Battle against the force of years of pent-up hormones?"

"I mean, stop me from getting *married*. There are such

things as affairs that don't involve recentering your whole
life."

"True," said Najma, "but were you ready to hear that?"

"Probably not," admitted Gita.

"So OK, what's happened has happened, it's all in the past
now. Experience. Don't let that mother of yours get you down
with all that nonsense about girls from Good Families. Any
sexy prospects on the scene out there?"

"Zero." Gita twisted at the curves in the telephone cord.
She couldn't help remembering that Najma was telephoning
her from Noah's house. He was probably in the lab but would
be home for dinner. It wasn't envy that Gita felt but an inner
evasiveness: she didn't want her mind to settle on what it was
like to press against someone in a broad and comfortable bed.
Najma and Noah were still claiming it was an unresolved
relationship, no possession on either side. Najma had always
wanted to work in India, but there were no jobs there in the
sort of chemistry that Noah did. After graduation, Najma had
actually taken Noah with her to India, and while her grandmother was no longer alive to scream at the dark apparition,
Najma's parents had immediately recognized his sterling vir-
tues. They offered to pay for a big wedding, but Najma had
vetoed the idea. Since then, Najma had moved back to Calcutta, where she lived with her parents, married brother's family, two maiden great-aunts, and one neighbor who had come
to dinner thirty years ago and had stayed on, sleeping in his
bed under the stairs. She was out all day and for weeks at a
time as a feminist activist. Yet despite the distance and the
passing years, she and Noah had somehow remained fixed
stars on each other's shifting horizons. At least once a year,
he sent a ticket. Najma explained that though she was for
economic equality in principle, imbalances in the world economy absolved her of guilt in accepting a dollar-bought ticket:
depending on her rupee income would make the foreign travel
connecting them as a couple impossible.

"Zero men! What's this, Gita? In a college with at least a
thousand students, maybe about six hundred men, and then

maybe sixty or so male faculty . . . you just can't be looking *hard* enough."

"Anyway, I tell you, why push things if they're not happening?" After a few meaningless dead ends after Norvin, Gita had come to believe that if things weren't clearly propitious there was no point hazarding any sort of entanglement.

"Not happening! You're in this ideal position to comb through the new crop of men, the long-awaited sons of feminists. Didn't Betty Friedan have any sons? Gloria Steinem? Too bad old Simone and Jean-Paul never got into reproductive mode, or there might be some fabulous Frenchman on the scene. Sons of feminists will be pretrained as supportive. There won't be all this show of being house husbands who are actually terribly interested but sorry, just now with the need to understand the American psyche through popular culture and that fabulous show on television . . ."

Gita giggled. "You saw him do it? He would even get out his chef's apron and wield a knife a little."

"I most distinctly remember trying to distract Noah so he wouldn't get any bad ideas about mixing football or 'L. A. Law' with the food! Anyway, as I was saying, keep an eye on those students. Or should they be renamed *stud*-ents, these sons of feminists who are marching toward Professor Das for inspection. We've all heard rumors of the teenage male sexual peak . . ."

"But they're so young!" Gita wailed. "And confused. You're outrageous, Najma!"

"We'll rename the entire educational system. '*Stud*-ents and *fuck*-ulty engaged in intellectual *intercourse* on the *come-puss*.' "

"Attending cull-*asses* and *semen*-hours," put in Gita. Both women laughed. This had all been part of a joke making the rounds at Berkeley years ago, in which Professor Ratnabhush-italingam-Hernandez had supposedly delivered a lecture on "The Cunning Linguist and Higher Education." At the time Gita had felt uneasy whenever the joke was told. She would make a point of turning the conversation toward the fact that she'd never actually been Norvin's student. Firoze too, if she remembered correctly, had never seemed to find this particularly funny.

"By the way, Noah heard from Firoze a couple of months ago," Najma said, perhaps whipping along the same trail of associations. "I tell you, I have to mend my ways and start writing letters or I'll lose track of everyone. Have you ever thought of all the people you swore undying friendship with at some time or another and how few you continue to even know? Chilling! Anyway, I rang up Firoze when I got here. He spent that year in India, you know. Now he's all done with law school and has a job in New York working in immigration law."

"Immigration law," said Gita. "Good God, don't tell me he's actually helping people be inculcated into the American capitalist system! All that carrying on about the Third World and the need for political engagement. What a *maha*-phony—this is just like Norvin and his housekeeping."

"No, *yaar,* you got it wrong," began Najma, but Gita was not interested.

"Speaking of people who're actually doing something in India, you haven't told me how things are going for you."

Though her eyes were beginning to prickle with sleep, she listened contentedly as Najma described how they had set up crèches and cooperatives in the Calcutta slums. "The old issue," Najma said, "giving women a decent chance to earn. Believe me, Indian women are hardly unaware of their own oppression. You should listen to a few of the folk songs or stories. It's just that the social system is so based on dependence, many women don't have the clout to do a damn thing about it."

Firoze and Ravindran were out for an evening walk in Lodi gardens, taking turns to wheel a pram in which Ravindran's small daughter, Meenakshi, had lolled off to sleep. Firoze was visiting Delhi for a symposium on human rights, and Ravindran taught computer science at the Indian Institute of Technology. The October evening had brought a splash of coolness to the shadows of the trees and the interiors of the old stone tombs, ayahs gossiped as children played and couples sat entwined, galaxies unto themselves. A few dusty men lay flung out, elbows over eyes, fast asleep in the grass. Passing Firoze and Ravindran from behind, or coming toward them, was a constant stream of joggers, sprinters, and serious, panting walkers. Some wore coordinated track suits and had on stereo headphones.

A middle-aged woman with pancake makeup slightly askew with sweat was bustling along with her elbows jutting rhythmically. Her bulky running shoes seemed quite out of place with a flimsy chiffon sari. Her hair, piled up in a bouffant, seemed unnaturally black. On nearing, a trace of white along the central parting gave the bottled source of the black away. As she walked, the woman inclined her head or called out greetings to certain people—an elderly Sikh gentleman with bristling mustaches and a Doberman, a stout young woman in a fashionable outfit and glasses—but she looked through most of the other people she passed.

"Take a good look at that dame," said Ravindran as she bore along toward them, and they stepped aside with the pram. She walked by as though they were simply not there, not even a flicker of the eyes acknowledging their existence in three-dimensional space.

"Why? Who is she?" asked Firoze.

"Remember Gita from Berkeley? That's her mom." Both men now looked after the retreating figure of Kookoo Das, her elbows pumping as though in an aerobic version of *bhangra* or break dance.

"How do you know?"

"Gita invited me to dinner last time she was here. I have survived an entire evening with this dreadful woman, her mom. She let me know that Dravidians like me are of inferior racial stock—not quite Aryan enough, you see. Then too, when I spoke, you could see her cringing because I don't have the correct British-style accent. Gita looked miserable. You could tell she wished she hadn't asked me to come. The father or stepfather or whoever he is was a real club wala, a back-slapping old chap. Anyway, I pass Mrs. Das whenever I come here to walk with Minni, and the bloody dame simply does not care to remember we've met. After a while I stopped saying hello."

"Poor Gita," said Firoze, looking after Kookoo Das once again, but she had turned the bend. "No wonder she was always so mysterious about her parents. By the way, I heard from Najma that she and that professor character broke up."

"Heck, *yaar*, that was doomed from the start," said Ravindran. He began to laugh. "Remember the evening that the Empress of Unintelligibility was there and he brought out champagne, hushed the room, and demanded that we all toast his and Gita's matrimonial future?"

"Gita was looking awful that night," said Firoze. "Meek and weepy, with those clouds of smudged *kajal* under her eyes. Hardly the radiant fiancée. Seemed embarrassed as hell when we tried to congratulate her afterward."

"But who wouldn't have been uptight, *yaar*, with that post-post female raising her champagne glass and giving that little lecture on how refreshing it was to see people who still believed marriage was a viable concept in the posthumanist age of multiple and ambivalent subjectivities. *Hajaar* sarcy, I thought."

"Sarcastic? Ironic maybe. But if I remember correctly, Professor, umm, Kamashree made some good points about the gap between the signifier and signified in the words *husband* and *wife*. Didn't she advise that they be *spouse* and *spouse*? I thought that maybe she was trying to help out Gita, give her some warnings about not being Norvin's chattel."

"Come on, *yaar*, don't give her such lofty intentions. She was making fun of everyone."

Firoze was silent. He took over the wheeling of Minni. After a while he said, "Well, to tell the truth, I've always liked Gita and all, but it *was* sort of a farcical situation. That Norvin was a cartoon! Did he ever go on to you about his Parsi ancestry? Heck, cartoons are good for casual observation, but living with them can't be funny."

"Do you know why they divorced?"

"Like you said, it was doomed. We could all see it was just a matter of time before Gita became too smart for him. That girl, I mean woman, she had her hang-ups and all, but I tell you, she is smart as a whip. That funny way she would look at you sometimes—you could sense a whole lot more was going on under that ultrameek exterior."

Minni had woken up and was crying. Ravindran picked her up and began to fidget awkwardly in the bag over his shoulder. Then he handed Minni over to Firoze and set the bag down to unzip it for a full-scale search for a bottle. Both men climbed up a grassy hillock near one of the tombs of the Lodi kings. A bullock pulling a lawn mower was being guided back and forth by a scrawny boy in pants like a divided skirt and a shirt without buttons. Firoze sheltered Minni against his *kurta,* thumping her back, clicking his fingers, and pointing at the hump of the bullock.

"Gorgeous baby," said Firoze. Minni had a golden sheen to her dark skin and masses of tight black curls. When the bottle emerged, he took charge of it, smiling down at the contented smacks and snuffles. Over the last few years, with everyone he knew having babies, he had become an experienced honorary uncle. "What a girl!"

"Of course, her mom would have wanted us to heat up the bottle and all," said Ravindran. "Anyway, we were talking about Gita. So what happened with that guy?"

"I don't really know why it came to a head," said Firoze.

"A head?" Ravindran raised his brows. Both men laughed, Minni, lying in Firoze's arms, looked up at him with bright interest.

"If it was one of them having an affair though, sex would only be the symptom." Firoze was suddenly self-conscious under the baby's gaze. What might she absorb now that would come out on some Delhi psychoanalyst's couch years later, facing modern Indian art and a box of discreetly placed Klee-nex? "Anyway, it's surely better for Gita. She's apparently got this great job out on the East Coast at some small liberal arts college. I hear about her now and then through Najma."

"Najma, our great connector," Ravindran said. "She makes it to Delhi once in a while. Hey, take a look, man, that bullock is having a good munch on the grass it just mowed."

"What an alternative for American suburbia," said Firoze, watching the bullock's jaw rotate. "No engine spewing fumes, and immediate recycling too! Really, there should be neighbor-hood associations that own bullocks, with everyone signing for a time slot when they want their lawns mowed."

"Don't be funny," said Ravindran. "In the U.S.? First of all, where are there communities like this, and second, what is the poor *bel* going to eat all week while everyone expects him to be a glutton on the weekend? For just a little mowing you'd have to change the whole bloody capitalist system around. Anyway, tell, what about you? No mention from you about any dames."

"No, *yaar,* no time," said Firoze. "Being at the crossroads of all these cultures it becomes harder and harder to find any-one who remotely understands. I don't think I'm cut out for this relationship business." Thinking that Minni was the first female he had held in his arms for many months made him hand her back at once to her father.

At first, Gita had thought she was happy. She had smiled when Norvin brought the best of Derrida, Foucault, and Lacan to bear on the telegrams they received from India. Mostly it was Standard Greeting Phrases, as found on the board of every post office, and in the introductory section of telephone direc-tories: Telegram number 16, "May Heaven's Choicest Bless-ings Be Showered on the Young Couple," and number 17, "Wish You Both a Happy and Prosperous Wedded Life." Yet in three cases, there appeared to have been a bad connection somewhere along the line, Ganeshan Kaka sent number 19,

"Sincere Greetings for the Republic Day, Long Live the Republic," although it was nowhere near January 26. Informed by the triumphant Kookoo Das, the sisters from Our Lady of Perpetual Succour dispatched number 32, "Wish You a Speedy Recovery." H. H. Pindapur had recently entered politics, so Gita was never sure whether there was a mixup on the phone or whether his aides had just sent out their most-used message: number 24, "Best Wishes for Your Success in the Election." In any event, Norvin was ecstatic. He displayed the telegrams at every dinner party for the next few months, and even took them into his lecture course to illustrate some point or the other about simulacra and semiotics. Furthermore, he had picked up Ayah's "May God bless you too, Baby." and would interject this as a stunning non sequitur at cocktail parties and faculty meetings.

They had been married at the city hall on Norvin's fortieth birthday, at 3:34 in the afternoon, the very moment that he had been born. ("Thank God he wasn't born at that hour of the morning," Najma had murmured, eyes dancing.) "This is what I call commemorating a midlife crisis in style," Norvin announced to all guests who came to the reception afterward. The meal had been catered by Tastes of the Taj—one of the many restaurants that had sprung up on the Indianized blocks of University Avenue. Norvin had squeezed into the raw silk Nehru jacket he had had stitched in Bombay many years ago. Najma drove into San Francisco to visit a Hindu temple, where she miraculously found a thick strand of jasmine for Gita's hair. In the posed wedding pictures that were to adorn Saroj Aunty's bedside table and Kookoo Das's sitting room, Norvin and Gita looked very much an acceptable bride and groom. Standing behind her, just a fraction taller than she, frizzy graying hair freshly cut, Norvin was plainly distinguished. With red and white dots arching over her eyebrows, wearing a Banarasi sari the reddest of reds (also from University Avenue), Gita might as well have been married in India. She was immensely relieved that the wedding had been planned too suddenly for Kookoo either to co-opt it or attend.

But the guilt of enjoying Kookoo's absence made her send an entire album of glossy color prints off to Delhi.

Gita's relationship with her mother had never been so good. The only criticism Kookoo voiced was that Gita hadn't labeled the Important Professors in each photograph she sent, especially the one who had received a Nobel Prize. Kookoo fluttered over the phone with Norvin and requested signed copies of all his publications, which she insisted she would read: "One only gets *one* son-in-law, after all!" Gita wondered what Kookoo made of the deconstructionist lingo. Dilip muttered a lot of "Jolly good"s. Vicky was made to be a good boy and speak on the phone, though he was clearly speechless with embarrassment. At the earliest moment that Kookoo could leave Vicky in safe hands, she descended in person to Berkeley to gloat over the man, the house, and the life that dear little Gita had finally had the good sense to procure for herself.

Gita had a paper due the day after Kookoo arrived. Though she had been trying to get it written in advance, preparing the house for her mother's arrival hadn't been easy. She knew all too well that Kookoo liked to inspect medicine cabinets when she went off to powder her nose in other people's houses and that, given a chance, she would peek into their drawers, closets, and diaries too. So first there was the issue of scouring the house to free it of all traces of Rachel: hiding the photographs, throwing out the tins of Diet De-lite, packing parcels of clothes and swimsuits for Norvin to send off by U.P.S. Gita got so involved in accomplishing this project that she even forgot her misgivings about Rachel. When Norvin refused to discuss details about the mailing directly with Rachel, Gita rang her up herself. She was astounded by Rachel's voice: very round and motherly, with bits of laughter and asides to "Sweetheart" about the next step in the Middle Eastern recipe they were cooking in the background. Rachel was nothing but cordial. Gita's observation that Rachel sounded nice caused Norvin to retreat, scowling, to the television screen on which boxing finals were being played. He was apparently doing research for a freshman-initiative class on sports and psyche. Gita sifted through the house and assembled Rachel's packages by herself, trying to keep down the panic that was spreading through her chest and up her throat. Ten days away and she hadn't even started to compile a set of references for her paper.

Then there was the issue of hiding the diaphragm and gel. After all, Kookoo would have the house to herself for happy excavations all day long while Norvin and Gita were on campus. The bathroom shelves behind the mirror seemed to shout the presence of contraceptives as much as the bedside drawer. Gita found an old cigar box in the basement. (Rachel believed that smoking cigars was an important contribution to the deconstruction of gender through parody and pastiche.) The box had a false bottom. After filling the top with sewing thread and secreting the box behind old shoes on the lowest shelf of the bathroom closet, Gita at last felt more secure.

"What's going on?" asked Norvin one night when Gita leapt out of his warm arms to ferret about for the cigar box.

"My mother's coming," said Gita, arranging her hair around her so that standing up with the lights on she could be modest. The one problem with Norvin unloosening her hair as soon as they got to bed was that, these days, she had to wash it almost every morning. That took up at least a precious hour of time. Since Norvin's house was out of walking range, she also had to be ready to catch a ride with him if she had classes. Once upon a time, mornings had brought her the best concentration.

"So you're hiding this stuff? Don't tell me your mother still expects you to be a virgin!" Norvin arched his hairy chest back against the pillows and laughed aloud. Gita noted with distress that the signal that they weren't just going to sleep and yes, Materials Were Required, was receding with every spasm of laughter. She was so endlessly curious about experiences in this department that she regretted losing any chance for further explorations.

Once they had been formally "engaged" by the announcement at the dinner party, the inner slogans regulating slow traffic had faded in Gita's head. She was ready to indulge her curiosity, erasing the black rectangles that had been stamped over tabooed areas by mutual consent. But it had been Norvin who insisted on restraint. "How many men in the Eurocentric regions of the twentieth century can say they waited until *after* marriage?" he asked. "This is a chance to historicize subjectivity."

When they were properly married and in his futon bed with all interdictions lifted, Norvin poised above Gita and then went limp. He accused her of staring, "People usually close their eyes," he objected. Gita shut her eyes. They kissed and groped some more, but by then the champagne was catching up with Norvin and he slumped over to sleep, Gita lay in his arms, enjoying the warmth, the way he was matted all over with hair, and the regular rhythm of his breath. She did feel a little let down, but the sheer comfort of sleeping in an embrace extended such well-being that she felt safe, amused, ready to wait.

The next morning Norvin had an eight o'clock appointment with a dean on campus, so it wasn't until the afternoon that they could finally return to the interrupted project. Gita lay as if on a gynecologist's table, eyes squeezed tight and every sense tingling with curiosity. What was IT like? Their lips were kneading, but her attention was trained elsewhere. What was he doing now? She was dying to peek. Was that a hand? Why there? What would happen next?

"Relax!" said Norvin. "It could give my penis bad vibes." Then, gritting his teeth and vanishing into his own interior space, he set out to complete what he had begun. Gita lay very still, trying to decide what she thought of all this clumsy motion.

Not that Norvin didn't have Technique, and he was courteous about giving pleasure as much as he received it. Not that she didn't learn more herself after studying a copy of *Our Bodies, Ourselves* that Najma had given her long ago but that, until now, she had never closely examined because of the disconcerting pictures. Yet even as she became better acquainted with the topography of her body and his too, she remained something of a fascinated onlooker.

"What would the good Sisters say if such contraband of sin was found in your possession?" Norvin was still laughing.

"It's not funny," said Gita, putting her nightgown back on and taking off for a session of reading at the kitchen table. "You don't understand about my mother."

Indeed, he did not. Driving from the airport with Kookoo beside him in the front seat, Gita could already see an alliance forming. Kookoo's lipstick was smudged at one side, but apart from that no one would have guessed that she had flown for twenty-six hours straight. Every fold in her nylon sari was immaculate, and she had the expectant manner of a bathed and scented hostess beginning an evening of sociability. Koo- koo held forth on the dear little Punjabi lady sitting beside her until Frankfurt. Flying for the first time, she hadn't known how to buckle her belt and actually thought that on ascending into the sky they would all shrink to the bug size of planes viewed from the earth: "Our Indian villagers, you know, such children." Norvin swapped the tale of how in Maharashtra the man he bought vegetables from had calculated that if it was twelve hours to the shrine at Shirdi, then America must be double the distance and somewhere near Bombay. "He just couldn't catch the concept of a plane traveling so much faster than a bullock cart." Norvin laughed. Gita could have added the story of how, flying once from Bangalore to Bombay, a withered matriarch with a huge gold nose ring in each nostril had relinquished her carry-on bag to the baggage X ray at security and then, with consummate dignity, had proceeded to crawl in after it. But Norvin and Kookoo were chatting furi- ously in the front. Gita could not break in. She contemplated people in other cars and worried about turning in her paper one day late.

A table had been booked for them in a restaurant known for the Zen art of California cuisine. "But doesn't our little Gita cook for you?" asked Kookoo, adjusting her sari and looking around at the other tables.

"Splendidly, splendidly," said Norvin, with a smile that displayed even his wisdom teeth. He leaned over to pat Gita on the shoulder with such enthusiasm that the waiter pouring wine stepped back. "Gita is superb in the kitchen. I'm sure she must have picked some of this talent up from you."

"Oh yes." Kookoo smiled brightly back, though because of the smeared lipstick one side of her mouth seemed to be grimacing. "I love to whip up this and that."

"Cheers!" Norvin bumped at Kookoo's wineglass. "I love to cook too."

Gita stared. In all her life, she had never seen Kookoo even step into the kitchen. As for Norvin, since the night of the first hot tub experience, he had not cooked anything single-handedly. Admittedly, he was willing to help if asked and was very good at rinsing and stacking dishes in the dishwasher. Yet there was no doubt that he preferred someone else to take charge so he could keep an eye on the television.

"You must cook together sometime." Gita found the words rising to her lips even though she could not remember having agreed to say them aloud.

"You would have to guide me," Norvin said to Kookoo, but Kookoo had turned a sharp and disapproving eye on her daughter.

"Gita, you are surely aware that Professor Weinstein has better things to do with his time than cooking!"

For some reason, Norvin thought that she meant to be funny. "Fabulous, fabulous!" He began to laugh. "The hegemony of mental production in the corporate structure of the university. It's *texts* we produce for consumption, of course, and these aren't for every sort of palate. Kookoo, you're terrific."

It took Norvin an entire week to sense that something might not be quite right. By this time, Gita had somehow managed to finish the paper, though she feared the comments she might get back on it. She had also achieved the hurdle of getting a few meals to the table, though luckily Kookoo was so transfixed by Berkeley's restaurants that she was always willing to go out along with a running commentary on the appearance of the dear little waitresses, what people at the surrounding tables were eating, and any fragments of conversations she managed to overhear.

"Why are you like this around your mother?" Norvin asked as he and Gita drove down to campus together one morning.

"Like what?" asked Gita wearily. It had begun to drizzle through gray light outside, and she realized she had forgotten her umbrella.

"It's like you're sulking or something. You hardly say a word."

"She doesn't give me a chance."

"Nonsense, sweetie, you've got to let go of these adolescent attitudes. She's told me she's proud of you, she identifies with your getting a Ph.D. What an amazing woman! I was blown away by her story about getting a full scholarship to Radcliffe but being held back by the relatives. This is something Rachel should have heard if she thinks discrimination against women's education was bad in her day. Then too, the other night while you were working and we chatted over some Kahlua, Kookoo got sort of carried away. She actually began to cry as she told me what it was like for her as a young widow. Quarantined in the house, wearing white. Can't you appreciate the courage it took for her to remarry and give you a home? And to a man from a wrong caste?"

Gita stonily looked out the window. Not much of a home! she wanted to say. But she stayed silent. All her life she had felt as though Kookoo was a center of gravity, pulling everything away from Gita and toward herself. With Kookoo on this prolonged stay, Gita felt as though she had no space of her own to take stock. She seemed to be losing the power of speech. In her mother's presence she rarely smiled: it would be giving too much in the battle over possession of her soul.

"Quit sulking, OK?" Norvin reached over and tried to take her hand. Gita did not twitch. Things were like this in bed too these days. There was a traffic light up ahead, and after a moment Norvin had to withdraw his hand for the stick shift.

Kookoo, on the other hand, felt that Gita did not sufficiently appreciate Norvin. "You're just too young," she announced one afternoon. Norvin was off at a dissertation defense, and Gita was unloading the dishwasher. Kookoo sat at the kitchen table with a shawl pulled tight around her, elbows resting on mail-order catalogs.

"He's given you everything," said Kookoo. "A green card, a lovely house, a washer and dryer. I don't mind if you want to study a little now and then, but the way you're always rushing off with your books just isn't right for a wife."

Gita silently piled silver knives, forks, and spoons into their respective compartments.

"He's already told me how much he wants children but how he's willing to wait until you finish up your Ph.D. Look how selfless he is. Do you think most men have this sort of consideration? Do most men take their wives out to dinner all the time? I didn't even go to college because of you. If you had any respect for him you would give him what he wants as a way of expressing your gratitude. Not many men of our age would even think of *noticing* a little thing like you, let alone giving her so much security."

"Our age" had become the new social formation in the household since Kookoo had discovered that she was less than five years older than Norvin. Gita began to stack plates with a clatter. Her heart was thumping in her throat and her fingers were quivering. One of the stoneware plates slipped from her grasp and smashed against the brick-colored kitchen floor. Bending, Gita noticed grimy spots: the floor needed swabbing again. Why had Norvin fired that woman who had done the cleaning when he was carrying on a commuting marriage with Rachel?

"You even break his things," observed Kookoo. She turned away to flip through a catalog. "If only Mother Superior could talk to you," she said.

The combination of guilt toward Norvin and sheer relief to be alone with him again had brewed potent emotion when Kookoo finally left. Gita found herself watching Norvin across the room as he read a journal, immensely grateful for the way his jeaned legs crossed at the ankle and the lamp glinted on his glasses. They caught each other's eyes at public gatherings and, on passing, briefly and circumspectly held hands. She turned to him generously in bed. In retrospect, she could never remember whether he had actually stopped talking about his Parsi connections at this time, or whether she had simply stopped noticing. During these months, Gita's poems won a campus award and two were published in a literary magazine. An article on how early British collectors of Indian folklore deleted all references to social change so as to preserve an "authentic" India had been accepted by a journal. She was studying for her orals outside the framework of classes, enjoying the ways in which pieces of knowledge fit together. The spring had blown with sweet scents, and sunsets had bloomed high and red.

Norvin had started new research on Japanese avant-garde drama. Now that his book on American images of India was safely under contract with a university press, his new dinner-party line was, "India is over: it's sad but true that academic interests are built into socioeconomic trends. Just take a look at the *Asian Studies Newsletter* and you'll see that all the jobs these days are for China and Japan." When Gita looked discomfited, he would add, "Of course, Gita's research takes the colonial discourse bandwagon, not to mention engaging the subalterns, who are really hot these days."

That summer, Norvin set off for Japan, while Gita took up a fellowship to do research at the India Office Library in London. Both Saroj Aunty and Kookoo had campaigned for a visit in India, but since Norvin was also scheduled for a series of distinguished lectures in Singapore, Melbourne, and Nairobi, he really did not have the time. Gita longed to see Saroj Aunty, detecting a blowing emptiness in her letters. But she just could not face another bout with Kookoo carrying on about how she could possibly have left Norvin to iron his own shirts on the mornings of his public presentations.

Language had been a major problem for Norvin in his new research. Japanese was not among his twelve languages, and he did not have the patience to slow down the accumulation of articles on his vitae by taking intensive Japanese classes. Instead, he hired a Japanese graduate student to accompany him as translator and research assistant. Gita hadn't paid much attention to his arrangements before she left; she was preoccupied enough with organizing her own work. In London she worked late into each night, and often wished that Norvin would send real letters instead of Fujicolor postcards.

She did not have to be told anything on her return. She heard Norvin insert Japanese terms into his conversation and listened to his new theory that the custom of bowing was related to swaying in synagogues. He was wearing a Kyoto workman's denim jacket and had taken to waving a plastic cigarette with a deceptively real glow at its end, through which one could suck peppermint flavor. In the refrigerator there were leftovers from a sushi party that Ryoko, the graduate student, had just orchestrated. (Yet sushi being perishable, Gita felt obliged to throw everything out.) At a Drama Department reception, she observed Norvin drawn to where Ryoko stood, abruptly bobbing to the twists of conversation. Ryoko was tiny, pretty as a white-faced china doll, with sorority-girl pastel sweaters, pleated wool skirts, and unexpectedly thick ankles. It wasn't jealousy that Gita felt so much as the sense that the ground was speeding away from under her and she just might have to vomit.

Gita had a job as a teaching assistant that semester, and Norvin was at last teaching the sports and psyche class that he had been planning for years. Between class preparation (which for Norvin included late-night viewings of games he had taped) and both trying to write, it was easy to avoid each other. Finally, Gita couldn't stand the ambiguity.

She broke into the silence over dinner one evening. "Is it this marriage?" she blurted.

"It's not that I'm not fond of you," said Norvin, looking not at her but at his own reflection in the French windows.

Gita didn't want to ask, "But love?" since Norvin always

dismissed this as a bourgeois word. Instead she said, "I could get a place of my own. I'm earning enough now, and anyway, I'll soon be on the job market."

"I know you can look after yourself," Norvin said. He tried to smile at her, but the muscles wouldn't quite cooperate. His face was very sad. "I guess I should talk to my therapist. But I do want to tell you that I know that being monogamous means a lot to you; it's not that I've been unfaithful."

"Thank you," said Gita. She looked at her hands, placed neatly in her lap. Unsaid sentences jostled with unshed tears, and after a while she stood up to do the dishes.

The apartment that Gita moved into was so small that the bed swung out of the closet with a crash of springs. There had been no property jointly owned, but Norvin let her take a few dishes, sheets, and towels. She worked very hard on completing her dissertation, and tried to avoid the routes that Norvin walked across campus. During the day she knew with certainty that it was a good thing that they had parted, whether or not her leaving precipitated him into recognizing that he was obsessed by Ryoko. There had been so many ways in which that marriage had made her tight and resentful. She could think of a thousand reasons why she was much better off alone. Yet in bed, she found herself straining to adjust around the absence of his body. She still slept way over on the right side of the mattress and had to force herself toward the middle to take up more space for herself. He had been so warm, matted all over like an exotic blanket. And quiet. He slept peacefully, hardly moving, reaching for her if she turned away. Sometimes, remembering Norvin's cuminlike smell, Gita would feel that her fates had gone sour, curdling into disparate fragments of sorrow.

"*Sala* third-class rascal!" said Ganeshan Kaka, gnashing his false teeth so they wobbled back and forth in his mouth. He slapped down seven lines of cards onto the ivory-inlaid coffee table. "Doing all this nonsense with our Gita?!"

Saroj took her time to deal her own cards for their game of double solitaire. Seeing Ganeshan Kaka in an agitated state always sent a smile creeping over her face, no matter how hard she tried to suppress it. An immaculate white *kurta* hung loose around Ganeshan Kaka's shrunken frame, and his eyes, lidded like a young sparrow's, were intense with indignation.

"Bloody B.C., M.C.: all that he is, I don't mind saying it! Come on, girl, that ace is simply lying vacant. Are you playing or what? If that dirty scoundrel comes to India I will personally go to meet with him. To the airport itself I will go."

B.C., M.C.: *bahen chut, mata chut.* So Norvin's sisters and mother were getting it too! The image of Ganeshan Kaka, five foot one and ninety-seven pounds, waiting to accost Norvin in the sweaty crush outside Bombay Customs, tickled too vigorously at Saroj's stomach. She could no longer keep the giggles from sputtering out as she maneuvered a succession of spades to the space between her and Ganeshan Kaka. "Tukaram!" she cried. *"Kakala naryal pani nahi dila kay?"*

"That and all is yokay," said Ganeshan Kaka, holding up a palm in a gesture reminiscent of his elephant-headed namesake. "Coconut water and all I don't require. Just you pay some attention to these cards, please. These days you are too distracted only, getting out of practice without Harishbhai to play with."

Saroj stopped giggling at once. She moved a few more cards and then rubbed a finger over one among the many empty spaces in the inlay work on the table. "By the way, Kaka, do you have any idea where to get these things repaired? Of course, I wouldn't expect *ivory*, what with what's happening to our elephants. But at least *some* sort of white filling so this table doesn't gape at us like some old crone."

"Yim-possible," said Ganeshan Kaka. "That sort of old work is no longer done." He wheezed, peering down at his cards through his bifocals. "Baba, forget all this inlay and all. Go in for Formica. Everything in this country is going down, all the crafts and all: produced for tourists. Whole the world is downgrading. Nothing in our India is the same as before. Now hurry up, girl, pay attention to the game."

"Drink up your *naryal pani,*" said Saroj, lifting the frosted glass off the tray that Tukaram now proffered. "Don't refuse it. It's good for you, Kaka. The way you're losing weight it seems like you'll just shrink to a point!"

"Heavy breathing," said Ganeshan Kaka dolefully. "Whole the time I am having this heavy breathing. *Sala,* this is age: what else? Seventy-seven years! Then too, with all this Mars passing through the world . . . My nephew Ramamurthy is forever asking me to come again to the U.S. for further check-ups. But I tell you, that place is hell."

"Hell?"

"Hell. *Sala patal* it is on the other side of the world. The main thing, I tell you, is: over there, does anyone know his neighbor? No! Bloody three months your Kaki and I were there. Not once did we talk to the neighbor. We get down, we go to car; next-door *wala* does the same. But he doesn't say anything so we also continue quietly. But, Baba, how long can you continue like this? After some time I started to wave, "Hi!" Just like that, just like an American: "Hi-ee!" But those neighbors, they mumbled something and carried on as if I was from outer space. They weren't Indians, I tell you that. Here in Juhu-Parle and all, look at all the going and coming between houses. Whole the time we are receiving some dish that a neighbor has prepared, or someone or the other is dropping in for predictions. Out there it is bloody hell, everyone in his own box. This proceeding alone is not human, I tell you."

"You're right," said Saroj in a subdued voice.

Kaka gave Saroj a sharp look. "Anyhow, how you are keeping, girl?" His voice, which had been squeaking with indignation, grew low and kind. "Putting on or what?"

"A little." Saroj pulled her sari over her shoulder to cover the bulge of flesh where her blouse ended.

"Due to the influence of Jupiter," said Ganeshan Kaka. "By sixty-six years, seven months, and three days that cycle will be ending. Be careful about indulgence, girl. Don't just eat for entertainment purposes."

"Anyway, tell me something about Gita," said Saroj. "Poor thing, out there working herself to the bone. Is there any romance on the horizon?"

"Paper," said Ganeshan Kaka. "Where is that bloody bugger Tukaram? Paper *aan!* Pen I have got already in my pocket." He sat and began calculations. Date of birth, date of question, time of question. A star, with numbers dancing around it, took shape on the piece of paper.

"Definitely! She will get a very good boy! Within five months, eighteen days, and seven hours, I predict it. *Sala*, why did nobody ask me about that bloody bugger American? With his name and birthdate I could have seen so many things."

"You once told me that sometimes people just have to live through things to find out about them," Saroj said. She didn't want to remind Kaka that when Harish was first ill, Kaka had assured them that he would pukka-positively recover.

Firoze Ganjifrockwala

Why is it that some of us go back to live in India and some of us stay on in the U.S.? I'm sitting in the Frankfurt airport in a haze of exhaustion and displacement, my carry-on bag tucked between my ankles. What the hell am I doing returning to New York? The question hasn't stopped bugging me ever since I turned away from my parents and went into security at Bombay's Sahar airport. As we embraced, I noticed how tired my father looks, his skin hanging so loosely on his face that his eyes seem bloodshot and huge. And my mother seems to have shrunk, her head bent forward, shoulders hunched. One arm was still in a cast from when she slipped at the end of the monsoon. But with the other arm she held me tightly, whispering blessings in my ear.

There is a constant stream of people in this airport, rivulets from many sources coming together to flow out in new combinations through different gates. There are Arab gentlemen gliding along in long white robes, immaculate Swiss couples speaking to each other in brisk, flat tones, several African children clambering over their sleeping mother, two women who looked like they might be of Indian origin (Ugandan? Canadian?) and both in pantsuits with artificial pearls, bent toward each other in conversation. An Indonesian delegation of short men in batik shirts has just gone by; a troop of healthy-looking hostesses, perhaps German, wheel their suitcases past; and some American college kids with backpacks arrive with raised chins to study the schedule. With a patter of shutters, the flight arrivals and departures are switched on the board overhead. What am I doing in this place? If I had

not got on the plane, it would now be time for an afternoon
nap, the fan in my room rattling.

There was this prof chap I once landed up in a seminar
with in those days when I was wandering across departments
at Berkeley. He'd been a campus hero from the faculty side
during the sixties, but now he seemed sort of tired. Pale, lined
face, gravelly voice, faded jeans jacket—I can still picture him
exactly. He used to say that there are two kinds of social
theorists: those who view life as spectacle, and those who see
it as predicament. I understood at once that Marxist scholars
clearly belong in the second camp, and actually, most feminists
do too. You look at things and see their imperfection, and
then you try to figure out a way it could all be changed. What
was intriguing about this fellow was that from his writings it
was clear that he saw us all as landed in a bloody horrible
predicament: capitalism, racism, sexism, nuclear arms, envi-
ronmental crisis, all the rest of it. But then if you went to see
him in office hours or anything, he would hold forth with
funny stories, spectacles of the first order. Crazy stories, like
how some Indian students who'd been Naxalites before coming to grad school had once left their elite college and gone
off in theatrically rumpled white kurta-pajamas to a village to
raise everyone's consciousness. They got a grand reception,
lots of tea and pakoras and marigold garlands and rope cots
pulled out for them to sit on. By the end of the day, just when
they thought they were making good progress on uniting the
masses against oppression, they learned that actually the
rumor had gone out that they were here to view marriageable
girls. Every house where they'd been received had daughters
who'd served the snacks. Apparently, the villagers were pretty
much just humoring these potential sons-in-law. They listened
to the speeches and smiled.

Anyway, telling stories like this, it seemed like this prof chap
had a vision of the world in which, within the huge predicament, most human interactions were a bloody absurd spectacle. I still wonder whether his stories meant that he'd given
up, or whether he'd just accepted that there are some things

too enormous to always keep in your mind or to tackle directly. I can see that teaching could be a form of political activity if you change the perspectives of your students. Choosing teaching and letting other fronts of action slide, maybe he had just accepted his own limitations.

Learning limitations is tough enough, but living with them is a constant struggle. I keep wondering if I should have tried to stick it out in India. Not just now, in the airport, but also when I'm in New York. The thought keeps pestering me: in the office when I talk to people who've been forced to leave their countries, on the subways when I see old people, in my empty apartment that registers flushing toilets, squeaking bedsprings, keening kettles, and unhappy babies from all the apartments around. My parents aren't exactly in the prime of their lives. I was born to them late, when they'd given up hope of ever having kids, and my mother dismissed what was to be me as menopause. If I were a good son I'd be living with them now. But just from the few months I was there after I'd graduated from Berkeley, I knew that I couldn't stand to be cooped up in that apartment. The Malabar Hill mansion has long since been torn down: The only tokens of it are in the huge urns on the gateway and the banyan tree at the back of the property. Otherwise we're boxed in among thirty-two floors looking out toward Marine Drive. It can be a peaceful place, too high for the city's noise, too high even for crows, with strong breezes and a beautiful view of the sea. Comfortable living too, meals appearing at the right time, and clothes left in the laundry basket reappearing freshly ironed from the dhobi. But I couldn't stand it. I couldn't take being reduced to a child. The old servants who smell of strong beedi tobacco always call me Baba. My father waits up for me to come home at night before lumbering off to sleep himself. My mother flits in and out of my room to tidy up my drawers and check on whether I am happy. Then too, the bloody phone, right in the living room, and the way both parents like to contribute to any conversation. "Who is it? Kaun? Why is she calling now? Tell her that we hope . . ." And the old beaked aunties who *chuck me under the chin and declare me* ketlo *sweet, but when will I have a* real *job, isn't it time? I just couldn't and still can't handle it.*

What I really wanted to do when I finished my degree was activist work. But those bloody amoebas just about wiped me out. You can't have a stomach raised on boiled water and expect to mingle easily with the proletariat. Not that I could mingle easily anyway—there were days when I just felt like getting some pigmentation injected into my skin. Currently there are these racist contact lenses available to make brown eyes blue or green, but I frankly wouldn't have minded some contacts that would have made my light brown eyes a penetrating black. Well, there are *other Indians as fair as me: Kashmiris, or Saraswat Brahmans; I still can't put my finger on why everyone treated me so much like a foreigner. I took off my Reeboks and got Bata Keds instead; I left my best North Face backpack at home. I only wore clothes of the roughest homespun* khadi. *But all the same, I never really mingled. I know, I know, it might have been more appropriate to wear polyester safari suits if I really wanted to look like a modern Indian.*

For example, on the train into central Maharashtra, where I was going to work with tribals being harassed by forest contractors, a ticket collector in his black-and-white uniform sat down at the end of my seat and stared through his black spectacles. Finally he asked, "What is your good country, sir?"

"India," I said.

He laughed, as though I'd said something witty. "That you might choose, and we will be very happy if you say so. But your native place? Originally?"

My native place? What was I to tell him? That originally, hundreds of years ago, some people bearing the eggs and sperm that would travel down in twists of DNA all the way to me had come as refugees from Persia? Or that one of my grandmothers was French? "Look, I'm from Bombay," I told the man.

Kirin Narayan

"Ha ha ha," was his comment. "So how you are enjoying this country? Visited our Taj Mahal as yet?"

I went to all that trouble to learn Hindi in Berkeley, but for my political work Marathi would have been better. Maybe I should have tried to take a reading course with that professor who was always carrying on in Marathi. Then too, even when I spoke Hindi, my accent was never quite right, my ds and ts always ended up being harder than they ought. Whatever I did in villages, people kept calling me Saheb. Just when I was beginning to get more comfortable, beginning to blend in, beginning to operate through my anger over the hopeless exploitation; just when it was all falling into some sort of productive rhythm, then wham, I'd bloody get sick. Jaundice. Malaria. Cycle after cycle of what my father calls Amoe-Baba and the Forty Pills.

I used to look down on people who'd come from the Third World to be educated in America and Europe and who then would just stay. I thought they were selfish, that it was their duty to go back. Like Gita: she never ever spoke of returning. I couldn't understand it, a smart woman like her and all she could do in India. Now I see that there were things about her background that she was escaping, that dreadful mother and who knows what else. I see that for each and every one of us, it ends up being not a matter of principles but of situations. Take Najma and Ravindran: they have families they can stand, situations they can live with. Sure, they don't have hot water available twenty-four hours a day, and they can't afford all the books they want to read. But they have some sense of home that makes them happy.

I'm too tired to listen closely to the announcements over the intercom, but I should start moving toward the gate. Got to stop at a water fountain so I don't get too dehydrated. Was I being a coward when I came back to the U.S. by the end of the year and went to law school instead? I can make all these rationalizations for how political action shouldn't take a nationalist cast so that caring for people like ourselves is all that counts. But I know this isn't the real reason I returned. Sure, *it's the usual thing for political activists to confuse the boundaries of social responsibility with nationality. When I'm in India some activist fellows pick on me for living in New York rather than some village in the hinterlands. I always have to take a few deep breaths so I don't get into a big fight or become apologetic. I now tell them, "Look, yaar, we all have to work with who we are. I'm not getting on your case for drinking beer rather than toddy brewed in the village. I don't know what your situation is, but for me it's easier to do something constructive elsewhere." The work I'm doing with refugees who are too powerless even to document that they've been politically persecuted turns out to be for no country at all but for very specific people. In a way, you could say that my work is to chisel holes in the borders between nation-states, to blur the meaning of "citizen."*

Hell, this bag is too heavy, I shouldn't have packed in all those pamphlets. My feet have swelled in their shoes. It will be nice to pull out a blanket on the plane and wedge a pillow against the plastic window frame. All this is too complicated to sort out now—I can think it through later. Wasn't it Gita who once quoted that Rilke chap to me, something about how if you live the questions long enough, one day you might find that you've lived your way into an answer?

6
What
Tribe?

A map of the world extended in pale pastels over the secretary's desk. It was the world but not the familiar one that Gita knew from geography classes, posters, or Norvin's transparent shower curtain. In this, the United States displaced crested England at the center. Golden and spacious, land of the free, the United States was flanked by two broad oceans. Canada offered salutations, and South America bowed to her feet. Bulky handmaidens, Asia, Africa, and Europe seemed to be bending toward her. India was split between two edges of the map. It was amputated at Assam on the side that should have comfortably cradled Bangladesh; sliced off at Punjab on the left. Trying to trace her forthcoming winter travel between Delhi and Bombay, Gita found that she had to jump back and forth between two incomplete Indias.

It was a Friday afternoon in the department office. The secretary had long since gone home. Other professors had retreated to their families. Gita had been staring at her computer screen, willing ideas for an abstract to flow forth. There would be a conference on women's contributions to South Asian studies in the spring in Berkeley, and if her abstract was accepted, the college would pay for a free ticket. Gita reflected that early British folk-narrative collections in India had been made by women—the daughters and wives of colonial officials. The collections put together by Mary Frere in association with her ayah, Anna Liberata De Souza, and Maive Stokes with her ayahs Dunkni and Muniya (and also a male servant called Karim) remained classics. Yet as the discipline became increasingly professionalized in England, folklore journals fell more and more into the hands of men, who tended to dismiss women's books as "unscholarly" and hardly ever printed their articles. That was the historical evidence, but how was one to fit this in now with contemporary debates? Gita racked her brains. Was this partly an argument about written genres, with the book less rigidly monitored than a journal article? No, that didn't quite seem the crux of the matter. The tension between lowly materials on which theories could be based and the prestige of the theories themselves was perhaps more the issue. Then too, one could work in a feminist angle . . . The hum of the computer was disintegrating into a growl of silence, echoing emptily through her heart and her head. She was hungry. Well, even if she had to think through this abstract, there was no denying that she had to eat. Sometimes the ongoing necessities of living seemed like a refuge from the academic pressures that swirled relentlessly around her, threatening to submerge every last moment of her life.

In the cool evening air outside, shriveled leaves rattled against the barks of trees. The parking lots were empty, traversed by white lines. Leaves somersaulted across the streets like the wraiths of forgotten marmalade cats. Leaves huddled together in piles on the sidewalks, hissing and crackling under Gita's brisk, booted feet. She walked across the bridge to town, pausing for a moment to peer into the rush of water glinting in the dark. Downtown, the ski stores, bath stores, and gourmet kitchenware stores were already closed. The churches were empty, spires rising into the night. The Safeway, though, was ablaze with lights. Gita could see lines at the checkout counters. Trudging on toward the health food store, with the wider world returning into focus, Gita found her anxiety over her work loosening a little. She smiled as she remembered her last visit to a large chain grocery store.

"Where are you from?" The ruddy-faced man behind the counter had asked Gita as he prepared to pack up her things. "Paper or plastic?"

"Paper, thanks. I'm from—" Well, what should she say? From the Whitney campus, from California, from Delhi? "I'm, umm, Indian."

"Gee! Indian!" He shook open a brown paper bag. "What tribe?"

"No, Indian from India."

"Really? India! So how long you been here?" His tired eyes were on her, his hands swiftly loading shampoos, paper towels, light bulbs, a carton of milk. What must it be like, Gita had thought, to be past middle age and working at a job like this, high school students by his side?

"How long have I been *here*? I guess about two months."

"You sure speak English good. Fast learner!" He had turned back to the cash register, issued Gita a weary smile, and deposited the receipt at the top of her bag. "Have a nice day now."

The windows of the health food store were misted from within. The door was thick with layers of hand-lettered posters offering everything from rebirthing and shiatsu to rooms available in cooperative vegetarian farmhouses, water signs preferred. A scent of ripe apples and incense pervaded the interior. A young woman with a gold ring in her right nostril and a crocheted African cap over her hennaed hair presided at the checkout counter. "Peace," she greeted Gita.

"Good evening," Gita replied, making her way toward the vegetables. Though certainly more expensive than elsewhere, these vegetables had a greater semblance to what she had been accustomed to in California. One of the most pathetic aspects of this move had been trying to buy lettuce at the chain store and finding only iceberg grained with brown. How Norvin, champion of arugula, radicchio, and organic lettuce mixes, would scoff. Pulling down a plastic bag, Gita felt her mind creeping to Berkeley. Six o'clock here meant three in the afternoon on that coast, the sun hanging bright over the bay. Norvin was probably showering just now after a game of squash. His face would be lifted to the hot water, the hair on his chest flattened by multiple branching rivulets. Gita shook herself: no, no thinking of Norvin. Thank God there were small organic farmers in this state. She swiftly bundled up a green rosette of hydroponic butter lettuce and moved on.

Lettuce, tomatoes, apples, *papads*, milk. Having collected what she needed, Gita joined the line and resigned herself to some people watching. In her few weeks here she was already beginning to recognize some of the faces. There through the door came Meg Stash of English, reputed mastermind of all campus gossip, eyes in her lean face shooting left and right to see who was here, who they were with, and, if possible, what they were buying. Here, sniffing pineapples, was the man from the used-book store, who cultivated a resemblance to John Lennon at his most shaggy era. There was the beautiful half-Italian dancer from Gita's lecture class lifting herbal deodorant from the shelf with a graceful sweep of her arm and swish of her golden hair. The motherly woman from the one-room department store where Gita had bought winter boots the other day was examining seven-grain breads; how odd that she should be here and not in the store across the street. Standing ahead of Gita in the line was a bespectacled, brown-haired man. Gita observed that he looked nice, examined the contents of his cart, and decided that he was shopping for more than one person. She promptly lost interest.

"Hey, honey!" Gita felt a hand on her shoulder. Emerging from the circle of her own silence, she turned to find Zelda towering beside her.

Gita beamed. "Hi! I tried your office earlier and thought you'd gone out of town."

"Heck no," Zelda said. "From this forsaken place, where is there to go?"

Like Gita, Zelda was on a one-year visiting position at Whitney College. She taught sculpture. They had first met waiting in line at the library desk as a student argued about overdue fines. Since then, they had spent many hours filling each other in on their lives. Zelda was lanky, almost six feet tall, and usually wore black. She also had a penchant for unmatched earrings. Just now there was a green fluorescent airplane flying from one ear and a silver wire bent in elegant angles in the other.

"I must've been lifting weights in the gym when you called," Zelda continued in her drawl that always sounded unhurried and amused. "Working on becoming this big macho woman who can bear men off to bed. I've been deep in job applications all week. Trying hard not to freak out about what happens if I'm unemployed next year. I know, suffering is supposed to make for great art, but I can't help worrying about what I'll eat. Speaking of which, what're you doing for dinner?"

"Let's just keep our fingers crossed over the jobs," said Gita, unwilling to let her mind crash off that precipice of uncertainty this moment. "Something should come up. I hope. No, I don't have any plans for dinner. So if you're free to—"

"No hot date?" Zelda asked. "Gee, Gita, hasn't the Heavenly Father taken any action?"

Pushing her cart past, the older woman who had been inspecting breads turned around and scrutinized them both.

Gita grinned. When Zelda had first heard about Ayah's assurances that God made a *jori*, she had thrown her head back with a great shriek of "Coo-oool!" A lapsed Catholic herself, she now took ongoing pleasure from intertwining Christianity and the pursuit of men.

"Anyhow, I'm going to India for winter vacation," said Gita.

"So?"

"So, what's the point of meeting someone just when you're going away?"

"Give me a break! How is one fucking month going to matter? For Heaven's sake, don't act so defeated. This sounds like one of those evenings when we all need to chill out from our work if it's made life seem so limited. How about rounding up Roberto and renting a video? Something romantic so we can at least remember how to dream?"

Roberto was another single person who didn't have a long-distance sweetie to lure him off campus on the weekends. He was from Costa Rica and taught mathematics. A compact man with a squat neck, deep-set black eyes, and hairy forearms, he was still nursing his heart after a messy breakup when he had moved away from graduate school and his boyfriend. Zelda had named their association of three The Society for the Protection of Single People. As she declared, "Heck, there're so many special-interest groups in this country, why hasn't anyone thought about the discrimination we single people have to put up with? Insurance, taxes, social events! Where do we guys get a break? Town to town, state to state, country to country, it's time to mobilize."

"I'd love to see a movie," said Gita. "You're right, it's exactly what I need." Pressed against other lives, her own sense of constriction loosened. There were still all those blue books to grade, and the letters of application to send out, and the abstract to think through, and the revisions for the dissertation. But the alchemy of another presence had made the weekend ahead seem spacious, the future swell with unknown possibility. "By the way, I made tons of bean soup the other day and could bring it all over."

"I have lots of cheese in my fridge from that department party," said Zelda. "And masses of salad ingredients that are going to get slimy unless they're eaten soon. I saw Roberto at the gym earlier and he said something about having baked bread." She leaned toward Gita, lowering her voice to a barely audible murmur. "Do you notice how old Meg Stash is hovering around the organic cookies trying to listen in on our

plans? Our threesome is really troubling the campus master-
minds. First they thought it was you and me, then it was you
and Roberto. Roberto and I are making for speculation, but
the general idea is that if I had to lean down to kiss him it
couldn't be possible. It's bugging the hell out of the gossip
Gestapo. How can there be closeness without a goddamn
couple?"

The lift man at Kalpana's apartment building knew exactly
which floor Saroj wanted. When he saw her, he set aside the
thick religious volume in Devanagri lettering that he was reading and smiled. The triangular grills to the lift pressed into
parallel lines as he opened the door. It closed with a squeak,
and there was a slight jerk as the lift started ascending. Saroj
looked around the wooden inlay of thick parallel bands inter-
sected at the corners with circles. This was the classic art deco
of the old downtown Bombay apartment buildings. She caught
sight of her eye in the mirror. The corners of her mouth tight-
ened in complicity with her own mission.

When the lift man let her out, she stood for a minute outside
Kalpana's apartment. A marigold garland was looped above
the door. Saroj pressed down the wisps of hair that had
whipped out like rays from the sun after the windy train ride
into town. She took a deep breath. Then she pressed the bell
and heard the chimes of "Do, a Deer, a Female Deer" repeating again and again from inside the apartment.

"Why darr-ling!" Saroj said when Kalpana opened the door.
"So glad you're at home. I was just on my way to the Sohan
exhibition and thought I'd just stop in to see if you'd like to
come along. Prabhaben says they have the best Kutch *ajrak*
prints in years.

"Come in, come in," said Kalpana, with the yips of dogs
resounding from an inner room. Her hair was still uncombed,
and over her sari petticoat she wore a dressing gown with oil
splotches and turmeric stains adding texture to the floral pattern. "I haven't had a chance to bathe as yet. The boy has

gone to his village, the *bai* has deserted. What am I to do? Cooking, cleaning, everything. Servants today are like this— you are so lucky to have old-old servants in your house. And then these dogs come in heat, and I have been chasing them all over the house to put on the panties."

"Panties?" Saroj lowered herself onto the false leather sofa beneath the showcase. She took off her glasses and wiped her face with a hankie from her purse. The Marine Drive traffic roared in through the open window, mingling with the rushing breeze off the sea. "What do you mean, dogs wearing panties?" she called after Kalpana, who had disappeared into the kitchen.

Kalpana handed Saroj a glass of cold water. "I tell you, it is the best precaution," she said. "If you have got one boy dog and one girl dog, what else you are to do? You can't just sit and supervise the entire day. It's too difficult to lock them in different rooms. They keep on crying and scratching: Baba, the noise! Panties is the best solution. Newborn size. Want to see?"

Saroj giggled as the two Pomeranians, Pinky and Tommy, came dashing out of an inner bedroom with a scurry of little legs and a volley of yips. They jumped around Saroj's knees. Pinky was white, and Tommy was black. They both had smudges of what apparently had been ceremonial red *kumkum* on their foreheads and were dressed in coordinated candy-striped panties.

"Now that the children are in boarding and all, it would be impossible for me to also look after puppies," said Kalpana. She sat down. "You should have seen the face of the man who sold me these panties. He asked, 'How old is your *baba?*' and I told him, 'This is not for a *baba,* this is for two dogs, a *kutha* and a *kuthi.*'"

"I'm sure he is still telling everyone he knows about it," laughed Saroj.

"*Aaa, beta,*" Kalpana crooned, bunching her lips at the dogs and thumping a hand beside her. Their constricted tails moved awkwardly.

"So, are you all ready for Ajay's visit in December?" asked Saroj.

"What is there to prepare?" Kalpana asked, not looking up as she petted the dogs. "You know how he is, my brother-in-law. Always an independent type."

"Our Gita will be here in December too." Saroj sipped at her water.

"Really?" Kalpana said.

"I think they'll both be here around the same time," Saroj observed. She set down the glass and nonchalantly examined the rings on her fingers. "Christmas holidays, I suppose."

"We should have a get-together," said Kalpana. "The children will also be coming from boarding."

"Come to think of it," said Saroj, lifting her hand so her diamond ring sizzled with light, "I don't remember whether Ajay and Gita have ever met. First Ajay was off being brilliant at his I.I.T., then he was at M.I.T. I really don't think they've ever even seen each other."

"Let's introduce them then," Kalpana said.

"What a marvelous idea, darling!" Saroj clapped her hands with a jingle of gold and green glass bangles. She sat forward. "You're a positive genius! Why haven't we thought of it before, all these years? We can *try,* of course. We *must* try. They'll have *so* much in common."

Kalpana looked alarmed. Her hands fell slack around the dogs, who whined and clamored toward the black-beaded *mangal-sutra* hanging over her bosom.

"You're *too* brilliant, Kalpana!" Saroj continued. "The way Ajay has been carrying on about how the Indian girls you advertize for over here are too young and too sheltered, it's *obvious* he's thinking of someone like Gita. You're so right to realize that divorce doesn't mean a thing in America. It's even *preferred* to meet a nice divorcée who'll have learned so much from the past mistake and will truly value marriage."

"Gita is a nice girl . . ." Kalpana began cautiously.

"But of *course,*" said Saroj, "and Ajay is not exactly young himself. It's a must that he meet someone before he's *com-*

pletely over the hill. Our Gita is so sensible, she's surely ready to overlook his handicap of being a bachelor so long. He needs a nice, understanding girl like her. You're absolutely correct to think of bringing them together."

"Both NRIs," Kalpana stated. "So many nonresident Indians out there in the States just now. I don't know about your Gita's caste and all, but anyway, Ajay has always said he is against casteism. Living abroad, I suppose, makes a new caste. They should understand each other."

"So true!" said Saroj. "And marriage is all a matter of understanding, isn't it? Children these days are blind to this elementary rule. They want love, they want this or that thrill and this or that item from a dream shopping list. They're all lonely but they don't listen. They try to do everything alone. Look how hard you and Prakash worked for Ajay, going through those hundred and one responses to the ad. Children don't see they need the intervention of elders."

Kalpana stared a moment at Saroj, her face still dazed. Ajay was actually a few months older than she, but being single without children or dogs, what could he know about life? Clearly, he was still a child. She drew herself up, adjusted the neck of her dressing gown, and issued a smile filled with the dignified authority of her freshly bestowed generational bracket. "Correct," she said. "Whatever people say, there's no doubt that when *elders* choose, marriages turn out for the best."

"Darling, you're *so* brilliant." Saroj beamed.

Ever since Gita and Norvin had divorced, letters from Kookoo were exceptionally hard to take. Coming home from a long day of classes, meetings, office hours, Gita was filled with trepidation as she neared the mailbox. In the middle of November, she trudged home one weekday afternoon though the landscape of bare trees, withered grass, and slate-gray skies. Her ears were still echoing from the voices of the faculty meeting, her eyes flickering with images of different students and their demands. Returning home was like retreating inward for renewal. She longed for a cup of tea. Yet in the mailbox was a dreaded envelope with Kookoo's slanted capitals and stamps displaying a chocolate-colored, turbaned man bending over a loom along with several sepia Mahatma Gandhis. Gita tore open the envelope and examined its innards without even going to the kitchen to put on a kettle.

Dear Gita,

That pretty wildlife card you sent for Divali has just arrived. I suppose that mail must be slow from that lonely little college, because it was actually five days after Divali had passed. Now that Vicky is growing up we didn't bother to have any firecrackers, but the neighbors did carry on with their bombs, and our nerves are still quite shaken. These days, with all the terrorists in the news, firecrackers that explode aren't quite the same.

How very clever of you to get a three-week trip out of your college. Such generous employers, who will support research at the Bombay branch of the Royal Asiatic Society Library without even knowing that Saroj lives in that city! She must be happy to have you for that long. As I've told you before, she seems desperate for company since Harish died. That's what comes of not having children of one's own. It's so very thoughtful of you to arrange to see her. I'm surprised that the archives at Delhi University couldn't help with your research. I suppose it must have something to do with those quaint little stories you like to look into.

You already know the little things we like from abroad, but since it's been so long since you were able to make time in your busy routine to visit us, let me remind you that your daddy would like two bottles of good scotch. He hasn't been feeling so well and Indian products are never the same. Not that I go out as much as I did in the past, but it never hurts to have another bottle of Charlie perfume. Brigadier General Dikshit requested that we ask you to bring him just one package of Marlboro cigarettes. Of course, this wouldn't be too heavy, and he has been so awfully kind sending round his army rations of brandy that we couldn't refuse. You can purchase all this duty-free so you won't have to spend any time on us by shopping. It would be very thoughtful of you if you brought a good physics book for your brilliant little brother. He is doing ever so well at St. Stephen's these days. It's really the finest place—just as good as in the old days.

I sometimes see that friend of yours, Ravindran, in the park. You would think he'd try some cold cream with that complexion. He even has a black dog, though mostly these days he seems to be with a baby. I don't know what school he went to, for he hasn't even learned the most elementary of manners. He never greets me. How such a person was admitted to a fine institution like the University of California is beyond belief.

Affectionately yours,
Mummy

P.S. Your daddy came across this most interesting piece in the *Hindustan Times* reproduced from some U.S. paper. Imagine the chances of being shot by a terrorist being larger than the chances of getting married! This is for nice girls with college degrees. No one has done a statistical survey of girls who went for Ph.D. degrees so there is, of course, no reason that you should be upset.

Quickly, as though the letter might ignite what it touched, Gita tore it up and tossed it in with the eggshells and cucumber peels in the kitchen trash. She squeezed the yellowish newsprint into a tight ball that joined the trash too. All this could be composted, bringing brightness to the Davidsons' summer garden. Then she filled a kettle and tuned in to exuberant African high life on the college radio station.

*   *   *

There should have been cafés in this college town, but so far no entrepreneur had identified this as the source for a minor fortune. The Society for the Protection of Single People had convened in a restaurant by the river. During these off-hours between lunch and dinner, the restaurant was empty. There was no need to worry about fellow faculty or students from classes listening in on conversations from the next table. A troop of mentally retarded teenagers brought in from a home for the afternoon were scrubbing and polishing the floors. A waitress counted cutlery, one eye on the hired help, dropping occasional pieces with a clang. For once, in this small town, a meeting in a public place actually had a sense of isolation and anonymity.

"We have a special present for your trip," said Zelda, passing a small box across the table.

"You shouldn't have," said Gita. "Zelda, what a beautiful box: Chinese satin trim, wow!"

Zelda was notorious for her love of boxes. She collected them in many sizes and shapes; she reused and decorated them and sent them off with new contents for friends' birthdays, weddings, arrivals of babies. When she had moved to Whitney, one-quarter of her truck had reputedly been piled with stacked and nested boxes. Walking down a street, it was not unusual for her to spy a discarded cardboard box and make a beeline to claim it.

"Wait till you see if you like what's inside." Roberto grinned, leaning back in his chair, hands locked behind his head so his elbows jutted up like large ears.

Gita opened the box. "Earrings!" she exclaimed. "Oh, how lovely. How different." The earrings had silver hooks attached to plastic oblongs, each one about one and a half inches long and half an inch wide, with a shiny red oval shape inside, gold thread twisted on the outside, and brushed-silver motifs drawn all over.

"We thought you could use some crazy earrings," said Zelda. She herself was wearing in one ear a cow whose legs, head, and tail waggled and in the other a simple coral stud.

"I've never had anything quite like this," said Gita. "Did you make them?"

"Sure, honey, select designs. You know that I sometimes make jewelry on the side." Zelda and Roberto exchanged a look. "Does it remind you of anything?"

"Not really." Gita took off the gold hoops bought in one of the glittering jewelry shops in Santa Cruz Bazaar with Saroj Aunty many years ago. She threaded the new earrings into her earlobes and put the old ones in the box. Then she shook her head, allowing the plastic to dangle and bump slowly against her neck.

"Very nice!" said Roberto, mustache stretching out over a smile. He smoothed down the mustache, or was it the smile? "Perfect. Ah, look, another person is here to admire your new acquisition. I see Charity of the Anthropology Department buying something in the bakery section. Did you meet her, Gita? She has lived in India."

"I've heard people mention her. You know, the India-India connection. People are also always trying to hook me up with the librarian who's of Indian origin from Mauritius. Isn't she on leave or something?"

"Writing," said Roberto. "She's married to Isaac in my department. Charity!" he called.

As the blond head by the bakery counter turned, Gita recognized the woman at once as a member of the couple she had seen driving around campus: the man with a long, intense face too young for the uniformly gray hair, the woman small and animated with hair cropped close to her head.

A few minutes later Charity was drinking tea among them. Gita was staring at her, dumbfounded. Charity had flecked green eyes that looked as surprised as a doll's, almost as though they would close if she were laid down. Her hair had the bleached sheen of a Californian surfer's. Yet her lips were moving to produce the unmistakable cadences of an Indian accent. This might as well have been Najma speaking.

"I'm *so* sorry," Charity was saying. Gita made an effort to tune into the substance of her words. "Really, I must confess that I've known you were here. I've been meaning to ring you up and invite you over, but I'm on leave and am trying hard to get one hundred and one assorted things written."

"What do you write on?" Zelda asked, also mesmerized.

"Gender stuff. I do research in the Himalayan foothills. My parents were missionaries in India, and I went to school there. Then after college here, I went in for anthropology so I could keep going back and forth." Charity smiled. Gita noticed that she was wearing traditional gold hoops very much like the ones that now occupied Zelda's box.

"So, you must have gone to Aspen School," said Gita.

"Aspen?!" asked Zelda. "It's a *school*?"

"Yes, an American school in India," Charity said. "How did you guess? Yes, of course I went there. Why? Do you know someone else who did?"

"At my school we used to recite this silly rhyme that was supposedly a big favorite at Aspen. It's *really* silly. Did you ever hear it? 'Oh come to me my love, oh come?' "

" 'I've loved you from my heart's bot-tom?' But first you must get rhythm! What about the clicking tongue and fingers?"

Gita and Charity burst into laughter. "What's going on?" asked Zelda.

"There was this woman who went on a train, and this guy asked her if she liked poetry . . ." Gita began.

"No, it was this boy, he was sitting on a bus—"

"Folklore!" cried Gita. "Multiple existence and variation. This is genuine Indian folklore. Someone really needs to do a study of modern urban forms like this in Indian English. My book is just about colonial collections, but this sort of thing really should be looked into."

"You're writing a book on Indian folklore? Really?"

"Mostly just archival stuff," said Gita. "You know, colonial attempts to understand the native mind, and how people went on to collect from their fellows. Basically how it might have fed into the construction of national and regional identities."

"I'd love to hear more about it. So where did you go to school?"

"A place you probably never heard of," said Gita, "and Zelda and Roberto, don't snicker! It was called Our Lady of Perpetual Succour Convent."

"Don't tell me! That place where the nuns supposedly did underwear inspection, and when you went on hockey tournaments you were supposed to fall down with your knees together?"

"That very place," said Gita. She grinned broadly. Hearing Charity speak, her own sense of difference was coming out of deep freeze. "So I guess you've heard all the stories about us repressed convent girls."

"The cousin of a friend of mine went there," said Charity. "Did you know Dinaz Ganjifrockwala?"

"She was in my class!"

"Well, I know her cousin Firoze. His family used to come up to the hills for vacations sometimes."

"I know him too, from Berkeley."

"Firoze is *wonderful*," said Charity with emphasis. "Really a good guy. Lives in New York, you know—we've got to get him up here for a visit sometime." She looked at her watch. "Look, I'm really sorry, but Isaac is probably waiting outside to pick me up this very minute. Here's my number, Gita. We've got to keep talking. It's great that you're here." As she stood up, she said, "By the way, I like your earrings."

"Thanks," Gita said, fingering the packages by her ears so the fluid squeezed back and forth inside. "Unusual, aren't they?" It was only when Charity had left that Gita turned on Roberto and Zelda, who were hunched over with laughter in their chairs, to ask, "What's going on? What's so hilariously funny?"

"When you don't see sex even when it's in front of you, it's time for a change of scene," said Zelda. "You might not have realized, sweetie, that these might be *functional* too? That the packages that I decorated with an indelible silver marker and tied in gold thread just might have something of use inside?"

"It's good luck for your trip," said Roberto.

"May God bless you too, Baby," said Zelda.

*   *   *

Gita woke in Bombay to the hoarse call of crows. She lay between the sheets and listened. There was the sound of a rough broom sweeping against the ground outside. A clatter of cans and a whir of a bicycle coming to a halt: the milkman making his rounds, pouring milk into the empty vessels held out in each doorway that he visited. Then there was a thud near the front door, the morning newspaper thrown by the paper *wala* from the gate. Gita smiled into the rich red behind her eyelids. In the background, like the hum of her innermost ear, she could hear the rush and retreat of the Arabian Sea.

"Bearah, bearah, chai!" Kookoo's voice rang from the living room. Gita rolled over, tensed. Calling scrawny Tukaram with his oversize white bush shirts and tightly wrapped *dhoti*s "bearer" just didn't make sense. Actually, Muktabai, the graying woman with a sweet demeanor and Marathi sari molded around her matronly thighs, was the person who brought the lemongrass-and-ginger-flavored tea in the morning. But unable to address her as either "nanny" or "girl," Kookoo preferred to give all her orders to Tukaram instead.

When Gita had emerged from the white-suited men and blinding lights in Delhi Customs, staggering a little through lack of sleep, Kookoo had fallen upon her. It was past 1 A.M. Delhi time, but the area outside the airport was thick with craning relatives, eyes rapt on the door from which travelers emerged with luggage wheeled before them. Taxi drivers squatted on the pavement, mufflers wrapped over their heads, puffing on their *beedi*s until their number was called for the taxi line. Just Kookoo and her salaaming chauffeur were there: Vicky had an exam the next day, and Dilip wasn't well. "Prostate problems," said Kookoo in an undertone when she and Gita were pressed into the backseat. "Like a woman's change of life, though of course you're much too young to know anything about *that*. His condition is nothing to worry about, of course—these little illnesses come with age."

But a pall was hanging over the house. Something had happened in the intervening years to the chic Western *House and Garden* look that Kookoo had striven, against all odds of climate and labor, to maintain. The plaster in the living room had developed large cracks, and the highest skylights were dusty. The flush in Gita's bathroom wasn't working at all, requiring buckets of water to be poured in. Mold was slick between the tiles near the tub, and since the main tank had a leak, water rationing meant that there were only certain hours that one could shower. In the kitchen, the servants had set up an altar with the radiant, red-garbed Santoshi Ma, a deity made popular through a film. The imported refrigerator had become asthmatic, a home to colonies of cockroaches. The house looked smaller than Gita remembered. Smaller, and with the air conditioners off for winter, invaded by the India outside.

Gita twiddled her toes and opened one eye. She was glad to be in Bombay rather than Delhi. Light was catching the blades of a young palm tree by the window. She wondered whether Saroj Aunty had come downstairs yet. Saroj Aunty's house, rising around her just now, had also shrunk in the intervening years. Its outer walls had been blackened by sea air. Inside, though, the floors still gleamed with a faint whiff of ammonia after their daily wipe by Tukaram. Fragrant flowers still floated in bowls placed all over the house. Saroj Aunty still changed her sari twice a day (three times—into a named one—if she was going out to dinner). The Maharaj still grumbled if you didn't eat. Gita inhaled slowly, feeling well-being creep over her limbs. It was such a luxury not to have to jump out of bed to sit at the computer or prepare for class. Anxieties that had become fused in every joint through the last few years seemed to be melting away under the high ceilings of this house.

"Good morning, good morning." Kookoo was here. "My goodness, you Americans sleep late! You can relax all day, but I must be off to visit your daddy in the hospital."

Why Dilip had to have medical tests in Breachcandy Hospital when there were perfectly fine facilities in Delhi had escaped Gita. It had to do with someone's uncle's cousin's friend being a Bombay doctor (though of course someone else's father-in-law's sister-in-law was in Delhi, making for some debate before departure). All in all, she wished Kookoo and Dilip had stayed in Delhi, or at least decided to take a hotel room instead of camping out at Saroj Aunty's. Dilip had made himself scarce before he was enrolled in the hospital. But Kookoo was as usual looming larger than life. Whenever Saroj Aunty was out of earshot, Kookoo took Gita aside to complain bitterly about the household arrangements, from the squatting toilets with mugs of water rather than toilet paper to how the servants looped flowers in front of all the paintings, even the modern ones, if they happened to feature gods.

"Morning," Gita said, stretching.

"That dreadful cook doesn't know about steeping tea separate from the milk," said Kookoo, sitting down on one side of the bed. She was wrapped in a lime-green polyester robe from the Woolworth's on Shattuck Avenue in Berkeley.

"Well, it's all mixed in a cup anyway," said Gita.

"Not that people know how to drink tea in America. Little plastic vials of cream that haven't even been heated. Dreadful. It's time to get up now."

"I heard you," said Gita.

Kookoo lifted a framed picture from the bedside. It was of Gita smiling from among fall leaves on the campus of Whitney College. As Kookoo picked up the frame, the picture slipped a little, revealing the edge of a different background. "Just like Saroj, never throwing anything, just layering," Kookoo muttered. She began to pick at the back of the frame. "Let's see what else she has in here."

"Don't pry, Mummy," Gita said. No doubt the fine print of old cough prescriptions had already been combed through in the bathroom cupboards; the flyleaves of books in the other guest room had already been inspected.

Both black-and-white and colored photographs fluttered into Kookoo's lap and onto the floor. "Why do you do this?" Gita asked sharply. She sat up and lifted a brittle black-and-white picture of a shriveled woman in white standing at sol-

emn attention, eyes fixed on the camera, as the grinning face
of a little girl peered from behind a hip.

"Ayah," Gita said. "Me and Ayah. I wonder what happened
to her."

"Dead, no doubt," said Kookoo absently. "My, you were
attached to her." She had taken to arranging the pictures on
the coverlet stitched from the silk of a soft old pink-and-green
tie-dyed sari. Gita tried to remember if she had ever known
the name of this sari when Saroj Aunty still wore it. In a
pattern that reminded Gita of Tarot cards from Telegraph
Avenue, Kookoo set Ayah and Gita in the middle. To one
side, she put down Gita and Norvin, posed bride and groom.
Beneath, there was Gita in the Our Lady of Perpetual Succour
uniform: a girl with gangly knees, fingering the edge of her
tie, too shy to look up at the photographer. On the other side,
Gita stood in the black and yellow robes of a graduate under
the campanile, waving the blank piece of parchment that stood
in through the ritual for the actual diploma. On top there was
Gita in a frilly frock sitting on the swing between Saroj Aunty
and Harish Uncle, who were both laughing and slim. Jimmy
Uncle stood, hands on his hips, in the background.

"The way Saroj hoards these things!" said Kookoo, picking
up yet another picture from the floor of Gita being garlanded
for a send-off to America from the Bombay airport. "She
should really get herself an album. Oh my, a double bottom
to this frame, here are two more. Oh—"

Gita recognized the first at once. It was a close-up of the
face of her own father. His head was turned to the side, and
though he wasn't smiling, there was a pucker around the
cheeks as though he just might. The studio sheen couldn't
disguise the darkness of his complexion. Gita saw her own
line of eyebrows on his face. "For Saru, Love, V. 1946" was
scribbled along one side.

The second was of her father with Saroj Aunty and Harish
Uncle. Saroj Aunty, in a sari Gita immediately recognized as
Nefertiti, stood in the middle. She wasn't wearing glasses yet,
and her hair was very black, pulled over the front of her sari

in a long braid. The men, wearing the long white sleeves and
baggy pleated pants of the fifties, stood on either side. Harish
Uncle looked a great deal younger, stronger, taller than Gita's
father. An extrovert even in a picture, he was waving at whoever the photographer was, his dimples deep and his teeth very
white. Gita's father wasn't smiling. From the extended forehead on his partially turned face, it was clear that he was
balding. His head was turned, just as Saroj's was. Both sol-
emn, they were looking right at each other.

"That's Saroj for you," said Kookoo, rapidly stuffing all the
pictures back into the frame. "Such a sentimentalist. Imagine
holding on to these old things!" A moment later, Gita smiled
again from among the reds and oranges of autumn. The larger,
mobile Gita was out by the living room windows, looking out
at the sea as she stirred fragrant tea. Those two tense faces
were still with her, and she didn't know quite what to think.

Saroj and Gita were in the garden. They had eaten a sumptuous lunch prepared by Maharaj, shared sweet *paan* as they
lounged on Saroj's double bed, and then had a nap. Now it
was late afternoon and they were awake again. Saroj had
changed into a freshly starched sari, but Gita, feeling rebel-
lious, had only rearranged her pleats. They sat on cane chairs
facing the sea. It was low tide, the rocks were showing, and
there was the smell of fish and brine blowing in on the breeze.

"He'll be here any moment," said Saroj, looking at her
watch. "Then we can have our tea."

"Saroj Aunty, you're horrible," said Gita, smiling broadly.
"So that's why you insisted that Mummy should go to the
hospital alone. If I had any idea that this was what you were
up to I might have shown some sort of filial piety and gone
along too. Delhi was bad enough. Everywhere I went, people
acted as though I should receive condolences. Not just Dilip,
who doesn't know what to say and still has one of those
wedding pictures of me and Norvin in his study, but every
other person in the entire social circle. You should have seen

the way people would sidle up close and in these lugubrious voices suggest that since there's been 'no issue' I could be remarried soon to some widower or divorced man. It took me a while to remember that 'no issue' meant 'no kids.' Then they'd begin to drop hints about these pathetic-sounding eligibles until I was utterly depressed. At least in America people pretty much mind their own business."

"Oh, shoo," said Saroj. "It's because we *care* about you, darling. Can you say anyone so busy minding their own business over there in your America cares like we do?"

"Well . . ." Gita played with the end of her braid. "Some good friends maybe. Life there is just so hard, so much worry about professions."

"And, darling, I don't like the suggestion that Ajay is pathetic, or anything like those other men you've heard about. He's *so nice.* Just wait till you see him!" Saroj gave Gita a coy, sidelong look. "I guarantee love at first sight!"

"Saroj Aunty, your fantasies . . . Come on, even you know romance like that doesn't exist. Let me tell you, I know the labels. *Nice* means ineffectual. *Handsome* means narcissistic. *Intelligent* means a compulsive worker. *Family-minded* means a mummy's boy."

"Shoo!" Saroj tittered. "Oh you! When you're young, life isn't worth living if there isn't some room for romance. Grand romance. Those labels might mean all those things, but you have to at least allow yourself the *illusion* of some perfection. Anyway, it's all a matter of compromise."

"By the way, Aunty—" Gita stopped herself from mentioning how Kookoo had dismantled the picture frame. "Aunty, tell me about my father."

Gita wondered if it was just her imagination, or had there really been a split second in which Saroj had no words? Saroj laughed. "Your father? Darling! What on earth do you want to know?"

"No one ever talks to me about him. I keep wondering what he was like."

"First of all . . ." Saroj looked out at the sea. "First of all, you surely must know that you look like him. Very much like him, male features transposed onto a girl's face. You're clearly feminine-looking, of course, but it's everything around your eyes, and then your size and your complexion. He was small too, just about my height. Your looking so much like him was one reason we all suspected that Dilip couldn't bear to have you in the house."

"I don't mean what he looked like, Aunty. I've seen some pictures and all, and then there was that character who played him in *Gandhi*. I mean, what was he really like as a person?"

"Vinay? As a person? Darling, he's been dead for years. I thought we were talking about Ajay."

"Tell, Aunty. You've never ever told me how you knew him."

Saroj sighed, stretching out her hand and examining the rings on her fingers. It was a ruby and garnet afternoon, to match the shades of red on the broad stripes of her starched Bengali sari.

"Well, you know how we all read Marx and Lenin and got involved in communism in those days before Independence, the days before the stories about Stalin began to leak out."

"Harish Uncle too?"

"No, not Harish—he was always much too involved in having a great time in the present to worry much about any Big Issues. Harish was always a lighthearted man. And anyway, I didn't even know him then. Your father and I were in the same communist cell. He was a fabulous speaker—it's really a shame that all this video technology wasn't around then to record any of it. We worked on a few productions of plays together, you know, Hindi translations of Brecht and things like that that we went off in groups to perform in the villages. Vinay . . ." Saroj Aunty raised, then released her round shoulders and let out a breath. "Darling! Anyone who met that father of yours couldn't help feeling that he was, well, magnetic. Magnetic! Small and quick and altogether *too* charismatic."

"And probably self-absorbed."

"Yes, that *too*, of course—why deny it? He was a man who needed a mission. It was such a letdown for him when we actually had achieved Independence and then there was Nehru without too much of a *real* commitment to socialism. And then the reports from the Soviet Union—Siberia and all the rest of it. He was so used to having a grand cause that would come before anything and everybody, poor chap. It was around then, at the end of the fifties, that he finally decided that he would settle down."

"So then he all of a sudden decided to marry my mother?"

"Well, Kookoo *was* awfully pretty," said Saroj. "You know, one of those fair young things with pouting lips. I believe she caught his eye at some wedding or other. And by then he was a legendary bachelor, one of those catches that no one ever thought would be caught—you know the mystique. Not that he was wealthy or anything, but he had connections, and castewise, he was a coup for Kookoo's parents with all their aspirations. They had the money to set it all up—it's just a shame at how they ostracized Kookoo when she remarried later. But speaking of *catches,* darling, let's get back to Ajay! Let me tell you, Ajay is simply brilliant, working over there at his Bell Labs."

"You're saying the wrong thing, Aunty!" Gita made a face. "Please! Don't you know I'm finished with brilliant men? They're never nice to their women."

Saroj laughed. "My, such wisdom!" A moment later she reached out and stroked Gita's arm. "Sorry, darling. I didn't mean to remind you of that idiot in Berkeley. Let me tell you, our Ajay is different. He's Indian. I've known him since he was in half-pants. Of course, he's a quiet chap, but we *all* know about still waters!"

"What's wrong with him that he agreed to meet me?" Gita asked, ashamed that her voice was straining under the weight of associations to Norvin. In an obscure way, she felt like blaming her father for what had gone wrong with Norvin. "Is he divorced too? Did he manage to bump off a wife?"

"No-no-no, he never married. He's another one waiting for

the *right* woman, someone just like you. Oh good, here is Tukaram. *Saheb ale kai?"*

Tukaram rolled his head. "He's come," he assured in Marathi, Adam's apple bulging. Behind him, Ajay had appeared on the steps.

"Then what are you waiting for?" Saroj raised her voice indignantly. "Why are you just standing there? Go, bring the tea, get the *dhokla!* Quickly, quickly. Tell Maharaj *masala* tea." As Tukaram sped into the house, her voice grew honeyed. "Ajay, sweetheart. My dear! *What* a surprise!"

Ajay, walking down the steps, was looking directly at Saroj. Out of the corner of his eye he had noticed the woman with the long braid. She looked around abruptly, then smoothed her hair back from its middle parting and looked out to sea. He glanced again, taking in her profile this time. She was pretty, yes, though certainly browner and more angular than what he'd imagined. He focused instead on Saroj's face, round as a fluffy American cat's, with gray hair blowing about her head.

"Darling!" said Saroj as Ajay stopped beside her cane chair. He was wondering whether to kiss her cheek or not. His codes for handshaking, hugging, and kissing always got confused when he was in India. The young woman's presence was crackling in his mind. He leaned down to kiss Saroj. "Hello, Aunty," he said.

"What a tremendous and wonderful surprise," Saroj said. "What *luck* that you showed up while Gita was here! You must meet Gita, Ajay. She's one of my most brilliant nieces. She teaches now at Whitney College. And Gita, darling, Ajay here is one of our I.I.T. geniuses. Now he works in New Jersey. Brain drain: you know how it is for India."

Gita had turned. Ajay wore black-rimmed spectacles and was somewhat thick around the waist. With his round cheeks and sensitive mouth, there as no denying that he bore a certain resemblance, if not to Shashi Kapoor himself, to other male actors from the Kapoor clan. He had nice shoulders too. And he smiled.

"Hello," said Gita.

"Pleased to meet you," said Ajay. He started to reach for her hand, but she had joined her palms. Feeling ridiculous, he returned her *namaste*. "Aunty has been talking about you."

"Sit, sit," said Saroj. "Here, take a chair."

"Yes, Aunty," Ajay said. "May I smoke?" After he had lit a cigarette and exhaled, he turned to Gita. "Are you really a niece or just honorary like me?" he asked.

"Honorary," Gita said.

"Which doesn't mean that I love you less," said Saroj. "Harish was the one who said that since we didn't have any children we should adopt the kids of all our friends as nephews and nieces."

"I miss Harish Uncle," said Gita. "His jokes! Why did the Malayali cross the road? Zim-ply. Why did the Guju go to London? To see the Big Ben. What do you call a mathematical Sindhi? Add-vani. The way he could mimic all the accents that the different communities use when they speak English, and build on all the bilingual puns. I wish he were here, Aunty. What do you do without him?"

"I manage," said Saroj, turning her head toward the house as she spoke. "I'm fine. These servants, what are they doing with the tea? *Tukaram!* Both of you amuse yourselves, darlings. I'll just go see what they're up to. We've made your favorite, Ajay: *dhokla*. I'll do the finishing touches."

"How nice, Aunty, you remembered."

"Of course!" Saroj smiled. "Do keep yourself entertained."

She disappeared into the house, and an explosion of shouts soon followed. Ajay and Gita looked out at the beach. The sea was a pale band of blue in the afternoon sun, and the sky was paler still. There were a few people wandering through the sand. Ajay had positioned himself so that the thinning spot at the back of his head wouldn't show. He was wondering if he'd offended Saroj by reminding her of her childless state; his mother used to say this was the greatest sadness a woman

could have. Gita was chiding herself for having brought up
Harish Uncle. Of all people, she should know better than to
blunder flat-footedly into the pain of absence. This guy probably thought she was insensitive, or even inane. Why hadn't
she stopped herself from reciting those silly jokes? She began
to edge her head toward Ajay for another look and found him
turning to her. Their eyes collided, then swerved away to the
sea.

The silence had begun to whir with tension by the time
Saroj returned. The servants followed her in a procession. Tukaram bore a tray with the tea things. Muktabai had canisters
of biscuits. Maharaj, stripped to the waist and wearing his
white *dhoti,* carried hot *dhokla* sprinkled with fresh coriander
and coconut. Saroj orchestrated what went where on the low
table. Then she ordered, "Now you must eat up. Have more,
Ajay."

"So kind of you," Ajay said. "Since my mother passed away
no one at our place can make it like this."

Gita sipped her tea. "Saroj Aunty, your tea here tastes just
the same. And this *dhokla!* It makes me think of all the times
I was a little kid in a frock, playing on your swing. This is
what I find so amazing about coming back to India. Everything follows the same old routines."

"Oh, shoo," said Saroj. "Nonsense, everything's changing
all the time."

"I can't keep up with the change," said Ajay. "Names of
roads, actors and actresses in the magazines, the politicians
you hear about, and now that there's TV, all the programs
and announcers . . ."

"Yes, all *that* changes," Gita said, "but households, they
remain the same. People's connections too. I mean, my mother
still plays her bridge. Her husband continues to have his pegs
at seven and Horlicks at night. The colonel next door still
plays old Hemant Kumar records when he's drunk. That kind
of thing. Or here at Saroj Aunty's we still have these afternoon
teas by the beach, and Tukaram can be trusted to be late in
bringing out things to eat. And then you always hear about

the same family friends and neighbors even if you didn't think of them for five years straight."

Ajay felt a wave of resentment. She obviously didn't know how the rhythms of a household could vanish. At one time when he visited Bombay, his mother would sit by his bed chatting and stroking his head as he drifted off to sleep. She had brought him morning tea. Now he was an outsider in the apartment. He had to wait till Prakash left for the office and the dogs had been fed before either Kalpana or the servants paid any attention to him. America or India, things were always changing, changing, sweeping close connections out of your life.

"I don't understand one thing," said Saroj, setting her cup down. "I want you both to explain. Just tell me, what's so special about your America? Why live there when we have *here*? I know there's the power of the dollar and all that, but, darlings, what about *life*? Why stay?"

Ajay and Gita looked at each other. They started to smile.

"Working phones," said Ajay. "One good reason. You don't have to dial and redial and get five wrong numbers before the phone goes dead."

"Libraries," Gita said. "It's just unbelievable, the sense of access when every book you ever wanted to see is available through interlibrary loan."

"And the smooth roads," said Ajay. "No honking, no cows. Sure, there are traffic jams, but nothing like here. Jesus! I'd hate to drive in this city."

Gita laughed. "Delhi is a little better," she said, "but then look at the price of petrol!"

"Lines," said Ajay. "Saroj Aunty, people in the U.S. actually know how to stand in line."

"Exactly," said Gita, "and not push and shove and swarm when a bus or train arrives." She was grinning at Ajay with such bright intensity that he had to look away before he returned a smile. When he smiled, his lips were tightly pressed and the teeth didn't show. "And the clean public bathrooms."

"Shoo," said Saroj. "We have *some* lines. Go to Santa Cruz

station to catch the two thirty-one bus, or wait for a scooter from Parle. Such efficient lines! It's *Delhi* where no one respects the queue system—it's not like that with us Bombayites. As for a bathroom, if you're in town there's always the Taj. Darlings!"

But Ajay and Gita were caught up in their own momentum. "Cable TV," said Ajay.

"Fewer amoebas," said Gita.

"Automatic tellers."

"Hot showers."

"Ice cream: thirty-one flavors."

"Actually, Ben and Jerry's is my favorite. By the way, we forgot sushi."

Ajay didn't care for sushi, so he grabbed at what he considered to be a close equivalent. "Tempura!"

Saroj had leaned back, basking in their conversation. She turned to each of them with her slightly cross-eyed smile. "Sushi-bushi. Jerry-berry. Darlings, I can't understand a thing you're saying. Don't you see you speak the same dialect? You're exactly the same kind of *American* Indian."

"Asian-Americans of Indian origin," said Ajay. "Truly speaking, I'm not sure we even qualify as a bona fide minority."

After tea, Saroj Aunty shooed Ajay and Gita off for a walk on the beach. "But you're both so young, you absolutely must have some fresh air. No, you know me and my arthritis. . . . Go on, darlings, don't worry if it gets dark before you're back."

To reach the beach, one climbed down a few steps and worked on sliding back the rusty bolt on the gate. The tide was still low, making for a spaciousness on the beach. A large area that waves had recently swabbed lay wet and polished, reflecting the sky. At Saroj Aunty's end of the beach there were bungalows set back from blackened garden walls, the air around them aswish with coconut trees. But walking north along the circle of beach, Gita could see that the deep green of palms increasingly gave way to the off-white and grays of apartment buildings. Only after the beach had tipped around toward Madh Island did a green band resume between the pale blues of sky and sea.

"When I came here as a kid," Gita said to Ajay, "Sun-n-Sand hotel was the only building on the entire beach over two stories high. Otherwise it was all low bungalows and shacks. Everything was so quiet."

"I remember," said Ajay. "We used to come for outings sometimes on the weekend. Juhu seemed far away then. But my mother could remember the days when you had to travel here by ferry."

Who at Whitney College would ever have known what Juhu was like twenty years ago, the vanished space living on in their minds? Gita walked beside Ajay feeling a benevolent past hang between them.

They were walking into the crowds and jangled noise that welled out from the main drag of Juhu Chowpatty. Here there were stands for fresh green coconuts, for savory *bhelpuri* that Harish Uncle had always decried as "instant amoebas," for Kwality ice cream ("calorific bombs") and poisonous colored ("cholera-cola") sodas. There were tarpaulins set up at an angle with bright balloons, and a series of prizes laid out on the base. Young men cultivating resemblances to film actors whose names Gita no longer knew poised before the balloons with air guns, shouting encouragement to each other. Carts clipped past with a jingle: mangy spots on the ponies' coats but brilliant pink feathers bobbing from their heads. Two monkeys dressed as urchin boy and girl danced around a gnarled man who rattled his drum. Real urchins with matted hair and snot on their lips presented outstretched hands toward Ajay, wheedling, *"Paisa, paisa."*

"Hutt!" said Ajay threateningly, digging his hands deeper into his pockets. "Look, there's even a Ramada Inn here now."

"And a Holiday Inn farther up the beach," said Gita.

Two bikinied white women, possibly air hostesses between international flights, wandered by with a retinue of young men in close pursuit. The urchins scampered after. "One rupee, I fuck you," a boy with a basket of roasted chickpeas called out as the procession went past.

"Look, can we walk closer to the shore?" asked Gita. This was the first time she had been out on the beach, and she hadn't been prepared for so much change. The breeze was sharp across the sea, and she wished she had brought along a shawl.

"Of course," said Ajay, touched that she seemed offended by the obscene word. "Watch out for the ball."

They were walking along the edge of a soccer game. Disembowelled green coconuts marked the goals. Ajay reached out a protective hand toward Gita as the torrent of players came running after the ball. Ahead, there was a silent demarcated area of sand from which a pair of disembodied hands emerged in folded salutations. A white cloth had been spread out where the body's feet should have been, and it already bore a splatter of aluminum coins.

"I've always wondered how the person breathes under there," said Gita.

"It's a gimmick," said Ajay, taking out his cigarettes. "A thin piece of muslin is laid on the face, and then just a fine layer of sand is scattered over. Probably the chap's helpers are watching from a distance, to make sure no one steals the coins. I tell you, it's a bloody shame that in this country people end up spending productive time doing things like this. Terrible for the economy."

Gita thought of the varied activities one might see on the streets and subways of New York, but the sense of vanished familiarity had made her too exhausted to point anything out. In the wet area ahead, she could see torn plastic bags and humps of withered marigold garlands washed up in pools of salt water. There were hardly any shells. Once she had been able to fill her pockets with tiny round shells of pale colors and intricate patterns. Ayah had always clucked when, for months later, the inner seams of her pockets shed sand.

There were fewer people right by the shore. The sea was quiet, the waves hissing forward in broad, low sweeps. A baby boy with a big spot of *kohl* against the evil eye on his cheek and DISCO emblazoned on his shirt was walking into the surging water. Hands raised from the elbows, he moved with the wobbly, bowlegged gait of a recent graduate from crawling. His mother, with a bright nylon sari tucked up around the waist, held out a hand. His father, pants rolled around the calves, stood watching. The boy needed no help. Step after deliberate step, he made his way through the foam. His chubby calves were wet and sandy. Catching Gita's smile, he gave her a deliriously happy chortle.

"Do you want children?" asked Ajay, who had noticed the transaction.

"I don't know, well, yes. I didn't want them when I was in graduate school. I guess that after I get tenure I might. Yes." Gita was all in a confusion. This interrogation seemed a little premature for a first meeting. But who knew, in arranged matters maybe these were the rules. After a minute she asked, "And you?"

"Of course," Ajay said with decisiveness. "I want children."

"Ah," Gita said.

Scattered images of possible futures rode in with the foam on the waves. As the sun swiveled slowly into the sea, Gita thought of how it was rising in Vermont, flushing snowfields. In Berkeley, the bridges and the town were probably resplendent with lights, the streets finally quiet, people inside their houses, asleep. Norvin and Ryoko were under the down comforter, light as a hundred clouds and covered with a patterned Merimekko duvet. And then, there was more night over the lapping Pacific.

Gita turned around to look Ajay full in his face. There was no doubt about it, with those plump jaws and that beautifully shaped mouth, he definitely looked like a Kapoor. "I've been hearing about you for years, you know," she said. "It really is nice to finally meet you."

* * *

The sun traveled on a few hours west to shine in through
the leafless twigs, through the glass dividing icy from warm
air, and straight upon the napkin stand and unevenly folded
New York Times on Charity and Isaac's kitchen table. Having
finished his coffee, Isaac was out shoveling the drive, and
Charity sat drinking spiced tea with Firoze.

"So the next time you visit you'll have to meet Gita," Charity was saying. "We saw her a few times before she took off
for India. Lucky bum! I'd only be more jealous if it was mango
season."

"Bombay in the May mango season is definitely not where
I'd like to be," said Firoze. "Your conceptions of India are all
warped by being so far north in those high, cool mountains."
He reflected a minute. "Still, those fragrant baskets of mangoes ripening in straw do make the heat bearable."

"I think you and Gita are really going to like each other,"
Charity said.

Firoze shook his head, smiling as he looked around the
kitchen. Wall to wall, it was a testament to domesticity: all
the implements that a wedding and two salaries could bring—
pictures of Isaac and Charity with their arms around each
other posted on the fridge, a fat cat asleep on the windowsill.
Last night he had slept in Charity's study and noticed the
framed wedding picture by her computer, a photograph of
Isaac beneath her embroidered elephant-headed Ganapati, a
blowup of them kissing hanging like a diploma from the wall.
Similarly, stepping into Isaac's study he had caught a glimpse
of Charity with chubby arms and curls, squatting with a doll,
placed before several gilded volumes with Hebrew lettering.
An older Charity smiled from beside a Yale mug filled with
pencils. Firoze couldn't help wondering why, if they had each
other to look at daily, they needed these photographs too. He
speculated that this was what happened when one joined the
Cult of the Couple: one surrounded oneself with paraphernalia
for daily worship, and then, as Charity was doing now, one
put in efforts to convert others.

"Frankly, I've always sort of liked her," Firoze said. "But

to tell the truth, there's this way that she disapproves of me. She's always made me feel as though I'm inept and can't do anything right, least of all carry on a conversation with her. Don't misunderstand, I think Gita is very attractive. But all that prim rigidity—it's too much for me to handle."

"Prim? Come off it, Firoze. Don't *lagao* stuff like that. What are you talking about?"

"You know what I mean. She's sort of uptight. Especially around men, I think. And then too, she's always been so unwilling to take any stand on an opinion."

"Sorry, Firoze, I don't know what you're talking about. None of this sounds in the least convincing. Are you sure we're speaking of the same Gita?"

"Well, yes, Gita Das—you told me yourself she's from Berkeley."

"First of all, let me tell you that she will hold forth at length about her very interesting research if you should care to listen. We had lunch together before she left, and were so engrossed in the conversation about our work that I almost missed my dentist's appointment. She has plenty of opinions to share, she just doesn't advertise them like most young academic males. And that second part about being sexually uptight: Baba, the first time I met her, she was wearing some sort of colored condoms as earrings."

"No!" Firoze had burst into a huge grin. "Not Gita!"

"Yes, Gita."

Firoze imagined Gita fixing him with those earnest eyes, acknowledging her own intelligence, telling him something. He pictured a moist condom hanging off her fleshy lobe, casting a shadow across the curve of her jaw, bumping amid the tendrils of young hair that hadn't joined her braid. He was glad that he was sitting at the table, but for propriety he also folded his hands in his lap.

Timothy Stilling

Serendipity. *What an exquisite word that is: a mater do-lorosa with serene pity for the odd twists of lives, for fate playing on human frailty. I remarked on this to Norvin when we had dinner together recently in Berkeley. But Norvin is Norvin. He could not help but disagree. I am increasingly suspicious that it is because literary critics are vultures on artistic creativity that he must always assert he is smarter than I. "Ah," he said, with that Cheshire smile of yellowed teeth. "Ah, but fate is sere, we rend it through our will. Isn't that a pity?"*

Serendipity. *Ink rolls sensually over glossy paper, but no further ideas are forthcoming. A car wheezes up the steep street outside my window. Can I be losing my inspiration?*

Lovely Ryoko, her face impassive as a Noh mask, looked at Norvin, at me, back at Norvin again, and speared the baby corn on her plate. Noh, now, is another word to play with. We were eating California Indian nouvelle cuisine. Norvin had made a point of assuring me that this meant Indian as in Native American. These days Norvin is interested by primitiv-ism. In fact, they were just back from a trip to New Guinea. Ryoko listened politely as he propounded his theory that male initiation rites among the highland tribes are related to bar mitzvahs. Norvin has also been rediscovering his essential manhood through drums and retreats. He reported that he took his drum along on the trip. The natives were apparently sure he was a forgotten ancestor whose skin had been bleached white from the trip to the underworld, over the seas.

Serendipity *was on my mind that evening because of an*

encounter that I did not reveal to Norvin. I had been attending a special session on my contribution to postbeat poetry at the Postmodern Language Association Meetings held in San Francisco this year. I was there incognito. I have always supervised the design of my jacket covers, and they have never, never carried my face. So, many people who know my name and read my work are unable to recognize me in person. Such is the power of the printed word. I revel in the oxymoronic trope of my anonymous celebrity.

Masked Noh anonymity, white / as the white / silence of serendipity . . . No, this is not quite right. I was standing in a crowd by the elevators in the large hotel, among the short, suited, self-important men and the women with a demeanor that informs you that though they may be intellectuals they always wear lacy underwear. I was making eye contact with a redhead I thought I perhaps recognized from one of my readings, or perhaps it was simply the association of red and read. Suddenly, the babble around me parted, and I heard a name I recognized. When I heard "Gita Das," I glanced down over my shoulder at the two men beside me. One had hair and the other did not, and they were both wearing gray suits with red ties. The red motif again.

"So those are your top candidates, huh?"

"Two of them aren't at the meetings this year. Gita Das is doing archival work in India."

"So what is she anyway? I know her work, of course, but it's hard to pin her down. Was her training in literature, history, or folkloristics?"

"I don't have the vita on me, and I don't quite recall. Whatever it is, her work is clearly the most unusual, and she can teach the courses we need. We'll probably be flying her in for an interview."

"She's not that woman who's married to Norv Weinstein, is she?"

"Oh no, you're mixing up the Asians, Bob—his wife is Japanese."

I was savoring the idea of Norvin being wiped out of someone's life as easily as a chalk duster slides across a board, when the elevator arrived with a "ping." We crowded inside. I found myself stomach to extended chest with the redhead.

"Hi," she said, lowering her lashes."Hi there, Timothy Stilling. I adore your poetry. It's expanded my subjective relations to sensuosity."

"Thanks," I said, trying to move back while she continued to butt into me. I suppose that this woman must have seen me at a reading. I remarked that she was not unattractive. But a little haughty distance might have been more compelling than this thrust of hers. Furthermore, I was on stage. Amid the whispers and murmurs all around the elevator I was sure I could hear the repeated "Timothy Stilling, Timothy Stilling, Timothy Stilling."

I got out on the fifth floor, and before the redhead could corner me for more conversation, I stepped into the men's room. I found myself standing at the urinal between the two men in gray suits and red ties who had been discussing Gita earlier. They now appeared to be regarding me with some awe, throwing me glances from either direction that induced self-consciousness not suited to bladder relief. At this point, who should emerge from one of the stalls but Norvin himself. He had a painted rattle under one arm.

"Hi there, Timothy," he called out. "Sorry I can't come to your panel. I have to go perform at the plenary session. So we'll be seeing you for dinner in a couple of days, right? We'll tell you all about our trip."

"Great," I said, shaking out the last few drops. I have always found it abrasive when Norvin uses "we": it is as though he wants to underline that Marie-Claire and others notwithstanding, I have always been "me," while he, three times, has been an established "we." I doubt that he will ever admit that it was I who Rachel first contacted. I had just won a poetry prize, and she wanted to interview me for a Radcliffe literary magazine. It was sheer coincidence that he had been tagging along from the dormitory and I hadn't been able to shed him yet. Certainly, he did more talking than I did at that interview,

*but it's on the record that Rachel thought the world of me.
The article she published is somewhere in the clippings I in-
tend to bequeath with other papers to the Library of Congress.
If I had tried to get her at the time I surely could have. It's
the same with Gita. Wasn't I the one who was carrying the
perfume from that talkative Indian couple? Wasn't I the one
she cast those lingering black eyes on first? I once received a
telephone call from her in which I'm fairly certain she confessed longing to have kissed me. And as for Ryoko, he met
her at the wine and cheese reception after my book was released. Norvin just follows in on situations where I have paved
the way, and he has no grounds to behave in this patronizing
fashion.*

*Masked Noh anonymity / silent, white successor of /
perfume-lipped serendipity. No, this won't do either. I probably foundered with "Noh"; the word is too short. I wonder
if Bunruku theater uses masks. "Bunruku anonymity" would
be better.*

*Norvin had already left when I started out the door of the
men's room. One of the two men, the hair-impaired one who
represented the institution where there is a possible job for
Gita, held open the door for me. This was my chance, I
thought.*

*"Let me tell you that Gita Das is brilliant, absolutely bril-
liant, far more brilliant even than the holder of a chair like
Norvin Weinstein," I told him. "Her magnificent intellect reverberates in my poetry from the mid eighties. 'To Ration the
Heart' and 'Nice, No?' are among the poems directly influenced by her when she was merely a graduate student. You'll
be very lucky if you can hire her at your institution."*

"Institution?" the man asked.

"Isn't she on your short list for a job?" I asked.

"What job?" asked the man. "Who are you anyway?"

*"My name is Stilling, and I couldn't help overhearing you
talking by the elevator."*

*"Stilling! Jesus, not the Timothy Stilling. Why aren't you
wearing a name tag? What a coincidence, I'm just on my way*

to cover your panel. Sorry, I wasn't on the elevator. I took the stairs because with this heavy day it didn't look like I'd have a chance to visit the Fitness Center."

"Who are you?" I asked. I couldn't help being pleased to be recognized, but it does put one at a terrible disadvantage to be famous.

Rather than say his name, he lifted up his name tag, on which his name and affiliation were spelled out. He was a reporter for the Chronicle of Higher Education. "I'm working on a special feature about contemporary poetry and the structure and influence of the academy. Thanks for the tip! That's great. I'll be sure to get this mentor of yours into the piece."

Why, I wondered, do all these little men have to wear the same gray suit and red tie? With this thought, I entered the conference room filled to capacity and slipped into the audience to observe the nervous panelists study their papers one last time or pour themselves ice water. It never hurts to monitor what is new in what the literary critics have to say about me.

But if they are to keep saying something, I must keep writing. Perhaps if I start afresh this poem will start rolling.

Red as the painted penis / sheath / of a highlands warrior / Neckties announce power / and echo / the anonymous rattle of serendipity . . .

7

An Arranged
Affair

Snow was deep in Whitney when Gita returned. White roofs slanted into white skies, and white smoke rose from chimneys. The twigs of trees had turned into the intricate fans of giant white peacocks that kept company with the snow people standing sentinel in many yards. Out in the fields, sun touched snow crystals with a dazzle of beams, as though Saroj Aunty had taken all her diamonds out of their settings and strewn them like a farmer sowing seeds.

The second Saturday that Gita returned, the Society for the Protection of Single People gathered in her house to eat dinner beside the snap and crackle of the wood-burning stove.

"The meeting is now called to order," Chairman Zelda announced once bowls had been filled with steaming vegetable soup and bread had been passed around. "The moment has arrived for confession. Is there anything that the Heavenly Father should worry about?"

Roberto set down his spoon and raised a hand.

"No! Roberto!" Zelda and Gita cried.

"And you didn't even go anywhere!" said Gita.

"Who? Where? Someone local? Oh, cool!" Zelda thumped the table with both palms. A papier-mâché chili and a cluster of translucent glass fruit bobbed on either side of her face. "Oh, tell."

"It is a complicated story," Roberto said. "It begins with Charity. She and Isaac had a guest, you must remember, that *wonderful* man whom Gita is supposed to know too: Firoze." He pronounced it Fee-ross.

"No!" said Gita. "I never even suspected . . ." Immediately worried that she might have sounded heterocentric, she added, "Oh yes, Roberto, he really is nice." She racked her brains across the years for more encouraging things to add. "Very striking, isn't he, those black eyebrows? Such a sympathetic and intelligent person. Intellectually courageous too—you should have seen how he didn't stick to the confines of any one department but kept taking courses all over the place. And I tell you, he was so unassuming! Never paid any attention at all to his dress. Oh yes, Roberto, Firoze is *really* a terrific fellow."

Roberto went on eating his soup. He bent over his bowl, his eyes on Gita, with no trace of expression showing under his beard. As soon as she finished, he resumed. "So, what happened is this: Charity invited me over for a holiday dinner. You know how it is with her and Isaac—they couldn't call it Christmas or Hanukkah so it all became the holiday season. As soon as I walked in I noticed this guy. He was helping Charity with the eggnog, you know, keeping track of the spiked and unspiked. He was fair, but he was dark too, one of those people with a face that is hard to place. I wondered if he was also from Latin America, or could it be the Middle East? Then I heard him speak in this deep, rich voice. I thought that perhaps he was Irish. I began to talk to him and learned that he was a Zoroastrian from India, but when he found out where I was from, he started to speak Spanish!"

"I told you Firoze had such broad interests," said Gita. "He was studying Hindi *and* Spanish at Berkeley. He even took courses in women's studies—isn't that wonderfully unusual in a man?" Again, she caught herself; she hadn't meant to imply that there might be something feminine about Firoze just because he was gay. She began to twist the edges of the paper towel standing in as napkin in her lap. "It shows great humanity, doesn't it, to not just be tied up with the concerns of the identity given by birth? There's really no doubt about it, Roberto, Firoze is a great guy."

"We got the point," said Zelda. "Now let Roberto finish his story."

"So, I started talking to this Firoze, and it turned out that he is representing one of my cousins in his immigration case. That made it seem even more like destiny. I was worried about getting a big, painful crush on a straight guy, so I told him some things about my friend in St. Louis and how we broke up. Firoze listened. He didn't suddenly have to go refill his glass and escape when he learned I was gay. He said it must have been so tough to move to a new place with a broken heart. My hopes grew. So I invited him for a tour around town the next day. He said yes. I tell you, ladies, I was in heaven!"

"And then what happened?" asked Zelda.

"I had little sleep that night. The next morning I came to fetch him. There is not too much to show anyone in Whitney, and I was beginning to feel ridiculous. First I guided him around the campus. When he saw that disappearing *n* on the main sign by the gate, he laughed. We talked about racism on campus and how undergraduates should be exposed to many cultures. Then we drove into town. But how long can you take someone around ski stores, soap stores, stores with little carved mementos? After some time we went into the used-book and music store."

"The place run by that guy who looks like John Lennon," said Gita, helping herself to salad. She was still conscious of having babbled on in a phony way, and she didn't want to risk saying more about Firoze.

"You got it. His name is Bill. I've always been wondering about that man. Last semester, when I was feeling trapped by the size of this place, I would go into that store and browse through his books and music. I picked up some fabulous jazz. He would smile a little and watch me from behind his register, but we never said much to each other."

"I've wondered about that guy too," said Zelda. "He's intriguing. I once wore this little purple miniskirt with purple zebra-striped tights, and asked him about all the Alberta Hunter, Laurie Anderson, and Pretenders records he had. Nothing happened. He doesn't wear a ring, but I had the feeling that he had someone tucked away."

"Now, I have to tell you that by the time Firoze and I had reached that bookstore, I was getting the idea that maybe Firoze was straight. It wasn't anything that he said directly, or even that he was taking much notice of women. I just could feel it. Small things I said that he did not pick up on—you know how it can be."

"Tell me about it!" Zelda theatrically sighed. "I'm always getting the same treatment from the opposite side. Sometimes you wish people would just wear badges telling you their sexual orientation and status of availability. It would be so helpful at every gathering."

"I'm not sure that even that's enough to sort things out," said Gita. "You might find out that someone is interested in women and available, but then do you think they'd sit down to introduce you to their pet neuroses before you got involved? It seems like you still could use a recommendation from someone else who knows them well."

"You mean, like a setup?" asked Zelda.

"Listen." Roberto spread his hands. "Do you guys want to hear the end of my story or not? There was no one else in the bookstore, just me and Firoze. I showed him some of my favorite jazz. Bill, the owner, watched us and he smiled. I smiled. Firoze smiled. Then Bill began to talk to us. He told us about this bar in town where the gay men get together on Friday nights. Firoze, he was cool. All he said was that he was leaving by Friday and thanks anyway. But I went. Can you believe it, I was in this fucking town for five whole months without ever hearing of this place and the Friday nights?"

"So, you see why the zebra tights had no effect whatsoever." Zelda shook her head and smacked her cheek with an index finger. "Bad try, Zelda."

"It did not take too long for me to tell Bill that actually Firoze was not my partner."

"Uh-oh," said Zelda. "Do I hear the rumbles of secession from our society?"

Roberto set down his spoon, flashing them an ear-to-ear grin. "Well, who knows? We have been seeing each other. The three of us could just change the name of the club and still be good friends."

"Do we have a motion?" asked Zelda.

"Or we could become the Parsi-Watching Society of Whitney," said Gita. "But then we'd have to make sure that Charity invited Firoze every weekend for observation." In a voice unsteady with laughter, she filled them in on Harish Uncle and Norvin. Laughter helped jiggle and melt the bad feelings associated with Norvin. It was only when she had finished that Zelda, the chairperson, steered the interrogation back on course, and Gita found herself admitting, "Well, yes, I did meet this guy in India. I don't know, he's Saroj Aunty's choice. He *seemed* very nice. Let's see, maybe there's a possibility. So, are you guys ready for dessert?"

Ajay had just come in from a dinner party in Murray Hall. The snow had started to scud against his windshield as he drove home, and now it was falling fast and thick outside. He sat on the sofa staring at the TV screen. Habit had brought him here. The TV was off, but he sat on the corner of the sofa so familiar to him that the cushions were shaped to his frame. He stared at the room's reflection, curved and distorted in the glassy screen. He lit another cigarette.

He was thinking about his brother, Prakash, and why Prakash's life made him, Ajay, so angry. One of Ajay's ex-girlfriends' therapists had had a guru, and Ajay had picked up the technique of not merely experiencing an emotion but looking inward to observe it. Apparently this was an ancient Hindu meditation practice. The anger about Prakash, Ajay now witnessed, had to do with the Marine Drive apartment, with its rhythms of noise and quiet. It had to do with there always being a servant in the background, Kalpana so ruthlessly competent, the kids on vacation with their singsong voices so full of rambunctious life. It had to do with dinners at eight-thirty with the television news in Hindi and *chappatis* still puffed with heat, the serials after the news that everyone watched, even the servants standing in the doorways. This is what Prakash had. Ajay wondered if he'd stayed on in Bombay if he'd have all this too.

Instead, what could he boast of? Several degrees in computer science. A job at Bell Labs. A thinning patch on the top of his head that all the creams and oils were not helping. He owned a condominium that was generally so messy it was embarrassing to have people over, even the maid who came in once a month and left the house reeking of cleaning fluids. He had a remote-control VCR he could watch from his bed. He had a cabinet full of liquors. Though he earned far more than his brother would ever hope for, that household still made him feel like a beggar—a beggar on crutches, standing at the gate, while laughter and argument flew fast from the house inside. Of course, he would never want to be around a woman as petty as Kalpana, so obsessed with her little dogs, recipes, and saris. He had always resented the way Kalpana had taken over the household from his mother. But even if Kalpana had banished his mother's bright posters of gods from every wall, and even if she had bought ridiculous arty mugs instead of using the old cups and saucers for tea, he still had to admit that it was Kalpana who stood at the center of the hubbub he identified as family happiness.

Ajay's mind moved on to the dinner he had just come in from: the men watching videos of cricket matches sent on from India, the wives who gathered in the kitchen amid a flurry of soft voices and swish of silk saris. He was the only one of the group who still came to these gatherings alone. He had tried bringing various American girlfriends, but they had never really fit. They always seemed to leak out of the kitchen and would want to publicly hold his hand. Their presences flustered the men who were forced to sit up straight and hold back on jokes like the one about the impotent Guju called Kamlesh, pronounced "comeless" in a nasal Gujarati woman's voice. Of course, not all American women were so unaware of how best to behave. Take Om Prakash's wife, who had started out as Vanessa from Tulsa. With time she had become Vinita, who faithfully watered a sacred *tulsi* plant grown from seeds formed in her mother-in-law's courtyard. While the other wives had developed brassier New Jersey accents, Vinita Bhabhi had begun to roll her head. She wore *kajal* smeared beneath her blue eyes, and on her forehead there was real *kumkum*—not just a stick-on dot of red felt.

The dinner tonight had broken up early, because of the children. It was hardly ten. The evening ahead alone with himself pressed against Ajay, squeezing at him, pulling heavily at his chest. He was so full that he had to loosen his belt, but his mind grabbed like a bratty child for the half-eaten chocolate bar lying somewhere in the fridge. That might lift him up. At least then he could watch TV, slip into someone else's world for a while. He thought of what might be on cable; but he continued to sit. He wondered what Gita was doing tonight.

From his pocket he pulled out an Indian aerogram. He smoothed the coarse blue paper across his knee. The letter had come a few days ago, and he had already reread it so many times he might have been able to recite it. But once again, he read through the letter, picking and weighing the words.

"Our darling Ajay" the letter began in Saroj Aunty's splashy handwriting. Her *i*s were dotted with full moons, and her *g*s, *j*s, and *y*s looped down to crisscross with the line below. It was large, abandoned writing that filled both sides of the form.

Our darling Ajay,

This will find you back in that country of yours. We are all despondent here, we miss you so much. You have grown up to be such a fine young man. There is no doubt that you will make some lucky girl *very* happy. I hope that wedding bells will ring *soon!!!*

By the way, our Gita was simply enchanted by you. She told me you spent a lovely day together. *Do stay in touch* [heavy underlining]. She needs to have more friends like you out there in the States. Keep an eye on her for your Aunty.

Of course, when you do meet a nice girl, I can arrange to have horoscopes matched. Remember, if you need a place to tie the "nuptial knot," this house is always ready. Just recently Girija Advani got married here. Do you remember her? The groom had dysentery, poor chap, but despite these problems it was a *lovely* wedding.

I worry so much about our Gita all alone in that Whitney place. Be sure to ring her up and send me a full report. Do write *soon*. I live in daily anticipation of your letter!!!

With love and kisses X O X
Saroj Aunty

Of course, Saroj Aunty always had a flair for exclamation marks and shameless exaggeration. But why would she lie about Gita? He had certainly noticed that Gita was smart and pretty. But since she was off so far up north, he hadn't thought about her seriously. He would never have guessed she was "enchanted" by him. The thought of someone being enchanted made him sit up straighter. Maybe she was home on a Saturday night, fondly reminiscing about the Chinese lunch they had had in downtown Bombay.

Ajay had been carrying around Saroj Aunty's letter for three days now. He had thought of calling several times, but whenever he went to the phone he stopped short and turned to something else. After all, Gita was Indian. He had never dated an Indian woman, and he was sure this couldn't be casual. Now things were changing there, but in the India he grew up in people became engaged to marry, they didn't just try things out with American open-endedness. Of course, Gita was living in America now, and she had even been divorced, but . . . Ajay stood up and broke two pieces of chocolate off the bar in the fridge. He pushed the pieces around his mouth, allowing them to melt and release reassuring sweetness. What the heck, she was an attractive woman, she probably wouldn't be home on a Saturday night, whatever Saroj Aunty insinuated about her social life. He took out his address book to compare the number he had with the one Saroj Aunty had underlined in a P.S.

He dialed, listening to the patterns that fell together as each digit extended into a tone. But before he completed all ten digits, he put down the receiver. He poured himself a stiff whiskey and tried again. Oh hell, it wasn't just ringing, but someone was actually picking up the phone. He tried to steady his voice.

"Umm, Gita? Hi, this is Ajay. Remember? You see, I got this letter from Aunty, and she had sent your number asking that I should check in on you. Of course, I was also personally, er, I mean wondering, how you are and if you arrived back safely. Travel isn't the same these days of world terrorism, but then I suppose most untoward incidents do get into the papers. I myself got back only recently and since then, I've been quite busy. Work, you know. So how are you doing?"

"Wait a minute," said a female voice at the other end when he finally paused. "I'll go get Gita."

Ajay took a deep breath. He was so focused on getting a cigarette lit so he could take a long, calming drag that he barely noticed that the unknown American female had called out, in tones echoing across phone lines. "Yo, Gita! Get your hands out of that soapy water! Our Heavenly Father is on the line wanting to have a word with you."

"Just look how brilliant our Gita is getting," said Saroj, opening up her purse and handing Kalpana a clipping across the table. "She is even inspiring famous poets!"

Kalpana sucked salted *lassi* up a straw. She smoothed the clipping out on the table and moved slightly away from it so her eyes would adjust their focus as she continued with her drink. She and Saroj had been out at an exhibition of Lucknow *chikan* embroidery. Now they had stepped into a café adjoining an art gallery for refueling before they proceeded on down the road to examine a new shipment of Gujarati tie-dyed *bandhni* saris. They sat at the end of a long porch divided by a corridor between two sets of tables. There was pink bougainvillea in blossom at the edge of the porch and abstract paintings by Bombay artists on the wall inside. Saroj had recognized people all along the two lines of tables when they arrived, slowing down her progression to the gracious pace of royalty. She now sat beaming out at the other tables, while Kalpana faced the proprietess and a hub of bustling waiters.

"What is postbeat?" asked Kalpana, trying to concentrate. "This is something about the postman making rounds or what?"

"Darling, you're so witty!" giggled Saroj. She waved and blew a kiss over Kalpana's shoulder, but by the time Kalpana looked back, it was impossible to say who it had been aimed at. "Isn't it wonderful to see so many friends? What with this impossible traffic, no one seems to visit Juhu anymore."

Rather than trying to read the whole article, Kalpana focused on the section highlighted with a red line and exclamation mark along the side.

> *Stilling attributes much of his inspiration to members of the academy. Among the scholars he cites as important to*

*his development as a poet is Gita Das, currently visiting
assistant professor at Whitney College. While only a graduate student, Professor Das directly influenced several of
the poems included in his prizewinning collection* Autumn
at the Heart's Bottom. *"Gita Das is absolutely brilliant,"
Stilling says. "Her magnificent intellect reverberates in my
poetry." The overlaps in creative influence within and
without the structures of academic institutions are well
illustrated in a case such as this.*

"Who is this fellow?" Kalpana asked suspiciously. She was
longing for *dahi wada* to arrive, and it was difficult to take
in anything else with good temper. "How Gita knows him?"

"Oh, someone she only met several times in her Berkeley
days," said Saroj. "It's all here in the letter. Actually she thinks
it is all some kind of joke. But he's quite famous and this is
a publication many people in the universities read, so all this
carrying on about her brilliance can't hurt her career. Look,
there's Jangoo Junglewala! I do believe he's coming in with
Jeroo—that's Jimmy's daughter. Did I tell you that Jimmy and
Proachie retired to Lonaula? They said they'd had enough of
city life. Oh my, these two down there are trying to avoid my
eye; this is extremely interesting. Was he her cousin or not, I
can't remember. I wonder if her divorce has come through
already."

"I have no idea," said Kalpana. "I don't know them." A
waiter in a once-white uniform was coming out, balancing a
tray at shoulder level. When he walked by and did not stop
at their table, Kalpana intercepted him with a sharp *"Jaldi
karo!"*

"Things are going so well for our Gita," Saroj said. "She's
even been called for a few job interviews. One is in New York.
She says that Ajay will be in California doing some consulting,
otherwise those two would have gotten together for a little
rendezvous! Probably he's told you too, they've been speaking
on the phone *quite* a bit." Saroj leaned over the table and
pushed at Kalpana's sari blouse with her finger. "All due to

you, darling—you're so smart in seeing that they might be compatible."

The *dahi wada* had arrived, soaked in white curds topped with brown tamarind chutney and sprinkled with roasted cumin and red chili powder. Kalpana leaned forward, anticipating the sensation of textures and flavors in her mouth. She smiled at Saroj. "Yes, so lovely that the children are getting along," she said, lifting a laden spoon to her lips.

Gita had a busy spring. Between keeping up with her classes, holding office hours, advising seniors on their theses, writing her book, and flying off for job interviews, it seemed as though she was always running. Yet amid all the pressure and activity, there was now a calm hub to which her life reassuringly returned: the presence of Ajay, twice a week, over the phone. He made her feel unusual, witty, competent. Even the simplest things she had said to Norvin used to be appropriated as a sounding board of his own quick intellect. Ajay, on the other hand, was not so much of a talker as a listener. He understood India. He knew Saroj Aunty. Reliability and appreciation were a good deal to ask from any man. Zelda had recently been brandishing a best-selling self-help paperback that warned that exciting men could not be trusted. Women, the book counseled, would do better to shed their expectations of thrilling heros and closely consider men whose bodies were not like film actors' and whose mannerisms had no macho panache. Ajay, Gita recalled, was handsome enough, but he was also slightly plump in a huggable way. She learned from him that he too had had a long drought period in which he despaired of ever meeting a suitable partner. He confessed his sense of heartache when he visited his brother's house, his isolation when he drove home alone after parties. Compassion for his loneliness coupled with a pact of camaraderie in getting to know each other tied Gita to Ajay with a knot that felt stronger than one spun from infatuation. Gita wondered: was

compassion a form of love? Or was she just ascribing to him
the pathos of her own unmatedness?

Several years ago, while doing research for her dissertation
amid the cramped stacks, low ceilings, and fluorescent lights
of the Berkeley library, Gita had pored through a number of
old British journals that featured items of folklore submitted
by collectors in many different regions of India. There was
one folktale that she now tried to remember. She couldn't
recall whether it was in *Indian Antiquary, North Indian Notes
and Queries,* or *Journal of the Asiatic Society of Bengal.* It
had been collected by a Parsi woman—something Wadia, if
she wasn't mistaken—and so she thought that perhaps it had
been a Gujarati folktale. The details of the plot were now
blurred, but she racked her brains trying to reconstruct how
it had unfolded.

[It started with a princess, that was certain, a lovely
and talented princess.] *Perhaps it was when she was out
walking somewhere that she observed a nest of sparrows.
There was a male sparrow, a female sparrow, and several
chicks. As the princess watched, their nest went up in a
forest fire. The male sparrow flapped away, but the female sparrow stayed with the chicks and was roasted to
a crisp. When the princess saw this, she was stricken. It
seemed clear proof of the unreliability of men. She vowed
then and there that she would never marry.*

[At this point, the story grew dim as the shadows of a
half-remembered dream. Was it the king who, filled with
sorrow over his daughter's decision, commissioned a girlfriend of hers to masquerade as a painter? Or was it that
the girlfriend, feeling pain for her friend, took it upon
herself to dress as a man and go off to another kingdom?
Or was it actually just a traveling painter, a man, who
happened to be on his way between royal families?] *In
any event, a prince in a distant kingdom somehow got*

his hands on a portrait of the lovely princess. He was overcome with love. He vowed then and there that he would marry her. But he also learned that this was a princess who had sworn she would never marry, for she thought that men could not be trusted.

"Help me," he implored the painter. "You must find some way that her mind can be changed and we can exchange wedding garlands."

[Gita wasn't sure if it was the painter who came back to the first kingdom, or if the prince now dressed as a painter in hopes of meeting the princess.] *The painter, though, set up camp at some distance from the palace. After some days, the princess was invited to come to view the paintings. There was a large frieze painted on one wall.* And also, there was a portrait of the prince.

"Who is this?" the princess asked, for though she had vowed not to marry, she could not help being affected by the depth of expression in the young man's face.

"This," said the painter, "is a gifted and wise young prince. But everyone in his kingdom is in mourning over him."

"Why is that?" asked the princess.

"The reason is that he has vowed not to marry."

"Vowed not to marry!" The princess's interest was fanned. "Why would he do such a thing?"

At this point, the painter pointed at a frieze. It was of a doe galloping away from a forest fire, as a buck and young faun perished. "He has witnessed this scene," said the painter, "and now he is certain that all women are unreliable, that they are fickle in love within their families, and that they desert men when the least problems arise."

"But that is extraordinary," said the princess. "I witnessed the same thing with a male sparrow and thought the same about men. But here it is a doe." She studied the frieze further and then commented, "But that doe is not all women, of course."

"He says that this is clear evidence that self-interest is paramount in the world, and that no bonds endure," the painter said.

"What ridiculous logic," said the princess. "I would like to meet this silly prince and explain why he is wrong."

And so she met the prince, and in the course of speaking with him, she understood that her own position was also extreme. By the time she realized she was in love with him, she had changed her mind about marriage. So they were married and both kingdoms rejoiced. And the painter—who was perhaps an itinerant artist, perhaps a girlfriend in disguise, or perhaps the prince himself—was the happiest of all with the success of the machinations.

Gita had been warned before she flew down to New York that though she and two other candidates were being brought in for a campus interview, it wasn't clear that budgets would actually permit a hire. This was a shame, for New York was the closest to Bell Labs in New Jersey. In any event, after flying to Austin, Tucson, and Philadelphia, her talk was all set and she had an infallible interview suit to wear. She was only frustrated that the interview was occurring at a time that Ajay was off doing some consulting and couldn't drive up to Manhattan. Though they spoke often on the phone, they had really only met twice, and that too in Bombay. After the first evening on Juhu beach, they had spent part of a day downtown where they had eaten a Chinese lunch, shopped at Cottage Industries, and strolled over to the Gateway of India, followed by bedraggled women who cajoled them for money until a troop of Japanese tourists wearing matched baseball caps rounded the bend.

Gita had finished her talk, answered questions, and was straightening the sheaf of paper on the podium when a man with a thick black beard approached her. He was wearing a bright Guatemalan sweater over his jeans, and for a moment

Gita thought he might be one of Roberto's New York relatives.

"That was an excellent talk," he said. "I'm really glad that Charity tipped me off to come hear you speak."

It was the voice that she recognized, the deep voice and the steady hazel eyes with intense brows. Firoze's face was thinner, its balance shifted by the beard. Studying him more closely, she could see flecks of gray by his temples and in the luxurious hair on his face. "You look so much older," Gita said. She caught herself. "I guess I do too."

"Yes," said Firoze. He took in the small dark woman before him. Though she hadn't actually grown, she seemed to be bigger, weighty with a new confidence. She was wearing a tapered mulberry skirt with matching jacket, her hair piled high at the back of her head. Understandably, she wasn't wearing her condom earrings but Navajo silver studs. "I'd be lying if I said you looked exactly the same. You look good, Gita."

"Thanks," Gita said. The chairman of the department where she was interviewing had appeared at Firoze's elbow. "This is one of my old friends from graduate school," she explained to him.

"Do you think you might have time to get together before you leave?" Firoze shifted his focus back to her after he and the chairman had shaken hands. "Or are you all booked up, breakfast, lunch, and dinner?"

Gita looked inquiringly at the chairman. "I don't know, really. I'm passed around according to the interview schedule."

The chairman was surveying Firoze as though he were an unannounced savior. The truth was, this was an extremely awkward time in the semester. There had just been a major conference here the week before. Students were clamoring to get their midterm exams and papers back. Das was the third candidate to visit in the last month. The faculty were jaded by having to attend talks, hold interviews in their offices, appear for entertainment. What with budget constraints, it wasn't like the old days when the university would pick up the tab if faculty went out to a restaurant with a candidate. It had been with great difficulty that the chair had managed to round up even half the department for dinner with Das the night before, and he knew that he would be the only person with her at dinner tonight. He had already spent much of his day with Das, showing her around campus and taking her in to deans. Frankly, though this young woman was quite charming, he had said just about all he had to say to her, and he would much rather watch "L.A. Law" tonight, and take his wife and kids out to dinner later on the weekend.

"Terrific! An old friend!" the chairman said. "I wouldn't want to stand between the two of you. Feel quite free to take her off to dinner, and then just return her to the hotel yourself. Her next appointment is nine tomorrow morning."

Looking sideways at each other, Gita and Firoze caught each other's eye. They broke out into grins. For Gita it was the sense of suddenly finding that there was a free period in a day of tests, and one could run headlong into the sunshine on the playground instead. For Firoze there was a feeling of having asked for something an adult surely wouldn't grant but encountering a miraculously indulgent nod and a pat on the head. With a complicitous bounce to their steps, Gita and Firoze emerged outside in the chill evening air. Traffic was dashing by with bright streaks of white or red light, a squeal of tires, and horns in many tones of imperiousness. In patches between tall buildings, the sky had the smoky luminosity of the day's last light. The buildings themselves were patterned with an uneven scatter of squares of light. They walked by a woman with a baby huddled up on a doorstep with a sign saying HOMELESS, PLEASE HELP. Firoze took out a dollar and handed it over without breaking his pace.

"Home food or restaurant food?" Firoze asked as they waited for the signal across the intersection to change. "I have all the ingredients for a good stir-fry."

"Home sounds great," said Gita. "I've ODed on restaurants recently. I've been traveling a lot. I remember you're a good cook, too."

"So we take the bus, then. I live right near Forty-second Street, way over by the theater district. It's the city at its most intense, a real jungle of drug dealers, hookers, peep shows, shrieking ambulances. And trash. But the apartment is up high. It's fairly quiet, with a little corner of the river in the view. Anyway, don't worry, I'll see you back to your hotel later."

They sat pressed together on the bus and exchanged synopses of their lives. The intervening years had added weight to what had never been a particularly close connection, and now they greeted each other as old friends. For Gita, Firoze was suddenly an ally rather than a member of a threatening enemy clan. She was relaxed and comfortable. Firoze, on the other hand, was recalling that odd energy that he had always felt sparking off Gita. He tried not to register the touch of her knee against his. Charity had cautioned him about there being a man at the margins of Gita's life—Charity couldn't say how serious it was—but Firoze did not want to allow himself any feeling that could topple headlong into disappointment.

The foyer smelled faintly of urine, and the doorman had a red nose. The walls of the elevator were spattered with some ancient dried liquid whose provenance Gita would not like to imagine. There were balls of lint in the yellowed light of the corridor, and the dull, close scent of laundry detergent mixing with grease from last year's dinners. But as Firoze had said, undoing the multiple locks on his door, the unsavory setting fell away as one entered his apartment.

A marmalade cat came to the door, breaking into a rasping purr as Firoze picked it up and advanced inside. It was a single T-shaped room, with a tiny kitchen at one end and a bathroom at the other. All along the top of the T was a line of window, speckled with lights that included a faint glitter of New Jersey over the river. In the corner near the bathroom a large bed was spread with a maroon comforter. An unfolding purple-and-gray Georgia O'Keefe iris hung over the bed. The larger area was dominated by an intricate maroon-and-black Bukhara carpet that Gita remembered from Berkeley. A sofa, a low table, bookshelves, and an extremely chaotic desk surrounded by shelves angled around the magnificent carpet. The walls were almost bare, except for Indian tribal jewelry hanging from hooks and a few woodcut posters with Spanish slogans that Gita also recognized from the old days. Firoze bustled about, switching on lamps, folding the newspapers that lay open on the sofa, moving a jumble of books off the table, picking up mugs and carrying them to the kitchen.

"This is Tigré Apsara," Firoze said about the cat, who was now sniffing at Gita. "Tigré for short. She's a great purrer, endlessly optimistic. I think she's responsible for my sanity in this city. What will you have? Wine, beer, tea, coffee, juice?"

"Wine, please," Gita called back, reaching out to stroke Tigré's soft, arching back and raised neck. But hearing the refrigerator open, the cat dashed off into the kitchen. Gita started to unpin her hair. Piled high, its weight was beginning to give her a headache. "Actually, I'm really hungry too. Can I help?"

"Not yet," said Firoze, reemerging with a bottle of white wine and two glasses. "But if you're hungry we'll get dinner on its way." He poured Gita a glass of wine and set a bowl of savory *chivra* beside her. As Gita fell on this first aid after her grueling day, Firoze brought a chopping board and some bowls, which he laid out on the low table. The cat had apparently been fed in the kitchen, for after a moment it joined them and set about an elaborate routine of licking and preening with an unbroken rumble.

"If I'd known you were coming I could have made some preparations," Firoze said, "but you're just going to have to be part of the process."

"So what can I do?"

"Peel garlic for starts," Firoze said, demolishing an onion with brisk swipes of a cleaver. "And, oh yes, why don't you choose some music?"

"All this garlic and onion!" Gita said. "Remember that lecture that Kamashree Ratnabhushitalingam-Hernandez delivered about the Jaina Return of the Repressed, that high-flown deconstructionist lecture that nobody could begin to understand?" Gita looked over at Firoze. He was absorbed with the onion, but she could see the gravity that had fallen over his face. "Sorry, I'd forgotten how much of a fan of hers you always were."

"Actually," Firoze said slowly, "actually, if we're letting each other in on our stories, we might as well be frank. I got involved with her after that talk."

"Really?" said Gita. "What on earth happened? My God, I had no idea." Her tongue was running ahead of her. "Not *Kamashree*. What was it like?"

"Music first, and then I'll tell you." Firoze neatly slid the sliced onions off the cutting board and into a bowl. He started on a carrot next, chopping at an angle as though he was sharpening a pencil. The cat crouched, watching the glint of steel with fascination.

Gita looked through his stack of records and chose a Brazilian samba collection. Firoze tried not to stare at her neat behind as she bent over the records, or to register the dense mass of black hair. A huge and lusty woman's voice soared through the room as Gita sat back down and began to work on the garlic. "I mean, you don't have to tell anything if you don't want to. It's just that Kamashree is legendary for her prowess. I've never known anyone before who actually experienced her up close. Oh, Norvin, of course, but I think that those were in the old days before either of them had become these famous academics."

"Oh yes, she did mention Norvin," Firoze said. He wondered how this related him and Gita, if they had both been, well, intimate, with people who were once intimate themselves.

Gita was thinking the same thought. But for her, it all tied in with the embarrassment of overhearing Norvin and Kamashree in his office that miserable evening of the reception. She wondered about the dismissive things Kamashree might have said about Norvin, and whether he had ever accused her of staring too. What was it that she had quipped about *Kama-*

sutra love secrets? Meeting Norvin with Ryoko, what might Kamashree now observe about the huge organs in Japanese erotic art? Gita smiled to herself, a tiny mischievous sparkle of grin that Firoze intercepted. He felt the space between them beginning to throb and longed to reach out and find her lips. Dinner be damned. Instead he refilled her glass. He stroked the back of Tigré's neck, until she broke into another crashing purr. Wordlessly, he moved on to pit and sliver the glossy bell pepper.

"So?" asked Gita. She was faintly aware that she might sound coy, but what the hell, with an old friend like Firoze one didn't need to worry. "Wasn't I going to hear a story?"

"How about a story swap?" asked Firoze, picking up the note of flirtation and dribbling it along until it could be tossed back in her direction. "One point about Norvin matched by one point about Kamashree? So, you get to ask the first question." He stopped chopping and had folded his arms, smiling. "I promise to try telling the truth and nothing but the truth without getting embarrassed."

"How did it begin?" Gita shot out.

"Well, you know that evening when you disappeared for the longest time, at some point she and I landed up beside the *samosa*s. I told her I admired her work. She looked me up and she looked me down with that stare of hers. Then she took out her appointment book. 'I'll be in town for two weeks,' she said. 'Are you free in the afternoons? How about three-thirty to five P.M.?' Well, yes, as a matter of fact I was free, it was summer vacation, and my work-study job was in the mornings. So that's how it began. And now you have to tell me, how did things begin with Norvin?"

"But what's there to tell? You know it all. You were there when he carried on about the Peace Corps and the Parsis."

"That guy certainly had quite a thing about Parsis; wasn't he trying to construct a genealogy that related Jews and Parsis or something? OK, so I get to ask the second question. What did you see in Norvin?"

Gita paused. This was an issue it was difficult to be honest about, even with herself. "I think I was very young," she said, choosing her words with care. "I think I wanted protection and affirmation—that's fairly human, isn't it? Norvin was very self-centered, but he wasn't all that bad. I think he has a good heart beneath everything. And to be frank, I was absolutely dying of curiosity about sex, but what with the Sisters at my school, and growing up in India and everything, I sort of thought I *had* to get married."

I'm absolutely dying of curiosity about sex too, Firoze wished he could say. Look behind you, there's my bed. But these were lines that men in movies could use while he had never been able to speak them.

Gita had surprised herself by saying that. Maybe it was because she was still on her best behavior with Ajay over the phone, always conscious of the impression she might be making. Editing herself in one context, the unsaid words came spattering out here instead. "And you, what did you see in Kamashree?" she asked after a minute, looking up to find Firoze's hazel eyes still on her face.

"Oh, I admired her!" Firoze said. He ruffled his hands over the cat's head and picked his words carefully. "She had such an incredible, forceful style. I was really overwhelmed that she wanted to see me. I felt as though I might get some hidden secret that would unlock the world if I hung around her."

"And?" Gita asked. She reached over and pulled Tigré into her lap, entwining the cat's orange fur in her long black strands of hair. She was surprised to find that she was bristling. After all, why should she care if Firoze had been so attracted to an old battle-ax like Kamashree? She tried to conjure up Ajay, a person who admired her wholeheartedly, but as usual it was difficult to imagine his features after those two meetings, beyond the fact that there was some vague resemblance to pictures in Hindi film magazines. "And so did Kamashree give you that grand secret and make you so very happy?"

"On the contrary!" Firoze said, startled by the sarcasm in Gita's voice. "If you really want to know, she just about broke my heart. I didn't realize that I was just a passing experience, another one of what she called her 'sex puppies' to add to the list. You've probably heard her joke, how if men can have sex kittens, women should have sex puppies. She only wanted to see me for an hour and a half in the afternoons, and only for those ten days. For all I knew, she had someone else coming in in the mornings. Not that she wasn't very brilliant and witty and skilled and all the rest of it, but in some essential way she was plain cold. I'm not sure she was ever entirely aware of my name. I have never felt so dispensable. When she left Berkeley, I wrote a few times but she never replied. I called and got her answering machine carrying a message for some other man. I guess she was too busy for me. It was soon after that that I went off to India. I felt like a piece of paper that's served its purpose, so it can be crumpled up and tossed away. It made more sense for me to get involved in other people's lives than try and figure out my own. Wait, now I can't remember what the question was that you asked."

"Actually, I had that sense of being thrown away once," Gita said, touched that Firoze had exposed something painful, and wanting to reciprocate. "It was Norvin's friend—in fact, I met Norvin through him. I brought all the good covent-girl rules to bear on slightly flirtatious American male behavior. It was a sort of cross-cultural misunderstanding, but I was depressed for what seemed like months. My friend Zelda says that the crucial thing in relationships is that both parties define the situation in the same way. It's when there are two different definitions of what's going on that you get into big trouble and very hurt."

"I don't agree that you can fix the definitions," said Firoze. "After all, the definition of what's going on keeps changing as people get to know each other. There's no stable point. I guess all you can do is keep talking." He reached out to stroke Tigré's soft fur too. Their fingers touched, but Gita pulled away.

"Yes, talking," Gita repeated, fixing her mind on Ajay's calls. She hadn't registered that she had recoiled from Firoze.

She felt satiated with the wine, the warmth, the conversation, and the fact that when she got back to Whitney there would be a man telephoning regularly. "But I guess that honest talk takes a certain amount of self-knowledge."

Firoze had felt a surge of electricity between their hands. He could feel disappointment starting to crawl on his heart like a limb coming to life after it had gone to sleep. He stood up briskly. Best to treat Gita as just an old friend. "Time to mix this on the stove," he said. "If you want, you can throw one of those blue rubber bands for the cat. She loves to retrieve."

It was past midnight when Firoze got back after escorting Gita to her hotel. Staring out at the diminishing lights through his window, he held his companionable Tigré Apsara, stroking her head and feeling her purr reverberate through his ribs and chest cavity. Then he turned his stereo up high and started to do the dishes. He chose Joan Armatrading, an album that Najma had recommended a long time ago. "Things can change," he sang along, "there's always changes. I'm gonna try some rearrangin' . . ."

It turned out that Charity had also been chosen as a participant for the conference on women's contributions to South Asian scholarship. Gita and Charity flew out to Berkeley together, chatting about many things. On arrival, they marveled at how the character of April could change from cruel to kind, all in the space of a few hours. In Whitney, the ground was dark with withered grass and muddy snow. The trees hung dank, their twigs bare but for the occasional twisted leaf. Berkeley, by comparison, was a wonderland of sunshine, blossom-scented air, and myriad shades and textures of green. During one of the long breaks in the conference schedule, Gita steered Charity across campus to an area near a pine grove and fountain that she knew was on none of Norvin's routes. They sat together on a bench, basking in the sun as Gita confessed what had transpired in her hidden phone life last night.

"This is positively the maddest thing I've heard of," said Charity, sunglasses glinting back a blue, elongated image of Gita. "This is *impossible,* Gita. You talk to some fellow for a month or two on the phone and then you up and decide you just might consider marrying him?"

"Is this what prolonged horniness will do to your decision making?" Zelda had asked in the same shocked tone.

"This is crazy," Roberto had decreed. "You're going against the Society's first doctrine: that single people are sane."

"I've met him," said Gita, smiling as she listened to all these voices. The sky was benevolent above them. Across the street, there was still a scatter of white apple blossoms in the outdoor café where she had sat so many years ago waiting for her March Man. She had talked to Ajay till 2:00 A.M. his time in her hotel room last night, and she had rarely felt so loved in her life. She had then fallen straight asleep with a glow in her heart, without her mind even attempting to slither up the hill and under Norvin and Ryoko's sheets.

"Sure, you've met him, but have you even *kissed* him? You can't make decisions like this based on the recommendation of some lonely old *budhi* who keeps herself amused by making trouble in other people's lives."

"Oh, shoo!" said Gita, hearing Saroj Aunty echo in her voice. "She's not just some lonely old woman. She's a genuinely great lady, a sort of empress dowager on Juhu beach. She had a wonderful husband too, while he was alive. You should have seen them giggle together after all those years of marriage. That was true companionship, Charity, even if the marriage was arranged. I mean, as an anthropologist you surely know that in India people have been doing this for generations. Compared with the older kinds of arranged marriage where people didn't even *see* each other before the wedding, this thing with Ajay is liberal. Liberal, Charity. I've talked to him for hours. I've even met him twice."

"But are you sure you love him?" Charity asked. "You

know as well as I do: living together isn't easy. Take me and Isaac. It's required a hell of a lot of love to tide us through all the differences in our backgrounds and somehow manage to coexist. Sometimes it feels like a daily struggle. Living together can be a major headache. Tell me the truth: do you love this man?"

Gita hesitated. Charity had cornered her on a point that she wasn't sure about. She decided to play devil's advocate for tradition. "What is love anyway? There are so many kinds of love, aren't there? There's being swept off your feet with attraction, and then there's affection too. A stable love isn't something that comes immediately. You start with compatibility and a shared background, and, you know—a commitment to go on together and make all the adjustments you need to make. Then the love comes."

"Definitely. I agree that love gets deeper the longer you're together. But I still think that there has to be an initial boost of some sort. Do you *lust* after this Ajay? Do you respect and enjoy his mind? Forget all this adjustment business. Do you find him an attractive person?"

"He's very nice."

"That's not what I mean."

Gita watched a golden retriever jump into the fountain near them and emerge shaking itself in a spray of bright drops, causing a couple sitting on the rim of the fountain to stand up, laughing. "What I remember," said Gita, "is feeling at ease and admired. There's no doubt that he's a good-looking guy. But to be really frank there weren't a lot of fireworks. I can't trust that kind of charge anymore. I mean, look where I landed up last time just because Norvin was a great kisser. Ajay isn't flashy. He's quiet but solid and dependable. I feel a lot of tenderness toward him. I feel like it could become love that, well, that was like a place to rest. I'm fed up with all these show-off American academic types."

"Look, if you generalize from that nut case Norvin to all American men I'm going to take offense. If you're in the mood for generalizations, you might want to think a minute about

Indian men. I had a thing about them for years. I don't know what it was: some sense that if I could marry an Indian I'd be validated. You know? That my ties to India would have a meaning even if I *am* blond and blue-eyed? OK, technically green-eyed, but you get the picture. It took my developing that tie for myself through a career that finally shook me out of that fantasy. I could start warning you about how blindly self-centered Indian men can be: you know all the flutter that goes up when a son is born. A son! That sense of being oh-so-special just because of being a boy can ruin a man for life."

"I haven't noticed that American men are that different when it comes to being self-centered and thinking they're very special," said Gita. As Charity spoke, she was thinking of how she had come back from school as an eight-year-old to find the household jubilant over a shrieking little bundle, a boy. An image flashed before her of Dilip carefully unwrapping a Five Star candy bar for Vicky, a toddler, while Gita stood by, a selfless big sister with no right to ask. From her last trip she could still hear the squabbles between Vicky and Kookoo over whether he should be bought a motorbike since all the other guys at college had them. "Anyway, didn't you just say we shouldn't generalize?"

Charity sighed. "I shouldn't talk if I haven't met this man. I know, some Indian men are different. Look at Firoze and what a great guy he is. All the same, I really worry that you're doing something stupid and rash."

"What you don't see," said Gita, "is that Ajay cares about me. This thing is all being planned with sense and responsibility. We've even talked about translation between our computer programs so I can finish the manuscript if we commute. We share references, Charity. We can laugh over small things like how Chinese food is completely different when it's cooked in India or America."

"Big deal," said Charity. "I hear it's different in China too. Come on, Gita, don't tell me you're planning to discuss Chinese food all your life!"

Gita laughed so happily that Charity's voice softened. "Give yourself time," she said. "I know this uncertainty on the job front has been really hard on you, but don't think that a man is going to solve things. If anything, a man complicates everything."

"This has nothing to do with my job prospects," Gita said tightly. "I have no intention of being supported by a man. I heard from New York that they're not hiring this year, so that easy commute is out. Philadelphia ended up hiring at a more senior level. I'm hoping to hear from Austin or Tucson any day now."

Thinking of the uncertainty stretching before her made Gita's joints ache. She fiddled with her bracelets. She bit her lips. The bells in the campanile played the theme from Masterpiece Theater, and students with bright backpacks began to pour out of buildings. A line began to extend out the door of the café across the street. "I wouldn't mind a cold coffee," she said.

"Or a frozen yogurt," said Charity.

"You know . . ." Gita started.

"What?"

"Yesterday I went for a walk by myself up to the rose garden, a beautiful place like an amphitheatre where I used to go with Norvin years ago. It's fabulous up there now—you wouldn't believe that roses could smell in so many sweetnesses. It was getting dark as I walked back. On one of those sloping roads near there, I passed this couple on the street. They must have just parked their car. They looked like they were coming home from a long day at work. She was carrying dry cleaning on hangers, and he had groceries in his arms. They were chatting about something. The way they smiled at each other made me want to cry. Do you know what I'm talking about?"

"Tell me about it," Charity said. "I used to watch couples like that too. You saw them close their front door behind them and you thought of how you'd go home to an empty apartment and look at the cans and Top Ramen on the shelf."

"Exactly," said Gita. "Or heat up congealed old *dal*. Ajay

understands the feeling too. He calls it the stray dog sense. You know, looking on hungrily from the edges of life."

"Now that's getting dramatic," said Charity. "Being single isn't that bad and being married isn't all that spectacular. At least when you're single you can choose what you want for dinner and sit right down to work immediately after. Those two, your ideal yuppie couple, could very well be quite miserable. Coke addiction, affairs, the question of whether they should have a baby, *maha*-trauma over the price of the new BMW. They were probably grinning like that out of nerves, or guilt, or because some TV program told them to."

"Come off it, Charity—can't people just be happy with each other?"

"OK, whatever. I'm just trying to say that marriage isn't a solution. I know, you think it's easy for me to say that when I'm with Isaac and we both have jobs in the same place. But we have these constant struggles about how he can pursue Judaism when I'm not Jewish, and what will happen if we have kids, and why he never wants to know more about India. Being together is a blessing, but it's also bloody hard work. I really think that you should spend some solid time together with Ajay before you actually get married. Try out the day-to-day. Why not go in for cross-cultural syncretism: call it an arranged affair for a while, and then see if you'd like to be married."

"Affairs are different," said Gita, laughing. "By deciding on marriage straightaway it's giving us a security, a structure, in getting to know each other and adjust. It's not so miserably ambiguous. But yes, I am going to see him. He has this conference in Boston in early May and he'll drive up after that."

"At last!" said Charity, taking off her sunglasses and giving Gita a mischievous grin. "Wah! At least then you can finally kiss. And . . . "

"Oh, shoo!" Gita grinned. She wondered what Saroj Aunty would think if things went further than a kiss. A light breeze brought her the scent of cappuccino, and the sunshine was warm on her limbs. Ajay's voice on the phone had been soft as a caress. To be held again. She shut her eyes. Send him, Heavenly Father. It is spring. Soon it will be turning even in Vermont.

Kalpana had been visiting some relatives in Andheri, a suburb close to Juhu. Her new servant, a Nepali boy smitten by Bombay films, had responded to the urgency in Saroj's voice by passing on the Andheri number, so Saroj had contracted her right in the middle of a *Dynasty* video. After speaking to Saroj, Kalpana had sent out for a rickshaw, even though the afternoon was glaringly hot and her relatives implored her to finish this episode and stay for a nap. Saroj's downstairs rooms were cool, the fans rotating in a frenzied assault on the April temperatures. Saroj was dressing for a benefit concert she would have to attend later in town. Kalpana sat at the edge of a bed as Saroj looked through her saris. Each sari was in a cardboard box and had a name inscribed in Saroj's large, looped writing.

"So that's the news," Saroj said. "They've made up their minds. End of August is what they want."

"He wrote to you first?" asked Kalpana, hot and bewildered after her rattling ride. She could still smell fumes of exhaust that must have lodged in her nose. "But he should have contacted Varun's Daddy. Varun's Daddy is the elder brother."

Saroj smiled, pulling down Moonlight on the Ganges. She opened the box and smoothed a hand over the pale blue and silver silk brocade. "Harish brought this sari from a trip to Benares in 1956," she said. "I'd often wear it on full-moon nights, especially for parties on the terrace."

"Or was it your Gita who informed? This Ajay, always bad at writing, especially since his mummy went up."

"They both wrote," said Saroj. "Separate letters, but saying basically the same thing. Darling, they want to have the wedding here. In this house. We'll set up tents in the garden, the same way we did for the other weddings. There've been three so far, you know—all these children growing up! Of course, if they want the wedding here they had to give me notice. I have to find a good Brahman, talk to our flower seller by the railway tracks in Vile Parle, go down to Bhuleshwar to look for bangles, ask Kookoo about the gold she wants to put in. Weddings take a lot of work and preparation."

"But *we* are the family," said Kalpana. "We will be giving her one full set of gold. We must have her measurements. Stupid fellow, Ajay—how will it look to our relatives? What will people think when Varun and Tarun are ready to find good matches? Of course, they're still young and all, but we have a reputation. We need to have at least one reception from our side. Why are her parents allowing it? How they can agree to a daughter's wedding in your house?"

"What do you think of these?" Saroj lifted down Gitanjali, a buttery yellow Orissan weave. She also unwrapped Cleopatra, an orange South Indian silk bordered with purple. "Which one? I think *jhari* work might be too dressy, better to go with a nice patterned silk. Yes, I spoke to Kookoo this afternoon. Thank goodness for the direct dialing we now have. Sometimes it's easier to reach Delhi than another part of Bombay. By the way, what happened to your *nimbu pani?* They didn't bring it yet? My goodness, these servants are getting worse by the day. *Tukaram! Muktabai!*"

"And what did her parents say? Don't they want their daughter's wedding to be in Delhi?"

"Well, of course they're surprised," said Saroj. She looked as though she'd eaten a pot of sweet cream. "But I suspect they're relieved. Even though Gita got this job at Whitney, Dilip is clearly terrified that she'll end up as an old maid divorcée and his financial liability. But it's not as though *they* were so busy introducing her to Bombay's best eligibles."

"He doesn't live in Bombay," said Kalpana. "He has a green card and he is going for citizenship out there."

"Come on, darling, always so *literal*. We'll have a wonderful celebration. I'm sure that Ajay will be calling you soon. It's easy to tell an old aunty but harder with one's own family. They want to keep it small. That's good, as we can avoid this catering nonsense. We'll get Maharaj's cousin to come help. I wonder if Manjuben can come down from Surat to draw *rangoli* patterns in front of all the doors and out by the swing."

"Has anyone looked at their charts? What your Ganeshan Kaka says?"

"Kaka isn't well these days," said Saroj. "Asthma, you know—he calls it heavy breathing, dear man. We'll have him look it all up when he's feeling stronger. Now *this* is one of my favorites." Saroj pulled out Rup Tera Mastana: purple and orange.

The name bounced into music in Kalpana's head. "That's a film song," Kalpana said. "I never knew you named saris after films."

"And events or places, or trees, or titles, or just pretty names," said Saroj. "It was Harish's idea. All languages, all cultures." She stood beside her open cupboard, reading along a line of boxes. "Nefertiti, Liv Ullman, Waste Land, Flame of the Forest, Meena Kumari, Pied Beauty, Fourth of July. Frankly I don't think that red and blue are much of a combination, I really should give this sari to someone. I think that H. H. Pindapur brought it back from a cricket trip to the West Indies. Have I shown you Yoko Ono yet? No? It's the latest, one of Prabhaben's Sohan wonders! I almost named it Woman after that beautiful song by John Lennon. Someone or the other had sent me a record of his hits and this is one song that just *mesmerized* me. Gita and I used to sit and listen to it again and again. Such a talent, poor fellow. Woman is so generic, Yoko Ono is definitely better for a sari like this! The only man's name I have is Idi Amin. Black and *truly* evil-looking! Ah, here's Tukaram." He had appeared at the door, stirring a glass.

"It's not auspicious to wear black," said Kalpana, gulping the cold *nimbu pani*. It was the correct amount of tart lemon and sugar, with just the faintest tickle of aromatic rock salt. She wiped her mouth with a hankie she pulled out of her bra. She was still shocked that Sarojben went on wearing bright colors, not a widow's white. There was some story about Harishbhai making her promise to always wear the finery he had collected, even after he died. These people were rich; even their grandparents were English speakers. They could challenge traditions. Staring at the cupboard filled with saris, Kalpana repressed envy to reflect that only a woman without children or dogs could have the time to sit and name each one.

Ajay had just driven into town in a rented car. He was late. It had been raining on the highway up from Boston, the trees dripping and the roads slick. The suit he had bought for the occasion was tight under the arms. He wished he could have had a shower before meeting Gita. But here he was, sitting across the table from her in a Chinese restaurant. A vegetarian Chinese restaurant at that, brown rice, no MSG.: Jesus, this might as well be California! Gita had her hair down. She was crisp and cool in a pink silk *kurta* with jeans. Ajay tried to remember what she looked like in a sari but he couldn't quite.

"I'm sorry about this reception we have to go to later," Gita said. "It's for this famous poet everyone thinks I've influenced, and I feel fairly obligated to be there. Actually, he's giving a reading this moment over at the university, which is why I could catch a ride up here. Someone or the other will drive him back to Whitney. I'm sorry that this happened to be going on the night that you arrived."

"No problem," said Ajay. "You can introduce me to your colleagues."

"So how was the conference?" Gita asked.

"Oh, fine." He wished she wouldn't look him so square in the eyes. He wondered if it would help if they held hands. While he was driving he had rehearsed their running into each other's arms. His speedometer swerved with every vision of the passionate embrace. But when he actually found her sitting at a table in the restaurant, they had just nodded and tried to smile as he muttered apologies for being late, and she said she was grading papers anyway and glad to have the extra time.

Ajay hailed a passing waitress. "Can you bring me a beer?" he asked.

"One for me too," said Gita. After they emerged from consulting the menu and placing orders, they faced each other again. Ajay looked above Gita's head to the No Smoking sign on the wall. He was relieved that she had ordered a drink. In his experience Indian women were vegetarian and puritanical. Neither his mother nor Kalpana even ate eggs. After she was widowed, his mother had given up all heat-producing vegetables like onions and garlic. She had also fasted according to the lunar calendar. He imagined what his mother would say about his sitting across the table with a woman—a divorced woman—who was drinking beer. He swiftly thrust the idea out of his head.

Gita was trying to remember how they had broken the ice that first day at Saroj Aunty's. It was hard to believe that she had spent so many hours on the phone with this man sitting across the table. She wondered which set of rules they would play by, those of convent Sisters or U.S. soap operas, and how the evening would end. Maybe he'd grown plumper since the winter; she hated to admit it, but truly, he didn't seem quite as good-looking as the image she'd been carrying in her head. Perhaps it was that vague Kapoor connection again; all those handsome male film stars seemed to balloon as they got older. Yet with Ajay she was going to be happy. With him she would grow infirm. "Tell me"—Gita leaned forward with her most welcoming smile—"what do you miss most about India when you're not there?"

Ajay reflected. "Hot puffed *chappatis*," he said. "That's one thing. How about you? Or I guess you make your own *chappatis*?"

"I don't have time to make *chappatis* here," Gita said. "Make the dough, roll it out, turn it on a pan, and puff it on the flame? No time! Pita bread is fine for me, or even whole-wheat tortillas." The smile had fallen from her face as she spoke. I can't believe he wants me to make *chappatis*, she thought. Next thing I know he'll tell me I shouldn't sign a job contract and should devote myself full time to his kitchen.

"What do *you* miss about India?" Ajay asked.

"*Chappati*s are a symbol of women's oppression," Gita continued. "It's always the women who stay by the stove so there will be hot *chappati*s to serve to the men."

"Or servants," Ajay said. He wanted to get her off the *chappati* issue quickly. He wished he could light a cigarette. "Too bad there are no servants in America," he reflected.

"There are, for rich people," said Gita. "Anyway, in India look at the way people treat their servants. Even Saroj Aunty. It's one of the few things that I don't think is perfect about her. That whole houseful of servants, just for one person! Sometimes I think she keeps them all just to give her something to fret about. Did you ever hear her shout at them? She acts as though they are retarded charges or something. My mother's the same way."

Ajay thought of pointing out that servants were fed well and given a place to live, which was more than much of the population could hope for. But he was in no mood for an argument. If she had been a man, maybe he would have pursued his point. This evening he wanted amiability above all. After all, this was their first weekend together. Gita's *kurta* was unbuttoned, and as she reached over for the rice, he had an exhilarating glimpse of brown cleavage contained in white lace. He sipped his beer. "I miss the trains," he said. "You know, long train journeys where everyone talks to everyone else."

"Yes!" said Gita, her face coming to life. "And they all share food. Just last trip when I was coming from Delhi to Bombay with my mother and stepfather, I was in a compartment with this fat man who bought snacks at every station and insisted that everyone sample whatever it was. 'Time pass' is how he explained it. My mother hissed about hygiene whenever he left the compartment. But I liked the idea of 'time pass': everyone together, passing the time."

Ajay couldn't think of any story to counter this with. He

drummed his fingers on the table, wishing Gita would lean forward again. Then he reflected, "I like time over there. It's so much lazier."

"It just rolls along," said Gita. "The mornings with everyone's routines unfolding, the long afternoons with tea. Time there is something you can soak in like a hot, scented bath." She was looking at Ajay with gleaming eyes. "And the light. The slanting winter sunshine . . ."

"The light," Ajay agreed, turning away. He couldn't bear her eyes. They almost seemed to scorch his skin. When she talked about soaking in time he had an image of the hours they might spend in bed. At least twice a month on the weekends they had agreed to commute.

"And the concerts," continued Gita. "The ones that go on all night. Those long hours with all the music carries you off into another state. Here the auditoriums all shut at twelve, just as everyone is getting warmed up. There you have it again, time getting sliced up. I actually said something to this poet chap once about rationing time and he used the idea."

Ajay didn't go to too many Indian concerts, and he absolutely never read contemporary American poetry, so he nodded. He knew that Saroj Aunty had always been keen on classical music. In his home there'd never been a craze for that stuff; his mother had liked devotional *bhajan*s, and the rest of them listened over the radio to songs from films. He was used to exhaling through a pause like this and missed having the prop of a cigarette. "Cricket matches," he finally said. "I miss those."

"What about them?" asked Gita, her voice hardening. She could see Kookoo and Dilip taking off with H. H. Pindapur for several days when a test match was on, leaving instructions for Gita to be a good girl, eat all her food, and go to bed on time with Ayah. The picture eerily extended to Norvin lying on the couch on a Sunday afternoon, reading Baudrillard and watching sports on TV while she was dying to get out for a walk in the Berkeley hills.

"Well, you know, the excitement," said Ajay. "I haven't

actually sat through too many matches recently, except for the videos that the guys in New Jersey get. But I've *lived* through dozens of them. What was so wonderful about cricket there is the way everyone participated. Everyone carried a radio. People even came to bloody class with radios. Wherever you went, you were an Indian among Indians, rooting for your team."

"You say 'everyone' and you leave out the women," Gita said. "I remember all that radio excitement as something just for men. I've always thought cricket was really *boring*. I have no patience for football, tennis, all of that stuff, especially when it's on television." Calm down, she told herself, calm down. Why be so feisty with this poor chap?

"Don't worry, don't worry," Ajay said, trying not to get alarmed. "Look, if you don't like TV, we'll buy a house with a den and I'll watch it there. I've been looking for an excuse to move out of my condo and the market is good these days."

Gita smiled at him. He was drumming his fingers on the table and still wouldn't meet her eyes. He was a good man. Even if a den sounded like American suburbia. But what was it that Charity had said: that marriage was all negotiation anyway? Was it Firoze who had said that you just had to keep on talking?

Saroj Shah

It's too wicked of me to be taking Kookoo to town on the train. But how could I resist? At least I'm taking her in the off-hours just before lunch! Anyway, Ladies' Second is never as crowded as any compartment with men. The way men all hang out of the open door: my God, during rush hour it can be up to thirty or so spilling out, a pleated fan of bodies with an uneven band of black hair and a layer of light shirts. I've sat in the car at the Parle railway crossing watching the trains run by, wondering just how all those men coming and going to work manage to keep their balance.

Of course, I know that everyone in Bombay thinks I'm mad to take the train to town when I do have a car and driver, and I can even afford the petrol with these ridiculous prices. But it's simply more convenient to travel by train. None of this silly stopping and starting at every traffic signal, with street children shoving things in through the window that they want you to buy: yellow car dusters, the latest editions of Midday, flashy packets of cheap agarbatti, bunches of absolutely exhausted roses. I'm not saying that there aren't vendors on the train too, but their aggression isn't focused on one person in quite the same way. Then too, it's easier on the lungs to be clear of those big red BEST buses, or lorries carrying construction workers, all billowing and belching clouds of evil smoke. I also love the entertainment on the train: watching and overhearing all kinds of people. I tell you, it's any day better than most films that come to town, whether Hindi or foreign! So there was every reason for me to take Kookoo with me on the train. Of course, I can't deny that I was being

*just a little perverse to insist she ride with me in second class.
If she was going by train at all, she'd of course have preferred
first. But Kookoo being what she is, who can help stirring up
a little mischief now and then?*

*Kookoo and I took a rickshaw over to Santa Cruz station.
We're waiting now on that segment of the platform where
women stand in groups. Kookoo is beginning to get flustered.
It is off-hours, the midmorning, and so the office goers have
already gone to town. All around us now there are Gujarati
and Maharashtrian housewives with hankies tucked into one
side of their synthetic saris and gold chains tucked into their
bosoms because we all know about chain snatchers on trains.
There are college students giggling in groups, holding their
books and pencil boxes, and all wearing variations of* salwar
khameez *with ribbons and dangles, and slit* dhoti *legs. There
are a few fisherwomen, with large baskets under their arms,
and complete bouquets of flowers sticking up out of their hair.
I don't see that Kookoo has anything to complain about, but
she is already drawing her sari closer around her and refusing
to look in my direction.*

*Kookoo did not take the news about Gita and Ajay well. I
haven't mentioned this to Kalpana, or both these women
might band together and form an association devoted to Family Rights. The way they're carrying on! You'd think that a
wedding is just for the family, and doesn't the least* bit *involve
the young people getting married and their desires.*

*"Why your house?" Kookoo asked over the phone. "That
girl has always been so difficult. What will people say about
Dilip if she gets married at* your *house and not at ours?"*

*"That's what she wants, darling," I said. I did not point
out that if Dilip cared so much about what people thought he
could have shown more interest in Gita's life years ago.*

*"Even the convent school didn't help Gita," Kookoo said.
"So disobedient. It was that Ayah who spoiled her. We were
ready to approve the marriage in Berkeley because of the
groom being so distinguished. But then she had to go leave
him, all for this career business of hers. Sometimes I think we*

should never have even allowed her to go to college. Who is this Ajay? What, she met him at your house? How could you, Saroj?"

The next thing I knew, I had Kookoo on my hands. I swear, she actually flew to Bombay! And let me tell you, Indian Air-lines prices are not what they used to be, even if the schedules are undependable and the service isn't getting any better, to say the least. Of course, she had some complicated story about needing to pick up Dilip's X rays and consult his doctors, but it wasn't as though Dilip was exactly tagging along. I could see very well that Kookoo wanted to start early in meddling with the dear girl's plans. Really, that woman should have been a politician, she has the wiles. Wiles, I tell you—what was Vinay doing when he married that woman?

I'm not just saying all this about Kookoo to be petty. Be-lieve me, I have zero illusions that Vinay might have married me. In the days when Vinay and I were close, he had abso-lutely no intention of ever getting married. I knew that, and it was my risk. But isn't that what youth is about: idealism, passion, risk? Sometimes I wonder what would have happened if society had been different then. Look at what's going on in the West these days. People shacking up all over the place, women bearing babies without any need for ring or man. Film actresses are already doing it here. The way everyone studies film magazines, I predict that within a decade this alternative for women will be quite fine in our cities too.

So, Kookoo has landed on my head. Oof! This morning, when she barely had arrived, she was already launching her campaign, insisting that she had to go at once to the Kala Niketan on Marine Drive to choose the wedding sari. We're in May now, and the wedding is in August. Why the rush? I asked. I told her that there are Kala Niketans all over Bombay, she could go to the Juhu branch or the Santa Cruz branch, but no, those were all suburban and inferior, and they just wouldn't do. She had to go to town at once and to that very Kala Niketan because there are dear little doorkeepers with uniforms, and one is served ice-cold Campa Cola as brocades are spread out over the counters.

Now it's not as though my fondness for saris is a hidden fact. You would think that Kookoo might remember that I have many years of experience in finding beautiful saris, and that she might want to consult me. At least she could inquire about what kind of sari I might be planning to present to our Gita. But no! Even though I was tempted to let her go out and rot in the heat, I also worried that she would pick out something so dreadful it would absolutely ruin the occasion. Though it's so hot these days, I decided to escort Kookoo. I gave the driver the day off and told Kookoo he was ill. I also told her that taxis were on strike. If we were to go into town at all, it would have to be by the suburban train.

I'm an old hand at the trains. I've been doing it since my communist days when I had only two saris and slept on the floor and carried well-thumbed copies of Marx and Engels and Trotsky. I was so young and earnest: yes, me, earnest! The joke is, I was carrying on in this ascetic way in my father's mansion, letting my two saris be washed by the servants and spreading my mat on a marble bedroom floor of a size that could have accommodated at least four pavement dwellers' families. Harish, of course, poked endless fun at all this later. When I married him, I gave up most of my pretensions and accepted that God gave me this life in a particular privileged class and why not enjoy what I had while also keeping an eye on how things might be changed. But one habit I never gave up was my traveling by Ladies' Third Class, even when Third was abolished and we have to call it Second.

The chocolate-and-yellow pedha-colored Churchgate local slides into the platform, and the mad dash for the door begins. Kookoo just stands back. She doesn't want to touch any of these women. I literally have to push her on, and let me tell you, in spite of her dieting, she is not light. Though we are almost the last ones to get in, we not only manage to get a toehold inside the compartment, but we are actually able to squeeze into two seats facing each other. One of the ridiculous *features of the newer compartment designs is that the plastic benches are molded into three seats. But it's always four women who squeeze into a row, so, all around, everyone ends up with a cramped behind.*

"One might get lice," hisses Kookoo, pulling her sari up around her head. Already, the procession of hawkers is picking its way through the compartment. A small barefoot boy selling long chains of safety pins stops in front of Kookoo, followed by a woman with uncombed hair waving trays of stick-on felt bindis *in all sizes and colors and designs. The college student next to Kookoo leans over her and begins to rummage through the tray. Kookoo strains backward as the girl chooses some interesting* bindis *that look like exclamation marks, turquoise blue with tiny synthetic pearls inscribed on them. She models one on her forehead and turns to shout across the compartment and point it out to her friends.*

I am already enjoying the scene on the train. Another boy, no buttons on his shirt and a terrible sniffle, comes by with gajras of jasmine for the hair. How can I resist? I've always loved flowers! I buy two and offer one to Kookoo. She just waves no. She is bending forward trying to see out the window, which is difficult as a little boy in a pale green Baba suit reading Micky Mousse *is standing against it. So I twist both strands into my hair, even if my bun is not what it used to be.*

"Are you comfortable?" I shout at Kookoo over the rattle of the train, the burble of talk, the cries of vendors. "Think of how not taking a car helps pollution. Darling, we're actually saving trees just by sitting here."

Kookoo just barely twitches one penciled eyebrow. She is glaring out at the hutments near the tracks, where men with their buttocks turned to us are relieving themselves.

Not many people get in at Khar Road, but in Mahim we have an installment of women in shimmering synthetic burqas, *which they lift to show their faces once we pull out of the station. In Bandra, we have some girls in frilly frocks calling, "What, men!" who look like they've just made the pilgrimage* to Mount Mary. But it is in Dadar that the crush grows. Among those who push in are a blind singer who bellows varkari *devotional poems and shakes a can, and a man without legs who pushes himself along, holding out one callused hand. Some of us give them a few coins. I hear loud clapping and deep voices, and turn around to see a few* hijras, *standing tall and manly with bright saris pulled across their stuffed and not-so-stuffed bosoms. After all, it is Friday, and we all know that on Tuesdays and Fridays the* hijras *have the right to go around begging, and even taking handfuls of goods from shopkeepers. They break up, each setting off to comb through different sections of the compartment.*

The hijra *who is coming our way is young and not badlooking, though she's wearing as much makeup as one of those Grant Road prostitutes in a cage. She is wrapped in a synthetic sari with huge flowers all over it. The sari needs washing, and the blouse doesn't match. By the way the blouse flaps around her arms and is anchored in front by safety pins, you can see that it is a castoff from someone else. Her hair is pulled into a thin, untidy plait. She claps her palms together and then stretches out a hand. Most of us sitting on the two sets of seats facing each other give her a little something. After all, it's not the* hijras' *fault, poor things, that they are born with bodies that aren't male or female, and so become this subgroup in society. But not Kookoo—she has no intention of paying the least attention.*

There is now a girl standing between us, a nice-looking girl, maybe Punjabi, wearing a lovely handloom salwar khameez and trying to keep a cardboard model of something or the other out of the crush. I have to peer over this girl's hips to find that Kookoo's face is averted.

"Madam!" calls the hijra *in a rasping voice, holding her hand in front of Kookoo's nose. "Madam-ji!"*

Kookoo draws in her breath. Her back is ramrod straight, and she lets us know she is occupied with whatever it is that she is viewing out the window. The other women have begun to watch her too.

"*Madam-ji!* De, na. Bhagavan apka bhala kare."

Even this offer of receiving God's graces does not make Kookoo twitch.

The hijra *keeps repeating this until Kookoo can stand it no longer.* "Shoo! Get away!" *she snaps.*

"Paisa *giving?*" *wheedles the* hijra. "*Madam,* paisa!"

The other hijras *must have cleaned up elsewhere, because they now join their friend. They all crowd around Kookoo. I suppose I could intervene, but frankly, I'm enjoying the fun. I wonder if Kookoo has ridden public transport ever before.*

"*Madam-ji, Madam-ji!*" *the* hijras *chorus. One begins to twitch a hip and draws in an outstretched hand down by her crotch.* "Paisa *giving!*"

The Punjabi girl turns her head and catches my eye. We both try not to laugh. "Let me hold your model for you," *I say.*

"Thanks," *she says.* "It's for a cooler. I'm on my way to town to show it to some clients."

I can't really see what's happening now, because the hijras *are crowded in so tight around us. Not that I would want to see everything. The first* hijra *seems to be hiking up her sari. Oh, no! The ultimate* hijra *threat, to flash whatever genitals they have down there. The sari is getting higher and higher. Kookoo shrieks.*

"Dirty pervert! I'll report you to the police!"

At this, all the hijras *begin to bray with laughter. But the word* police *seems to scare them, for as soon as the train stops at Grant Road, they jump off and blow extravagant kisses in to Kookoo through the bars on the window.* "Rashmi, Rashmi, I got a seat!" *Someone summons my Punjabi friend, and she takes her model from my lap. A moment later, Kookoo and I are facing each other again. She is shaking, her face under its pancake mask twitching out of control.*

"You have always been stark, raving mad," *she says.* "You have been the worst influence in Gita's life. Everything disobedient she has ever done is entirely due to you."

I'm startled. This isn't the kind of showdown one expects on a train, after all.

"You have always tried to take her away from me," Kookoo continues.

With this I find my tongue. "It didn't do much taking," I say. "What else would she have done in her vacations?"

"You've always acted as though she's your daughter. I can't help it if you can't have children of your own. You should mind your own business and not meddle with other people's children."

"Where is all this possessiveness coming from?" I try to laugh it off. "My, Kookoo! You might have given Gita more love and attention when she was growing up if you really felt this way. You should have stood up to Dilip when he wanted to hide her away."

"Don't think I haven't heard rumors of the coat hanger, and how you almost died from the loss of blood," Kookoo sneers.

"Who told you that?" I ask. Either people are playing drums for a religious procession outside or it is my heart.

"A little birdie," says Kookoo, with prissy lips.

I look at her, and I look at the women around us who are listening in even if they don't all follow English. It's absolutely never constructive to talk to someone when they are that angry, and especially not in a public place.

"Birdie, birdie, num-num," I say loudly. This is that ridiculous line from the Peter Sellers movie in which he plays a Sikh extra in Hollywood, invited to a fancy party. The government tried to ban the film since it represented Indians as such numskulls, but all of us saw it and laughed. In fact, it was one of Harish's favorites.

It does my heart good when I see that beyond Kookoo's bouffant, the Punjabi girl with the model has heard me utter this nonsensical line. She has gone into stitches of giggles, her eyes like half-moons brimming with tears of laughter. Catching my eye, she raises her hankie to wave. The jasmines in my hair are giving out the sweetest, calming fragrance.

"Kookoo," I say, leaning forward, "darling, don't be ridiculous. Whoever said that love could be rationed?"

8

Dial an
Indian Song

The days were getting longer, and though it was
past seven by the time Ajay and Gita set out from the restaurant, it was still bright outside. They drove in Ajay's rented
car along the two-lane highway as the fresh greens of young
leaves darkened on the trees and deep reds filled the sky.

"I suppose this is what is known as riding into the sunset,"
Ajay said, pressing harder on the pedal.

"Unfortunately, we still have this reception to attend," said
Gita. She was playing with the end of her braid, wondering if
Ajay's suit was too formal for the occasion. Would she introduce him to the Whitney crowd as her fiancé or would she
just let them guess? Was he dressed too much like a computer
nerd for this academic gathering, where there would surely be
jackets over jeans? Was it better that she had left her diaphragm buried in the drawer with her underwear, or should
she have presumptuously taken it to the bathroom, with more

gel beside the bed? Why hadn't she thought of buying some of what Najma had always called the "American erasers"? But what would Ajay's response be? They had plenty of time anyway, why rush things along? On the other hand, it *was* finally spring, with all the birds and beasts in full fettle and sweet scents stirring the breeze.

Parked cars already lined the road on either side of Meg Stash's house when Ajay and Gita arrived. Laughter, conversation, and the smell of liquor drifted out of the front door. Charity was having a cigarette out on the porch, looking down meditatively at the Siberian irises. When she saw Ajay and Gita she hid the cigarette behind her back.

"Boy, what a reflex!" she called down to them as they climbed the steps. "After smoking behind the bathrooms in boarding school, I see Indian skin and still feel as though I'm doing something really bad. Hi, you must be Ajay. I'm Charity. I've heard a lot about you."

"Very nice to meet you," said Ajay. Gita had told him that Charity had grown up in India, so Ajay started to join his palms in a *namaste*. He rapidly extended this into a gesture to brush his cheek when he saw that actually Charity was reaching out her hand. "What a pleasure!" Ajay said with an enthusiastic handshake. "Do you mind if I stop here a moment and also join you for a smoke?"

"I'm going to step inside," said Gita. She watched Ajay lighting his cigarette, thinking of a clip that often showed at the U.C. theater before films: a cigarette and liplike ashtray chasing each other until they met with a sighing sizzle and a No Smoking sign flashed on. Maybe Ajay would give up smoking sometime. Thank God this first introduction was going well. Charity looked Ajay up and down, thickened torso and all, but she didn't give any visible signs of disapproval. "See you in a minute."

The moment Gita stepped into the crush inside, she caught Timothy Stilling's eye. He had grown even balder in the intervening years, and the image of an enormous ivory phallus flickered in her mind. He was talking to someone, but his eyes gleamed just for Gita as he gestured a hello. Gita waved too, feeling strong and confident. She stepped up beside Timothy, panicking only at the last minute, when she saw that it was the college president that he was talking to.

Timothy leaned down to place a meticulous kiss on the cheek.

"You're looking good," he said. He turned to the president. "Do you know, umm, Gita Das?"

"Indeed, indeed, I don't believe we've met before," said the president, a dark man with jowls who looked like a cross between a film actor and revivalist preacher. They had actually once spent several minutes talking at a party, but he had not bothered to remember. "Of course, I read the article in the *Chronicle* and was very happy to learn that we had such a distinguished faculty member. So young at that! Very nice to meet you."

"Actually . . ." began Gita.

One of the president's secretaries sidled up to whisper that a certain trustee had arrived. Gita and Timothy were left standing together. Timothy was looking right at her with those clear blue eyes in the harlequin face. Gita stood up straighter and looked right back. There's no doubt that he's a flirt, she thought. A smile spread across her face. He smiled too, never taking his eyes off her. Not wanting to flinch, Gita tried some conversation.

"So, what *was* the story with that clipping?" she asked in a nonchalant voice. "I'm very grateful you've made me so notorious and everything, but all the same, it did seem a little excessive since you used our conversations for just two poems—"

"Gita! I've been looking for you!" Firoze now stood beaming beside her. He put a paper plate with vegetables and dip down on the chair behind him and gave Gita a warm hug. He smelled of roasting onions and a lemony aftershave.

"Have you been cooking?" Gita asked.

"Yes, actually, at Charity's. We made some terrific *chole*. You should have been there."

"My old friend Firoze," Gita said to Timothy. "Firoze, another, well, another—old friend, Timothy, who I also knew years ago in Berkeley. He moved to France later. Are you still living there?"

"As a matter of fact," said Timothy. Having shaken hands with Firoze, he was fixing her with his eyes again. "My, umm, ties there were terminated. I'm a free spirit now, ready to fly wherever I am lured."

"That's nice," said Gita, guessing that this meant that he had broken up with Marie-Claire. Why did he keep looking at her like that? But she was absolutely not going to let her eyes drop as they had in the old days. "You must be enjoying the open possibilities."

Timothy sighed. "Yes . . ." he said. "And of course, I'd love to hear all about what's been happening with you. You're looking lovely, you know . . ."

Firoze had been watching without pleasure as these two stared at each other. Gita had sounded so sensible over that dinner, it was really a disappointment if she was still drawn to the glamour of powerful older men. "So, how are you, Gita?" he asked. "I tried to call you a few times. You should get Call Waiting."

"Oh, I'm fine," said Gita, relieved to have the excuse to break the deadlock of looks. She turned to Firoze. "I'll be moving to Austin at the end of August. Yes, it's a tenure-track job. I'm really happy about it; you know I took sort of a risk in writing a dissertation that slipped through disciplinary divisions. I love the place too; it reminds me a little of Berkeley."

"Congrats!" said Firoze. "I heard from Charity that the New York job had fallen through; they're not hiring this year, right? Well, who knows, maybe they'll reopen the search later. You might enjoy living in New York. By the way, did Charity tell you that I'm swapping my apartment with Roberto for the month of July? It's great that you'll still be in Whitney."

"I'll actually be desperately trying to finish my manuscript then." Gita's brows puckered. "I'm going to India in August. But I'm sure I could take time off for tea once in a while."

"Ah, India. More research?" asked Timothy. He had caught the admiration on Firoze's face, and this made Gita look even prettier. That pearly pink *kurta* brought out the sheen in her eyes and her strong teeth. Her hair, as always, was glorious. Why had he never written a poem about drawing his fingers through it? Perhaps he could go in for a phase of poems with the languorous roundness of words like *coconut* and *monsoon*.

"No, not exactly research," said Gita. What should she tell these men? This was the moment she should announce the marriage, but she couldn't bring herself to do it. She was aware of Firoze swaying slightly, back and forth beside her, and could feel a tightening in her own pelvis as though the two were connected. She was aware of Timothy's burning blue eyes, the incline of his chest as he bent forward. Stop it, Gita, this was not what women with fiancés were supposed to register! The spring was really making her crazed, or maybe it was only the slither that presaged the descent of yet another egg. At this moment, Ajay appeared.

"Ah, let me introduce you to my, my—*friend,* Ajay," she announced as he took up the third position nearby.

The red light on Gita's answering machine was flashing insistently as she and Ajay stepped into the house. "Do you mind if I listen?" Gita asked, throwing her tie-dyed red-and-brown shawl toward the sofa.

"Go ahead," said Ajay. He set down his suitcase and walked around the room. The shelves were crammed with books. There was a Kangra miniature on one wall and a Paul Klee on the other. The cushions on the sofa were in mirror-work cases. Standing in this room crowded with color, Ajay suddenly felt constricted by the solidity of her person. On the phone she had seemed light, almost ethereal, yet here she was with her own defined tastes. This was upper-class, artsy taste. At his own home they had preferred Formica, and he had tended to fill the walls of his condominium with batik damsels from Colaba Causeway as well as paintings of sunsets and horses from New Jersey flea markets.

There was a hesitant message from that stuck-up poet fellow, saying that he was in town and he was calling from Meg Stash's, and he was hoping that Gita was planning, umm, to attend the, umm, reception. Another beep and a strangely accented voice, some Roberto saying that he and Zelda were driving up to Canada and did she want to come along? So, other men had her number. Well, this was America, and she didn't want to marry *them.* The third message started with a buoyant woman's voice. "Hi, babe, this is your old ayah. I've got to escape this campus, and can't make it to the reception, but now listen here to the Lord Almighty . . ." Gita abruptly turned down the volume. She leaned close to the machine, a smile breaking over her face. "Zelda," she mumbled, looking very pretty and guilty.

Ajay sensed that the message had something to do with his presence there. Gita had mentioned Zelda before, and now it hit him with chilling force that this Zelda, whoever she was, not only knew all about him but would possibly hear every detail of what happened this weekend. Hadn't that Charity woman also said something about having heard a *lot* about him? With all his American girlfriends he had hated the sense that there were friends watching and passing judgment from the sidelines. It had always made him feel as though he was in bed with an audience filled to capacity, some with binoculars, some with notepads or clicking laptops. He'd just assumed that Gita was different. He sat heavily on the sofa and bounced the tips of his fingers against each other.

Gita was obviously flustered when the machine clicked to a halt. "Will you have some tea? I can make it *masala* style à la Saroj Aunty's servants, or I have herbal too."

Herbal tea too, Ajay thought; probably she didn't eat sugar or drink coffee. No doubt she read labels for preservatives. She wouldn't approve of his pretzels or potato chips. What had he gotten himself into?

"And then there's some brandy. You want some of that? So this is the place I've been renting. I put a lot of my own things out so it feels more like a home ..." Gita spoke rapidly as she showed him around. She could hear herself prattling. There was still the big question ahead: how would this evening work out? Should she take him upstairs now for a viewing of her bed? Should she mention that the sofa downstairs could also be pulled out?

Sitting on the as-yet-assembled sofa, they were both more relaxed after a few drinks. "So, heard from Saroj Aunty lately?" Ajay asked, edging his feet out of his shoes.

"Yes," said Gita, from the other end. She sat with her legs tucked under her and hair falling about her shoulders, down below her waist. "She's getting our horoscopes compared."

Ajay laughed. "Well, if it gives her something to do. I don't believe in that stuff myself. My mother, of course, would have had that done before we were even introduced."

"I bet your mother wouldn't approve that I was divorced," Gita said.

"No," said Ajay. "But these astrologer buggers are touchy. What will Saroj Aunty do if they say we don't match?"

"Oh, knowing Saroj Aunty she'll probably bully Ganeshan Kaka to recast the charts until they fit." Gita smiled, playing with a long, long strand of hair. Gleaming hair, fragrant hair. Ajay caught his breath. His previous girlfriends had all worn their hair in matter-of-fact career styles. He vaguely remembered some book that described the things you could do with hair. Maybe it was *The Joy of Sex,* which he had once stolen glances at in a friend's bathroom.

"Here, I'll do some predictions," said Ajay. "Show me your palm." This usually worked with American women, but as soon as he took her hand, he could see the absurdity of posing to her as a font of Eastern mystical wisdom. Too late, though—he had to continue. "Oh, what a fine long life, and yes, a strong imagination ..."

Gita wasn't listening as he rambled on with the usual things that people who looked at your palm said. Her body had tensed around his touch. Her breath was focused around his hands. They were warm, broad hands, almost the same shade as her own skin. She leaned closer, willing him to kiss her, her hair spilling into his lap.

Ajay obediently lunged. It was an awkward kiss, teeth bumping and his glasses getting dislodged. It was certainly worth another try when they had both loosened up further. Gita grinned as they parted, and he took off his glasses to wipe them. "Do you know what Zelda said?" she asked, reaching out for another sip of brandy.

"What?" said Ajay. "When?"

"Well, on the answering machine. She was talking about condoms! Don't forget, she said, this is the age of AIDS. Plunge into the Arranged Affair, she counseled, test it out before marriage. I can't believe she left this message on the machine when she knew you'd be coming in with me! Zelda; she's as outrageous as Saroj Aunty. But Saroj Aunty speaks coyly about romance, and with Zelda it's exuberant sexuality. You'll have to meet Zelda. Do you know, she once even gave me some earrings she had made out of colored condoms?"

Ajay froze. It offended him to hear her talk this way. His mother wouldn't, Kalpana wouldn't. So far she had never said anything like this over the phone. It was fine for American women to be forward, it was even fun, and yet, they were never the sort one wanted to marry. But for a girl raised in India! Maybe girls of Gita's circle in Delhi spoke like that. Kalpana had been making dark insinuations of "those people" being different. He had an image of the Indian gatherings in New Jersey with Gita leaving the kitchen to burst confidently in on the men telling that old joke about the new immigrant who wanted to eat dog but had been horrified by the part served, Gita joining in the laughter as Ajay tried to pretend she didn't belong to him.

Gita was still laughing about those earrings, but Ajay was frozen. Shameless girl, she had probably drunk a little too much. He looked into her open mouth with its archly pointed uvula, and he saw his universe cracking. The continents were disintegrating into many Indias and Americas. People were falling apart into many selves. Objects were scattering, colliding, coming together only to separate again and form new combinations. Being Indians in America wasn't enough to make a choice. In fact, in this debris of everything familiar, there were no grounds for a proper decision.

Gita saw the shutters slam down on Ajay's face. But what started out as a wave of rejection curved and rolled, becoming relief. All evening it had bothered her that they hadn't once looked at each other eye to eye for a long, steady gaze. Not that she would have wanted him to stare probingly like Timothy, but she had hoped that he would look at her directly and see all of who she was. She understood that to fit his life she might have to sever parts of herself, a Cinderella's sister hacking at her toes. She couldn't do it. Not again. Even *if* Saroj Aunty had ordered one hundred wedding invitations on the finest, red-speckled rice paper. Gita knew she would be responsible for the talking that severed her and Ajay, and it was with a soaring sense of strength that she began.

These days in Juhu there were always bulldozers rattling or men swinging blows around rusty, exposed girders. Shacks went down, and apartment buildings grew up from head-loads of brick and sand carried by emaciated famine victims turned construction workers. Saris fluttered from the terraces of the apartment buildings; Lata Mangeshkar's multibillion-rupee voice pierced from radios to meet the bass thump of The Who. Men shouted for bathwater. Maruti cars that endlessly tinkled the first lines of "Jingle Bells," "We Wish You a Merry Christmas," and "Santa Claus Is Coming to Town" when shifted into reverse backed day and night out of parking spots under the buildings.

Because of the population boom, the postman had changed the times of his delivery. He now walked under the coconut trees up the cleanly swept Shah driveway in the midmornings, as a pressure cooker hissed in the kitchen and a distant thump from the back of the house signaled that someone was washing clothes. Often he did not have to slide the letters under the door, for Tukaram would be squatting outside, elbows on his knees and a bulge of tabacco in one cheek. When Tukaram brought in the mail, Saroj would put down the newspaper she was reading to take charge of the day's haul at the dining table.

On a morning in late May, she received what looked like a sizable stack, but it had been inflated by the presence of *India Today* and the *Herald of Health*. There was a postcard from Tehmi and Jer, two spinster sisters who taught piano and went on vacation once a year to the Matheran hill station. There was a black-rimmed death announcement in Gujarati; someone unimportant, Saroj hoped, hiding the card under the magazines. There was a yellow inland envelope embossed with the three-headed lion. It looked like Manjuben's son in Surat— maybe he was due for a visit soon. Another postcard was packed tight with the nearly illegible writing of her friend Didi, who lived alone in the hills. No glossy American aerogram.

"You know about the marriage in August?" Saroj asked Tukaram in Marathi. He leaned against the doorframe, waiting for orders about what Saroj would drink. It might be salted *lassi* with roasted cumin, instant coffee, slightly sweetened *nimbu pani, masala* tea, a fizzing Thums Up, Gold Spot, or Limca. The postman's changing his times had upset the old routines. "Gita-baby's marriage?"

"*Ho, bai.*" Tukaram nodded.

Saroj had lifted up her glasses to read one of the postcards when the phone rang. "Darling!" Saroj exclaimed. "For you it must be the dead of night!"

Tukaram edged some tobacco into his mouth as the *bai* talked on. Since she was lunching alone today, he was wondering how much food might be left over for the servants to take home. He noticed that she looked alarmed and was holding the black receiver with both hands. When she put down the phone, her face had changed. She looked as though she had just woken up from a heavy summer afternoon's sleep. Her face was puffy, her glasses were askew. In a low voice she asked him to dial Kalpana's number.

Tukaram tried several times, laboriously studying the squiggles the *bai* wrote on a scrap of paper so as to match them up with the squiggles that had to be pulled around all the way to the right. Finally he got through. She started talking. Her voice trickled at first, then, as she went along, it grew louder and faster. Finally, she began to laugh.

"Well, anyway, Kaka said that their Marses were poorly aspected," she was saying in English. "He wasn't sure about the Saturn-Venus conjunction. Also, it was an absolute numerological nightmare for Gita to even *think* of hyphenating Das. Still, I don't doubt that this experience has been good for them. We'll just have to try again. Did I ever tell you that Harish's cousin Max, you know, Maheshbhai, has a daughter out there in Queens? She's younger than Gita, of course, one of what they call an ABCDEFG. Come on, darling, *of course* you know what I mean: American Born Confused Deshi Emigrated From Gujarat. It wouldn't hurt to have Ajay invited over there for dinner, would it? *Such* a shame when young people have to be alone."

Tukaram squatted. He rocked back and forth on his heels, listening to the flow of a language he didn't understand. He was thinking about how his wife might be able to pick up a few more clothes-washing jobs in that apartment building down the road, about the rising price of potatoes, about why his son had taken to wearing a saffron headband and going off on demonstrations all day when there was a rumor that more jobs might be opening in the cloth mills. If the *bai* was not going to decide what she wanted to drink, he would like to stand up and have some water himself. But he knew better than to move. As she spoke on, he reflected that since Saheb died, she spent too much time talking into that black receiver with unseen voices.

Gita spent much of the summer working on her book. Her computer hummed, her printer whizzed to and fro: the manuscript grew, draft upon draft, thick piles of paper gathering on her desk. Around her Vermont turned lush with deep greens and the whirr of crickets. In the late afternoons she would often take a break with Zelda. The Society for the Protection of Single People had momentarily been disbanded for lack of an adequate quorum after Roberto's defection, but Gita, Zelda, and Roberto still gathered together along with Roberto's man, Bill. Charity and Isaac were off visiting Isaac's relatives. Many other faculty members had also left for the summer. Despite the influx of a few summer students and tourists passing through, the town of Whitney felt deserted.

Zelda was teaching Gita how to drive. With many warnings about being careful about the gears, Charity had left them with her small Japanese car. Under Zelda's direction Gita gripped the steering wheel and proceeded along the back roads: past fields filled with black cows, tall silos, and white farmhouses set back from the road.

"You're doing great," said Zelda one afternoon in June. They had been out driving and now were back at Gita's house, sitting under the hanging geraniums on her porch. They each held a cold glass of juice livened up with sparkling water, and a bag of blue corn chips lay propped up between them. "The next step is to buy yourself a good little car and drive it down to Austin."

"I wish you were coming too," said Gita. "It makes me sad to think about starting from scratch with friends."

"Tell me about it!" said Zelda, stretching out her long legs. "I feel the same way about moving to Philadelphia. I don't know a soul there. And of course, the way these things are timed, I was *just* getting to know this actor up in Burlington before he went off on a summer tour. By the time he's back, I'll be moving. I guess that becoming these snails who crawl around with homes on our backs makes us self-sufficient. But what about love? I guess it's time that we learn how to be happy spinsters, babe. Let's cut loose from the crap about needing a man to make us complete."

"I don't know if divorced people count as spinsters," said

Gita, waving at the plump young doctor she had consulted a few times, who was now driving by in his Jeep. A neighbor's child, balancing on her pink bicycle, stopped short so she would have two hands to wave back. "I see what you mean about feeling complete, though. I'm still so relieved about that narrow escape from boring security with Ajay that I haven't been hankering at all for distraction. Also I'm really enjoying spinning out the chapters in my book. I'm frankly sort of excited about having a real, tenure-track job."

"Work and friends," reflected Zelda, thoughtfully pulling at the cow that dangled in one ear. "That's what we need to aim at for our happiness. All that stuff that Freud said about work and love didn't make enough room for love that wasn't sexual, I think. Who knows, though, I haven't read the dude myself; like most people, all I know about him is secondhand."

"Well, a little of that sexual sort of love wouldn't hurt once in a while," said Gita. "True, love comes in all sorts of packages and shapes, and it's a big mistake to feel impoverished just because the romantic content isn't always at hand. But I think that above all we shouldn't get too set in any definition of what will make us happy. The trick seems to be learning how to be content with all kinds of situations. I've never felt so much at peace with being alone in my life. But then too, everything is in limbo because of the move. It's when time stretches on and on without a break in sight that a situation becomes intolerable."

"Talk about the ultimate mirage!" said Zelda. "Time can seem unchanging from the distance, but get up close and you can barely keep up with the unexpected bumps and twists and sceneries."

When Zelda left, Gita checked her mailbox and found that she had a postcard and two letters. There had been a postal strike in India for several weeks so both the letters were old. The postcard was a Museum of Modern Art reproduction of the Rousseau painting in which a fleshy white woman with long black hair reclines nude on a couch in the forest, while a lion and a dark native stare through the foliage behind her.

Love, Stars, and All That

Gita,

Is the imagination hyperreal? Are symbolic inversions t(r)opical tropes? I think of our meeting as attended by such questions and the obscure progressions of emotion/art/criticism. I travel east to Manhattan, you travel east to India. Do our trajectories intersect?

Timothy

This time Timothy had included an address in San Francisco. Gita propped up the card by one of the paned windows. But the window was open, and a breeze blew it down behind the radiator. Gita didn't notice, for she was already reading the aerogram from Kookoo:

Dear Gita,

We were very glad to receive your call. Your daddy and I were most relieved to see that you showed some sense and didn't give in to Saroj's ridiculous plans. I never heard such nonsense in my life! Why should you be forced to marry someone just because he is her sidekick's brother-in-law? I had met that woman at Saroj's a few years ago, and believe me, she was very shallow, going on about her doggies. You certainly wouldn't want to be involved in a family like that.

We are all recovering from that dreadful scare you gave us. Your daddy's health is much better. Vicky has applied to the engineering program at the University of California. Because of my good relations with Professor Weinstein, I have taken the liberty to write asking him to look into the admissions. If you have any contacts there, please act at once. I hope that your brother being in America will be a chance for you to get to know him better.

If you should ever want to get married again, be sure to inform us first. Remember, you do have a family of your own to turn to. Your daddy joins me in saying that we hope you will be happy, and you should never hesitate to let us know what we can do to further our hopes.

With love from your
Mummy

Gita refolded the letter, wondering if she imagined a chastened tone in it, and what might have brought this on. Then she slit open the envelope of the second letter, which was obviously from Saroj Aunty. The two pages of stationery with speckled patterns of a *bandhni* sari along the rim were crammed full of Saroj Aunty's floral writing with all its circles and loops.

Gita darling!

Of course I was disappointed, as you could pick up so well, even with those silly staccato silences from satellite transmission, so every tenth word gets swallowed up between the seas. But I'm so glad, darling, that if you found you both didn't get along that you had the courage to take a stand on that *right then and there!!!* Too many relationships just carry on because of what other people might think. When people love you, as I do, they will accept whatever it is that makes you happy.

I'm proud that you are enjoying being alone. It's something I'm having to learn late in life myself. In my day, girls were brought up to believe that they *needed* a partner, and it makes me glad to see that things are changing. At one time, when a sad thing had happened to me and I had no hope for my future, I had sworn I would never marry. But within a few years, I had changed my mind. I was so lucky that Harish turned out to be such a nice man who made me laugh and helped me live life with *pleasure!!!*

I will *completely* understand if you never want to even contemplate the idea of hooking up with any man again, but I can't help hoping, darling, that someone *wonderful* will show up on the horizon. Wedding or no wedding, I still plan to give you my best Patola sari the next time you're visiting—I hope soon! And if you don't want to have children, remember, you can always adopt the children of your friends as your favorite nieces and nephews! All the good stories for women don't have to be about marriage and motherhood.

X O X your ever doting
Aunty Saroj

Gita reread this letter with a large smile on her face. She looked around for Timothy's postcard but couldn't find it. Then she watered the blossoming plants, set up a table fan, and switched on the computer.

"Oh my God!" said Firoze. "I can't believe you did it!"

Gita stood in her doorway, shaking her newly light head from side to side. Her hair rustled like wind in a grove of trees. It flopped over her eyes and against her cheeks. Then she stood still and raised both hands to smooth it back, running her fingers through only a few inches before they were released.

"So, what do you think?" she asked Firoze.

"Well, it's fashionable . . ." began Firoze. Why was it that women always thought that short haircuts were alluring and sophisticated, while men really preferred long tresses? It was kinder to give positive feedback, though. "It looks good. I like the curve around your face. It must be very cool."

"I was just so fed up with being that Woman with the Hair, you know, all the exotic mystery. I feel like I shed a whole persona. Life feels a lot lighter. The time it used to take me to wash and comb it: you wouldn't believe, it was like caring for a shadow self."

"Can I touch?" asked Firoze, surprised that his tongue had actually spoken those words.

"Sure." Stepping out into the porch, Gita leaned over. Firoze rummaged one hand around her head. The hair slipped between his fingers like the current of a stream.

"Very nice," said Firoze. "Very soft."

"That felt great," said Gita. "Did you ever have an ayah who massaged your head as a kid? I used to have this wonderful ayah who would bring out coconut oil and rub my head, telling stories, if I was ever upset or couldn't sleep. Saroj Aunty wondered later if all the hair that grew was because of those rubs."

"Possible," said Firoze. "I've had my head massaged by barbers in India. My ayah mostly tickled my back. Is this ayah you're talking about the same one Najma used to quote: something about luck and how Jesus Christ would despatch a good *jori?*"

"Heavenly Father Bhagavan," corrected Gita. "Frankly I don't know about this *jori* stuff anymore. Isn't the idea of the one and only fated match sort of improbable? Anyway, how was your trip? Did Roberto leave everything for you in the apartment? Is there anything else you need?"

"I brought some books," said Firoze. "But I left Tigré Apsara for Roberto and Bill to look after."

"That happy cat," said Gita. "Tigré Apsara—isn't that the name of a make of shoe?"

Firoze grinned. "Yes, actually, one of Bata's models, I believe, something like what they call pumps in the U.S. I saw ads for those shoes while I was in India."

"It's great." Gita laughed. "I love the improbability of those two words together, a fierce Spanish tiger fused with celestial damsels from Hindu mythology. I'll have to buy Saroj Aunty a sari she can give this name to! I should get an animal too; I guess that when things are rough you have some company."

"Absolutely, it's like therapy," agreed Firoze. "Sometimes my job really wears me down: you know, hearing tales of such horror from refugees, and trying so hard to prove that they were politically persecuted, even if the question hinges on things like whether they refused to be conscripted into a guerrilla army. The irony is that this government will usually admit people as refugees from regimes they've opposed. But it's much harder to make a case for refugees from regimes they've supported, like those down in Central America. Anyway, when all this becomes overwhelming, I get recharged with a shot of sweet Tigré's purrs."

Gita, listening with interest, had noticed that the space between them was humming, crisscrossed with fine, iridescent rainbows. Like a cat's purr, the hum rose up around a sense of perfection centered in this moment. "I really want to hear more about your work," Gita said. "It's great that you're actually able to help people through what you do. Come on in. Some lemonade? Tea?"

"Tea, thanks," said Firoze. "You'll have to tell me more about that book you're writing, too." He followed her inside as Meg Stash, who happened to be driving by, slowed down her car to take a good long look. By the end of the afternoon, most of Whitney had been alerted that the Indian woman was entertaining a handsome stranger.

A few days later, Gita and Firoze went on a bicycle ride in the afternoon. They glided out along the tarred road beyond the hospital, until it merged into a beaten track smoothed by farm vehicles. Wildflowers bobbed by the roadside, and horses came to stare over a stile. The air was golden around them, the sky very blue. But clouds outlined with gray were billowing in over the horizon.

"Hindus would love this part of the country," said Firoze. They had just cycled past a farm with a tall silver silo and a herd of hairy black cattle lounging in a field. Some looked up from what they were munching, tags dangling jauntily from one ear, making Gita think of Zelda.

"Why?" Gita asked.

"You know, all the cows, and then the enormous Shiva-*lingam*s towering up into the sky."

"And stocked full of seed too!" said Gita, laughing. "At least at certain times of year." She looked over at Firoze pedaling beside her. What was it about him that made it OK to say things that usually would be reserved for close girlfriends? "You know, you could start a Hindu-Watching Society."

"A *what?*" asked Firoze, who had swerved to avoid a stretch of pebbles and missed the end of her sentence.

"It's a long story," said Gita. "I'll tell you sometime when we're sitting down. Also, you never finished telling me that story of how your great-aunt got possessed by Queen Victoria."

Firoze smiled. "Actually, we're all possessed by cultural others in one way or another, aren't we?" he asked. That was the difference, Gita thought: in the past he would have lectured on about this point, but now he could simply say it with a smile.

"Except, at this moment in time it can be sort of hard to say what makes for a cultural self and what's an other," Gita called over her shoulder as she overtook him. "People like us are this impossible collage, aren't we?"

"Tell me about it!" Firoze shouted back.

Crossing the railroad tracks, they got off their bicycles and walked side by side. "You know," Gita reflected, "when I first came here I used to see everything in terms of dichotomies: America was this big lonely place, and so when I thought of India it was mostly in terms of happy things. I also used to think there was a space I could arrive where I'd understand everything and be contented ever after."

"But then you got older, and you saw that everything is mixed up, every horizon opens onto another even more complicated one, and no solution is ever final," said Firoze.

"Exactly," said Gita.

They were on their way back, nearing the horse farm, when the storm burst. Rain spilled from the sky like a water main broken loose. Rain set the trees quivering wetly. It splashed along the unpaved road in rivulets, making the bicycle wheels lurch and slide. Gita and Firoze pulled up alongside a red barn. It had no eaves to take shelter beneath, but the door was lightly ajar. They left their bicycles by the road and climbed up the slippery embankment to take refuge in the barn. The air inside was warm and sweet with hay. A low growl greeted them, followed by a chorus of little mews. They could not see much in the darkness within the barn, but it sounded like a mother cat with her kittens.

Firoze dropped his voice. "Better not go too far inside. They're probably not too used to human beings."

"No problem," said Gita, wrapping her arms around her and trying to warm up. "We can stand in the doorway."

Firoze was wet too but more aware of the goose bumps on Gita's arms than his own. "Here, let me help," he said, vigorously rubbing a hand up and down between her shoulder and her wrist.

"Thanks," said Gita "Brrr. That's better."

After a moment they sat down together in the doorway. Gita moved closer to Firoze. He drew an arm across her shoulders, anxiously awaiting her move away. But she sat still, relaxing into his warmth. In the green fields before them, the wet horses had also gathered in a huddle.

"You know, in New York, there's this service called Dial an Indian Song," Firoze said, trying hard to distract himself from the situation at hand.

"No, really?" Gita asked, looking over at him. It was disconcerting for their faces to be so close. She felt a warm flicker of anticipation as she looked under that line of brow and met his eyes. "Tell!"

"Because of your name and all, I thought you'd be interested. You know, there's this huge Indian immigrant population in Queens. There's even a television program on Sunday morning, complete with clips of dances from films and astrological predictions. Anyway, I read about this Dial an Indian Song service in *India Abroad,* and so I tried it out. It's a 900 number, subsidized by a store called Patel Produce and Provisions in Queens."

"So then what happened?" Gita asked.

Firoze switched into a woman's speeded-up, Gujarati-accented voice. *"Namaste* and hallo. You have reached Dial an Indian Song, Big Apple's premier service for lovers of India. This week at Patel Produce and Provisions, beautiful mangoes are specially priced at seventy-nine cents only, Brooke Bond Red Label Tea is three fifty-five per five-hundred-gram box, Elephant Brand Basmati Rice is eight dollars seventy-five for five pounds. Come now and enjoy these and many more savings! If you are calling from a touch-tone telephone, press one for latest Hindi film hit, two for Hindi goldie, three for South Indian special, or four for international selection. If you are calling from a rotary phone, hold the line and you will be connected to a live operator during the hours ten A.M. to ten P.M. only. Dial an Indian Song changes daily, so check in with us tomorrow. Thank you and *Dhanyavad. Jai Hind!*"

To Firoze's satisfaction, Gita's shoulders were shaking with laughter. "So which did you press?" she asked.

"Four, of course," he said, "for international selection. What I got was a song by the New Pardesi Music Machine. It's this Sikh group from Birmingham. Really quite a rousing hit called 'Telephone,' all in Punjabi but with English words thrown in. I'm not great at identifying musical instruments but it seemed that there were *tabla*s, electric guitars, and synthesizers together. From the resemblances between Hindi and Punjabi, I guessed that it was about this guy who is always trying to reach a girl called Rani each day of the week. He starts out with her answering machine, but by Saturday he ends up finding her as she's out shopping in Soho."

"So they end up together," said Gita, tightening her own hold on his back. It was a good, strong back, smelling faintly of sweat and testosterone.

"I guess so," said Firoze.

In a voice so casual she could have been inquiring about the weather, Gita asked, "So, do you think you'd like to kiss me?"

"OK," said Firoze. "I mean, yes!" He put a hand on her cheek. They looked each other in the eye and then leaned gently together.

"Acid rain," said Firoze between kisses of a rising intensity. "Taste the—"

"—tang," finished Gita during the next pause, a few moments later. "Do you know this is like a Hindi—aaah—"

"—film . . ."

After a while, Gita paused in a frantic exploration of the

shape, curve, and taste of Firoze's ear to laugh. "We're in the compulsory wet scene. You know how every Hindi film has got to have one? Rain, boating accidents, waterfalls, tidal waves . . ."

Her hard nipples and laughter pulsed against Firoze's chest, and he pulled her closer. "I guess we should run around some trees," he whispered. "Do you have any idea which song it would be appropriate to break into?"

The rain passed as suddenly as it started. The sun came out, the silos glistened and steamed. Gita and Firoze pedaled back to her house, where they toweled each other down and promptly went upstairs. In the long, suspended evening, Gita even dismantled the earrings that Zelda had given her to find that they were indeed most satisfactorily functional.

"So tell me, Kaka," Saroj asked, "why is it that sometimes your predictions don't work?"

"Heh, heh," Ganeshan Kaka cackled from his armchair. His false teeth were out. Thinner than ever, he sucked in his gums. With every year, Saroj thought, Kaka looked more and more like a light, featherless bird. "That and all is the great mystery. You have planets, you have numbers, and then, *sala,* you have got the human *choice.* Planets simply open up possibilities— it is for the people to act."

"So are you saying that when a planet starts to do something, it could begin a cycle of change, not that the change immediately shows?"

"What else I have been telling you? Look here, girl, when are you going to start listening to your Kaka's words?"

He lay back in his armchair, hooding his eyes and breathing with difficulty as Kaki, his diminutive wife, came in with two cups of the coffee. Scolding him in Tamil that Saroj couldn't understand, Kaki poured his coffee in a foaming jet between two steel glasses. The aroma of Mysore coffee powder mingled with the heavy scent of Nagchampa incense in the room.

"Yanyhow," said Kaka, leaning forward to take a sip of his

coffee when it was cool. "The truth is, if you love someone, it is very difficult to do fair predictions. What you want for them gets hopelessly mixed in the interpretation. What to do?" He laughed again, bursting into a cough, but then struggled for air to add, "Hopeless. *Sala,* this is life!"

"It's life," agreed Saroj.

One Saturday evening toward the end of the summer, Gita had a party to celebrate the mailing of her manuscript. She had swaddled the paper, still warm from the Xerox machine, into a box, and Firoze had driven with her to the UPS station. Soon she would have to start frequenting bookstores and liquor stores to collect strong cartons for her move. For the moment, though, she was celebrating the end of a long journey, of discovery and of hard work.

"Though you could say that all endings are arbitrary," Firoze said as he arranged chicken breasts and thighs on the grill that Charity and Isaac had lent them. He and Gita had split the cost of flying Najma out for a visit during her current trip to California. Under Najma's exuberant direction, they had soaked the chicken in yogurt and spices as though preparing it *tandoori* style. Without an earthen *tandoor,* though, no one was sure just what the outcome would be.

"I know, I know," said Gita, mussing the back of his head. "I know that I'll have the reviewers' comments and the editors' comments—"

"—and the proofreaders' blue pencil marks," put in Charity.

"And then I'll sit down to revisions again, and someday I hope to read reviews and have people read my name tag on elevators at conferences and say that they read my book. But for now, it's done."

"Enjoy it, babe," said Zelda, taking a swig of beer.

"How long were you working on it?" asked Isaac, hands in his jeans pockets. These were Charity's friends, but he was trying hard to fit in.

"I don't know, exactly. Years. It depends where you start

counting. I first thought of this idea for a dissertation when Norvin asked me what I was working on the first time we met, and I was too shy to admit I didn't know!"

"Some of my best inspiration has come at weird moments too," Charity said. "Somehow it's never when you're *trying* to have an idea."

"Like love," added Zelda. "It's usually when you've absolutely given up."

"Don't ask me *why*," said Najma, eyes bright in her round face, "but I'm reminded of this story of your ayah's. You know, the one about the king and the prime minister that you told me that time I was really depressed about not getting a fellowship, but then later I got an even fancier one that I wouldn't have been eligible for if I'd accepted the first?"

"The one about everything being for the best?" asked Gita. "Really? I told you that? I'd forgotten that I first heard it from Ayah. I've seen it in so many collections since then."

"Tell it," said Firoze, flipping the chicken.

Gita recollected for a minute. Once again, she was a small girl beside a bastion of safety—Ayah—lying on a mat through a hot afternoon. Ayah's steady voice reverberated across the years. Unhurried, speaking ungrammatical Hindi, Ayah was telling one more story in which things turned out right.

"Okay, so there was a king, and he had a very optimistic prime minister," Gita began. "Whatever happened, the prime minister would say that it was a good thing. So once the king was out hunting, and he somehow fell and injured his foot, and he lost his little toe."

"Right," said Najma with a huge grin, "and the prime minister said it was a good thing."

Gita was slightly distracted by a car waiting to turn farther down the road. After nights with Firoze, even the spasms of red turn signals gave her a thrill. There was a swarm of butterflies out. Across the fields extending beyond the house, the mountains were luminously green.

"Why don't you tell it?" asked Gita. "Really."

Najma took charge, crossing her arms. "So the king, poor

fellow, mentioned this to the prime minister, and the prime minister as usual said that it was a good thing. The king was in pain and very irritable, and he got so furious that he actually fired the prime minister. 'Lost my toe? My royal toe? What do you mean it's a good thing? Get out!' And the prime minister said, 'Very good,' and he left."

"This is beginning to sound familiar," said Firoze. "I seem to recall it from some school reader."

"So what happened is this," continued Najma. "The king went hunting, and a great mist fell, and he got lost. It got to be dark, and he finally fell asleep under a tree. Then, in the dead of night, the guy woke up to find himself surrounded by some thugs. They bound him and they trussed him, and they laid him out as a human sacrifice to the goddess Kali. But at the last minute, they realized that he was missing one toe and so he was an imperfect offering. So, just when he thought that he was about to die, they actually let him go."

"That's right," said Gita. "I think that in Ayah's version there were tribal people, not thugs. Anyhow, it's the same thing for the plot, sort of a symbolic equivalence."

"When the king got back to his palace, he sent for the prime minister at once. He pulled him out of retirement right then and there! He told the prime minister his story. 'You were right,' he said. 'It was a good thing that my toe got cut off or I wouldn't be here today. But why did you say it was 'very good?' when I sent you away?' The prime minister smiled, wise old sage that he was. He said, 'You see, if I'd been with you, I would have been killed even if you were let free. So you never know how one event makes another possible.' "

"In other words, all's well that ends well," said Isaac.

"Actually, I just read this story in an ethnography written by this Indian-American anthropologist, all about a swami who tells stories like this," said Charity.

"Really?" said Gita. "Sounds like something I should read. I didn't do much on modern folklore, but I bet that a lot of the stuff I looked through has variants that are still alive."

"Hey, honey," said Zelda, "no good stories ever really end. They're just *always* getting remade and retold."

Najma and Gita stepped inside to work on the *pullao*. "So, I haven't asked you what your plans are with Firoze," said Najma as they peeled soaked almonds, preparing to sliver them and then brown them in *ghee*. There were already finely sliced onions releasing a rich fragrance from the stove.

"No plans," said Gita. "I mean, I have my job, and he has his. Come on, Najma, you're a fine one to ask me about plans!"

Najma laughed. "Any fights yet?" she continued. "Or at least good arguments?"

"Well, one or two," Gita admitted. "The amazing thing is that I don't think I ever really argued with Norvin, I was so conditioned to defer to a man. It's odd, isn't it, that by clashing you sort of hit right up against the hidden contours of another person? In a way, a little conflict can help you understand the topography inside. Know what I mean? You get to love a person in all kinds of ways. We're still learning. Maybe a *jori* isn't destined but you make it happen."

Firoze had swung in the screen door behind them. "Chicken's ready. Gita, can I have a plate?" he asked. He had caught her last sentence and grinned. "Make it happen," he repeated, drawing an arm around Gita. Resting her head on his shoulder, a smile rising up through her heart onto her face, she glanced down to notice that pressed beside her clean sandaled foot, his battered black Reebok did, after all, look nice.

"So, it looks like God is good and luck is with us," Najma said, surveying them with a big grin.

"And why not?" said Firoze. "Well, by the way—"

"—may God bless you too!" said Gita.